PENGUIN BOOKS

My Fat Brother

Jim Keeble grew up in Cambridge. He lives in London, not far from his thin brother. This is his first novel.

My Fat Brother

JIM KEEBLE

PENGUIN BOOKS

PENGUIN BOOKS

Published by the Penguin Group
Penguin Books Ltd, 80 Strand, London WC2R ORL, England
Penguin Putnam Inc., 375 Hudson Street, New York, New York 10014, USA
Penguin Books Australia Ltd, 250 Camberwell Road, Camberwell,
Victoria 3124, Australia
Penguin Books Canada Ltd, 10 Alcorn Avenue, Toronto, Ontario, Canada M4V 3B2
Penguin Books India (P) Ltd, 11 Community Centre, Panchsheel Park,
New Delhi – 110 017, India
Penguin Books (NZ) Ltd, Cnr Rosedale and Airborne Roads,
Albany, Auckland, New Zealand
Penguin Books (South Africa) (Pty) Ltd, 24 Sturdee Avenue, Rosebank 2196, South Africa

Penguin Books Ltd, Registered Offices: 80 Strand, London WC2R ORL, England

www.penguin.com

First published 2003
1

Set in Monotype Garamond by Intype London Ltd
Printed in England by Clays Ltd, St Ives plc

To my brother, Ben, for all things fraternal

Thanks to

Dudi, Anthony W, Jeremy, Sue, Paul, Martin and Susy, Jane Mc, Sister Emma and Sister Monika. My parents, David and Valerie, for everything.

A special huge hug to my agent, Stephanie Cabot, and everyone at William Morris, and another one for my editor, Louise Moore, for her faith and wisdom.

And, most importantly, all my respect and love to Jessica Grainger for being there.

People say we look alike. Scott and Jes Barron. We're the same height – six foot in our heels – mine are blue Campers from Covent Garden; his are brown Clarks from Mr Shoe in Morden.

'You look like brothers,' they say, pleased with themselves.

'We are,' I say.

'Always have been,' says Jes.

It's the chin. Kirk rather than Michael Douglas. 'Bum chin,' they called us at school, me first then him. Jes got the slightly better features – a stronger jaw, a straighter, more elegant nose, thinner eyebrows and those deep brown eyes, set in gently curved, brooding sockets.

I have grey-blue eyes and my brown hair is starting to ascend each side of my forehead but both my grandfathers remained shaggy until the day they died so I should be okay. Jes's hair is darker. Sometimes people think he's Italian. They always think I'm English.

My brother was Jeremy on his birth certificate, but Jes from the moment he arrived home and Mum cooed into his cot, 'Jessy, Jes . . .'

At the time, 'Jes' seemed a strange, foreign name. Now it seems well . . . very now. 'Scott', in contrast, seems very . . . then.

I was named after my mother's nationality, after her nostalgia for a childhood spent roaming the Pentland Hills outside Edinburgh. Apparently I was a Celtic retort to my father's Anglo-Saxon surname. I've never liked the name Barron, with its élitist or desolate connotations.

I liked it even less after our father left us, when I was seven and Jes was two. At the time, I asked Mum if I could start using her maiden name, Henderson, at school. She smiled thinly, patted my head and said, 'Please don't make a fuss now, Scott,' in her strictest Scottish tone.

Unlike my mother, I have an accent as English as afternoon tea. On the rare occasions I've been abroad, salesmen hawking carpets, pottery or snowstorm Virgin Marys have always shouted, 'Ingleeesh!' before any other nationality.

I'm thirty-one, Jes is twenty-six. But he's fatter than me. He looks a little like Elvis, during the peanut-butter-and-banana years.

I stand on the scales in my small North London bathroom. The needle stops quivering at eleven stone nine pounds. That's 163 pounds if you're American, or about 73 kilos if you're anyone else. I've been down to eleven two (156 pounds, 70 kilos), but that was after a nasty bout of diarrhoea.

In contrast, Jes weighs sixteen stone. I know this because he told me a couple of weeks ago. He rested his hands on his paunch, and said happily, 'Sixteen stone. And I've only been married a year.'

So, I'm thinner than my younger brother. It's not that I don't work at it. You have to remain vigilant: you can't let yourself go. I run most days. I've been running for years.

'From what?' asks Ellie, flicking through this month's *Vogue*. Ellie is my girlfriend of eight months. She's Jes's age, twenty-six, attractive to everyone as well as me, and likes to flash her smile at older men to control them (her words). She's five foot eight (more in her daily heels), with a neat bob, face and body like a French actress. You wouldn't guess she was from Surrey, until she opens her beautiful, blossom-lipped mouth.

She's a commissioning editor for a minor women's magazine and dresses in clothes that everyone else will wear in six months' time. If Jes is now, Ellie is, well, later. When I walk into bars with her on my arm everyone turns to look.

'Nothing,' I reply, because I don't want to think about it too deeply. 'I'm not running from anything.'

Thankfully she does not pursue the question as she's just arrived at an in-depth article about Gwyneth Paltrow's shoe collection. Neither of us likes to talk about our feelings, which might be one of the reasons we're together.

Today I ran four miles in twenty-eight minutes thirteen seconds, according to the fancy Nike watch Ellie got me for my birthday. You can store the time of each run to compare them. I'm getting faster. I run to keep in shape, to get out of the house – I work from home – and to ogle the yummy mummies who push their prams between eleven a.m. and three p.m. on Hampstead Heath. Recently I've been finding young mums very attractive. Which is strange. I have yet to share this development with Ellie.

Ellie says she likes me because I am a writer. She says

she's hopeless with words – she is, really: she confuses 'ambivalent' and 'ambidextrous'. She says she likes my small but sensitive poems that don't rhyme, don't use long, complex or challenging words and don't mention God (funny that I should use negatives to describe what I write, but there you go). She likes the fact that I make money from my books and that my name sometimes appears in national newspapers, albeit on pages that no one reads.

Today is the launch of my third book, a collection of poems entitled *Men and Other Mammals*. I'm early, as I'm early for most things. Nothing if not organized, Ellie says, which in her sweet tone sounds like sweet reproach. She teases me frequently about my Virgo characteristics – characteristics I didn't realize I had until she started making fun of them – such as my need to plan carefully ahead, to make lists, and my inability to flick through magazines thinking about nothing in particular.

My brother Jes is more forthright. He thinks I should be more relaxed, whatever that means. 'Take it easy, won't you?' is one of his preferred refrains.

Since there are at least forty-five minutes to go until my book launch, I walk into Green Park where I decide to rent a green and white striped deck-chair for a pound and sit in the afternoon sunshine.

I'll show them. I can be impromptu. I can relax.

It's actually a really nice afternoon for mid-September in London, one of those warm days that were termed 'Indian summers' when I was young. The sun beats down, a light breeze makes the leaves tremble and insects buzz merrily, oblivious to their impending autumn demise.

Alongside me in the ranks of green and white stripes are old people in sun-hats complaining about the heat, a few office workers hiding between meetings, and a smattering of foreign tourists, most of whom seem to be kissing so passionately that their deck-chairs are in danger of collapsing.

I sit in the sunshine and wonder why I don't feel more excited. My third book is about to be published. I'm a relatively successful writer. I have a pretty girlfriend, who says she's 'really into' me (neither of us has used the L-word yet). But something doesn't feel right. I'm not looking forward to my launch. In fact, I'm dreading it. I just feel . . . I don't know . . . a fraud?

You see, I'm supposed to be an expert on the male condition because I write poems about men. I'm even known in some sections of the press as the 'Lad-Lit Poet' and on one unfortunate occasion as the 'Male Muse'. It's embarrassing. I'm no *Zeitgeist* commentator. I just write poems to entertain, to make people laugh.

The truth is, I don't know much about men. I don't know much about myself.

Am I happy? Relatively.

Am I inspired? Not really.

Do I love my girlfriend? Maybe.

As for my work, I never even planned to be a poet. It just sort of happened. I always wanted to be a novelist. In fact, if someone held a gun to my head, which is unlikely given that I live in a quiet middle-class street of North London, I would admit to feeling uneasy about people calling me a poet.

Ditties. That's what my father called them once. 'Just little ditties.'

Sitting low in the green and white striped deck-chair, I manage to relax for just over eight minutes. Then I reach into my bag and take out my new book. It feels smooth and more substantial than my other two collections. It's the first time I've had a book out in hardback, which might not mean much to you but to an author it's the equivalent of finally making the first team after several seasons in the reserves.

My first collection, *Uptown Guys*, was a flimsy, dull-coloured paperback. It was published six years ago, after Barbara Smiles, my ironically named agent (her lips never curl upwards), battered several small publishing houses until Oak Tree Press relented. They paid me five hundred pounds and printed 1,500 copies. No one thought they would sell, which accounted for my paltry advance and the fact that Barbara was able to negotiate a hefty 35 per cent royalty payment on every £6.99 copy.

'Just like George Lucas's first deal for *Star Wars*!' she declared, in her strident Yorkshire accent. No one was more surprised than Barbara when the book sold faster than the new Bill Bryson.

'MEN, READ THIS! THEN DARE TO GIVE IT TO YOUR WOMAN!' screeched one national newspaper, and the second print-run topped five thousand. Before I knew it, I was 'a lyricist of male inarticulacy' and I couldn't find words to express my stupefaction.

To date *Uptown Guys* has sold twenty-five thousand copies. I might not be George Lucas, but those royalty cheques do allow me to shop at Waitrose. And now there's even talk that one of my poems might appear on the London Underground, to entertain the capital's commuters. As a poet, these days, it doesn't get any better than that.

The initial print run for *Men and other Mammals* is 10,000 copies. On the back of the shiny electric-blue cover there's a photo of me looking like the kind of guy who would have an electric-blue book. Rugged, yet sensitive. The kind of man who knows the names of the Arsenal back four, what years were good for Rioja, how to cook duck, and when a woman just wants to be listened to.

The only thing is, I don't know the names of the Arsenal back four, I don't know about Rioja, apart from its country of origin (Spain, of course), and I've never cooked duck. I do listen to women, though. I'm fine as long as I don't have to say anything.

Clasping my hardback book like a shield, I step from the deck-chair on to the path. A few faces look up – a silver-haired granny and a group of olive-faced French exchange students. As they watch I drop the book from chest height. It hits the path,

SPLAD!

A solid, happy slap. The book lies there, blue on grey. The silver-haired granny gives me a worried glance, as if I might be a recent escapee from a maximum-security mental institution. I smile to reassure her. It's just a ritual I have, dropping the book. It helps it all seem more, I don't know . . . real.

My book launch takes place in the private members'

club of a minimalist London hotel. Despite having loitered in the park for almost three-quarters of an hour, I still manage to be early. A twenty-something PR from the publishing house is busying about without anything to be busy about. Miranda is thin, blonde and attractive, in a junior-newscaster sort of way, and she flashes me a smile, which is one of the reasons she's a successful young PR: it makes me feel instantly important. I ask if I can buy her a drink and she points out politely that all the drinks are free. 'Maybe another time.' She grins, and I know flirting is part of her job but I can't help feeling warm. In that moment I fancy Miranda. But I have a girlfriend and I'm a Virgo so I'm loyal, or so Ellie tells me.

The book launch begins well. I'm relieved. The room fills quickly with journalists, editorial staff and a few writers from the same publishing house who are here because I came to their launches. My editor is standing alongside the marketing manager. Even the managing director is here in his corduroy jacket, which must mean they hope to make more money out of me. And, of course, there's my agent Barbara Smiles, the woman who made it all possible. She stands sipping vodka martinis as if they're about to be made illegal. She's a small, thin lady who looks not unlike a two-thousand-year-old corpse dug from an Irish bog, only slightly prettier, immaculately dressed in her trade-mark black suit, tailored so sharply that she appears almost cut from cardboard.

'You look smashing, Scott-lad!' she exclaims shrilly, kissing each cheek with dry lips. 'Doesn't he look smashing, Gordon?' she remarks to the man next to her – another writer she represents, who seems somewhat embarrassed to be monopolizing my agent at my book launch. I smile an ambivalent but gracious smile, and walk on.

Near the bar, among the junior publishing staff vying to maximize their consumption of free booze, I spot my three closest friends standing in a protective huddle as if under attack. It's rare to see them together like this: they only ever meet through me, and don't really like each other. I wonder, sometimes, if they represent different sides of my own personality.

There's Brian, the small big-city lawyer in his grey suit. I'm friends with him because he's a little self-conscious like me, and we manage to convince each other that we're cooler than we are.

There's Dr Simon, in his out-of-hospital Bohemian look – black jeans, black Marks & Spencer turtle-neck and Doc Marten shoes, trying not to drink his wine too quickly. We met at sixth-form college in Cambridge, and have been drifting apart slowly ever since. I'm only friends with him now, I suspect in my darker moments, because I'm nostalgic – the past is one of my favourite places.

And there's Big Barry in a thousand-pound suit, two-hundred-pound loafers and slicked-back stockbroker hair, eyeballing every woman in the room. Big Barry is perhaps my best friend, by which I mean he makes me feel the best. In his company I sometimes think I'm almost as brilliant as Barry believes himself to be.

Brian, Simon and Barry are all in their mid-thirties, and each of them is as single as the day he was born.

It's been a long time since we've all been together like

this. To be honest, I wasn't even sure that they'd all turn up. In a city like London, it's hard to stay in touch with people, even if you call them your best friends. People are too busy, too tired, too put off by public transport and high taxi fares. At least, that's our excuse.

I walk up to my friends, and they smile at me, one after another. I know what these smiles mean. In the perpetual competition that is our relationship, tonight's event sends me to the top of the leaderboard. They're each happy for me in their own way, but they cannot hide their jealousy.

'Top totty!' intones Big Barry, turning his back on Brian and Dr Simon and glancing past me at Miranda while clasping my shoulder with his over-size fingers. His hand is not unlike the large felt ones handed out at sports events so fans can wave at their teams.

'Cool venue, Scott-man!' chirps Brian, who was born in Los Angeles and never fails to be impressed by places that have appeared in glossy magazines, much to my embarrassment.

'Where's Ellie?' asks Dr Simon, downing the last of his wine and looking around nervously. He doesn't like Ellie, a view shared by my other two friends.

'She should be here somewhere . . .' I say, glancing around the room.

And in that instant I wonder if Ellie and I will get married and, if so, whether our wedding will be like this – my uneasy friends, the warm champagne, the gentle, detached enthusiasm of strangers, and my own enthusiastic detachment. As I think about it, I realize two things. First, our wedding will be nothing like this: it will look like a magazine article, in her parents' large garden with a *fantastic* marquee and the latest fashions. Second, this is the first time I've ever imagined getting married to anyone.

I look for Ellie, but she's nowhere to be seen. I suffer a sudden snatch of jealousy as I wonder if she's having drinks with some fashion photographer (they *are* all gay, aren't they?) or some actor (they *are* all gay, aren't they?). I'm annoyed, she said she would come, and despite her profession she sometimes does what she says. I know she's not too keen on my friends, with whom she has little in common, but this isn't about them.

Jes is also absent, but he called to say he had an article to finish and might not make it. We both know he won't come. This is how we are – we see each other more than some brothers, but not as much as we could if we really wanted to.

Jes lives in Morden – South-South London, which is a place that looks like it sounds. It's at the end of the Northern Line, and then you take a bus, which isn't such a bad journey, but Jes doesn't seem to feel the need to go out like I do. He lives with his wife, Sam, who's from Huddersfield and pretty in a Sinéad O'Connor way – a good way, in my books. They met when Jes put an ad in the *Brighton Echo* offering piano lessons. By the time Sam could play a C-minor scale they were in a major relationship. Sam learned *Für Elise*, and they got married at the age of twenty-five. It was as easy as that.

It's Tuesday night. Sam will be sitting on the sofa dozing in front of *ER*, one of her many telly addictions, tired from another day as assistant picture editor on the *Daily*

Telegraph travel desk, gazing at beautiful images of far away places while rain spatters the windows of a small cubicle in the Canary Wharf tower. Jes will be in the spare room hunched over this week's 'Shoppers Report' for the *South London Gazette*, determined not to use the same word twice in a three-hundred-word article comparing the prices of margarine.

Secretly I'm glad he isn't here. He would have noticed my general shiftiness, my unease, and he would have asked me why I was feeling like that. Jes doesn't hold back. Unlike me.

I think Jes, too, will be glad he's not here: he wouldn't want to see his older brother praised for his latest book while he himself struggles with dreams of being a world-famous travel writer stalking the planet with a fully charged lap-top: 'Morden's Chatwin or Paul Theroux.'

He can get jealous, my little brother. I understand his sibling rivalry, but I wish sometimes he could see my side of the story, how it can be hard always being the leader, the first to break new ground. I mean, he never had to suffer that bowel-expanding fear of the first day at school, the first spelling test, the first exam, the first date, the first driving lesson, the first sexual encounter. It was me: I was always the guide, the trail-blazer, the pilot through choppy water, especially after our father left. There were times when I used to wonder if I'd been put on the earth simply to prepare the path for Jes.

But I suppose Jes did one thing first. He married the woman he loved.

One of the reasons we see each other less these days might be because of Ellie. Jes, I feel, doesn't like Ellie. Sam, I feel, hates Ellie. We went to their house just once, and Ellie smiled and made conversation like it was a work party, chatting about fashion shoots in the Seychelles and parties in Milan – maybe because she was nervous but maybe because that's what she likes to talk about – and Sam kept fingering the hem of her own skirt, bought at Next two years previously. We left early, and Jes seemed relieved.

'Why have you never bought me flowers?' asked Ellie, as we drove back north, and it struck me that I always buy Sam flowers because it makes Jes smile.

At least my mother has come to my launch. She stands listening to the managing director, looking slimly elegant in her best black dress and pearls, her white hair neatly and expensively set for the occasion. She's still attractive at the age of fifty-nine. She nods as he continues his lecture, happy not to be talking. My mother uses few words. She prefers to listen.

I wander over, exchanging a few pleasantries here and there. I find it hard – like Mum, I'm not good at talking to people, smiling at faces I don't know, saying similar yet personally tailored things, but it's something you can learn, or so Ellie tells me.

I kiss my mother, which I know she hates, but it's my party and I'll be affectionate if I want to. She suffers this ignominy with good grace, even saying, 'Thank you, my darling . . .' in her soft Scottish brogue. I give her the pained look that I've been giving her since I was little: it says, 'I don't want to be here.' In return, she smiles the smile that says, 'I know, but you have to be.'

She holds out a copy of my book with the electric-blue cover. *Men and Other Mammals. New Poems by Scott Barron.* 'Will you sign it for me?'

So I sign my book and the managing director tells me what a lucky boy I am to have such a charming mother and I agree, while thinking that he is only five years older than me, married with a small baby, yet he sounds like he's hitting on my mum.

Then he taps his glass with a gold pen and makes a speech, predicting greatness (large sales), and toasts me. I blush and take out my small piece of paper, crammed with tiny writing, and I thank everyone. I thank my mother for her continuing support, and she blushes behind her rouge. I thank my editor, who grins possessively. Then I read one poem that I've carefully selected because I hope it might get a small laugh.

MEN

Men are people who clean the loo just once a month and only
    when asked by a woman,
Who know distances, heights, and weights of all things except
    peaches or babies,
Men are mammals too, with hair on chests, and toes,
Who sometimes eat pies
To feel happy.

It gets a small laugh.

I conclude my speech by saying, 'I hope you like the book, or at least buy it,' and most of the crowd smile.

By ten p.m., I'm a little drunk. As I break away from a group of people I hardly know, I spot my mother at the cloakroom, taking her black wool coat from the young pony-tailed attendant. I hurry over to her. 'You're leaving?' I ask, a little hurt. I've been looking forward to a drink with her and basking in some maternal praise.

'I'm feeling a wee bit tired,' she says softly, pulling on the coat. I move to help her, but she nudges me away. 'You go and have fun with the lovely Eleanor,' she says, with a small smile. My mother likes Ellie. They got on well the two times they met, gossiping about supermodels and the latest handbags. In some ways I think they're similar – both beautiful, both somewhat reserved in their emotions. I'm a little worried that that's what I look for in a woman – the reserve, the coolness. Is it true that men seek to marry their mothers?

I think about telling Mum that Ellie hasn't shown up, but I don't want to disappoint her. Instead I ask if she's got enough cash for the taxi back to her hotel, which of course she has, being an organized Scot, and I kiss her one last time.

'Run along, you silly boy,' she says quickly. I think about offering to wait for a taxi with her, but I know she'll tell me to stop fussing.

I spend the next quarter of an hour searching for my three friends. I haven't had a chance to chat with them, and I feel bad. I know they will resent it, but I hope they realize I've had to do the rounds, do the chat, do the business.

I look in the obvious places, bar, toilets, by the buffet table, but I can't find them. I wonder if they've left already. Then I catch a glimpse of Big Barry in the hotel foyer chatting to a young blonde woman who, as far as I know, has nothing to do with my book launch. He seems ensconced. Beyond, Dr Simon is standing at the exit. He sees me and waves. 'Sorry, mate, I'm on early shifts at St Mary's . . .'

'Where's Brian?'

'He wasn't feeling well. He said he'd call you.'

Dr Simon shakes my hand quickly, we nod at each other (a farewell first formed fifteen years ago), and he leaves. I feel irritated. Looking around I can see no one I want to talk to. Barbara is browbeating the managing director, who for once can't get a word in edgeways. Some of the junior publishing staff are dancing drunkenly to the bar music, but I don't want to join them. I don't dance. It's time to go.

By the cloakroom I overhear Miranda talking to one of the junior editors. 'I'm not sure Barron's quite as witty in real life,' she says, in a low voice, while the twenty-something editor nods slowly, his eyes fixed on her breasts. I turn away hurriedly, zip up my coat and head out into the rain.

In the taxi, sliding though London's now wet September streets, I call Ellie three times, but there's no reply from her mobile or her house. In her absence I conjure a conversation with her, admonishing her for not having made it to my book launch. I know she'll have an excuse, maybe even several, but I feel a little let down. After eight months we should be edging towards loyalty, shouldn't we? Isn't that what couples do?

In my head I suggest that perhaps we should think about modifying our priorities, to concentrate more on 'us, not work', which may be easier for me to say since I have nothing to do over the next couple of months but sit back and wait for the book figures to scamper in.

'Us? Do you really think so?' my invented Ellie asks, green eyes wide.

'Yes, darling. Some things are more important than work.'

As the taxi chugs through Camden, I imagine that somehow she's let herself into my flat, run a bath, put on a Van Morrison CD and is lying in a tub full of suds like a luxurious hussy in a chocolate advert.

'Scotty, oh, Scotty,' she'll coo, and I'll slip into the hot water, then slip into her.

But Ellie doesn't like Van Morrison. And she'd never be a luxurious tart.

My flat is cold. The heating hasn't come on: the timer is stuck firm and resolved. I bash it a couple of times, but it remains stuck.

There are two messages on my answering-machine.

'All right, Scott? Hope the launch went well. If you want to call tonight, please refrain between ten and eleven. It's *ER*. Speak soon, Jes.'

The voice on the second message is more tense: 'Scott. We need to talk. Give me a call when you get this.'

At least I don't have to walk home. She comes to my flat. I'm surprised how much I plead. 'No, Ellie . . .'

'I'm sorry. I don't feel it's right any more. We just don't connect.'

'Connect?'

'I admit when I first met you I was impressed by your words, your poems, how emotional and deep they seemed. I couldn't wait to get to the depths of you. But now I wonder. Maybe you just save your feelings for your writing.'

'My feelings? What are you talking about? You never worried about my feelings before. Where is this coming from?'

Ellie remains quiet, which infuriates me. Usually she hates talking about feelings almost as much as I do. I wonder if she has latched on to this theme as an excuse, exaggerating the issue as an aid to rejecting me. Then I wonder if someone has coached her on it.

'What about you?' I bark at her. 'You're not exactly the most openly emotional person I've ever met!'

'See?' she says, almost triumphantly. 'That's just it. We don't connect.'

'How can we? We never talk about anything!'

'That's not my fault! It's you! You're so . . .' She seeks a word that lies just beyond her reach.

'What? What am I, Ellie?'

'I don't know!'

'Cold? Uncommunicative? Repressed?'

'Yes. All of those things.'

She pauses for a moment, putting a finger to her mouth

as if to bite the nail, before remembering she has painted it deep red, this season's most fashionable hue.

'You're just like your friends,' she snaps, with a practised glare.

'No, I'm not! I'm nothing like them!' I shout angrily, half aware that in saying this I am rejecting my best mates. She's knows what she's doing, pretty Ellie. My friends have been a constant bone of contention between us: she dislikes Barry, Brian and Simon, calling them the 'Freak Bunch'. She thinks they're socially awkward, the greatest sin in her book. She knows talking about them like this will make me mad.

'Anyway, this isn't about them, is it? It's about us!'

'I'm sorry, Scott. There is no us. It's over!' she declares categorically.

'Ellie . . .'

'Please don't make this more difficult –'

'But I love you.'

She looks away, and I feel a glimmer of hope, a stab of possibility, which reminds me of the first time we met when she glanced at me at the magazine party and I hardly dared dream that maybe, just maybe, I had a chance of achieving the impossible.

She looks back again. 'Unfortunately, Scott, that's the first time you've ever said that to me.'

She's right. I've had the feelings – missing her, needing her, wanting to protect her from skinheads, traffic wardens and unscrupulous sales assistants at Harvey Nichols – but I've never been quite able to formulate the words.

In this case, as in the past, emotions have seemed less

powerful than words. I've not been able to connect one with the other.

But now I know. Now I am certain. I think.

'I love you.'

There. I've said it (again).

She looks at me coldly. 'Two months ago those three words might have been enough.'

Three words, two months. I was never much good at maths.

Ellie snatches up her new Gucci satchel and car keys with a dramatic flourish. I step to the door and block her path. 'Didn't you hear me? I love you!'

She stands there, lovely jaw clenched. 'No, you don't, Scott. You're just saying the words.'

'I mean it!'

'Go on, then. Say it again.'

She looks at me, like a gunslinger must look into the eyes of his victim. I know that this is a huge moment. I know that I have to perform, that I have to express my innermost, deepest, most visceral emotions. But I can't. In that split second of thinking about it, I've lost the moment, the instinctive passion. As she knew I would.

'I . . . love . . . you,' I say weakly. As soon as the words vanish into the air, I know I've blown it.

'It's okay, Scott. I don't love you either.'

'But we have great sex!' I stammer, immediately regretting it. Ellie looks at me witheringly. I stumble on, 'It's been eight months! We can't throw it all away now!'

She moves towards the door.

'Please, Ellie.'

She glares at me once more. I step aside. She opens the door. ''Bye, Scott,' she says softly. The door closes. For a moment, I watch the rain pattering on the window.

When I run outside, her car is gone. I call her mobile.

'Hi, this is Ellie, can't speak now. 'Bye-eee.'

I call and call and call, but she doesn't answer.

''Bye-ee.'

I sit on the closed toilet seat staring at the luxury blue toilet paper Ellie bought just three days ago. She'd stacked ten rolls neatly beside the cistern, an act I'd believed then to be a symbol of commitment. Now I realize it was merely a parting gift.

The sixth poem in *Men and Other Mammals* is called 'Girlfriend'.

GIRLFRIEND

I have a girlfriend now.
She is round in the best places, but straight when she needs
    to be — on motorways, in whisky bars and bed.
She makes me glow like gold at dusk, or at dawn like the
    Readybrek kid.
I'm happy that she's a friend.
But happier that she's a girl.

2

Six days later, I get up enough courage to call *Zap!* – 'For the Woman in Every Girl' – and ask to speak to Ellie. I get put through to her assistant Serena.

'Oh. Hi, Scott.'

'Is she there, Serena?'

'Er . . .'

'I'd really like to talk to her.'

'I don't think she wants to speak to you, Scott.'

'Please, Serena. You've got to help me.'

'She's got a new man.' Serena blurts this out as if confessing to a triple homicide, breathing heavily afterwards, the relief all too evident. I wonder if Ellie has ordered her assistant to do this, so that there's no blood on her own hands. 'He's some moneybags at Goldman Sachs,' she whispers conspiratorially. 'A bit of a dickhead, apparently.'

She's added the last bit to make me feel better. So Ellie was single for just under a week, a record for her.

I feel so stupid – because Ellie's absence at my book launch wasn't the first warning sign. Every time I'd called her recently, I seemed to get her answering-machine. Some days she hadn't returned my call, and I'd had to call back in the evening. She claimed that she was up to her eyes at work, and I felt sorry for her – even guilty for bothering her. Then, one evening, she'd told me she didn't want to stay the night at my place. 'My flatmates are on my case. They say they never get to see me these days,' she'd said, with a beautiful smile.

Why didn't I see it coming? Am I so blind?

In retrospect, I suppose it started going wrong that Friday night a couple of months ago when Ellie and I went to have dinner with my friends at some Italian restaurant in Fulham. It was going to be the first time she would meet all three of them together. I was really looking forward to it – an evening with my beautiful girlfriend and my best mates. It was a turning-point, I felt, in my journey towards fully fledged grownupness. It was going to be a 'special night'.

It was certainly special.

Barry and Ellie took an instant dislike to each other. During the meal they interrupted each other's stories, ignored each other's questions, and refused to pass each other the pepper. I sweated profusely, trying to interject words to calm them down, to ease them together, but to no avail: they were too similar, both craving centre-stage.

After the meal, we headed downstairs to the sweaty dance-floor where Barry informed me that my girlfriend was a stuck-up cow. Brian got drunk and called Ellie a princess to her face, while Simon looked bored out of his mind – until he returned from the upstairs loos to inform me that Ellie was at the bar being chatted up by an Italian waiter. 'Better keep an eye on that one!'

We departed soon afterwards.

Back at her flat I challenged Ellie about the waiter. She

didn't even have the decency to blush and admitted that indeed he *had* tried to chat her up. 'It's not like it doesn't happen every day,' she said pointedly. I remember thinking at the time that this was a strange way to reassure me. In the end, she made me feel embarrassed for doubting her, then proceeded to rip into my friends, whom she accused of being cold, dull and nerdy.

I feel so stupid. Because Ellie's gone. And my cold, dull, nerdy friends aren't calling.

At two in the morning I lie in bed listening to the downstairs academics having loud, clumsy sex, while upstairs Mat and Emma's baby tries to scream out its kidneys. I pull the duvet over my head, but this exposes my feet, which are freezing. The heating is still not working, adding insult to injury.

As Dr Philippa moans below, and baby Adam screeches above, I thrust my head under the pillow and try not to think of being alone. I try to picture reassuring things, like post offices, green hillsides, or toast with various jams.

Sex, ejaculation, impregnation, baby. Then, many decades later, the last gasp. At each end of life we're just a shudder, a release. But sex, I guess, is more fun than dying.

BABIES

I like babies, even though I'm a man,
But I couldn't eat a whole one.
Some people were babies once upon a time,
Like Churchill, Bill Clinton and Drew Barrymore.
But some, I suspect, were never newborn,

Just adult from day one.
I think of Stallone, Mrs Thatcher and Gandhi,
Who came out ready-made, with biceps, handbag and
  spectacles.
Me? I was a tot once, and in one respect I have not changed.
I still like breasts.

I open my eyes at five a.m. and stare at the ceiling waiting for baby Adam to start crying again, which he does precisely seventeen minutes later. At six a.m. I go running before sunrise for the first time in my life.

Up on damp, misty Hampstead Heath I feel damp and misty. My head, back and legs ache, but I compensate by trying to imagine it's the same pain Scott of the Antarctic felt, remote from the world, striding back from his silver medal at the South Pole before heroically freezing to death.

I've always had a thing about old Scott of the Antarctic. It's not just that we share a name. Ever since I was a little boy I've been fascinated by pictures of him, stern-faced, standing strong, even when wearing some ill-advised fur outfits. He's always seemed the ultimate Englishman – tough, determined and silent, with morals as rigid as his body after a few weeks frozen to the Antarctic ice.

I want to go to Antarctica one day. I'd like to stand in the middle of nothing, with no one around to bug me or break up with me.

At the bottom of Parliament Hill Fields I finish my run in a flurry of whirling arms and juddering knees. I've done three miles in nineteen minutes and fourteen seconds, which goes to prove that, if nothing else, getting dumped makes you run faster.

I call Ellie six times, but the phone cuts straight to her answering-machine. Five times I listen to her voice before I leave a message. 'Hi, it's Scott. Hope you're okay. Would you give me a call if you get a moment?'

In desperation, I get up the courage to call Brian, then Dr Simon, then Big Barry, but none of them answers. They've all got real jobs, earning real money. They don't have time to chat about relationships at 2.36 p.m. on a Tuesday. I leave a message with each of them, as brief and detached as I can be: 'Hi, it's Scott. Just to let you know, Ellie and I split up. We're both fine. It was probably for the best anyway.'

That will make them happy.

I lie on the sofa and stare at the ceiling for an hour while the television mumbles to itself in the background. My legs ache from their unaccustomed early-morning workout. I feel sick. I feel tired, but I can't sleep. My stomach hurts. I want to moan to someone but there's no one to call. Mum would only tell me to stop feeling sorry for myself and be strong, and I'm not ready to hear that yet.

Shortly after six p.m., the phone rings. I grab at it, miss and fall off the sofa. The answer-machine starts to click in as I grab the receiver. I hope it's Ellie. I pray it's Ellie. Please let it be Ellie.

It's Jes.

'All right, Scott?'

'Yeah. Not bad.'

There's a small silence.

'What's up, mate?'

'Nothing.'

'You're sure?'

'Ellie dumped me.'

Another small silence. I think about hanging up. Then Jes speaks again, concern and warmth in his voice: 'Look, I'm cooking for Sammy Friday night. If you're not too busy why don't you come over?'

I wait until Friday afternoon for a better offer, but no one calls so I get on the train to Morden.

Jes and Sam live in a small rented terraced house that they can only just afford. It's cosy, with bright walls – yellow, orange – wooden floors and a scrubby garden where Jes hides and smokes pot when Sam's mum comes to visit from Huddersfield. In each room they've hung a few of Sam's photographs taken on rare foreign trips with the *Daily Telegraph*. They're mainly portraits – a bored machine-gun-toting soldier leaning against a Roman statue, a wide-eyed Thai boy wearing nothing but an oversized Disney T-shirt, and a particularly surly Swedish fisherman waving a large grey fish. She seems to have a knack for capturing people's moods. You get the sense that you know exactly what the subject is feeling.

I like Sam. She's forthright but kind. She says what she feels, but she's careful not to hurt people. And she seems happy most of the time, which is more than a lot of people I know.

Their house feels like a home, if 'home' means a place that's not too tidy, nearly always warm and smells vaguely of coffee and marijuana.

Jes and Sam are warmly welcoming.

'The bitch!' declares Sam.

'Fancy a Stella?' asks Jes.

I suppose I should be more grateful. They've taken pity on me. And Jes has cooked (usually he's more Oliver Hardy than Jamie Oliver in the kitchen).

'Bangers and mash. Comfort calories,' he announces, with a big grin, his flabby stomach protruding proudly beneath a large apron emblazoned with a smiling penguin. He has never been a fashion guru, my brother, but there's always something cheerfully exuberant about his wardrobe. Ellie had to bite her nails to suppress her comments whenever she saw him. I guess I'm just used to it. It's been twenty-six years.

The kitchen is snugly warm, the opposite of my own. And for once the wedding-present wide-screen television remains switched off, although the VCR timer blinks happily.

'How was the book launch?' asks Jes brightly, helping himself to more mashed potatoes.

'Fine,' I say noncommittally. 'Everyone had a good time.'

'Yeah, sorry we couldn't make it,' says Jes, a little too hurriedly. 'I told you about the deadline thing, and Tuesdays are always busy for Sam. She didn't get back until after ten.'

'Don't worry. Ellie didn't make it either.'

'Cow,' offers Sam.

'What's the print run?' asks Jes, changing the subject.

'Ten thousand.'

'Wow. They must really think it's going to be a winner.'

'A winner. Yeah. I guess so . . .'

There follows an uneasy silence. I sense Jes is jealous, but trying to hide it. I haven't talked with him about my writing in a long time. It wasn't always like this. I remember sitting up late in my rented flat in Gospel Oak, my youthful brother haranguing me for using too many similes in my poems, before falling down the stairs, a bottle of vodka in hand, shouting, 'WORDSWORTH WAS A WANKER!' at the top of his voice.

At my first book launch, in the luxurious surroundings of the *Camden Chronicle* smoking den – a vague area between the coffee machine and the ramshackle toilet – Jes insisted on being DJ and made a drunken speech extolling the virtues of his newly published brother. He had just come back from a couple of years bumming around the world with his best mate Zeb, and was in his first year doing English at Sussex University, pursuing a less than healthy fascination with Samuel Taylor Coleridge.

My second book, *Men Matter*, was published in his final year. It won the Tattershall Prize, but you still might not have heard of it, poetry having a profile in the mass media somewhere between sewage filtration and Finnish election campaigns. It was about the time of Jes's final exams, during which he failed to sleep for six nights straight, replacing Coleridge's opium with Pro-Plus and Red Bull.

He was predicted a first in his degree, but lack of rest

and his penchant for rewriting exam answers landed him a 2:1. The fact I'd barely scraped a 2:2 at Bristol wasn't much consolation. Unlike Jes, I'd never had the desire to be good at my subject. He got a second-class degree and *Men Matter* sold 22,000 copies.

In the warm orange kitchen we sit in silence. From the front room comes the gentle hum of Cuban music, one of Sam's favourites. She likes anything foreign, preferably female. Jes has hipper tastes: he loves talking about new rock, old jungle, post-big beat and pre-garage, especially with his trendy friends. I, on the other hand, know little about popular music, or any other kind of music for that matter. I'm always getting the singers' and bands' names mixed up. It can be quite embarrassing.

The clock ticks. Time passes. I realize I haven't seen my brother in two and half months. I try not to watch as he takes his wife's hand beneath the table and gives it a little squeeze. Is it an ordeal for them, having me here?

Sam breaks the silence, loudly. 'Jes has been writing this piece –'

'Sam . . .'

'That's great, Jes. What piece?' I say, quickly, wanting to show enthusiasm.

'A travel piece,' continues Sam.

'It's nothing,' Jes interrupts her.

'What's it about?' I ask.

'It's nothing, I said.'

'Come on, Jes.'

'You don't want to hear about it.'

'Don't I?' I retort, a verbal jab back at him.

'It's really good,' says Sam, 'one of the best things he's written.'

'Leave it out, Sammy,' Jes grumbles, annoyed by my interest, which I know he has interpreted as patronizing when, in fact, I was just trying to be brotherly.

'So what's the subject-matter?' I ask, as nicely as I can.

'I told you, it's nothing. I don't want to talk about it.'

'Why not?' I press, wanting to wind him up a little.

'Impressions of South London,' interjects Sam. 'That's what you call it.'

'Because you don't care about what I write.'

'That's not true, and you know it.'

'I mean, why would you? You've just published your third book.'

'There's this great line,' intones Sam, trying to stop our incipient argument. We turn to look at her. 'South London is made for people who dream of living elsewhere.'

'That's a good one,' I say, a little too quickly to sound genuine.

'It's not,' says Jes, defensively. 'It's crap.'

Sam looks pained.

'So, when can I read the finished product?' I ask, and I'm honestly intrigued. Jes's writing is very different from my own. He doesn't try to entertain, or be funny, or to make people like him. He's blunt. He uses short sentences and difficult words. He's hard work. I wonder how he's described his home patch.

'Look, it's nothing,' says Jes, conclusively. 'I've only just started it.'

So we leave it at that. As usual.

For dessert Jes and Sam have double-choc-honey-dip ice-cream. I decline, having already consumed far more than I would usually eat for dinner. After his second bowl, Jes pats his stomach and Sam reaches over to smooth her hand over his flab, stroking gently as if he's carrying a baby and she's waiting for it to kick. He kisses her, on the back of the neck, and she shivers.

'Well . . .' I say, decisively.

'Why don't you stay the night?'

'Thanks, Jes, but I think I should head back, you know?'

'Why?' asks Sam. 'Hot date?'

I look down at the table, for effect, and it works.

'Sorry, Scott. I'm sorry . . .'

'I should go.'

The phone rings.

'Look, if you don't stay the night,' says Sam, going to the phone, 'I'll cut off your bollocks with the breadknife and feed them to Gigsy.'

'Next-door neighbour's Dobermann,' explains Jes.

While Jes goes upstairs to make up the spare room, I put the plates into the dishwasher, keen to show gratitude for their kind hospitality. I line up the wine glasses, and before I can help it I find myself downing the remnants of Rioja from each glass. I don't know why. Maybe I just want to be drunk.

I set the dishwasher going, and stand, for a moment, admiring a picture on the wall of my fat brother and Zeb, a guy who, ever since I first met him – three years old, cut knee, howling his head off – has promised more than he's delivered, planned more than he's done, and looked cooler than he is. The photo must have been taken fairly recently, and shows them wrestling in the back garden. It makes me smile. Jes was always a bit of a rough-and-tumble kid. He often got into scraps at school, nothing malevolent, just boyish fighting. I've never been in a fight in my life. I used to rough Jes up a bit, but only when he was little. As soon as he got bigger I stopped and, to his credit, he realized how much I loathed scrapping. Perhaps that's when I first started to run, scampering away from school-yard confrontation.

I look around for another open bottle of wine, or some whisky or anything vaguely alcoholic, but they have evidently failed to restock after their last dinner party – Jes and Sam's friends aren't ones to leave a house until all alcohol has been ritually consumed.

So I head to the downstairs toilet at the end of the hallway. As I pass the living-room door, I overhear Sam talking to her mother on the phone. '. . . Jes cooked, can you believe it? Yes, it was more than edible, thanks, Mum!'

I smile.

'. . . because Scott came over, his girlfriend just dumped him, poor guy.'

I stop smiling.

'No, I didn't like her, but that doesn't mean I can't feel sorry for him. I don't know why she dumped him . . . Oh, come on, Mum, he's not that bad. Yes, all right . . . he can be a little needy sometimes. But he's a writer. They're all a bit self-absorbed, it goes with the job.'

I hurry to the toilet where I sit until I hear Sam finish her call and go upstairs to bed.

*

In the spare bedroom Jes has laid out an inflatable blue mattress, as if for a war-zone invalid, or a teenage runaway. Next to it, in pride of place, stands his most expensive and prized possession: a Yamaha Clavinova electric piano with weighted keys that he plays intermittently when not writing things that nobody will read because he's too insecure to be judged.

I used to play the piano once. My father got up at six thirty every morning to make me practise. But I had no ability. I couldn't hear my mistakes. I tried. He would sing to me, la-la-la, do-re-me, scales and melodies, but it made no sense: the black and white keys were just black and white keys.

One morning he didn't come into my room. I woke anyway, as I always did, and went downstairs to play, waiting for him to appear. At breakfast I asked him why he'd been absent and he coughed and said, 'I think you need a bit of time to practise on your own.'

I gave up three weeks later.

Jes had lessons from an old Czech woman. He was her star pupil. He even played at her funeral.

On the wall behind the piano is a series of pictures – the symbolic photographic union of two people's lives that occurs after marriage. I glance down the images of Sam through the ages, looking as I'd expect her to look – small and pretty, even as a little girl, with a smile that suggests she will never do exactly what people ask.

Between Sam and Jes is the bridge – the marriage picture, smiles and hope outside St Peter's, Huddersfield. They have their arms round each other, but somehow Sam seems in charge, protective almost. My brother is leaning on her.

To the right of the wedding photo is a large clip-frame containing Jes's gallery: twenty or more snapshots thrown together haphazardly, an illustration of his lack of artistic prowess – thank God he married Sam. There are old pictures of Jes as a baby, Mum holding him on her knee, another of Jes and Sam, on their second date this time, smiling as if they already know they want to spend the rest of their lives together.

I peer closer at the jumbled photographs, wondering if I'm in any of them. Instead I notice a picture that I want to take out and tear in half. It's a black and white snapshot of my father. I keep the few pictures I have of him hidden away, buried under unloved pictures of rainy holidays with ex-girlfriends. But here Jes is displaying him brazenly, within the frame, within the fold. The symbolism is obvious: Edward Barron is part of his life.

I am annoyed. Jes has always been so lenient with our father. I know he was only two when Edward Barron walked out on us, but that's no reason to forgive him for the ultimate betrayal. Because of Jes's softer approach, our father has always treated him differently. I remember the few times we visited him in the South of France, he would always ask Jes what he wanted to do before me. It felt like a punishment. I stopped going to see him about ten years ago, but Jes continued to visit once a year. Maybe he still does.

In the picture our father is standing by a large open doorway, smiling as if to say, 'Catch me if you can.'

He left three years after Jes was born, two days after my seventh birthday party when he'd dressed up in a rented Batman costume, his belly hair protruding slightly from the tight shirt, and handed out birthday cake to my sugar-loving guests. Batman wasn't one of my favourite super-heroes, but I was grateful that he'd made an effort.

During sleepless nights I worried under my duvet that it was my fault he'd gone away because I hadn't shown more gratitude for the Batman outfit. Then Mum explained he'd gone away because of her, which made me feel a little better even though she was crying her eyes out. I tried to tell her that it wasn't her fault either, it was his, but this made her cry all the more.

My father was a bastard, in the literal as well as the figurative sense. His father worked for one of those great British companies that ruled the world when there was a Great British Empire rather than a Great British Suburb. My grandmother was a pretty young secretary to the East Asia manager on floor three. She fell for a tall, debonair insurance clerk from the fifth floor. The only problem was, he was married, with three children, which he only revealed when Lillian Walpole discovered she was pregnant. At this point Charles Barron pointed out he could never leave his wife and kids, and she accepted a meagre yearly allowance and a flat off the Finchley Road in which to raise her son, to whom she proudly gave her impregnator's surname.

'Father came round every Christmas Eve with a new dress for Lillian and a tin of Murray Mints for me,' my father told me with a smile one 25 December, trying to explain the boiled sweets he'd given me with my new Lego set. They tasted horrible so I took them to the park and threw them into a rubbish bin. When he asked me where they were I said I'd eaten them all, they were so nice. He smiled, and patted my head.

Edward Barron joined his father's great British company from university, and worked there until it wasn't so great any more and the new German owners sacked him. He left us shortly afterwards and went to work for a computer firm in France where he shacked up with a diminutive French secretary eighteen years his junior, who resembled a smaller, dumpier version of Cher, without the musical ability. 'My little foreigner,' he called Mireille, as if he was the great liberator, freeing her from Nazi oppression.

He didn't leave us with much, my father, apart from the psychological stuff. I guess the one thing Jes got from the father he never had was his singing voice. My father's mother was Irish somewhere back. I remember him singing 'The Fields of Athenry' while he shaved, and I imagined those fields, which were always green and dotted with happy picnicking red-headed families.

FATHERS

I had a father once. Perhaps we all do, except Jesus and
*   Vampires.*
My father wasn't Jesus or a Vampire but he did like loaves
*   and fishes, and never ate garlic.*
Fathers are meant to fix things like taps and cupboards and

the hearts of young boys rejected in love by eleven-year-
old girls,
But my father just fixed his hair each morning with Mr
Right-Sheen hair pomade.
I wish my father had been Jesus because he could have turned
water into wine at parties.

I feel suddenly morose, like the beginning of a hangover. I turn from Jes's picture gallery to the bookshelf, seeking a trashy novel to stop me reminiscing and send me off to sleep. In front of the books, as if on guard, is a small stuffed toy penguin, another reminder of Jes's childhood fascination for the stubby little birds. I smile unexpectedly at the memory of a room filled with penguin toys, penguin books and a couple of impressively tacky penguin duvets.

I don't understand why people love penguins. As far as I'm concerned, they're smelly, useless birds that spoil the perfect empty landscape of Antarctica. But my brother became addicted to them at an early age, buying any sort of penguin paraphernalia he could get his little hands on. I used to think it was because he was like them – fat, small and wonderfully gullible. I'd tease him constantly. 'Penguin bum!' I'd shout, enjoying his wails of protest.

On the bookshelf are all Jes's books from college, the masterpieces – Jane Austen, Gerard Manley Hopkins, Dickens, Thackeray, Graham Greene, Scott Barron.

I look again.

There I am, on the sacred shelf. To my surprise, my brother has put my three books in pride of place between

Collected Works of Keats and his guru, Samuel Taylor Coleridge. I can't resist taking out the first edition of *Uptown Guys* to see what I wrote in it for him. As I do a photograph falls on to the floor. I pick it up.

It's a colour picture from the late seventies. I wish I hadn't seen it. It shows two small boys. The older one is smiling cheekily. The younger one, almost half his height, holds on to the other's trouser leg, frowning out at the world. It's me and Jes. I must have been about eight, he about three, a year after our father left.

There's no hiding it. In the photograph I am fat. I have a wide, chubby face and dimples. I'm wearing a blue T-shirt stretched over a tight little belly. My arms are thick.

'Fatty!' they used to shout at school. 'Porky!'

'Lard arse!'

In the picture I am holding a Mars Bar, my chocolate of choice. I'd consume at least three a day. Mum didn't seem to mind. I guess she had other things to worry about after our father left and, anyway, she said a certain chubbiness was normal in young boys. I tried telling my classmates this, and regretted it almost immediately.

It wasn't until I hit puberty that I started to slim down, helped by my purchase of a set of exercise weights from Argos that I used religiously every evening before dinner.

I take the photo of the two fat brothers, and slide it underneath a large pile of old magazines. I glance inside the cover of *Uptown Guys*. The inscription, in my unruly hand, reads,

To Jes,
Thanks for all your love and support.
You're the best,
Luv, Scott.

The dance music starts soon afterwards. Jes is big on dance music – unlike me he loves to dance; he has done since he was little. I pull the sleeping-bag over my ears, wanting to block out the tripping drums and thumping bass. I can guess why the music is playing.

Then I hear the bed groan, Sam's quick laugh, and the rhythmic squeak, creak, squeak.

I try not to picture it, my fat brother and his pretty wife having sex. And in not picturing it, another image burgles into my head: Ellie, above me, rocking back and forth. I shake my head to banish her, but all I can see is her face, a puzzled frown, eyes wide, lost in the moment for once, as we make love and she whispers, fiercely, 'Screw me, yes!'

I pull back the sleeping-bag, get up from my inflatable mattress and go to the electric piano. I flick the setting on to 'Vibes' and play a note, a vibrating, farting D. I play 'Three Blind Mice' with both hands, from memory. It's quite good. Then I play 'Frère Jacques', but I can only remember the right hand. It's less impressive. The squeaking from the next room stops.

I flick swiftly to the Clavinova setting, and embark on an ambitious version of the *Pink Panther* theme, a wild improvisation that sounds only a little like the original. I tap my feet and start humming along with a few cha-cha-chas.

Jes opens the door. He's wearing nothing but tartan

boxer shorts, his voluminous belly hanging over the elastic waistband like butcher's meat. For a moment we look at each other, and in that look I see him as a five-year-old, when I ate his portion of Neapolitan ice-cream while Mum was out of the kitchen, starting with the strawberry, my favourite, and finishing with vanilla, his favourite. Maybe he's seeing me at the same moment, the mixture of elation and extreme guilt on my freckled face. 'I was just messing around,' I say.

'Sammy's got to work tomorrow,' he growls gruffly.

'Of course. I'm sorry.'

'Do you want a lift to the station in the morning?'

'That'd be great. Thanks.'

He presses both hands to his stomach, as if trying to smooth it down, or pack it inwards, and I notice how thin his legs are, as if they can hardly bear such weight.

'Sorry about the piano,' I say, softly.

'No problem.'

'I'll be quiet.'

He nods, once, turns and leaves the room.

'Good night,' I say, to the empty doorway.

I get out at Kentish Town station. It's raining, big fat gobbets of rain, unkind and vindictive. I decide to shelter in the Café du Nord but it's full, except for a table outside, half-way under the blue awning, which is taking a pounding from the rain. Under it I sip a large mint tea and look out at the delivery-vans snarling and cars growling and the people going to and fro all irritated. I watch men sheltering in the doorways opposite, and they all look glum.

It's funny: this is where it began, my professional writing career. Sitting in the Café du Nord, jotting down notes, drinking milky (non-fat) cappuccinos by the dozen.

I suppose you could say I've always been a writer. I think I started around the time my father departed, scribbling down stories, plays and anecdotes in the notebooks Mum used to get from drugs companies at the hospital. But I never recorded a diary of my own reality, my own thoughts. Instead I'd spend hours in my room creating imagined lives, an imagined life, involving a character called Scott Barron who was bigger and better than me. I'd wait for Mum to get home, dying to recite my latest instalments. Usually she'd apologize, say she was too tired, and I'd end up reading them to Jes, who complained that he'd much rather be watching *Blue Peter*.

Perhaps because of my literary hobby, I did well in English at school – in stark contrast to most other subjects – and somehow got into Bristol University, where I did less well studying English literature.

After Bristol, I decided to try and make it as 'a writer'. I wasn't sure what this meant, other than getting up late, going to the pub in the afternoon, and worrying about death, but nothing else grabbed me and I had hardly any money so very little to lose.

My break came three doors down from the Café du Nord, in the shabby offices of the *Camden Chronicle*, whose editor, the overweight, chain-smoking Charlie Smith, was bored enough by my pleading to grant me a weekly column depicting the characters who lived in the streets of Kentish

Town, under the title 'Kentish Gents', for which I was paid a handsome £75 a month.

It was under this awning, in rain similar to that which is currently tumbling out of the late September sky, that I wrote my first poem. I was bored. I gazed across the road at McDonald's and started to write about the skinny young man at the till in his jaunty red-paper hat, about his vanquished hopes and grimy-grey dreams. Charlie refused to publish 'Ronald of McDonald's,' saying poems were for exam papers and unread literary reviews. He held out until he realized that if he didn't use my poem he'd have to write the column himself.

Barbara Smiles called the next day and informed me that she was a literary agent. She also informed me that she hated modern poetry, but her boyfriend at the time – a millionaire venture-capitalist living near me in Tufnell Park – had shown her my poem, in tears. 'It touched a nerve, or something,' she said, in a vaguely disgusted tone.

Whatever it was that had made the venture-capitalist cry, Barbara Smiles wanted more of it. She would read ten of my poems and make a decision on representing me.

I went away and wrote twenty in a week, about Kentish Town men – the homeless tramps, the Bosnian stallholders and the millionaire venture-capitalists who populated the streets of NW5. I wandered, just watching, and was amazed by how easily I seemed to perceive these men's feelings, their frustrations, their hopes, their fears, and how easily I manipulated these perceptions into non-rhyming verse.

I was astonished when Barbara said she was impressed

enough to represent me. The venture-capitalist wasn't so lucky. He got the boot the following weekend.

I walk home even though the rain has only eased a little. I reach the top of my street where the slight slope starts to descend past the terraced houses and dog-shit-bottomed trees with ragged leaves. There, by the alleyway between the two blocks of flats, a homeless man sits on a duffel bag. He's old, maybe late sixties, maybe more, wearing a threadbare black suit and short black wellington boots. He'll be asked to move on because the flats are getting more expensive by the day and he's an eyesore. The owners are sure to call the police.

The old man sits there, a square of sodden cardboard over his head. His flesh is white, his face a mess of grey stubble and blotchy red marks that may or may not be lacerations. But his hair is carefully slicked back, combed with Brylcreem or some such product, in the manner of a forties movie star, just like my father's used to. He stares out at the world, eyes watery from the rain.

I know part of his story just from looking at him: that he has no woman in his world to admonish and encourage him, no one to pull him from this alleyway and hold him. I cross the road to avoid his croaky plea for cash.

As I pass by on the other side, I don't know his name, age or background. But I know that he is lonely.

3

My friends finally call. Each of them sounds relieved that Ellie and I have split up, glad that they will no longer have to deal with her cutting tongue, pleased that I am once again like them, back in the fold of the single, clumsy, thirty-something male.

'Sorry to hear it,' says Brian. 'But let's face it, you guys were completely incompatible.'

'Tough luck,' says Dr Simon. 'Still, it's better than getting stuck with the wrong woman for the rest of your life, don't you think?'

Then, to my surprise, they both recommend that I undergo psychiatric counselling.

'It's not that expensive,' says Dr Simon, a man not prone to spending money. 'I should have gone after Kathy dumped me.'

Brian is even more zealous, being from Los Angeles. 'I'm telling you, it'll cut your recovery time in half, at least. Go, talk to someone. You need to emote.'

The only one not to recommend relationship therapy is Big Barry, who gives me the number of a Dutch girl he met in Bali.

I stay in bed, feeling cold. With Ellie, staying in bed was as thrilling as a childhood midnight feast. It didn't happen often – Ellie was not one to lounge. I'd wake at nine thirty a.m. on a Saturday to find her in the other room inscribing the following week's schedule on to her palm-pilot. Or she'd be gone to the shops or the gym, having left a small Post-it note attached to the bedpost saying: 'GET UP, LAZY BONES!'

My happiest moments came when she was hung-over and would nestle into the duvet with primeval feminine lasciviousness. I'd lie there alongside her, holding her lightly (not too tight because then she'd ask me if I thought she was a security blanket or a rugby player), my front against her back, my cock hardening against her arse, and if I was very lucky, and the planets were aligned correctly, and a butterfly had beaten its wings in some Amazonian rain-forest, she would turn her beautiful head and flutter her long thick eyelashes – which were, occasionally, her own – and whisper, 'Okay, Scotty. Fuck me.'

But today I lie in bed alone. I can't move. I try to think of the future, of plans and projects, but I can see nothing, feel nothing ahead of me. So instead I stare at the white ceiling and try to imagine that I'm in frozen Antarctica, with no sign of human life before me. I imagine the ice, the howling wind, the empty white sky. I want to feel a calmness, a distance from the world. But I just feel alone. Maybe polar exploration isn't all it's cracked up to be.

Why am I not happier? I have a book published. I'm healthy. I'm thin.

But I'm miserable. My agent has no news. I have no poems in my head. I have no girlfriend.

I lie in bed and do what every man does when he's been dumped. I think about my exes.

It's not that I want to go out with them again. That would be too sad. It's just . . . I hope they still think of me. I hope that their memories of me sometimes make them smile, even though they're not the sort of women prone to random acts of smiling.

I worry sometimes, about the type of women I'm attracted to. They are usually less than sentimental. Not frosty, but not the warmest either. Let's put it this way: in four of my five main relationships I've been the one to say, 'I love you,' before my girlfriend.

The first was little Jenny Rowan, who took pity on me in my last year at sixth-form college. She was part of the 'cool set' at school, which seemed to include anyone who wasn't me. She wore black fishnet tights and snogged me at a seventies disco. After four months of resistance (mine, not hers), we had sex. She dumped me the following week. I have no idea where she is now, but I know two things: she's still talking about getting a tattoo, soon, and she hasn't thought about me in over a decade.

The second was Susan Fraser. She wrote a fashion column for the *Camden Chronicle*, which was surprising since she had no sense of fashion at all. She wore Marks & Spencer dresses and sensible shoes, and we spent almost two years together while I worried about my writing and she learned to speak Spanish. We never managed to orgasm together, but we had a strange knack for finishing each other's sentences. I reckon she still thinks about me occasionally, even though she's married with two kids and living in Barcelona.

The third on the list is Lucy Sanders. We went out for

seven months just after my first book was published. She worked in a bookshop in Tunbridge Wells where I did a poetry reading. Over a post-event pint of Guinness, she confessed to wanting to be a writer and I, being a published author and all, tried to help her with her ideas. She listened to my advice for a few months, then went on a creative-writing course. We lost contact. Her first novel has just been sold to one of the big three for £120,000. I'm pretty sure Lucy Sanders doesn't think about me much, since she's currently the most famous lesbian in the country.

Then there was Ellie. The ice queen of them all.

The only one of my longer-term girlfriends who said, 'I love you,' before I did was Naomi Lewis. She was half Australian and a computer specialist who did temp-agency work. We met at a party Barry invited me to, and I fell for her soft smile, pretty laugh and thin, delicate fingers. She didn't read much, but loved films. We went to the cinema two or three times a week, that rainy autumn, and she was always so funny, so cutting about the performances, the plots, the terrible sickly scripts. I loved her wit, her spark. Unlike my other girlfriends she had no problem talking about herself. She told me she loved me after three weeks of dating.

My mother didn't like Naomi. She thought she was too wishy-washy, too uncertain about her plans. My friends thought Naomi was a bit of a waster, drifting from job to job, never finishing anything. Then she got offered a ridiculously highly paid position at some bank in Sydney, the city of her birth. I told her she should go, it would be good for her career.

I know Naomi still thinks about me. I know she still smiles at the memories of our ten months together. We email, occasionally. Just last month she sent me pictures of her second child, Tommy, the two of them on a hammock in the backyard. She was smiling that smile, looking tanned and gorgeous. I have to say, her husband Mitch is a pretty good photographer.

I call Dr Simon at the hospital. After I've spent a few minutes listening to 'Greensleeves' being played by a chimpanzee on a xylophone, he comes to the phone. Before he can chide me for bothering him at work I ask whether he really thinks I should go and see a psychiatrist.

'What have you got to lose?' he growls, grumpily.

'My pride.'

'Listen, Scott, everyone goes these days.'

'Do you?'

'Me? No. I'm a doctor.'

'So why should I go?'

'It might make you feel better to talk about your feelings.'

'I don't want to talk about my feelings. If I need to get things out, I write about them.'

'Maybe it could be good material for you.'

This stops me. I have a sudden vision of Woody Allen lying on a couch pouring out his heart in a witty and humorous way. Perhaps Simon's right. It might be good for my career.

'Look, Si, you talk to Jes sometimes?'

'Sure. You know Jes, he likes to keep in touch.'

'Do me a favour, will you? Don't tell him I'm thinking of . . . you know . . . going to a shrink.'

He chuckles. 'You mean a mental-mechanic? The brain-plumber?'

'Simon –'

'Head-quack, thought-police . . .'

'I'm putting down the phone.'

'Dream-doc, mind-mender . . .'

The next day I catch a tube to south-west London, where I feel overwhelmingly hungry. I purchase three Prêt à Manger sandwiches and eat them hurriedly, one after the other. I spend a few minutes reading the labels on the back of the packet (a comforting habit – I like to see how things are put together), then take out the address written on a scrap of paper.

Lindsey Stevens was Brian's suggestion. She's somehow connected to the firm he works for. 'She's good with beginners,' was all he said.

The building is an old red-brick Victorian office block now converted into plush Chelsea flats. According to a polished brass sign by the double door, it had once housed an obscure office of the British and Overseas Railway Development Board. Where men in pinstripes and bowlers once tracked the progress of steam trains across Africa and Asia, connecting the points, revealing the hidden recesses of the dark continents, now – I imagine – Lindsey Stevens sits in her big leather armchair connecting the points, revealing the hidden recesses of her client's dark minds.

I don't want to go. Because it's weak. Or so my mum would say.

After my parents' divorce, our school suggested Jes and I should see a child psychiatrist. I wanted to go because it meant missing maths, but Mum didn't believe in it. 'Putting silly ideas into people's heads that were never there in the first place!'

I hesitate. I hear her words now, as I stand at the big double door.

'People should just learn that things aren't always simple!'

But I want to go, partly because visiting a shrink feels like something a writer should do so it might be good for my career. But I also want to know if Ellie and Sam and my friends are right. Am I cold, detached, and too self-absorbed? Because I don't mean to be. I don't want to be.

I ring the bell, looking around to see if anyone is watching. In the rickety lift I take out my scribbling pad and scribble:

Resist brainwash. Mouthwash for the mind?

Then add as an afterthought:

Carwash – why do men love cars?

I'd expected the waiting room to be full of tearful middle-aged women, dribbling young men, anorexic girls and mad-staring old guys – somewhere between *One Flew Over the Cuckoo's Nest* and a morning television chat-show. But there's only one other person here, a man about my age, in a suit. He nods at me, then returns to his copy of the *Financial Times*.

To my surprise, Lindsey Stevens isn't some posh sixty-year-old wearing pearls with a hint of a German accent. She's in her late forties, a wiry woman dressed in jeans and a dark woollen sweater. Her voice is soft and gravelly, an accent that occasionally hints at Essex origins. The only problem is, her breasts are quite large for her slender size, and I have difficulty keeping my eyes off them.

I sit on the brown-leather couch. The office is wood-panelled and there's a globe in one corner next to the high windows. I imagine the bowler-hatted men turning it carefully, one with a fancy silver pen, sleeve rolled up, drawing in the lines that will connect up the world. A world full of certainty, exactitude and resolution. A world opposite to mine.

My heart is beating faster. My palms are damp. What if she discovers something really wrong with me and I end up sectioned in a mental institution? The anvil in my stomach shifts slightly and I'm afraid Lindsey will hear the clunk. Then, in a flash, I imagine us naked on the couch, her on top of me as I grab her ample breasts, and I shake my head to rid myself of the vision. I mean, it's probably not good to begin the first session with your psychiatrist by imagining her having sex with you.

'So, Scott, what brings you here today?'

'I don't know. I just ... I haven't ... I'm not ...' I stammer.

She smiles, and I wonder if she knows I've been thinking about having sex with her. Can psychiatrists read your thoughts? Are we all that transparent, following well-known patterns, well-trodden paths? Are we all the same?

'I haven't been feeling great. That's all.'

'Right. Well, let's begin with an easy one. Can you describe how are you feeling? Right now. The first words that come into your head . . .'

I think about this. And I'm honest with her. 'I don't really know. It's just . . . I don't know.'

'What do you think brought you here this afternoon?'

'I feel a bit . . . I don't know. I feel a bit . . . heavy?'

'That's not an uncommon feeling.'

A short silence follows.

'I usually like to begin by getting to know the client a little bit. So, why don't you tell me about yourself?'

I try. Honestly I do. But I've never been very good at pouring my heart out to strangers. I come across as distant, shy at best, cold at worst. Perhaps if I'd been born in Sicily and attended the musty confessional on a weekly basis, I'd have no problem with it. But I'm from south-east England and at school they told me to stop crying when Michael Crawley punched me in my fat little stomach: 'Barron, you are a dreadful moaner.'

Needless to say, I don't tell Lindsey this. There is a short silence in the room, during which the clock ticks.

'What about your family background?'

'Mum's Scottish, from Edinburgh.' My stomach grumbles. I sit up in the chair. 'My father's English, but he's living in France. I guess you could say I'm a bit all over the place, family-wise.'

Your parents are separated?'

'Divorced.'

'How old were you?'

'Seven.'

'That must have been hard.'

I nod. My stomach rumbles again, deep and angry.

'Do you have any sisters or brothers?'

I fart. I can't help it. It's fat and loud. 'Sorry.' I blush.

The smell is impressive. Lindsey puts her hand to her mouth, suppressing a giggle.

'One brother,' I say quickly, trying to pretend nothing has happened. 'He lives in South London.'

'I see,' says Lindsey, attempting to regain her professional composure. 'Do you guys get on well?'

A simple question, you would think. But I don't answer. I sit there, unable to speak. I hope Lindsey's thinking that I'm debating her question, so I scratch my head a little to look like I'm thinking. And then I am thinking. Because I have a nagging sense at the back of my mind that there is something I should tell her. Something I need to say. But it doesn't enter my head.

So instead I answer her emotionally charged question as men traditionally reply to emotionally charged questions – with a fact devoid of emotion: 'He's five years younger than me.'

'You're the eldest?'

'Yes.'

'Do you like being the eldest?'

'Er . . . sure. It's okay. I mean, it's not like I had any choice in the matter.'

She nods slowly at my attempted witticism, scribbling a note on her pad. 'What happened after the divorce?'

I hesitate once more, then describe how our father left us, how he shacked up with a Gallic midget Cher lookalike, and how my mother made innumerable sacrifices to raise us, trying not to make it all sound like a Maeve Binchy novel.

'Did your mother remarry after your father left? Were there boyfriends?'

'No. It was just me and Jes. She always said we were the men in her life.'

Lindsey makes another note. I feel like I'm being interviewed for a job I don't know anything about, that I don't even know if I want.

'Did you ever feel like you had to compete with your brother for your mother's affections?' asks Lindsey, looking up once more.

'Well . . . No. Why? Should I have done?'

Lindsey Stevens smiles again. 'It's not compulsory, no. It's just quite common for siblings to feel resentment for each other, especially in single-parent households.'

'I don't think I feel resentment,' I lie.

'So you're a writer . . .' says Lindsey, changing the subject, breaking the silence.

This is evidently her tactic, to keep things bright and breezy, keep asking general questions, in the hope of catching me out. But I won't be caught out. She won't find anything wrong with me. 'Apparently. I'm a poet, sort of. I write about men and their feelings.'

'I know. My nephew gave me one of your books last Christmas.'

'*Men Matter*?' I ask, a little too enthusiastically.

'I think that was it. Very funny. I enjoyed it.'

'Thank you.'

'Why did you decide to start writing about men?'

I know the answer to this one. I've given it on several radio book shows, from BBC Leicester to Bittern FM, 'the Voice of the Norfolk Broads'. 'I don't know. I think maybe I felt a bit isolated from men after my father left. I guess writing about them is a way of reintegrating myself into male company.'

Lindsey nods, and makes a note, as if I've just revealed something about my inner psyche. I feel relieved. Maybe she thinks I'm opening up, letting it out.

'Why did you choose to be a writer?'

'Er . . . I'm good with words. I think I always have been. I read a lot when I was little. And I like stories. I used to write stuff, I had these notebooks Mum used to give me.'

'What sort of stories?'

'Anything, really. Stuff I'd make up, ghosts, space aliens, monsters, you know. When I was on my own I'd make up all these stories where I'd be the hero, fighting off invaders.'

'Would you say you were lonely as a child?'

'A little bit. The thing is, I was . . .' I don't want to say it. Lindsey looks at me, waiting. 'I was fat. For a few years. I got teased a bit.'

'The usual stuff?'

'Yeah. You know, "fatty", "chubby", "lard-arse". Children can be cruel.'

Lindsey looks at me. 'So can adults.'

I nod, slowly. Lindsey scribbles something once more. 'I have several clients who are writers,' she says, and I detect just a hint of pride in her voice.

'We're a deviant lot,' I say, noncommittally.

'They all have different explanations for why they write. Some say they're dissatisfied with reality, and feel a need to invent their own. Others have a highly developed fear of death and write, so they tell me, because they want to leave something behind, a sort of memorial, I suppose. Why do you think you write, Scott? The first answer that comes into your head.'

I think. Then I realize I shouldn't be thinking, I should just be answering. 'Er . . . it pays all right. And I can get up late.'

Lindsey laughs, or at least pretends to. I wonder if I should tell her that actually I haven't been getting up late recently. I've been waking at five a.m. after two hours' sleep. I haven't got up late in months, even when I was with Ellie. After all, this is the real reason I've come here. But Lindsey seems to enjoy discussing easy things, like families and writing, and anyway the hour is nearly up.

'So, Scott, how was it for you?' she asks. I wonder if I can hear just a hint of flirtation. 'Not too torturous?'

'No. It was fine.'

'Do you fancy coming back next week?'

To my surprise I say yes.

Outside, I head up and down a nearby street. I try to remember what Lindsey talked about, to piece together what I might have learned for my forty-five pounds. Something about being the eldest and writers writing to leave something behind.

I end up on the King's Road. The sun is easing weakly through a misty cloud. Ahead, a couple are strolling, looking chic and confident in the autumn afternoon sunshine. I can tell the woman is beautiful just from the way she walks, her soft, assured saunter. The man is taller, thickly built, and dressed in a cool roll-neck sweater. He swaggers as he strides.

As they near, and I try to look without looking, I see that the woman is Ellie.

My heart bursts.

I walk into the side of a bus shelter. 'Ow! Shit!' I crumple to the ground.

An old Asian man stares at me. 'All right, mate?'

I look up, trying to pretend I haven't just walked head first into a bus shelter. As the couple turn the corner the woman glances at me, prone on the concrete, and I see clearly that she's not Ellie, just someone who looks a bit like her, another West London brunette beauty.

'Shall I call an ambulance?' asks the old Asian man, gently. I shake my head, and gingerly ease myself up, clinging to the side of the bus shelter. As I do so, a red double-decker bus pulls up. On the side is a long poster advertising the latest John Grisham. John stares down, arms folded, judgemental as a prosecutor.

I run down the King's Road until I get to Sloane Square. I know I have two options: to go back to Lindsey Stevens and tell her all about Ellie and how I'm hurting, or to find a bookshop.

I find a bookshop.

In Waterstone's, my book is in the New Titles section at the front of the store. I grab a copy and hold it to my breast. I stand for a moment until I realize I now have a large card attached by sticky tape to the front of my sweater. I peel it off and read.

Men and Other Mammals
Barron's brand new collection of short poems is as hilarious and poignant as his previous works, but this time a gentle melancholia lends the writing a softer, yet perversely sharper resonance. His poems contrast the sweet recollections of childhood with a bitter sense of contemporary apathy. Barron tells us what it is to be a man at the beginning of the twenty-first century.

John Nesbitt, deputy assistant manager

I go up to the information desk and ask to see John Nesbitt. He appears from behind a stack of pink self-help books. He's almost bald, with the face of a twelve-year-old and a deep voice that seems better suited to a fifty-year-old bank manager. 'Thanks for your write-up,' I say.

'No problem. Liked the book. Funny, you know funny ha-ha, not funny strange.'

I nod, modestly.

'Hey, since you're here, do you want to sign some copies?' he asks brightly, as I'd hoped he would.

'Does it do any good? I mean, signing?'

'Some people will buy a signed copy of anything. And

the publishers won't take them back once they're signed, so we'll have to sell them.'

I sign twelve copies. In each, I cross out the printed version of my name with a single line, as authorial tradition dictates, and sign in my own swirling hand.

Scott Barron

Me. In ink. I begin to feel a little better.

'Ever done any writing yourself, John?' I inquire, wanting in some way to thank him for being there in my moment of need.

'Writing? No, mate. To be honest, I'm not much of a book guy. I'm jacking it in next month – emigrating to New Zealand with the girlfriend.'

'You've got a job out there?'

'Naw. We're just gonna bum it for a bit, you know? Live a little.' He lowers his voice. 'Here, you might as well sign the lot. I'll be twelve thousand miles away by the time they find out.'

Back at my flat the heating is still not working. There are two answering-machine messages. The first is from Barbara: 'Good news, Scott! Not the other good news, which is still in the pipeline, but different good news! Call me!'

I call her. She takes a breath, then exhales: 'Good Life Muesli!'

'What?'

'The crunchy breakfast crap that actress advertises on the telly. They want your poems!'

'For the telly?'

60

'No, you daft bugger, to put on the back of their cereal packets! So Mr and Mrs Welwyn Garden Suburb can pretend to be cultured over breakfast!'

'Wow. A cereal packet.'

'Four thousand minus commission, which, if you recall, is twenty per cent for merchandising.'

'Muesli. Wow.' It's not London Underground, but it's a start. I mean, a lot of people eat muesli.

'Wait, wait! Julie, get me the muesli fax!'

There's a dramatic rustling of paper while I imagine my poem sitting alongside a tastefully photographed bowl of hazelnuts and sultanas. 'Here's the slogan they want to use . . .' Barbara pauses, putting her training in advertising voice-overs to good use. 'Put the Goodness Back in Your Life!'

A moment passes. I don't know what to say.

'Okay, it's bloody crap, but it'll sell your books.'

'It's great. Thanks, Barbara.'

'Remember, Scott-lad, every little counts!'

The second message is from Big Barry: 'Hear you're in the market for a new bird. Got just the gig. Totty-tastic. Give us a tinkle.'

4

As usual Big Barry has talked me into doing something I have no desire to do.

The invite is in gold lettering:

Sixty seconds to find true love!
The new craze from the Big Apple!
Join us to find The One!

It's difficult saying no to Big Barry. You try.

'Don't you like women, Brains? Are you not of the male gender? Do you not have a penis, testicles and spunk that needs liberating from solitary confinement?'

'Barry . . .'

'There'll be some great-looking gash. Don't you like great-looking gash?'

'Barry . . .'

'Thursday night. The Pacific. Only fifty gold ones.'

'Fifty quid?'

'You're a top author. You can afford it.'

Big Barry calls me Brains partly because I once won a crossword competition in the *Bristol Advertiser*, and partly because when you get to know him, he's insecure about his own intelligence, even though he earns six hundred thousand a year investing other people's money in companies no one has heard of. Barry McGee is from Galway, although you wouldn't know it from his Cockney accent, meticulously cultivated over three years at Bristol where we both wrote for the *Collegiate*, a flimsy little-read student paper. I was the 'Student News' reporter, spending all night editing and re-editing two-hundred-word articles about rent rises at Whiteladies' flats, or blocked toilets at the university sports ground. Barry was the eponymous 'Mr Party', outlining the best Bristol had to offer in the way of free alcohol and easy women. Needless to say he was avidly read by the few students who bothered picking up our free paper while I was not.

Now Barry is a thirty-five-year-old millionaire who still delights in free alcohol and easy women.

'Thursday night, Brains. Gash galore.'

I call Ellie again. Again her answering-machine clicks on, but I sense she's there checking her caller display. I curse my technological incompetence – I have no idea how to block my number.

So I walk half a mile to a phone-box, preparing a hundred different devastating put-downs and insults in my head. This time, to my horror, she answers.

'Hello?'

'Ellie it's me, I just want to talk to you.'

'Scott?'

'I'm sorry about everything. Can I see you? There's so much I want to say –'

'I can't deal with this right now. I'll call you some time. 'Bye.' And she puts down the phone.

I stand there, by Kentish Town station, holding the phone, which buzzes angrily at me. I grip it tighter. Then, to my surprise, I find myself hammering the plastic receiver against the metal casing of the phone-box. It breaks surprisingly easily.

It takes me two minutes to race back to my freezing flat, a criminal on the run. I lock the door and cover my head with my duvet, trying not to think of Ellie with her new money man.

On Thursday afternoon I go to see my editor at Oak Tree Press. Eric Maloney sits in his swivel chair and tries not to swivel, although I can tell he is excited. 'My wife loves Good Life Muesli,' he says, swivelling slightly.

'I've never eaten it. But you see it in Waitrose.'

'Well, Scott, it's a good product. A damn fine product. Who knows? Maybe one day we'll get the bus.'

'The bus?'

'The big guys get them – you know, Clancy, Michael Owen, Posh Spice. A big red London bus. Book title, mugshot, two decks high. Imagine that.'

Eric Maloney is in his late thirties, but still has a boyish enthusiasm for success that perhaps stems from his New York upbringing. He didn't like me at first, or so he told me, but when the first print run of *Uptown Guys* sold out, he found himself liking me more. Now he loves me. Not only do my books make money but he can say he edits a modern poet. As far as he's concerned, it doesn't get any better than that.

'I was having dinner the other day with McCabe at the *Observer*. He was droning on about the lack of classical structure in modern poetry, all this tosh about how your poems were nothing more than ditties, how time was ripe to get back to the alexandrine and what-not. Anyway, I told him to put a sock in it, because the reason you sell so well is that people today just don't like structure. A world without barriers demands art without barriers.'

'I guess so.'

'And people want emotion, Scott. Raw emotion. They want it real. And emotion isn't structure. It's instinctive, immediate. That's what you do so well.'

'Thanks, Eric.'

He lights a cigarette and artfully blows two smoke-rings in front of a framed black and white poster of a young Alain Delon smoking a cigarette and blowing smoke-rings. 'Cup of tea?'

The phone rings. Eric picks it up, listens for a moment and hands it to me with a polished smile. 'Darling Barbara. She says she's got some news that she'll only share with her favourite poet.'

The receiver smells of tobacco and stale breath, like the phone in my father's study for what seemed like years after he left.

'All right, Scott-lad. It's good-news time!'

'What good news?'

'*The* bloody brilliant news! The Beeb wants you! Television calls! Your agent is a miracle, she's got you a fifteen-minute slot, reading your own poems. They wanted an actor, but I said no! He can do it, Scott Barron's a looker, he's a charmer, he's a bloody star in the making! And they said yes!'

I listen hard, trying to make sense. 'What are you saying?

That the BBC want me to do a programme?'

'Exactly. And you're going to be bloody brilliant!'

'That's great, Barbara, but what will I —'

'Keep smiling. The future is bright. Give Eric a kiss from me.'

Eric is impressed, as Barbara Smiles intended. She's a smart player, my agent. Calling me at the publisher's means that everyone here will get excited too, raising my profile another small rung up the ladder to big marketing bucks.

Eric steps outside his office, beats a spoon against his *Reservoir Dogs* mug and announces that I'm going to be a TV star. The bored assistants and PR girls applaud. Miranda pretends to smile.

At the lift, Eric pauses, a hand on my shoulder. 'Any feelings about the next collection?'

'Er . . . not really. Not yet.'

His eyes narrow, something else he's borrowed from the Alain Delon poster. 'You are happy with us, aren't you, Scott?'

'Yes. Of course.'

'Well, I was thinking, and it's just a suggestion, but hear me out – after all, I have some experience in developing the careers of brilliant young writers . . .' Eric smiles, glancing round conspiratorially to check he isn't being overheard by the empty atrium. 'Women.'

'Women?'

'You should write about women. How they feel. What they think. A complete change of tack. Catch them unawares. Women, it's a huge market . . . I don't have to tell you that.'

I think about this. I have no better idea of how women think or feel than most men. I don't even know how *I* think or feel. My poems sometimes give the impression they are about me, but they're merely inventions, glimpses into a fabricated soul. I've been making up stories since I was old enough to read *Pinocchio*. But writing about women? That would be the biggest lie I've ever told.

'That's interesting. I'll certainly think about it.'

'I'm here for you, Scott. Any time.' He cups his hand to his ear. 'What's that I hear? What's that I hear?'

I look at him. 'What can you hear, Eric?'

'The bus, Scott. The big red bus is coming.'

I meet Barry in the bar of one of those cavernous London restaurants to which celebrity chefs lend their names in order to get awestruck customers like me through the door. By the time I arrive he's half-way into a bottle of Pol Roger.

'Up, up and away.'

'This is going to be terrible.'

'Relax, *compadre*. We're here to have a laugh. F-U-N! Fun, fun, fun!'

Bass music thumps out from behind a pair of large gold doors. I'm feeling a little nervous, but I'm wearing my lucky pants – black Calvin Klein briefs that Ellie said made me look like a male model, almost.

Big Barry is dressed big: a black suit that's cut so slickly it seems sculpted to him, exaggerating his big chest, his big neck showing signs of a recent shave, his big Patrick Cox shoes. But, then, everything about Barry is always big

– his chest, his hands, his head (literally, and figuratively). He's a big spender, a big noise, a big deal. But he has a big heart. Most of the time.

Big Barry picks up the champagne bottle by the neck like a club and thumps open the golden doors, a prize gladiator entering the Colosseum. I feel small in his giant presence, a sword-bearer or entrails-sweeper, happy enough to be following.

Nobody has ever accused Big Barry of under-confidence. But if I had the courage, I would accuse him of sometimes seeking new conquests at the expense of spending time with his friends, in particular me. As he strides towards the tables, I know he hasn't asked me along because he wants to find out how I'm feeling about Ellie, or about my new book, or about anything except whether I feel as lucky as he does tonight. I'm here to be his sidekick, someone to talk to until he can make contact with the opposite sex.

To punish him I decide not to tell him about my television prospects. I smile at the thought that, when he finds out, he'll be mildly offended he wasn't told first.

The concept for the evening is distressingly simple. Thirty men sit on chairs down one side of the room, facing thirty women sitting on the opposite side. We all wear stickers with our names written on them in black felt-tip pen. We are separated by eight trestle tables, end to end. Each man has sixty seconds to introduce himself to the woman opposite and say something witty/charming/sexy/engaging/life-changing. The compère then rings a bell, 'CLANG!', and the woman has sixty seconds to make her pitch. Once that minute is up, the men shift one seat along. At the end of the process, you write down the names of the members of the opposite sex you want to go on a date with. Those who coincide head together to the bar or bed. Those who don't . . . well, the photocopied sheet leaves that to the imagination.

'TAKE YOUR SEATS, LADIES AND GENTLEMEN!'

It's well organised, I'll give them that. We each have a number, and approach our designated chairs like the market cattle we are. Everyone starts scribbling notes on the white cards provided, anxiously preparing minute-long biographies.

'Come on, Shakespeare! This is your game, ain't it?'

'I don't know, Baz.'

'You're a writer, for Chrissakes! Just write one of your "short, witty, brilliant poems".'

'This is different.'

'What's the difference?'

'I dunno . . . It's just more . . . personal.'

I've written four lines. Barry has a series of extravagant squiggles on his card, which he flourishes like a banknote. 'What's that?' I inquire, knowing that he will be more than happy to talk about his own presentation.

'Target points. Likes, dislikes. Current position. Future goals. Hit the target, bang, bang, in, out, on your way. It's simple.'

I sit down opposite my first 'date'. Count to five, then look up.

'Hi.'

'Hi.'

She's wearing glasses. That's the first thing I notice.

Then I notice the mousy hair pulled back in a severe ponytail. Then I notice her fingernails – scarlet. Before I can notice anything else a bell rings.

CLANG! CLANG!

Round one.

'Hello. Yes. Er . . . I'm Scott. I don't . . . er . . . well . . . How to put it? How indeed? Er . . . I don't normally do this, I mean, like . . . blind dates. Not that this is a blind date, is it? But it's not like we've met before. No. Have we?'

Around me I sense a huge swell of energy, the surging of male voices, a one-way assault of desire and hope. I want to look at the woman opposite, but there's no time, no point. Seconds are ticking away. I try to make out what I've written on the card.

'Okay, here goes . . . I'm, well, my name is Scott, oh, God, I already said that. I was born in Cambridge, I'm thirty . . . thirty-one years old, my mum's from Scotland, my dad lives in France . . . and, er . . . er . . . er . . .'

I stare in panic at my white card, which is now just a series of indecipherable black swirls, like Jes's paintings when he was six – I took them down and threw into the bin, to his dismay and Mum's reprimanding anger.

'Yes, well. Yes. There we go.'

Now I do look at the woman opposite, and she's smiling thinly, trying to exude sympathy.

'Oh, and I run, yes, I run . . . every day, really. I mean, it gets me out of the house, you have to get out of the house, don't you? I run up on the Heath, four miles, that's what I run, just about . . . Hampstead Heath, do you know it? Of course you do, I mean, if you live in London, which you might not, oh, shit –'

CLANG! CLANG!

I stare at my lap. It feels like the end of a boxing round in which no punches were landed, the crowd still waiting for blood. I am sweating more than my deodorant was designed to cope with.

'WOMEN DO YOUR THING!'

CLANG! CLANG!

I look up. She's staring at me, like I'm a target, an object. Her words come out in measured syllables, not spewed but constructed.

'My name is Laura Mercer, I'm a management consultant for one of the top five. I'm a Pisces but I don't like fish. I like long walks, swimming in foreign waters, Coen Brothers movies. I've jumped out of an aeroplane twice, with a parachute . . .'

She leaves space for me to laugh, which I don't as I'm too nervous, so she laughs herself, quickly.

'. . . I speak Spanish, at least to a conversational level, my favourite colour is magenta, I own my own flat in Battersea, my last holiday was to Cuba where I learned to salsa, I'm passionate about opera, as long as it isn't German, and I can cook, up to a point.'

She keeps her eyes focused on me as she speaks, hardly blinking. And I realize this is what she does for a living. The pitch. The analysis. Sell the vision, the product. Which isn't such a bad thing – I mean, that's what we're taught to do these days, isn't it? We've imagined everything before it's happened, written out our target points, visualized our goals. No wonder we're all so ironic: we wait for things to turn out the way we planned and when they don't, we laugh at them to hide our disappointment.

'I like to dance, drink fine wine and go to the occasional art exhibition, but never, ever to a musical, I simply loathe them. I travel when I have time off, usually Europe for long weekends, especially in the wintertime. I haven't always been single, and I'm not looking for a father for any children, but if the right man comes along I have no issues with commitment. Laura Mercer. Remember that name.'

CLANG! CLANG!

She's timed it to perfection.

I smile weakly. She smiles weakly. I move on to the next chair.

Just before the bell chimes again, Barry leans close and stage-whispers, 'Didn't fancy yours much.'

I improve slowly. Here's how I do it: I drink ten plastic cups of cheap red wine; I try not to stammer; I make things up. After all, I'm a writer. The funny thing is, as soon as I start to invent, I find it easier to talk about myself or, rather, someone I've just invented out of the hot, perspiring, red-wine night.

'Hi, I'm Scott, I was born in Edinburgh but moved to Islington when I was five. I teach English at a comprehensive school in Surbiton, I'm divorced but no children, thank God. I'm a Leo, I like clubbing, never miss Ibiza although, yes, I agree it's a little *passé*, but we've been going since eighty-seven. I voted for Tony, but I'd say I'm more of a free-market man and, as for European integration, well, fine, as long as we don't get Italian rock bands . . .'

At half-time I seek refuge in the toilets, along with a dozen suited men. We all studiously avoid looking at each other.

Back in the main room, Big Barry is chatting away to two women at the bar, both of whom are on my list of four prospective dates. Other women are sitting on their own, as if waiting for someone to ask them to dance.

I feel like laughing. Sixty seconds to find a mate. Why don't we just sniff arses?

What the fuck am I doing? Get out, out, out!

CLANG! CLANG!

And so it goes on. The auction of our self-esteem.

'Hi, I'm Cindy.'

Cindy is my twenty-fourth date this evening. She doesn't look at me, but stares down at her card. Because I sense she's not looking at me, I sneak a glance at her. She has red-wine stains around her lips. Her hair is straight but somehow it doesn't seem like it wants to be that way. She's wearing a roll-neck sweater that looks like it's been pulled over her head too many times, made from the sort of cheap fibre Ellie would laugh at, then burn.

This being the second half of the contest, the women go first. Cindy still doesn't look up. She has a London accent. 'Hello, er, Scott. I'm Cindy. I don't really like that name, I mean, it's a doll, isn't it, and who wants to be called after a doll? I know I don't. I guess I could change my name, so any suggestions would be gratefully received . . .' She takes a quick swig of wine, snatches a swift glance at me. She has brown eyes. I smile back, trying to make her

73

feel better. For the first time tonight I feel a connection to the woman opposite. Because Cindy is more nervous than me.

'I suppose I should tell you what I do, because that's one of the definitions we look for, isn't it, like what music the person likes, films, things like that? I suppose. Well, I'm a . . . um . . . I work for the Inland Revenue. Yup. I'm a tax collector. It's not great fun, but it pays quite well. And I work in an office with a view of the river, which is nice, because I like the river. We get good holidays too, and I love to travel, you know, backpacking and all. I've been to a few places recently, er . . . Bolivia, Morocco. I just got back from South Africa . . . I live in Queen's Park, a nice flat, sort of . . . but I often dream of . . .'

CLANG! CLANG!

She stops. Her time is up. Her dream cut short. She still doesn't look at me, but takes another swig of wine.

CLANG! CLANG!

For some reason I abandon the fictionalized Scott Barrons I've created for the last dozen women and start to tell the truth again.

'I'm Scott. Um . . . I'm a Virgo, but not a typical Virgo because a typical Virgo would, um . . . would know what the characteristics of a Virgo are. Anyway, I . . . I have a brother called Jes, who's younger than me. Yes. He's five years younger and he's married to Sam, who's cool. They seem happy. They live in Morden, South London – you know Morden? I didn't, but I do now. Obviously. He's a writer, sort of like me, and sometimes I think he's better than me, but I'm more successful. I write poems. I've had three books published. You might have read . . .'

There is a squeal. I look up. Cindy is sitting there with red wine dripping into her lap. Her plastic cup lies on the table still rolling from side to side. 'Sorry, sorry . . . oh, God, I'm always doing that. Oh, shit . . .' She pushes back her chair, mumbles an apology and hurries to the toilets. I feel like following her, to tell her it's all right, but the bell rings, the men stand, and I move on down the line.

I lie swiftly to the remaining six women, all of whom work as lawyers or finance executives or something, and the final bell tolls.

'BRAVO, BRAVO!' chirps the compère, betraying great relief that her evening's duties are coming to an end and she can go home and laugh about the sad thirty-somethings trying to find love as if it was something they could buy off the shelf like sunglasses or stock options.

'NOW WRITE DOWN THE NAMES OF ANY PEOPLE YOU'D LIKE TO SEE AGAIN ALONGSIDE YOUR OWN NAME ON THESE STRIPS OF PAPER, AND PUT THEM IN THE HAT OF LOVE!'

I look at my strip of white paper. Now when it comes to the crunch I don't want to meet any of these women. Apart from maybe Cindy, just to buy her a drink and tell her it was okay about the wine-spilling. So I write, CINDY. And next to it, SCOTT. Then, for a laugh, on a second piece of paper I write BARRY, and next to it, CINDY. Because Cindy has left and it might wind Barry up as he looks for her.

While the compère and her little helpers sort out the strips of paper, I join Barry at the bar. He's ordered another bottle of Pol Roger and is chatting to the most attractive woman in the room. 'Scott, this is Nancy. She works in advertising.'

'Hello, Scott. Find anyone to your taste?'

'Dozens.' I smile.

Barry pours me a glass of champagne and we toast each other. Then he shifts his body just slightly so that he's turned himself towards Nancy, blocking me from her. 'So, Nan, what was this concept for British Airways again?'

The compère comes around with the hat of love. Suddenly my heart is thumping. What if no one wants me? What if I've just been rejected by thirty women in a single singles night?

Nancy excuses herself and heads for the toilets. Perhaps she's embarrassed about the number of men who have doubtlessly put their names next to hers. I wonder what she's doing here, as pretty as she is. Perhaps it's a bet. All the men glance at her, apart from Barry. He's too big to show he's interested.

The compère hands out the paper strips, and I see people's eyes shut or open depending on what they're given. Then she's at my side. Judgement is nigh.

'Here you are, Scott.'

I look in my hand. Three strips of paper. I breathe out. At least I've not been rejected. I look at the names.

SCOTT. LAURA.

SCOTT. BARRY. Alongside it Barry has scrawled, UNLUCKY! and drawn an ejaculating penis.

Good old Barry.

The last strip of paper reads, SCOTT. CINDY.

I look up quickly, seeking out Cindy's face. Because she must still be here – she wrote the strip of paper. I really want to talk to her, to tell her it's okay about the wine, to make her feel better, to save her from any feelings of shame.

And then I see her. She's laughing, despite the red stain on the front of her dress. And in front of her, offering her a sip of Pol Roger champagne, is Barry. She's holding up the piece of paper that I wrote for him, as a joke. BARRY. CINDY.

'So how did you do, Scotty-poos?'

I turn and Laura Mercer is at my side. She hands me a plastic cup of red wine. 'I forgive you, you bastard.'

'For what?'

'For not choosing me.'

'I . . . er . . .'

'I guess women who know what they want really scare men like you.'

I look at her. Her eyes are focused on mine, or at least she thinks they are, but she's a little too drunk to focus on anything, even with her honed presentation skills.

I glance over at Barry. He has his arm round Cindy's shoulders. Beyond, Nancy is surrounded by six men, jostling each other for a second of her voluptuous time.

For some reason, in this moment, I think of Jes.

'C'mon, Scott . . .' says Laura.

Jes would do what he felt.

'Sorry, Laura, I've just got to go and talk to someone . . .'

I stride over to Barry and Cindy. Barry's body is blocking the room from his prey, but I duck round him, being slimmer, and appear at Cindy's left shoulder, the one without Barry's large hand on it. 'Hi, Cindy.'

She turns and blushes. 'Oh . . . hi. I'm so sorry about the wine . . . I'm just so clumsy sometimes.'

'It's fine. No problem. I'm always spilling stuff. Isn't that right, Barry?'

Barry doesn't reply.

'Was Barry telling you that it was me who wrote his name by yours, for a joke?'

Cindy looks confused. Barry's glare turns homicidal.

'We're old friends, you know, from university and, well, we like to play jokes on each other. I'm sorry. It was silly. But, then, the whole evening's a bit silly, isn't it?'

Cindy nods. Barry is now shifting from foot to foot, as if limbering up for a run, or a fight. But I feel big. I feel tall. I smile and say, 'I was just getting a cab home. I live near you, I think, I'm in Kensal Rise. Perhaps I could drop you in Queen's Park?'

Barry has had enough. 'Me and Cindy are just going to China White for a drink. Aren't we, Cindy?'

Cindy looks worried. 'Er . . . well . . . if it's all the same to you, Barry, I don't think I need any more to drink. I should be getting home.'

'Nonsense. As we say in Ireland, the night is getting younger . . .'

I look at him – we both know they say no such thing in Ireland, but he ignores me.

'But of course it's up to you, Cindy. You must decide how you feel,' he says, gently, his hand firmly on her right shoulder.

Cindy looks panicked, as if she's no idea how she feels. I sympathize. I put a hand on her left shoulder. 'I can drop you off in the cab. It's no problem.'

So we stand, two men, each with a hand on one shoulder of the woman we're pursuing. It's going to be the survival of the ... what? The fittest? The smartest? Or the man with the best information?

'I really should get going, Cindy,' I say, gently insistent. 'Where exactly in Queen's Park do you live?'

Cindy looks from me to Barry. 'Sorry, Barry. I think I need to go home. Perhaps another time.'

As we get to the door I can't quite believe that I've won a woman from under Big Barry's nose.

'I think I'm going to be sick,' murmurs Cindy, as we get into a mini-cab, and she leans her head against my chest.

SEX

Women think men need sex to love.
Men think women need love to sex.
But the truth is, men like love more than sex,
Because when she loves you
You get laid all the time.

*

I wake with a searing headache. I have no idea where I am. Everything is different – smell, temperature, the lumpy mattress beneath my backside.

OH, JESUS!

There's a face next to me that I don't quite recognize. Mouth slightly parted, tongue black with wine, a small

79

pool of dribble gathered beneath a small chin.

Then I remember. Almost everything.

And I feel as dark as a hole.

I look at Cindy next to me. She's not moving. I watch to see her breathing. Come on, Cindy. Nothing. Oh, my God, she's not breathing. She's dead.

I don't know her. I mean I know her name and that she wears a black Wonderbra and likes oral sex . . . but that's it. And now she's dead. I'm the last person to see her. To touch her. Shit. What will I say? What will I tell her parents?

'So, how did you know our daughter, Mr Barron?'

'Well, how can I put it, Mrs Shavers? She was very drunk and so was I, but somehow we ended up in bed together. She rode me like Lester Piggott till we both came, almost simultaneously. At this point I wanted to go to sleep because my hangover was kicking in, but she seemed to wake up a little and commanded me to perform oral sex on her while she hung her head out of the window and howled like a banshee.'

'Oh.'

'Yes, Mr and Mrs Shavers. If it's any consolation she came three times. In the space of an hour.'

Then Cindy moves, gruntingly, stretching across the futon, kicking me in the balls. I forgive her for this because I'm relieved she's alive.

I try to push her back to her side, but she's locked there, crucified across her bed, on home territory. My head is pounding as if someone's trying to nail my cranium to the pillow. I need a drink of water, or something, anything to help me feel better.

I get up from the lumpy futon, hit my shins on a low metal table and sprawl headlong into her dirty laundry basket.

'Go to sleep . . .' she growls, in a voice that hardly seems like it could belong to the same sweet girl who folded my lucky Calvin Klein's so carefully before performing fellatio.

I want to leave. I'm not sure why. I pull a pair of knickers off my head and reach for my jeans. As I do I feel dizzy suddenly, my head cold with sweat, and I know I'm going to be sick so I dash from the room. I just make it across the narrow hallway to the bathroom, opening the door, pulling on the light before I vomit out takeaway curry long and hard into the toilet bowl.

'What the hell?'

I look up. Two men are lying in a double bed, staring at me as sick dribbles down my chin.

'What are you doing in the bathroom?' I ask, innocently enough.

'What? This isn't the fucking bathroom!'

It does seem unlikely now that this is the bathroom. My spicy vomit is starting to seep out of the wicker wastepaper basket on to what looks like an expensive Persian carpet.

'You fucking idiot!'

I run from the room, snatch my jeans, shirt and shoes and dash at speed for the front door. The lock is caught. I can hear footsteps, shouts.

'Cindy, what the hell is going on? Cindy –'

'Shut up, Billy, I'm sleeping –'

'Your fucking boyfriend just threw up in my bin!'

I jiggle the lock, drop a shoe, and sprawl out into the

corridor. The door swings shut. SLAM. I hurtle down the stairs, two flights, holding my one remaining shoe, and out into the street.

It's raining. Of course.

I'm half-way down the street before I realize I've trodden in dog shit without a shoe, I've left my lucky pants on Cindy's floor, and I have absolutely no idea where I am.

The road sign says ENDEAVOUR ROAD NW6.

WHERE AM I?

It's funny how you can feel so alone after the closest intimacy with another human being. I woke next to Cindy and I felt a sudden and intense need to protect myself. From what? From being hurt? From hurting her? From having to embark on a deeper and ultimately painful excursion into each other's emotions, into each other's unchangeable past?

I feel like shit. I've deserted a woman I've just slept with. There was me thinking I was so superior to Ellie, that I would never treat anyone with the disdain with which she treated me, and now I've done the same thing. Maybe I was wrong. Maybe I'm no better than her.

I wait for a taxi, but no cars pass. I begin to shiver, gently.

I start to walk, glad that I'm still a little bit drunk despite the vomiting, and therefore capable of walking huge distances without any sense of time or fatigue. I decide I want to find John Nesbitt from Waterstone's, Kensington, before he goes to New Zealand with the love of his life and ask him one question: 'Tell me, John, what is it to be a man at the beginning of the twenty-first century?'

5

I'd forgotten my mother's sixtieth birthday. We've all done it, haven't we? Please say yes.

There are several reasons I'd forgotten it. Perhaps because of my pounding hangover, perhaps because over the past few weeks I've been a little self-obsessed. Anyway, there is definitely some excuse.

It was Jes who reminded me. He always reminds me of such things, my dear conscience-inducing brother. He's given me twenty-four hours to redeem myself.

Sarah Henderson, once Barron, now Henderson again, is going to be sixty. She was born and raised in Edinburgh before meeting her English prince Edward at Jesus College Cambridge in 1963. They met in the college JCR watching Kennedy's assassination, the packed room hushed as they all stared in disbelief at the President's head exploding again and again, while Jackie threw herself at his side.

Apparently my mother burst into tears after the sixth time blood splattered from Kennedy's temple, which is unlike her and must have given Edward Barron a false impression of an emotional, impressionable young beauty, ready for the plucking. He put his arm round her and they cuddled close as the youthful President was shot in the head one more time.

My parents were brought together by an assassination. She should have known.

In 1963, my mother was a very attractive woman. There's that strange moment in the life of every teenager when you pick up a picture of your parents in their teens, and wonder what it would have been like to hang out with them. Would they have been your mates? Would you have fancied them?

Without being too Oedipal, I think I'd have fancied my mum. There's a picture of them going to a May Ball in Cambridge in their final year. She's wearing a short dress that ends a couple of inches above her knees and she looks gorgeous, sexy, even. My father is wearing a tuxedo, a devilish goatee etched on his face, his arm round her as if he's afraid she might escape.

No. I don't blame him for seducing her. I just blame him for walking out on her.

Not that I'm unnaturally bitter. I mean, so what if I come from a 'broken home' – a phrase I quite liked when I was younger because it suggested something that could be mended. It's normal, these days, for people's parents to be separated, divorced, living with different people in different countries.

And Mum, well, she dealt with it. I have to hand it to her. A seven-year-old and a two-year-old. And a career. A difficult, demanding career as a histopathologist, cutting open stiffs to find out why they died, analysing organs, cancerous, diseased tissue to decipher what went wrong. What went on inside. The irony was that she had no idea what was going on inside my father;

what was growing, spreading and finally killing off his love.

'It's not you, Scott, my love. It's me,' she said, crying her eyes out. She didn't realize it was him. His own disease – his arrogance.

She worked part-time at the hospital, then as Jes got older and started school she went back to work full-time. She was called out at weekends and at night, when she would come into my room and whisper that she had to go to the hospital, not for long, just a quick emergency biopsy, the neighbours would keep an eye on us, there's the number.

I'd nod, and fight the urge to stick my thumb in my mouth – after all, I was eleven and a grown-up. When I heard her locking the front door, I'd rush downstairs to check the lock, then the back door and the patio doors. I'd grab a couple of Mars Bars, then rush back up to my bedroom, leaving all the lights on. I'd turn on the radio, meaningless words filling the silence, and I'd read book after book, munching chocolate, until she returned. At the sound of the key in the door I'd switch off the radio and my light and feign sleep. It always seemed very late, but probably wasn't, given that the neighbours were still up watching television. She'd kiss my nose before slipping to her bed. In the morning I'd find chocolate marks on my pillow, but Mum never mentioned it.

Sometimes Jes would wake, crying for her. I'd go to Mum's room, open her drawer and take out an item of clothing – knickers, socks, bra, T-shirt – and take it to him to hold. Then I'd go to the kitchen, carrying my jabbering radio, and juggle back up the stairs with a cup of milk and some of the chocolate biscuits that Mum only let us have on Sundays. This made him so happy I wondered sometimes if he waited until Mum left before crying, knowing I'd feed him. He'd smile and gobble down the biscuits like a baby bird.

As we got older, Mum worked harder, became a registrar, senior registrar, consultant. It's not easy to manage a career and two boys. No wonder she didn't have time for men. There might have been the odd night, who knows?, but no one explicit, no 'uncles' offering crap toys or 'friends' who appeared at breakfast time. Which was lucky because I don't know how I'd have reacted. I mean, I like to think I'd have been okay with it, but jealousy has always been one of my favourite emotions.

Now she's sixty. Or about to be. And I would have missed it if there hadn't been a message on my machine from Jes, a subtle yet careful reminder.

'Hello, Big Brother. Need a lift to Sarah's big six-o Saturday? Call if you do. Jes.'

I feel better the moment I get off the train at Cambridge station on a bright Saturday morning. Wind blustering like a loud-mouthed boxer, armies of small leaves rattling. Blue sky, scudding clouds, like a child's painting of autumn.

The taxi takes me along Trumpington Road, the pavements of my childhood, scenes of infant battle and adolescent derring-do. Then turning off to Grantchester and the fields I once owned in my head. Like royalty returning to a kingdom after decades in exile I feel joy and sorrow. All has changed, yet much is the same.

86

The house still looks ugly – the pebbledash 1930s cube with its big back garden, bought by my parents in 1978, six months before my father departed.

Maybe you've heard of Grantchester. It's a surprisingly literary village. Jeffrey Archer lives there, at the Old Vicarage with its tennis court and the sculpture of sheep in the garden – his readers, my mother calls them. Next door, the Orchard Tea Rooms once welcomed Virginia Woolf, Ted Hughes and E. M. Forster, who frolicked among the apple trees. But its most famous literary connection is the war poet Rupert Brooke, who lived there for several years and extolled its virtues in print.

At the small red-brick primary school we were indoctrinated into Brooke's poems as intensely as Chinese schoolchildren were force-fed Mao, or Soviet offspring the works of Lenin. Twenty-six little voices, chanting sweetly along with the skylarks in the fields beyond:

> *'God! I will pack, and take a train,*
> *And get me to England once again!*
> *For England's the one land I know,*
> *Where men with Splendid Hearts may go.'*

A reviewer in the *Cambridge Evening News* once went so far as to call me 'The New Grantchester Poet', even though I hadn't lived in the village for fourteen years. I wrote her a letter protesting at being compared to our beloved Rupert Brooke, when the simple fact is I can't stand him. He's the embodiment of a ridiculous fairytale vision of England, of village cricket, warm beer and garden parties, while he himself is portrayed as the perfect Englishman – strong, stoic, unselfish, who gave his life for his country. But do you know how he died? England's darling war hero?

From a mosquito bite.

It turned septic, he got blood poisoning and coughed his last on a French hospital ship in the Greek Mediterranean. How heroic is that?

> *If I should die, think only this of me:*
> *That there's some corner of a foreign field*
> *That is for ever England.*

Bzzzz. Bzzzz. What's that? Oh, no! Watch out, Rupert, it's a mosquito!

There are times when I feel depressed going home to see my mother. I hate the dust that clings to the rooms, the absence that lives in a house where one partner has died, or decided to fuck off with someone else to somewhere else. I loathe it. The soft musty scent of rejection.

But on this day I am excited. I'm happy to be home, to be out of London. I've bought the biggest present I've ever bought anyone – a seventy-pound bunch of flowers from Paula Pryke, a magnum of champagne and a silver Tiffany's teardrop necklace (£250), very now, quite sexy, even, that I selected carefully in Harrods. And I have news that I know will make my mother both proud and excessively excited. She loves television and occasionally watches *Word Up!*

I arrive to find her in the garden with Jes and Sam. She's holding a bunch of flowers. Shit. My bouquet is ostentatiously bigger and more expensive than the one she cradles. As I approach I see Jes eye it. My mother smiles at me. 'You're looking thin, Scott.'

Perhaps it's because she's a clinician that she uses few words, and those she chooses are often as sharp as her scalpel.

'Haven't you been eating?'

'Just running a lot, Mum.'

'Not like your brother, eh, Jes?'

Jes looks down for a moment, contemplating his stomach, which juts forth proudly.

'It's his winter hibernation layer,' smiles Sam, who can always be relied upon to deflect my mother's less delicate and thought-out comments.

'Happy birthday, Mum,' I offer, handing her the flowers.

'Oh, they're lovely.'

'Impressive flowers,' says Jes.

'You too, mate. Great minds, hey?'

We walk towards the house and I am regretting the champagne. Buying it in Harrods food hall made me feel lavish and better about myself. But now I feel worse, like Jes and Sam will think I am trying to show them up.

'Och, Scott, such a shame about the lovely Ellie . . .'

I look at Jes, who looks away. I am momentarily livid. I'd rather not have told Mum about our split (my dumping) until after her birthday. But Jes had to get one over on me.

As we near the kitchen door I take my mum's hand and lead her into the house, ignoring Jes's small glare.

At lunch I open the champagne and Jes tells me I'm doing it wrong, that you hold the cork and twist the bottle instead of the other way round, and I'm tempted to say,

'Bring your own bloody champagne,' but I don't, for the sake of birthday conviviality. Once we start drinking the mood thaws and I laugh at all Jes's jokes. I don't think he suspects I'm over-compensating. I feel unusually hungry and have a second helping of everything. Jes, in contrast, takes a single slice of lamb, declining his favourite roast potatoes, perhaps still smarting from our mother's comments about his girth.

After the main course there is a pause, a warm, fuzzy, well-fed lull, and I look at Jes and Sam laughing together at something, her hand on his arm, and my mother, smiling as if to herself, here on her sixtieth birthday with her two sons and one daughter-in-law. She seems happy. And I can make her happier. 'Mum, guess what? I'm going to be on TV.'

My mother looks up. Jes moves his arm from Sam's hand.

'Crazy, isn't it? The BBC want to do this programme with me, *Word Up!* Reciting some of my poems.'

'Och, Scott. That's so . . . brilliant.'

I've always loved the way she says 'brilliant'. The way she rolls the R, flicks the Ls, her Scottish vocal heritage.

'Well done, Scott. That's great,' says Sam.

Jes just smiles.

'It's only a one-off. And I'm on with another writer.'

Of course, Barbara hadn't told me at first that I would be sharing the programme with the acerbic and occasionally downright rude Northern Irish novelist Pat O'Neill. But, hey, at least I was going to be on television.

'Och, Scott, I'm so proud,' my mother says happily. 'We

must celebrate. Jes love, will you not go to the cellar and pull out the seventy-one Pétrus? We'll have it with the cheese.'

Jes looks up. 'The Pétrus?' he repeats.

'Really, Mum, it's not such a big deal,' I say, a little embarrassed.

I feel guilty, Château Pétrus is her favourite Bordeaux, 1971 the year of my birth. Jes pauses as if waiting for her to change her mind, but she is adamant: 'It's my birthday. And we have lots to celebrate.'

The afternoon sun fills the garden and we drink coffee on the patio, my mother crowing over my silver necklace and the silk scarf Jes and Sam brought for her. I am drunk, and all the better for it. My anger and guilt have fizzed and slipped away with the champagne and red wine, and I'm enjoying the sort of post-lunch drunkenness that fills you with satisfaction and hope.

Sam takes our picture with her fancy Minolta, the three of us, and I wish I could look at the developed negative the moment it's taken to see if we have finally banished the absent father, or whether he's still there as a haunting space behind us.

Then my mother takes Jes's hand, and I know she's doing this because he seemed quiet towards the end of the meal and she wants to show him that her love is equal. We follow the narrow muddy paths to the river Cam where Rupert Brooke once danced before going off to get killed by a mosquito.

My mother and Jes walk together, chatting. She throws

back her head, laughing like a girl, the low sun glinting in her silver hair. I feel good. There are rare instances when you know a moment is beautiful, even when you're still in its sharp, shining midst. Walking alongside the river Cam with my mother, my brother and my sister-in-law, the sun warm and bright, I know this is such a moment. Out of nowhere, unplanned, unhoped-for, even. I know, as the wet grass licks my ankles, that I will remember this afternoon for a long time to come.

I catch up with Sam, who seems to be waiting for me by the fence. I feel a little nervous. I haven't spoken to her since the dinner in Morden when she agreed with her mother on the phone that I was needy and intro-spective. I wonder if I should ask her about it to see if she really thinks this of me. But before I can form the right words in my head, she smiles and says, 'Looking forward to telly fame?' in a friendly, cheerful voice.

'I dunno. Bit nervous, I guess, but it's not like it's *Richard and Judy*, is it? I mean, no one's gonna see it.'

'Don't you believe it. I'm calling half of Yorkshire. My brother-in-law on the box.'

'Don't you dare!'

'Your mum's dead proud.'

'We like to make Mum proud.'

'Jes is happy for you too. He's just not showing it.'

'I'll take your word for it.'

Ahead, Jes is helping our mother over a stile into the next field, his arm on her back as she climbs carefully, her movements slow and exact, the surgeon's deliberation. I decide to continue this conversation about my brother,

Sam's husband, partly because I hardly ever get a chance to chat with Sam on her own, and partly to prove to her that I don't always think about myself. 'You know, Sam, sometimes I just can't figure him out.'

Sam stops. She looks beyond, at her husband of a year. 'It's hard for him . . .' she says quietly. 'There's your mum, one of the top pathologists in the country, published in all sorts of journals, giving papers at conferences all around the world. And then there's you, his big brother, the bestselling author, about to star in his own TV show.'

'But he's talented too,' I say, haltingly. I mean this. He's a good writer. He could be a great writer. 'It's just sometimes he seems to find it hard to get it going.'

'I know,' says Sam, a little too emphatically. She stops, realizing what she's just said, a chink in the armour of invincible support for her husband.

Beyond, my mother laughs at some story Jes is telling her.

'Maybe it's because he's afraid of failing,' continues Sam, who has evidently decided that she needs to explain herself. 'I try to get him to submit stuff to the *Telegraph*, but he always comes up with an excuse. He's terrified that if he's rejected we'll all think he's useless.'

'What? That's crazy. We all think he's brilliant. He's so creative, he's such a great person. He does so many things I could never do. I mean, look at the way he cares for people . . .'

'Yeah. St Jeremy.' I try not to think about my brother's charity work, volunteer Saturdays, and the fact he cooked me dinner after Ellie dumped me. Sam flicks a strand of

93

hair from her eye. 'Sometimes I wonder if he does all that do-good stuff because he knows he won't have to compete with you or your mum because you guys have other things to worry about.'

'It's not a competition,' I say, weakly.

A flock of ducks spurt into the river, yacking and spluttering. I want to smooth over the cracks that have appeared, to rebond us all. But the moment has gone, the warmth and hope have slipped. We walk on. I help Sam over the stile. As my feet hit the muddy ground on the other side of the rickety wooden fence, I feel sad. Guilt and regret are returning. Something shifts inside me, a valve opening. I feel alone.

'Shit. I dunno, Sam. At least Jes has you.'

'I'm lucky to have him.'

'Sometimes I look at you two and I think you're so great together.'

'Thanks.' Sam smiles. 'I think so too.'

'I wish I could find that.'

'You will.'

'You're so perfect together.'

'Listen, Scott . . .' Sam stops and looks at me, squinting against the sun. 'I'm sorry Ellie dumped you. I'm sorry we make you feel lonely.'

'It's not that.' I look away.

'Come on. You've got so much,' Sam says, gently.

'Did I go after the wrong things? Did I just make the wrong choices?'

'We all have to make choices.'

'Or do you only know what the right things are when

94

it's too late?' I look back at her. 'How do you do it, Sam?'

'Do what?'

'Connection. Commitment.'

'That other C-word. Choice. A choice you make once, to love that person, to be with them whatever they do, however they behave.' She glances beyond, at my brother. 'It's a choice you then make again and again, every day. For the rest of your life, I guess.' She looks back at me. 'Loving someone isn't just about holding hands and kissing in public. Sometimes it's just as hard as not having someone to love. Harder, maybe.'

'Do you think I made my choice too late?'

'Why are you so gutted about bloody Ellie?' She shakes her head, almost angrily.

'I . . . She . . .' I mumble, cowed a little by her harsh tone.

'She was a bitch, Scott. Just let it go.'

'All right, all right.'

'Stop feeling sorry for yourself. You've got so much. I hate to say it, but sometimes you're a little bit too caught up in yourself to see what's really there.'

'What does that mean?'

But Sam has moved on, walking away from me, hands in pockets, fast, straight and strong.

I sit on the bed in my old bedroom. It's been a year since I was last here. Apart from the shape (four walls, a door), it's unrecognizable. The walls are now flowery with some dreadful Laura Ashley wallpaper, the wardrobe would not look out of place in a Spanish bordello and the bed is a brand new pine queen double, with a flowery duvet that matches the walls.

The only thing that remains is the large bookcase on the far wall, filled with books neatly ranged in alphabetical order, the English classics and a smattering of American authors – Hemingway, Steinbeck, Salinger. They were my mother's: she'd had them for years, she said, although she read very little when we were young. I, of course, read them all, arranging my mini-library like a billionaire recluse, proud to be continuing my mother's tradition.

It's not just the room that seems different. I look at my reflection in the sideboard mirror and I seem like another person, hair receding slightly but not so I can't hide it, lines around eyes and mouth. I finger the scar where I cut my ear on the door at the age of ten – how did I manage to do that?

So Sam *does* think I'm selfish. She thinks I'm too self-obsessed, too caught up in myself. But I'm not. Am I?

I mean, I can be generous, caring, selfless. I spent almost twenty years looking after my younger brother. I cared for him after our father left, and Mum had to work. I helped him with his homework, I bought him cider from the off-licence for his fourteen-year-old parties, I didn't tell Mum when I found cigarettes in his schoolbag. I drove him and Zeb to a New Order concert in Manchester (and even paid the forty-pound fine we got after I put the car in a resident's parking bay because they were both complaining that I was taking too long to park). I gave him condoms so he could lose his virginity at the age of sixteen (one year earlier than me) to Katie Murphy, a Nirvana freak with matted dreadlocks who, everyone agreed, was by far the most beautiful girl at Hill's Road sixth-form college, Cambridge.

My own deflowering had taken place four years earlier at the age of seventeen, in this very room, my bedroom, with Jenny Rowan and her fishnet tights. She wasn't the most beautiful girl in the sixth form, but not the ugliest either. Mum was away, Jes was banished to watch TV in his room, it was over almost before it had begun.

'Have you finished?' asked Jenny, smoothing down her home-stitched denim skirt.

'Er . . . yes.'

I remember the condom lying there, us both staring at it as if it was some strange sea-creature washed up on a beach. Jenny departed soon afterwards with a mumbled farewell – she was never one to get emotional – and I scrubbed at the carpet with something bleachy and industrial, which only served to make an impressive stain. For several months afterwards I kept a ratty rug at the foot of my bed, to cover up the spot, to hide my scuffed-up secret.

It's still there, despite my mother's attempts at interior redecorating. Looking at it now, I realize you wouldn't notice the spot if you didn't know it was there. It seems a pathetic trophy, the sole reminder of my first sexual intercourse. I wonder how many spots in how many houses there are like this – small sad memorials to brief moments of pleasure.

As I gaze around it, the room fills with sounds, voices, spectres of Scott Barron, through the ages. My tears after our father left, my friend Johnny Ashby making fun of my miniature snooker table, Jes breaking my Atari video game the day after Mum bought it for me. The nights I would sit in bed with a chocolate bar, reading Steinbeck by torchlight until after midnight. I rest a hand against my stomach, remembering a time when I was fat like my younger brother.

There's a knock on the door. Mum stands there holding a glass of whisky. 'Sleepy?' she asks, and I suddenly feel ten years old again.

'Yeah. You heading to bed?'

She nods. 'I was just going to say goodnight to Jeremy and Samantha, but I think they're having a wee talk.'

We both listen, but hear nothing.

'Happy birthday,' I say, to break the silence. She smiles, steps into the room and sits on the bed. I feel comfortable and uncomfortable at the same time. I move my foot to cover the small sex stain. 'So, work's almost done?' I ask.

'Retirement party next Friday.'

'That's great. Who's organizing it?'

'Old Dickie Bennett.'

'He's not that old.'

'None of us is getting any younger.'

'Don't be ridiculous, Mum. You're fitter than I am.'

I expect her to smile at this, but instead she looks into her whisky glass, as if searching for the future in the swirling gold.

'Time passes quickly . . .' she says, soberly. I'm surprised at this – my mother doesn't usually get nostalgic, philosophical, or emotional. She's a scientist, after all. I try to think of a reply, but I'm unable to come up with anything that doesn't sound trite. So I just nod, and she continues, 'When I came upstairs just now, I had this sudden memory. I don't know where it came from. It was when you were both little, just after Edward left. I came upstairs one morning and Jes was standing there, in his pyjamas, outside your room.'

'Really? What was he doing?'

'Nothing. Just waiting. I don't know why I remembered it.'

As she says this, I remember it too. Some mornings I'd open the door and Jes would be standing there, two years old and three feet tall, clutching a toy penguin. I'd ask him what he wanted, but he'd remain silent, impassive, almost. Once he followed me to the bathroom and I had to close the door in his face to stop him watching me have a dump.

We sit there, my mother and her elder son, on the bed, memories both welcome and uninvited playing through our minds. I want desperately to break this moment of reflection. 'So you're retired now,' I say lamely. 'No more stiffs to slice, meat to mangle?'

She seems relieved that I've changed the mood. Her voice is lighter, more energized: 'It's a strange profession, Scott my love. In the last few months it's seemed . . . how can I put it? A little pointless. Why do we bother finding reasons after the event, once it's too late?'

'I don't know. To make the future better?'

She looks at her whisky, turning it, the light dancing in the glass. And from nowhere I ask, 'Mum . . . do you think I'm selfish?'

She looks at me, smiles, and kisses my cheek. 'Sometimes you are, my love. But aren't we all? That's human nature.'

I go to bed in my Laura Ashley Spanish bordello, but I can't sleep. In the next bedroom I can hear Jes and Sam, raised voices arguing, indecipherable yet antagonistic. Sam is shouting, shrill and hard, and I recall her words from the riverside: 'Loving someone is just as hard as not having someone to love.'

6

Okay, maybe I am selfish. But all men have an innate instinct that makes us try on our own shoes first before we put ourselves in someone else's.

I sit in Lindsey's office telling her over and over again that I'm worried I'm too self-centred. 'Am I going on a bit?' I ask at last, when I finally need to breathe.

'Do *you* think you're selfish, Scott?'

'A little bit. But we all are, aren't we?'

Lindsey doesn't answer, nursing her mug of tea.

I continue, almost enjoying this opportunity to rabbit on, to chuck out whatever comes into my head. It's not something I do very often. 'I mean, I think, yes, maybe there are times when I'm selfish. I think sometimes I could work harder at putting others before myself. But nobody's perfect.'

Lindsey nods, slowly, sipping her tea. 'Do you feel a need to protect yourself?'

'From what?'

'Other people.'

'I don't protect myself. I'm the one who always ends up getting hurt.'

'Why do you think that is?'

'Because people can be bastards.'

Lindsey looks at me, as if trying to divine whether I really mean this. 'How do people hurt you?'

'They walk out on me. After I trusted them.'

'And why do you think they walk out on you?'

'They say it's because they can't get close to me.'

'Do you think they can't get close to you?'

'Of course not. I try to let them in . . .'

'Do you think it was your fault your father left?'

'No. Why should I? He was a wanker, that's all.'

'So who says they never get close to you?'

'Women. Girlfriends . . . ex-girlfriends.'

'Relationships end. Maybe these women were just not right for you?'

I nod. She's trying to make me feel better. Maybe she is worth forty-five pounds an hour.

Then Lindsey throws another of her curve-balls, a question that zips out of left-field, and clonks me on the head. 'Do you feel that your brother has walked out on you?'

'No. He's there for me, if I need him.'

'Do you need him?'

'No. I don't need anyone . . .'

'I see,' she says, with another of her enigmatic smiles.

I arrive at the BBC studios in White City on a damp, dark October evening. I've done little to prepare for my television début, except practise every one of my poems over and over again, recording myself on a high-tech digital dictaphone purchased at great expense from Dixons. I have also spent a few hours changing in and out of every item of clothing I possess, trying to ignore Ellie's voice in my head: 'No, the slate grey. Much better in front of studio lights.' Most of my wardrobe came from Ellie, in the form of free samples, which, she assured me, were very hard to come by.

I end up with two items of clothing lying on my bed, like armour before a battle – the slate grey cashmere sweater and a green short-sleeved shirt that I bought from a Hoxton boutique two years ago. I loved it and Ellie hated it.

I haven't talked to Jes since Mum's birthday. He seemed downcast as we headed our separate ways back to London, Sam silent and staring behind the Beetle's steering-wheel. In contrast, my mother has been overly excited at the prospect of coming to a television studio. She's bought a new dress for the occasion.

It's funny how everyone has advice for you if you're going on TV. I mean, most people have never been on the box but they still feel they know something about it.

Dr Simon suggests that I smile more on the right side of my face. 'It evens your grin up on the screen, especially when you're nervous. Michael Parkinson always does it.'

Big Barry has forgiven me about Cindy – he persuaded Nancy to go with him to China White and is hoping to get his hands on 'her shrubbery' soon. He advises wearing two pairs of tight briefs. 'Tighter the better. Just in case you get a stiffy on live TV.'

And Brian, who is the only one of my friends to have experienced the bright lights of television fame (he's from LA, after all, and was in a washing-powder commercial at the age of two), is characteristically adamant: 'Make sure you eat something. Those studio lights are damn hot, and you don't want to faint on live TV.'

Actually, I have to admit, I do want my *Word Up!* appearance to go well. In my imaginary future, Ellie will see me on TV and realize she loves me after all. Or if not Ellie, my future wife. She will be dark-haired, sultry, yet marvellously intelligent and caring – Liv Tyler, only shorter. She'll think, Wow, what a guy with his fresh skin and witty, yet sensitive poems. She'll call up the BBC, we'll be introduced on-screen by Cilla Black and our celebrity-strewn wedding will be featured as the last item on the evening news, a bit of light relief from famine and war.

I like the future. I dwell there quite frequently. After all, you can have a thousand futures. But only one past.

I'm still trying to decide on my clothes, draining my second can of Stella, when the BBC driver rings the doorbell. In a panic I throw the cashmere sweater to the floor and pull on my favourite green shirt.

I meet my mother in the BBC reception area. She's staying with friends in Chiswick, some doctors I've never met but who are apparently friends from medical school. I have to admit she looks good, the black Armani dress, hair cut short, slender as a model. She's wearing more makeup than usual, an impressive amount of foundation, but I put this down to her desire not to appear pasty under the television lights.

'You look great, Mum.'

'Thank you, Scott. Where did you get that shirt?'

'A shop. I haven't worn it in a while. Fancy a drink?'

'I'm fine.'

'No drink? Are you all right?'

'Tummy's been playing up a bit. I think I've been a wee bit stressed, what with retirement and all . . .'

'Stressed?'

'Well, not every mother gets to see her son perform live on national television.' She places her hand on mine, an unaccustomed gesture from my usually untactile mother. It's smooth. She takes hold of my fingers and gives them a little squeeze.

I'm really glad she's here. True to form, my friends have all made excuses – Big Barry has Belgian clients in town, Dr Simon is on call and Brian has a petroleum merger to finish. As for Jes, he just sent me a home-made card with a photo of my head cut out and pasted into the centre of a television set with the inscription 'TV STAR'.

Word Up! is a BBC2 late-night literary programme that, Barbara was eventually forced to confess, pulls in under a hundred thousand viewers on a good night. Most of these, I assume, have simply forgotten to turn their tellies off after *Newsnight*, but it does have a loyal and influential following – or so Barbara tried to convince me.

It's a small, hardly watched late-night television show, but I am nervous. I'll admit that. When an assistant asks me if I'd like anything to drink, I find myself ordering a vodka and tonic. She then leads me into a sleek, cream-coloured office with brown-leather sofas to meet the series producer, Megan Hyde-Jones. I'm surprised that she doesn't stand to greet me when I enter, until I realize she's already standing, all five foot of her. She's dressed in black, with bright red hair the colour of a stop traffic-light, which has been meticulously gelled up as if she's recently suffered an electric shock. 'Scott. So glad. Love your work. Simply love it. And so does Jenny.'

I turn and there, in a long black leather skirt and a black denim shirt, is a pretty woman I think I recognize.

'Hi, Scott. It's been a while.'

It strikes me. Oh, God. It's Jenny Rowan. My first ever shag. I turn bright red.

'Jenny's our top researcher. She works closely with me on all our live segments.'

'When I heard it was you . . . well, I had to get involved,' says Jenny, with what sounds like a hint of flirtation. She looks good, fourteen years on. Her dark hair is cut almost to a crew-cut, she's wearing deep-red lipstick, and her denim shirt is open enough to offer quick flashes of black bra. I glance down. She's no longer wearing fishnets, but she does have a small tattoo – a butterfly or a flower on her left ankle. 'How have you been?' I ask.

'Good. Life's busy, you know.'

'Right,' says Megan Hyde-Jones, interrupting our little reunion. 'Shall we run through things?'

We sit down and I have a sudden sneaking suspicion that the reason Jenny works so closely with Megan is that she is the same height. They go through the order of the programme and the poems to be read. 'There's just one small change to the list we faxed to your agent. I hope you don't mind. We'd simply love it if you wouldn't mind reading one poem from *Men Matter*.'

'Sure. Which one?'

A quick glance between Jenny and Megan. Jenny answers. '"Little Boys".'

'Oh.'

'I simply love that one,' crows Megan.

'Me too,' croons Jenny. 'It always made me want to cry.'

I look at her. Maybe I was wrong about her being unemotional. My heart beats faster. 'Er . . . all right. Sure. Why not?'

Megan smiles. 'I'm so glad Jenny suggested you for the programme.'

Jenny blushes. Or maybe it's just hot in here.

It's ten thirty p.m., forty-five minutes until broadcast. My mother, so the spotty male researcher informs me, is making some phone calls to her friends, ensuring they all have their televisions, or at least VCRs, on. My agent, Barbara Smiles, is on her phone. She waves, distractedly. I sip another vodka-tonic, slowing down now as I don't want to be drunk on live television, and the researcher escorts me to the Green Room.

Sitting on a green sofa is Northern Irish writer Pat O'Neill. We are being billed as representing the two faces of modern male writing – me the humorous, emotionally literate self-deprecator (if only they knew the truth), O'Neill the angry, inaccessible misogynist.

I hadn't read any of O'Neill's work until I knew I was going to be on *Word Up!* with him, but since then I have waded through three interminable novels about incest and land disputes in the border counties of Northern Ireland.

'All right, Barron. Haven't read yer stuff, but sure it's cracking. Paddy O'Neill.'

I shake his hand, which is warm and damp like a recently wrung-out sock. Pat O'Neill is probably in his late forties, with a face that seems to have been chiselled by a special-needs art-therapy student – no straight lines, deep incisions, a crooked smile that he employs regularly to link laconic sentences.

'Nice shirt.' He grins. 'Reminds me of home.'

As I sit down I realize my green shirt is the same colour as the sofa.

Jenny Rowan pokes her head round the door and flashes a smile. 'Glad to see you're getting on. If there's anything you guys need . . .'

'A blow-job,' cackles O'Neill, after she's departed. 'Great little slapper, in't she?'

I am about to boast about our shared past, myself and Ms Rowan, but I hold back. I feel increasingly in control. A sense, which you sometimes get in life, that this night is going to go well.

I accept the whisky O'Neill pours. We clink glasses and down the amber liquid in one. A shiver of excitement runs through me. Here we are, two writers, the writing fraternity, having a drink before wowing the British public with our literary talent. And O'Neill, Pat, Paddy, seems to like me. 'Problem with you Brits is you're so fucking magnanimous. The Provos blow up Canary Wharf, you bend over backwards to be nice to Sinn Fein. I'd fucking shoot the lotta them. And I'm a fucking Taig.'

'Yes. Of course . . .'

O'Neill pours more whisky, almost half a glass each. 'You need to stop being so . . . so fucking grown-up. You need to . . . say what you think. What you feel . . .'

'I suppose we did when Princess Diana died.'

'Fuck, yeah. Yer right there, man. Di's dead, man. Di's dead. I loved that woman . . . Jesus, man, imagine that blow-job. Those silky lips. A right royal suck. Man, I loved that woman . . .'

We toast Princess Diana, and the whisky sparkles in my throat.

Jenny Rowan pokes her small pretty head round the door again. 'Fifteen minutes . . .'

'C'mon, Jenny-babes, c'mon, sit with us, have a wee drink, just a wee one . . .'

'I'd love to, Pat, but duty calls. Er . . . perhaps you should . . . er . . . have a quick coffee or something before you come on.'

'Yer, fuck, whatever. Yer don't want a drink, fuck yer. Yer little twat!'

Jenny withdraws at this, and I feel anger rising. 'Come on, Pat, don't call her that,' I declare, boldly.

'Why not? She's a twat!'

'I've known Jenny a long time. In fact, we were at school together. She can be a bit officious sometimes, but she's a smart young woman.'

'Yer wanna shag her?'

'What?'

'Yer do. I know you do. Up the arse!'

He pours another two glasses of whisky, downs his, burps and announces he's departing to the toilets. 'Nose candy,' he mumbles. 'And I'm not fucking sharing.'

I sip the whisky, feeling strong. I've stood up to O'Neill, defended Jenny. I've done what I felt, I've followed my emotions. This is good.

Then I remember the advice of Brian, the infant washing-powder star. On a silver platter placed close to a bright spotlight is a pile of egg sandwiches. They don't look very appetizing, but I think I should soak up some of the alcohol I've been necking. I eat a sandwich, then realize I haven't eaten all day, so I eat two more, wiping congealed mayonnaise from my chin, smudging my makeup slightly.

I drink the rest of the whisky, knocking it back against my throat, holding the stinging liquid in my mouth until it mellows and sinks. I smack my lips theatrically. At this moment, I feel more like a writer than ever. Because this is how writers are. Whisky flowing, heart pounding, eyes clear as ice.

'Scott, there's a problem. A big problem.'

I look up. Jenny is standing there. I squint against the bright light.

'It's O'Neill. He's passed out in the loos. There's an ambulance coming. I think the bastard's been doing coke.'

My heart-rate triples. I try to breathe. Jenny sits down on the sofa. I sit at her side, hoping she won't notice that my shirt and the furniture are twins. The green sofa leather breathes out suggestively as I lean back. Jenny reaches over and takes my hand in hers. I feel an erection stir and silently thank Barry for his advice. 'Do you . . . could you, Scott? Could you do the whole thirty minutes?'

I look at her, her eyes are wide and pleading, and I know I can. Of course I can. I am Scott Barron. The poet. 'I'll give it a try, Jenny. If you want me to.'

I have just five minutes to prepare. I skim through my collections, picking out six extra poems that I think will get a laugh. Jenny returns with Megan Hyde-Jones. She holds out her hand solemnly. I shake it firmly and pour whisky into three glasses.

'To tonight.'

'Tonight.'

We drink, and the two tiny women escort me from the Green Room, their heels tapping down a dark corridor and up to a large door through which I enter into the big bright lights of Studio 5A.

My nerves have vanished. There are fifty or so people in the audience in seating that rises steeply from the stage. A pair of cameras point at two chic leather armchairs, lit by a bank of lights. In the right-hand chair sits the presenter, Catrina McLeod, a forty-something Scot with thin features and a cheerful interviewing style – I've watched numerous tapes. She smiles widely as I walk on to the stage, shakes my hand, then asks a few questions about how I'm feeling, whether I've been on TV before, how the new book is doing, just to ease me into things. Then the floor manager counts down and we're live on air.

'Welcome to *Word Up!* Tonight's programme features the work of popular poet Scott Barron. Unfortunately those expecting to hear Northern Irish novelist Patrick

O'Neill will have to wait for another time. Pat was taken ill today and has not been able to make it to the studio. We all wish him a speedy recovery . . .'

I sneak a look at the audience and I think I spot Jes, but it's not him and I feel a quick stab of disappointment. I thought there was an outside chance that he would show up. He does the unexpected at times, unlike his older brother. Then I glance again, and to my surprise I do see a familiar face sitting behind my mother and Barbara Smiles in the second row. It's Brian, in his pinstripe suit and Bristol University tie – a mark of solidarity, I'm assuming. He grins, his expensive black-rimmed spectacles glinting in the hot studio lights, and salutes me like a soldier on parade.

I smile back, a silent thank-you. I feel my heart thumping, excitement and fear. I'm the sole interviewee on a nationally broadcast book programme. In the front row, my mother is on the edge of her seat, and I realize she's incredibly nervous, trying to wish the right words into my mouth. She wants to take care of her son in front of under a hundred thousand viewers, like she used to take care of me as a child. But there's no time to dwell on my mother's love, or Jes's absence, because Catrina turns to me and begins our conversation.

I cope with the first few questions without a hitch, I mean I've done publicity before, the simple stuff about how I started writing . . .

'I won a writing prize at school and I guess I never looked back.'

. . . why I write about men:

'Well, I suppose I'm a man, I have feelings, and this is my way of expressing them.'

. . . do I think modern poetry is really poetry?

'Hmmm, that's a hard one, but personally I consider any free expression of emotions and thoughts as poetry. Something doesn't have to follow a structure or rhyme to be emotionally true.'

Next Catrina asks me why I write one poem about penguins in every collection and I raise my eyebrows, a little too theatrically perhaps, and lie: 'I just like penguins . . .', which gets a gentle laugh. I can hear Brian laughing louder than anyone, and I feel warm and thankful that he's there.

I breeze through the first couple of readings, poems I know off by heart so I can glance up at the camera, give myself a little to the audience. I'm amazed at how good I feel, no nerves, no trepidation, and I'm glad Jenny agreed to bring out a glass of whisky, because I can sip it between readings to calm myself.

Time is passing smoothly like water flowing. I sense a little sweat in the usual places, but the three deodorants I've applied are doing their job beneath the green shirt. I feel bright, shiny, sparkling in the lights.

I take another gulp of whisky and read 'Fathers', slowly. I try to put as much feeling into the words as I can, and as I'm reading I actually begin to feel a little emotional. I read out the final line, 'I wish my father had been Jesus because he could have turned water into wine at parties . . .', and, to my happy surprise, the audience laughs. Even Catrina joins in. I close the book and see Jenny Rowan behind one of the cameras, grinning broadly. She raises her thumb, a childish gesture, and in that instant I remember her at school, campaigning to be head of the student council. I wonder, just for a second, whether fate has brought us back together.

Catrina clears her throat. 'Thank you once again, Scott. That's certainly one of my favourites, and my father's favourite, he always wanted to change water into wine . . .'

The audience laughs again, small, late-night-television chuckling.

Now Catrina asks me a couple of questions about my own father, and I sense my mother is on the edge of her seat once more, concentrating, brow furrowed, as if uttering a spell or incantation to defend herself against painful memories of the past. But she has nothing to worry about, because I keep my answers light and humorous, and only slightly evasive when talking of my parents' separation. I give enough to appear open, yet say nothing I wouldn't share with someone sitting next to me on a bus. 'We get on okay now. I mean, maybe I'll understand him better when I'm a father myself.'

'Is that something that's likely to happen soon?' asks Catrina, with a raised eyebrow, her signature quizzical look.

'Well, apparently you need someone else to make that happen, so not in the immediate future, no.'

'I take that to mean you're single?'

'For the moment.'

Catrina smiles and I sneak a glance at Jenny, who also smiles, a little flushed, I think. Catrina breaks off from our conversation to do the top-ten fiction and non-fiction bestseller lists. I drink some more whisky and look at the big studio clock, which shows only ten minutes to go. I allow myself another quick smile. Somehow I'm carrying the show. Somehow I'm saving the day. Barbara Smiles looks on proudly.

Catrina asks me about future projects. I tell her I'm exhausted from the publication whirlwind of *Men and Other Mammals*, a nice fib that will help explain why I'm looking a little peaky, if the makeup lady's magic is wearing thin. I mention that I've got some vague plans, and then I say something that surprises me, because I had no idea I was going to say it: 'Perhaps my next book might be about brothers. You know. The old fraternal relationship. The rivalries, the unspoken love. That sort of thing.'

'How intriguing. An area that is somewhat under-explored in modern writing.'

'Er . . . yes. It could be interesting.'

I sip the whisky. Catrina smiles again. My mother sits forward in her seat again. I imagine Jes watching the television, scowling at his presumptuous, pretentious brother, while Sam tries to placate him. Well, tough. I'm the one on the telly.

Catrina begins the wind-up to the show. There are five minutes to go.

'It's been a pleasure, Scott. I wish you all the best for your work on the theme of brotherly love, we all certainly look forward to your words on that . . . Now, I believe you've got one more poem for us tonight, one I think many of us know and love. Ladies and gentlemen, Scott Barron, reading "Little Boys".'

There's applause, and I stand. I don't know why I stand, maybe it's the applause, maybe it's because I feel more confident than I have in a long time. The cameraman jerks back his head in surprise, rising to follow my head. There's a brief silence, as I stand there, facing the camera and the audience, the centre of attention, the star of the show, Scott of the BBC. I feel dizzy, just for a second, so I place my foot forward to balance. The dizziness passes.

I look into the camera for a moment, and I don't know why, because it's very unlike me, but I wink. I wink at the camera. The audience stirs, surprised by my cheeky audacity. I glance at the book of poems. Then I look up once more, and just manage to suppress an unexpected whisky burp. In the second row Brian is dabbing sweat from his forehead with a handkerchief. I feel a little shaky, so I reach down and take a swig of whisky to calm my nerves. It tastes sour. My stomach gurgles.

And then I begin.

'"Little Boys" . . .' I announce, and as I speak I suddenly feel faint. My stomach rumbles again.

'"I was a little boy, once . . ."'

Suddenly sweat beads my forehead. My hands start trembling.

'"About a week ago but . . ."'

Shaking a little, hands, legs, I glance over at Jenny, her shining skirt, bright black leather, staring at me. Her mouth is a little parted . . . she's a little cracker, in't she?

'"I grew up yesterday . . ."'

I'm drunk. I hadn't known it until now, but it's crept up on me, like a mugger. I should never have stood up, because now I feel terrible. I have to breathe, so I stop the line, breathe quickly, in-out. I try to swallow, the back of my throat is swimming with spit.

'"When my father left us . . ."'

White light, hot-cold, face burning. Oh, God. I'm not feeling well. I can taste . . . what? Whisky definitely, but something else is mixing, swilling, a fatty, soured flavour. Egg mayonnaise. Oh, God, I can taste the egg mayonnaise, the gelatinous jellied egg. Suddenly I see the egg sandwiches on the silver platter under the bright light, creamy yellow oozing. I feel terrible. I'm shaking.

I glance ahead, seeking clarity, and I see my mother mouthing the words of the poem, word after word, wishing me, willing me, on. Brian is leaning forward, Jenny staring, blow-job lips, and I glance at the monitor and it's not me there, but my father.

Shit.

A picture of my father, me and Jes, at the seaside, buckets and spades. He's smiling, the English daddy at the English seaside. I look glum, a porky child with my fat little brother. Where did they get this picture? Why are they showing it?

My mother is still mouthing the words of the poem like some ancient incantation. Then I hear my father's voice, but it's not quite his voice. 'Keep going,' it says. 'Keep going with your little ditties.'

But my hands are shaking, my knees trembling, I feel faint. I sense sickness frothing through me, but I have to keep going, onwards and upwards once more unto the breach into the valley of death with a stiff upper lip.

'"When my father left us . . ."'

Sweat damp, I try to see the words on the page, because I know the next line is a long line, I know it's a long line because I wrote it, it's my line, but right now it doesn't seem like my line, letters merging, page spinning, spinning words, spinning letters.

'". . . and someone told me that love is not eternal . . ."'

I step forward once more, to steady myself, the cameraman stumbling to follow me. I try to get to the end of the next line.

'". . . before she put her tongue in my mouth . . ."'

I burp, quickly, egg and whisky, '". . . for . . ."', and then it all rushes up, a gurgling stream, spewing up through me as I say the last word, '". . . free . . ."'.

From my open mouth I vomit out egg mayonnaise and whisky. A rush of sick. I throw my hands up to my chin, catching most of the eggy spew, but then I heave again, spurting out more egg mayonnaise through my fingers. A glob of undigested bread chugs out of my nose. I thrust my hands up to my mouth again, but the sick spills over and splatters on to the studio floor.

I glance up, just long enough to see the faces staring at me, eyes wide, they can't believe what they're seeing. Jenny Rowan stares, her red lips parted in an expression of incredulity and disgust. I hear a chair scraping, Catrina leaping from her seat, as I stagger and heave again. This time I don't have time to raise my sick-drenched hands to my mouth and I simply lean over and spew out egg-mayonnaise-whisky on to the chic leather armchair Catrina has just vacated. A sharp pain shoots through my intestines and I double over, vomit running down my chin.

I hear a gasp from the front row. I look over to see my mother, standing up from her seat, about to rush on to the stage and take care of me.

I muster my forces, like an Englishman of old, raise myself up and look up into the vast bright lights for the last time. I speak, loudly and relatively confidently considering the circumstances, straight into the camera: 'I'm sorry, everyone. I think I had a little too much to drink.'

7

They say that bad things come in threes.

1. I vomit over myself on live television.
2. I am carried to an ambulance through the reception area at BBC Broadcasting House in front of my agent and the *They Think It's All Over* audience while my sixty-year-old mother bursts into tears and one of my best friends shakes his head in despair.

The Third Bad Thing could be Barbara Smiles's phone call at eight thirty the next morning. 'What were you bloody thinking? Do you realize what this means? After all the work I did! You're in the tabloids! You're a bloody laughing-stock!'

'I'm really sorry, Barbara.'

'I'm ashamed. After all I've done for you. It makes me wonder about being your agent any more. It makes me wonder about being anyone's agent any more!' With that she slams down the phone.

My head throbs. I know Barbara won't give up agenting – Barbara Smiles not an Agent is like Attila not a Hun – and as for dumping me, well, I probably deserve it. Perhaps the *Camden Chronicle* will take me back.

No. Barbara's phone call is not the Third Bad Thing.

The Third Bad Thing is still to come. I can feel it in my toes.

I wake early, as you do when something bad has happened, wondering why you are awake so early. For the first few moments I'm fine, it's like any other day. I squint, trying to judge from the daylight on the wall whether for once the sun is going to shine and then, bump!, like whacking my shin on an unseen coffee table, I remember.

I threw up on television.

It was undoubtedly the worst night of my life, apart from that evening twenty-four years ago, after my father left, when the large house in Grantchester was filled with the sound of a woman and two boys crying in separate rooms.

I blew it on BBC2. How could I have been so stupid? How could I have been so arrogant? I try to block out the images, the sounds, the smells, like a crime victim tries to erase the moment of attack. But I can't stop them coming – the bright lights, my cheeks burning as I stand covered in vomit, and Jenny Rowan glaring at me, speechless. Then there's my mother's face, so stricken and white, her eyes filling with tears.

I feel a physical pain – the tightening of the chest, the pounding head, the ache in my internal organs. I try not to think about it. I try to empty my head and not think about anything, but even a boy band on a slow day can't stop thinking.

Perhaps I'm really ill. What are the first symptoms of

mad-cow disease? Could I be the latest, most literary victim of CJD?

Thinking about being sick makes me feel sick, so I get up, head thumping, and dash to the bathroom where I lean lovingly into my blue Armitage Shanks toilet bowl. The porcelain is deathly cold against my cheek. I take a deep breath, slowly but methodically stick two fingers down my throat, and vomit once more for England.

As I sit gasping by the toilet bowl, I wonder if I have finally discovered my one true talent. I might not be much of a poet but I can puke like a champion.

This, I feel, is a low point. Here and now, spew sliding down my chin, staring at my speckled toilet bowl, I know that I'm more miserable than I have been for years.

As if to prove my state of wretchedness, I start to shiver, then cry. Short tears at first, without range, that swell along my eyes. Then I start sobbing, shoulders heaving, longer tears that trickle then stream, and I begin to rasp like a cow gasping for air. Maybe I do have CJD, after all.

I reach up to the small medicine cabinet and fumble around. Of course there are no aspirins, no paracetamol, just a few throat lozenges and a bumper bottle of chewable vitamin C. The bottle trembles and then falls, striking me triumphantly on top of my head.

I wonder what would happen if I overdosed on chewable vitamin C. Maybe I could defecate myself to death.

If I was more of an artist, a real poet, I would end it all here. As Barbara Smiles would no doubt inform me, it could do wonders for my sales. I could be the Janis Joplin of poetry, the James Dean of ditties, a star cut down in his prime. I'd be in the papers for at least two days: VOMIT-POET WRITES HIS OWN ENDING.

I could be the new Sylvia Plath, but with a better taste in socks. The only problem is my oven is electric, and I'm too much of a chicken to commit suicide. I just want someone to care.

I want Ellie to call me and tell me it's okay, she loves me after all. I want Brian to phone and say it could have happened to anyone, even him. I want Big Barry to tell me he still thinks I'm a great guy and a reasonably funny raconteur, even though I chundered on BBC2. I want my mother to call and reassure me that she wasn't really upset and overwhelmingly embarrassed last night. I want her to say that she's proud of me for at least having the presence of mind to apologize as she'd raised me to, live on air, before being carried off-stage by two ambulance men in fluorescent yellow coats. And I want Jes to call and mumble, 'All right, big bro, sorry but I didn't get to watch the show in the end, had some work on, but anyway I just wanted to say you're a top-notch geezer and the best brother any bloke could wish for.'

But the phone remains silent. I flush the toilet and wait for someone to call.

I wait. And wait. It gets to four in the afternoon and rain spatters the window with tiny angry taps, like skeletal fingers typing.

Where are my friends? I know Brian is too embarrassed to call, having witnessed my humiliation at first hand. But he could at least have emailed me – I would happily accept his teasing and ridicule. I just want the contact. Why hasn't

Dr Simon telephoned with consoling words, telling me that no one watches late-night BBC2, that people will still buy my book and, anyway, at least I'm healthy in body and mind? And why hasn't Big Barry rung up with a chortle and a chirp, suggesting we go and forget about it all with two Australian chicks he met in Dublin last New Year?

And then, in a moment of lucidity, I realize why.

Because I wouldn't call them if the roles were reversed.

I mean, look at the evidence. When Brian got fired by his first law firm, I didn't call. When Dr Simon's father died, I didn't call. When Big Barry went through two sexual-harassment suits in a month, I didn't call. Instead I waited for a while, until the heat had dissipated, so it would be easier to joke and laugh about things rather than offer support. I told myself it was all right, our sort of friendship wasn't about the heavy stuff. Our sort of friendship was about going out, being witty, keeping things light and fun.

Fun, fun, fun.

That's my motto with my friends. We go out, talk about football, even though they all know far more about the teams and players than I do (I have to memorize the sports pages for at least two days before meeting Dr Simon or Barry, or for one day if I'm seeing Brian). We talk about women, films, politics, and sometimes more weighty matters, such as the merits of Communism, our fears for European integration, and whether Ross could take Chandler in a fist-fight – Ross, of course, has the sportier physique, but Chandler is looking chunkier by the day and might win with a lucky punch.

But we never talk about feelings. About fears. About

what lies beneath. When Ellie dumped me, my friends didn't exactly rush to pick up the phone.

You see, our relationship is based simply on the fulfilling of mutual needs.

As far as I can tell, it works like this. For the lawyer, Brian, and the doctor, Simon, I am the cool artist, whose books they can point out to impress prospective girlfriends in Waterstone's – although Brian hasn't had a prospective girlfriend in months, if not years. To party-animal Big Barry I am the intellect, who helps him feel clever.

And what do my friends give me?

It's simple. With them I can be a follower. They are all older than me – Barry is thirty-five, Brian is thirty-four, Dr Simon is thirty-three. And each of them loves to tell me what to do.

I've always had older friends, even back at primary school. Partly it's because I'm shy, but mainly it's because I have always sought out those who are more experienced and better able to deal with the world than I am.

With my friends, I like being a follower. Because in my family I felt like I had to be the leader from the day Jes was born.

I suppose I could call them. But that would be an admission, a plea for help. And each in his own way responds negatively to signs of weakness. Dr Simon becomes overbearingly anxious, with a concern for your well-being that makes Mother Teresa look like Henry VIII. Brian becomes cold, desperate to avoid feeling responsible for someone more infirm than himself. And Barry just laughs: he finds weakness amusing.

I should get out of the house, at least. I should go for a run. I have to keep running. I need to keep thin. I must not let myself go. I must not give in. I should keep control. I must run, run, run.

I run as far as the newsagent two hundred yards from Kentish Town station. I pretend to breathe heavily as I enter the shop, just in case anyone might suspect that I've changed into shorts, 'Let's Do It' T-shirt and Nike Triax trainers just to go to the shops.

I'm not on the front page of any of the tabloids. I'm relieved, then inexplicably annoyed. It doesn't seem fair – if Elton John had vomited on live television it would have been splashed over ten pages, with a special souvenir pull-out.

At least I'm on the inside pages of three papers. The *Mirror* has a two-paragraph article that begins,

POET PUKES ON BBC2!

There's a grainy photograph taken from a television screen. A man stands, his hands cupped under his chin as some indefinable goo dribbles from his lips.

BBC2 viewers were amazed last night when poet Scott Barron, author of bestselling poetry collection *Men Matter*, threw up at the end of the live book-show *Word Up!*

Barron, who according to BBC sources had been drinking whisky heavily before the broadcast, apologized before being taken to St Mary's Hospital. He admitted live on air that he'd 'had a little too much to drink'.

The show's assistant producer Jenny Rowan told us: 'It's disgusting. Poetry is not rock and roll!'

Jenny Rowan. You've blown it there.
Shit. Fuck. Shit.
You stupid dipstick.
She might have been the one. She might have been your Sam.

Back at my flat there's a package waiting for me. I open it hurriedly. Inside, I'm surprised to find my lucky Calvin Klein pants with a yellow Post-it note attached that reads:

I HAVE CHLAMYDIA! I WISH I'D NEVER MET YOU! GET TESTED, YOU BASTARD!!

The pants have not been washed. But you can hardly blame Cindy for that.

For the rest of the day I hide under a blanket on my sofa waiting for my boiler to start working, wondering if Cindy's note is the Third Bad Thing and how I could have caught my first ever STD. The last time I had sex was two months ago, with Ellie, and I used a condom . . . didn't I? Can you get chlamydia from toilet seats?

Still my central heating defies me, so I make a pot of tea and console myself with an intriguing American programme on Channel Five about dogs who look like famous people. It's narrated by a poodle that's the spitting image of Tom Hanks. As I watch a segment about a cocker spaniel who resembles Bruce Springsteen, the phone rings.

It continues to ring. I lie thinking that, if I were famous, my canine twin would be a wormy whiny whippet called Cyril.

The phone stops ringing. My answering-machine clicks on. It's Jes. Normally I wouldn't speak to him, but I'm lonely and need human interaction.

'All right, Jes? I'm just watching the celebrity dog impersonators on Channel Five, and I reckon you'd be a big old beagle called Lucky.'

This seems to throw him. 'Are you sure? I always saw myself as a beefy British bulldog.'

There follows a small silence during which I realize that perhaps my brother hasn't called to discuss our canine *doppelgängers*. I pray he hasn't called to discuss my puke-tastic performance on *Word Up!*

Jes speaks, slowly and with measure. 'Look, Scott, there's something I want to talk about. Any chance we could meet for a drink tomorrow?'

We arrange a late-afternoon rendezvous at some trendy bar in Soho, and he says good night. I lie back on the sofa feeling happy that my younger brother wants to talk to me about something and that he didn't mention me being sick on national television, while a proud woman from Chigwell demonstrates how her dachshund is the spitting image of Sylvester Stallone.

8

I wake feeling excited, thirty-three hours after throwing up on BBC2. After all, I have a fun-packed day ahead of me. This is my diary: clean toilet; go to Archway sexual-health clinic for a penis swab; meet my brother to talk about something.

I try to remember the last time Jes and I met up for a chat. It's not obvious – there have been a few evenings at the pub watching football – Jes hates football even more than I do, but comes along occasionally to have a drink with my friends and feel part of the national obsession – and I've been out to dinner with him and Sam four or five times since they were married. But the two of us alone together, a whole evening stretching out in front of us to be filled with talk of our respective lives and, God forbid, feelings? That hasn't happened since ... And then I remember.

It was the day before the publication of *Men Matter*, in a wine-bar near Waterloo. Jes had just begun the last term of his final year, and was obviously highly stressed – he devoured seven bowls of peanuts. He kept biting his fingernails, and when they were down to stumps, he took out a pen and chewed that instead. It snapped and the ink went all over his face but he wasn't embarrassed, he just went to the toilets and washed it off, as if nothing had happened.

I, being the older brother, spent the evening trying to suggest ways he might cope better with his revision, how he might organize his time, what food he should be eating and what time he should go to sleep every night. I was trying to help. I realize now I might have been a tad insistent, but who else was going to give him top revision tips? Mum was too busy at the hospital and our father was as absent as a corpse.

To be fair, Jes listened. After all, I'd got through my university finals, I'd blazed the trail, so even if he disagreed with what I was saying, he had to give me the floor. The funny thing was, he listened to my lecture about timetabling work, about giving yourself time off every two hours, about getting sufficient exercise, running, maybe, until I started talking about different relaxation techniques: 'Yoga breathing, it's kind of circular, very easy, breathe in through your mouth, out through your nose ... Watch ...' I remember it clearly. He lost it.

'What the fuck are you telling me how to relax for? Look at yourself, Scott! You're the least relaxed person I know! You're so fucking uptight it's like you've got a bollard up your arse!'

The evening went downhill from there. Jes didn't come to my book launch. I didn't speak to him until he'd finished his exams. Soon afterwards he met Sam.

Now, two and a half years later, we're going to talk. I make a mental note to listen more, and to offer less advice.

It must be hard to imagine what it's like having a brother

if you don't have one. I can't imagine having a sister, although I wanted one desperately as a teenager (she could have introduced me to all her promiscuous friends). But brothers are different. Being men, they find it difficult to select words to express their intricate jealousies. They interact like strangers most of the time, then end up punching each other mercilessly in public over what, to everyone else, seems like an innocuous little argument. In contrast, I imagine sisters talk about things all the time, become firm friends, then end up scratching each other's eyes out in public over what seems, to everyone else, like an innocuous little argument.

Whereas sisters develop an intricate private language early on – as all women seem to – based on codes that are secret to men, such as tiny details of dress, hairstyle, and the amount of eye-shadow they should apply for a particular party, brothers find communication difficult except through action. If one is jealous of the other, he will take something from him, or push him, or challenge him to a Sumo match in the back garden. These actions sometimes dissipate their ill-feelings – a good Sumo session works wonders – but more often than not they merely act to bury them in shallow ground, from where they will rise again like horror-film zombies. At the end of the day, a game of headers and volleys is no substitute for a good chat.

I call my mother on the way to Archway sexual-health clinic. She hasn't phoned following *Word Up!*, but perhaps she's giving me space. I mean, what do you say to a son who's been sick on live television?

I listen to her answering-machine, the clipped tone, the clinical brevity: 'I can't take your call. Leave a message. I will call you back.' It makes me smile, hearing her cursory speech. For Mum, flowery language is for lawyers and hospital managers. Maybe it has something to do with her background – she's from Protestant stock in the Scottish Borders, a people for whom words are dangerous, open to misinterpretation and abuse. And she's lived most of her life in a foreign land – England – where her accent marks her out for comment and occasional ridicule. She mentioned once that in her first week at Cambridge she was laughed at for saying, 'Pass the tatties,' at matriculation dinner. As a result, she can be almost monosyllabic.

I recall my childhood, the long silences at the dinner table after our father left in which words flew above us like distant birds, never landing. Mum's never been very vocal. At school plays or sports days she never talked to the other parents, never shared their jokes and banter, only exchanging a few necessary words with our teachers. She was always distant. Polite, yet detached.

I think I reacted against her reticence, her mistrust of vocabulary. I started a secret quest to find longer and more elaborate words. It became a covert passion, sitting at night with a dictionary in my bed, underlining the most interesting entries. *Acquiescence. Invincibility. Sanctimonious.* But I was careful not to show off my new-found treasures, keeping them hidden, my personal pornography. At school, teachers would call me 'shy' and 'uncommunicative'. In contrast, Jes never seemed timid or withdrawn. At the age of five, he told a plumber mending the bathroom sink that the drains 'stink like putrid armpits'.

I wonder where my mother is on this Thursday morning. I wonder whether she could possibly be screening her calls, like I do, and doesn't want to talk to me. Perhaps she's really upset with me. Perhaps I've gone too far this time.

I leave a brief stilted message, concern discernible in my voice: 'Hi, Mum, just thought I'd call to say I'm fine, much better now, actually, sorry about it all. I'd love to talk, call me soon, love you, 'bye.'

Archway sexual-health clinic proves less scary than I'd imagined. A nice man called Charles, with blue hair and various facial piercings, asks me about my sexual history, whether I sleep with men, whether I inject myself with drugs and whether I've had sex with women in sub-Saharan Africa. I feel very conservative when I have to admit that I've done none of these things.

'We just have to ask,' concludes Charles, with a smile that says, 'Nerd!'

To my surprise and heart-thumping delight, the only other person in the waiting room for the blood test is a very attractive woman with a small nose wearing smart business clothes. I try not to look at her. She shifts a little nervously. And then it strikes me. What a great place to pick up women! Yes, guys, head to your local sexual-health clinic! Here you'll find vulnerable women in need of support and commiseration, you'll have a shared topic of conversation and, best of all, any woman there is likely to be up for sex, otherwise she wouldn't be in a sexual-health clinic in the first place.

The two of us sit in the waiting room, clock ticking. I look straight ahead as if the most fascinating thing I've ever seen is the chewing-gum studding the grey wall opposite. She stares down at a six-month-old issue of *Safeway* magazine. She crosses her legs the other way. I do the same, hoping this is some unspoken language between us. I think, desperately, of something to say. A first line. But what do you say to a gorgeous woman in a sexual-health clinic?

'I think I might have chlamydia, what about you?'

'Are you a drug-user, slapper, or both?'

'Nice weather for the time of year.'

I've almost composed my line, after several rewrites, when Charles appears, inquires, 'Ms Atkinson?', as if this could be either of us, and the pretty woman dashes from the room with visible relief, leaving me with no chance to ask, 'You wouldn't happen to know anywhere around here where I can buy laundry detergent, would you?'

Above her freshly vacated chair a poster reads, 'IS SEX PAINFUL?'

Another says, 'SEX AND THE OVER-50S. YOUR QUESTIONS ANSWERED.'

In a horrifying moment I experience a vision of my mother having sex. Does she? I know my parents did – they'd lock the bedroom door on Sunday mornings, classical music playing loud enough to deafen Beethoven, and we'd have to entertain ourselves until lunchtime, no whining, no exceptions. I wonder if there's any way she could have had sex since my father left. I don't think so. But maybe I don't want to think so.

I know my father has. He used to grab Mireille's floppy little arse at any opportunity, as if having to prove to us, his young sons, that breaking up with our mother was the best thing that ever happened to him.

I remember asking him about sex shortly before his departure. I wanted to know facts – we'd just had our first sex-education class at school. What did it feel like? This was evidently a question not dealt with in the *Dorling Kindersley Parents' Handbook*. My father coughed, scratched the back of his neck and coughed again. I had a brain-wave: 'Is it like having a really good poo when you're desperate?'

My father laughed and said, 'Yes. Sort of.'

ORGASM

It's a funny feeling,
Down below, like a day off school because of snow,
Or your first ever Slush Puppy.
Men shudder, judder, splutter,
'I love you,'
and sometimes even mean it.
Women, however, are more opaque,
wriggling out multiples, or fakes.
Unlike babies, we can make one on our own,
but it's much more fun,
to have an orgasm,
with a human you like.

*

A very large female nurse stands over me with a cotton swab. 'Don't worry, love. I see twenty-five cocks a day.'

I drop my boxer shorts.

'This might sting a little,' she says softly.

My screams can be heard in Liverpool. When I finish wiping the tears from my eyes, she informs me that I might feel some discomfort passing water for the rest of the day.

I change my clothes three times before going out to meet Jes, settling on twisted Levi's, a black cashmere sweater (another of Ellie's free samples) and my blue Campers. Then I head down the festering Northern Line to Leicester Square.

In Soho I wait in a bar called The Place, which is half empty, just a few drunken media types still pickled from lunch. There's a particularly loud table of twenty-somethings, women in stripy shirts and low-slung faded jeans, men in roll-necked sweaters who take it in turns to glance at themselves in the mirror on the opposite wall. The loudest is an older, skinny man wearing yellow sunglasses, his receding hair bleached blond in an obvious attempt to appear youthful to his employees. He's evidently the boss, lecturing like a schoolyard bully, cigarette dangling from thin lips.

A young pretty waitress with spiky brown hair and pink lipstick approaches the table and he takes her hand, continuing his lecture while she tries to think of a way to free herself. Not for the first time in my life, I wonder why women put up with men instead of clubbing us to death with baseball bats.

I'm early. Jes is late. I'm annoyed – with him, and with myself for being annoyed. This is the curse of the elder child, anxiously arriving way before the allotted time for every event. I was early for my own arrival, born a week before the due date. Jes, of course, popped out two weeks late.

I nurse a beer and wonder why Jes wants to talk to me. Usually he talks to his friends – Zeb, Mad Michael, Dan the Man – boys, now men, whom he's known since school, with whom he shared everything growing up, from skateboards to girlfriends, which at one stage seemed to have equivalent value. They talk for hours on the phone, they send each other's parents Christmas cards, they spend every New Year's Eve drinking cheap champagne and telling each other they'll always be mates. Which they will be.

It used to make me angry, this insistent camaraderie, it seemed so . . . false. I thought maybe it would dissipate after they all left university, but it hasn't. Recently Zeb and Dan carried Jes three miles home from a Clapham party. He was blind drunk, they got him into the house, put him to sleep on the downstairs sofa, and cooked Sam breakfast in bed the next morning to give him time to sober up.

My friends would have carried me outside the party, called a cab and gone back to try to find a woman to sleep with. At least, I hope they would have called a cab.

Another thing that rankles is this: Jes can drink me under the table. I know it's physiological, he's bigger (okay, fatter) than me, he can take more booze, but even when we were younger – me a lithe twenty-one-year-old, he a podgy sixteen – he could consume more.

He had practice though. From the age of twelve he took to siphoning off spirits from our mother's drinks' cabinet into a jam-jar, a thimbleful from each of the seven bottles to avoid detection – gin through whisky to the foul-smelling Bols Uncle Jack adored. He'd swill them round in the jam-jar, then slink off to the bottom of the garden to swallow the contents before climbing into my old tree-house for a sleep or a vomit.

I never told Mum.

Jes arrives twenty minutes late. I am angry, counting minutes, hot bile simmering. But when I see him, his large flabby bulk in one of the slimmest districts of London, I feel a sudden and surprising surge of . . . what? The desire to protect? Sympathy? Love?

He tries to squeeze past the twenty-something table, and the skinny bleach-headed man affects an exaggerated stare, and his co-workers laugh, and he mutters, 'Fat bloater,' and they all laugh some more. Jes ignores them. Maybe he doesn't even see them.

We shake hands, like businessmen. I shoot a glare at the twenty-something table, and they look away. 'Listen, Jes, this place is a bit noisy, do you want to go somewhere else?'

'It's cool. They do great cocktails.'

He smiles as he sits, and I recognize the smile from our childhood – he's excited about something. Maybe about meeting his older brother for a drink after three years.

If it's possible, he seems to have put on more weight. His jaw is a little saggier, his cheeks more puffed, his eyes less finely cut. He's breathless. 'You'll never . . . guess . . . what.'

'No, you're right, I won't.'

'I've got a travel-writing gig. Well, Sam got it for me. She sent in the piece I did on South London. I'm going to Bremen. It's a press trip for the *Daily Telegraph*. No one else fancied it, they're all too busy, so Sam suggested me. They read the piece and said sure, why not?'

'Bremen. That's great. What's in Bremen?'

'Big port, shipbuilding, medieval loveliness, and a museum devoted to the work of Paula Modersohn-Becker, founder of the Worpswede art colony.'

'Wow,' I say, mustering enthusiasm, although I bet even the people of Bremen don't like going to Bremen. I'm happy for him, though. He's obviously relieved that finally he's got the chance to write about something other than the comparison between Sainsbury's and Safeway's frozen-food sections. Even if it took his wife to organize it.

We order some expensive cocktails to celebrate and I give the pretty little barmaid my credit card, holding up my hand when Jes starts to protest. 'When you're a famous travel writer,' I say magnanimously.

He nods thanks, and then he's drinking and talking, telling me about the delights of Bremen, about how he's going to structure the article, about how this is his big break. His enthusiasm slowly softens me, like fabric-conditioner.

Jes has always loved travelling. He delayed going to

university for two years, backpacking around dusty impoverished countries with Zeb. When he returned, with some dubious ethnic rugs in his backpack and some dubious ethnic bacteria in his stomach, he was the skinniest I've ever seen him. He weighed less than me for the first time since he was ten. 'That'll teach you,' I joked, as he began a terrifying course of antibiotic pills the size of drink coasters.

'I'd go back in a shot.' He grinned, washing the pills down with a can of Guinness.

I have always hated the thought of leaving the British mainland. I don't see the point, all that stuff you don't know about. I mean, I can get foreign food in London.

'You never liked travelling much, did you, mate?' he says, reading my mind.

'No.'

'Hey, do you remember when we went to France for the first time?' Jes laughs, ordering more drinks. I try not to scowl: he's dredged up a memory I wanted buried. I was twelve, he was seven, Mum put us on the plane at Heathrow and our father picked us up at Nice airport. For the whole journey I was terrified – of losing Jes, of the plane going down, of being allergic to the aeroplane food, of the responsibility of it all.

'You made that video . . .' Jes laughs again, downing his whisky sour as if it's water. I smile, blushing slightly. I'd made a home video of myself – me in my bedroom looking studious, me in the garden running really fast, me helping Mum with the washing up, because I wanted to be sure that if we were kidnapped or the plane crashed, I would look good on the television news reports – you know the ones, where they show the grainy home videos of the missing person doing startlingly ordinary things for someone who subsequently gets caught up in extraordinary tragedy. I even marked it: SCOTT BARRON – MISSING PERSON.

We laugh together. Jes is bright-eyed, fat cheeks ruddy.

'You know my favourite trip when we were kids?'

He knows I know the answer to this but, apparently, ritual is part of the fun of family life. 'Would it be Edinburgh, Jes?'

'It would be Edinburgh, Scott. That first time. I was, what . . . four?'

I know what's coming next, although I'm surprised he's talking about this now. He hasn't mentioned it in years, probably since puberty.

When I was eight and Jes was four, Mum took us to Scotland for a summer. We stayed with our grandparents in a grey pebble-dash housing estate in Fairmilehead. I remember a curtly clipped front lawn, stodgy cakes that sat in your tummy for days, and a dizzying view of the Pentland Hills, which, if you lay on the floor just below the sill, filled the window with a blanket of green.

Bill and Betty Henderson were old, stooping, slow and fragile, yet they came with Mum to Edinburgh Zoo where I felt miserable and Jes fell in love with the penguins. If this is one of Jes's favourite memories, it has to be one of my worst. I recall being dragged around in the rain, pressing my nose against grubby glass to peer at shrubs and stumps that allegedly hid animals of spectacular interest.

'You know, I felt a sort of connection with the penguins,' says Jes, on his third whisky sour. 'I remember this keeper telling me that they need a layer of fat to protect them from the harsh environment they live in . . .' He laughs, and caresses his belly. 'Maybe that's why I've piled on the pounds. The harsh environment of South London.'

'You're looking good,' I lie, but he doesn't hear.

'Yeah. That day at the zoo was pretty happy. Gramps bought me that blow-up penguin, do you remember? The giant one, it took us an hour to inflate it . . .'

I'd forgotten. But now I remember. It was huge, at least four feet tall, an excessive symbol of elderly love – perhaps our grandfather knew he had only six months to live. I got a fluffy snake, because I'd thought they were the coolest animals in the zoo since they could poison all the others.

From then on Jes loved penguins. For some reason, he named the giant penguin Norman – he just liked the name. It stood like a Greek god at the entrance to his bedroom, guarding a kingdom of Norman acolytes – countless penguins of various sizes, hues and fluffiness.

'Remember when Norman burst?' Jes asks.

'Yeah. You were a bit upset.'

'That's life, hey? Deflating?'

'Yeah. Psssssss.'

Jes smiles at my impression of an inflatable penguin bursting and orders another drink. We clink glasses. If I was more sober perhaps I wouldn't say what I'm going to say, but I'm not so I do: 'Listen, Jes . . .'

He's gulping his drink.

'I have a confession to make.'

'What? You're not really my brother?'

'No. It's more serious than that.'

He puts down his drink.

'I put a hole in Norman.'

'What's that?'

'Yeah. Sorry.'

Jes holds his glass mid-air. His face seems less flabby. His brown Bambi eyes are suddenly locked on me.

'I got a pin from Mum's drawer and stuck it in him. I'm really sorry. I don't know what came over me. I guess I just don't like penguins.'

Considering I had forgotten all about my dastardly childhood deed, the relief of confession is surprisingly acute. And I would feel even better if my younger brother wasn't now looking at me as if he wants to be an only child, which, given his not inconsiderable girth, he could accomplish simply by sitting on me.

'You killed Norman?'

I nod, slowly. I am the Lee Harvey Oswald of the penguin world. As I try to meet my brother's piercing gaze, his face becomes chubby once more, blood rushing to his cheeks, and he laughs. And laughs. And laughs.

If you haven't heard my brother laugh, you should. I'm thinking of bringing out a CD – *Jes Barron's Big Laughs!* Most of the people in the bar turn to look. The blond skinny man exaggerates another stare. It's the original fat man's laugh, rolling up from the deep, a *tsunami* of laughter that washes over everyone in its path. I see people start to smile, one or two chuckle, some laugh along with Jes.

'You killed Norman!' cackles my fat brother. 'You killed Norman!'

Tears are flowing down his cheeks, he's lost it, and now lots of people are laughing, perhaps less with him than at him, the twenty-somethings giggling like teenagers.

'I said I was sorry. Are you okay?'

'Just, ha, ha . . . a bit, ha, ha, emotional, ha, at the, ha, moment.' Jes takes out a white handkerchief with which he dabs at his eyes. 'Oh, God,' he splutters, gulping for non-humorous air. 'You killed Norman.'

Then he focuses on me once again, and I wonder if the belly-flop on to my chest is imminent, Big Daddy, WWF Night of Steel, but instead he smiles and says, 'I hated fucking Norman. He scared the life out of me. I was so happy when he burst.'

And we both laugh like loons. It feels good, a shared moment, a connection.

The twenty-somethings stand to leave, and as he puts on his coat I glare at the skinny bleach-haired man one last time, and he looks away.

Over our fifth whisky sour I find myself asking how Sam is. I admit I heard their argument in Grantchester. Jes falls silent. I'm suddenly worried. Are they okay? And then, somewhere below the worry, a more evil sentiment emerges, small yet alive as bacteria, a small ugly hope that maybe they're going to split up and my younger brother will prove to be as useless at relationships as me.

Jes puts down his drink. 'Sam's pregnant. We're going to have a baby.'

I swallow the whisky sour too quickly and cough. My

heart pounds. 'Wow, Jes, that's great. Was it, er . . . planned?'

'Oh, God, yes. I've been wanting a baby for the last year. Sam didn't, so we've been kind of fighting over it. I even thought about replacing her birth-control pills with vitamins on the sly. But I think now that it's happened she's okay with it. You know, Scott, I've been dying to tell someone.'

'Does Mum know?'

'Yeah. I called her last night.'

I feel slighted, slightly, that I wasn't the first.

'But I couldn't wait to tell you,' hurries Jes, perhaps sensing my chagrin. 'I just wanted to choose the right moment, you know?'

I smile to reassure him, and dispel my guilt at feeling jealous. 'How long has Sam been . . . you know, pregnant?'

It's such a funny word, pregnant, so clumsy, so clinical. Where is the beauty, the compassion that the word should evoke?

'Eight weeks. I know it's a little early to be telling people, so don't go too wide with it. But I tell you, Scott mate, it's the best feeling. I feel like, I dunno, the one thing I want in life is to be a father.'

'Wow. That's great, Jes. Many congratulations.'

But I just sit there, not shaking his hand or hugging him or kissing him on both cheeks or giving him a big smacker on the lips, or whatever a normal, functional, loving older brother does to his younger brother when he's just announced he's going to be a father. No. I sit there, a little stunned, as if someone's just informed me that the Queen is dead. But Jes seems not to notice, perhaps overjoyed to be spreading his good news. 'The weird thing is, once Sam agreed to try, it was pretty quick. One shot and bam!'

'Super sperm.'

'Can you believe it, big brother? Me, Jes Barron, twenty-six years old, is going to be a father!'

There's something in his voice that snips at me, cutting. It's like, I don't know, like he's beaten me at something. At least, that's how it sounds to me.

'How's Sam?' I ask, to deflect his glory. This seems to work. He casts his eyes down, as if trying to make a decision. Then he looks up again. 'Actually she's been sick quite a lot. And moody as hell. Poor love. She even mentioned getting an abortion.'

'No? Sam wanted an abortion?' My jealousy vanishes, concern floods in.

'She said she didn't feel ready. She's scared of the responsibility.'

I recall Sam on Mum's sixtieth birthday. Did she know then that she was pregnant? Was there a deeper, hidden meaning to her line about loving someone being harder than not having someone to love? Did she mean Jes, or the child she knew she was carrying? 'She'll be fine. You both will. It's great news, little brother. So much to celebrate. What do you say to a bottle of champagne?'

At the bar I order the champagne – not the most expensive, but not the cheapest either. The strange thing is, when it arrives in its fancy ice-bucket I don't want to go back to the table. I glance over at Jes, but luckily he's on his mobile talking animatedly, probably to Zeb or Dan the Man.

I watch him leaning back in his chair, big belly protruding as if he himself might be in his third trimester, big jiggling arm dangling, and I try to picture him with a child, a small baby, diminutive on his lap and I can't. I just can't.

I mean, he's my younger brother. This isn't the way it's supposed to be. *I* do things first. I went through all the hard stuff first. At least I should be allowed some of the good stuff first.

I look around the room. There are probably a dozen women here, a few of whom I find attractive. But even if I was to go up to one of them (which I won't), convince her to go out with me (which I couldn't) and we ended up in a long-term relationship (which I have signally failed to achieve), it would be at least three years before I could be in Jes's position – in a loving married relationship, with a house that smells of coffee and marijuana, and a baby due in seven months' time.

I go back to the table, muster a smile, and start unwrapping the foil on the champagne bottle before I notice Jes is no longer talking on his phone. His cheeks are white and his jaws are clenched beneath his jowls. 'Are you okay?'

'I was just talking to Sammy. She's mad as hell. I forgot to take the washing out of the machine. Now she's crying her eyes out. I think I'd better go.' He looks up, apologetically, brown eyes wide like they used to be when he'd spilled something as a child. 'Sorry, Scott.'

He picks up his coat, pats my shoulder and departs, people following him with their eyes, the fattest man in the bar, as he picks his way through the tables and away back to South-South London and his pregnant wife.

I sit with the champagne. I open it and pour myself a glass. I feel terrible. There I was at the bar, wallowing in negativity, thinking my glass was half empty when in fact it is half full. I mean, my brother is happy. He's going to have a baby. It strikes me then, between the eyes, and I smile widely like some Soho street nutter.

I'M GOING TO BE AN UNCLE!

Back in Kentish Town – three-quarters of a bottle of champagne, one clumsy advance to the pretty waitress, quickly rebuffed, later – I wander home. I want to go to bed and sleep for days. I get to the top of the road and see the old homeless man lying in his alleyway. I think about crossing the road to avoid him, but across the road there's a group of teenage boys drinking Special Brew, and anyway the old man seems asleep, so I head towards him. It's only when I get level with him that I see his head is bleeding.

I stop. I look around. The teenage boys have gone. There's nobody to ask advice of, nobody I can pass the buck to. Bloody hell!

I'm not a bad person. I'm just not so good at doing good. I'll give money, I have a direct debit to several charities, but active service, no, that's just not me. Jes got all those genes.

Still no one. Shit, what if he's dead? But then he groans. I kneel down and he stinks of alcohol, which in my drunken state makes me feel like puking. On closer view the gash on his head looks less serious. I nudge him with my elbow. He stirs and grunts.

'No,' he says, emphatically.

'Are you okay?'

He looks at me, bloodshot eyes, yellowing at the edges. 'No,' he says.

Which is not the answer I'm looking for. I take out my mobile phone.

'No! No police!' he growls.

Great. I'm tired. He's mad, drunken and bleeding. I should just leave now, maybe give him a couple of quid and depart. I could be lying in a warm bath in three minutes' time.

Then I have a swift vision – Jes in my position, picking the old man up in his big jiggly arms and taking him home, making him a cup of tea, offering him a bed for the night. And to my surprise, and not inconsiderable horror, I hear myself saying, 'Listen, why don't I make you a cup of tea and you can clean yourself up a bit.'

To my considerable horror he says, 'Yes.'

In the flat, I sit him on a chair and hurry to the kitchen, flick on the kettle and run back to the living room where he's still sitting on the chair. He looks so strange in my flat, in his misshapen black suit and surprisingly clean wellington boots. And then I realize that, apart from Ellie, no one else has been in my flat for about two years – the Sky TV installation man doesn't count, nor does the plumber who comes every time my boiler packs in. This old man is my first guest since Ellie left. If he is a guest. Which, considering I invited him, he must be.

'Is your head okay?' I ask. He puts his withered blue-veined hand to his withered blue-veined head. His voice is gruff and phlegmy. I'm beginning to wonder if he has an accent – something Eastern European, or Mediterranean. Maybe he's an asylum-seeker. Or an Italian war criminal.

'Shower,' he says.

Oh, no.

'Shower, please,' he says.

Oh, fuck.

'Shower,' he says.

I give him an old towel from under the sink and some soap and he seems happy enough to close the bathroom door and embark on clattering noises. Now I dial 999. The operator asks me which service, I say police, the police operator asks me what the problem is, I say there's a strange homeless man in my flat, she asks if he broke in, I say no I invited him in, and she informs me that if I bother the police again without good reason I will be liable for prosecution.

What am I doing? I invited him in because I wanted to feel better about myself. I wanted to feel more like my do-gooding younger brother, but it's not working. I want to get rid of him, push him out and lock the door. But that would be even worse than not having invited him in to begin with. I'd be giving and taking away in the same breath. Bloody hell!

The old man exits the bathroom ten minutes later, his

head washed, wearing his same old ragged, bloody, alcohol-infused clothes. I rip some old clothes out of my wardrobe (brown cords, Bristol University sweatshirt) and hand them to him. 'Here. You can have these,' I say, magnanimously.

He looks at the clothes for a moment, perhaps weighing up whether Bristol University is a suitable academic establishment for him to be endorsing, then says, in his grouchy foreign accent, 'No. Want chocolate.'

'I don't have chocolate.'

'Chocolate.'

I search my kitchen for chocolate. I'm just about to give up, a little worried that the old man might have a blood-sugar problem and flip out if I don't return with a cocoa-based product, when I discover, like some ancient forensic evidence stored long after the crime, two Mars Bars in the freezer section of my small fridge. The relief is surprisingly intense.

The old man eats the frozen Mars Bar quickly, taking sharp bites, which suggest his teeth are still all his own. He looks at me as he chomps, at times inquisitive, at times blankly, as if staring straight through me.

I nibble the other Mars Bar and find myself loving the taste. With the first bite I feel a rush of warm nostalgia – hiding under my duvet with a book and a torch, nibbling slowly to make it last till the end of the chapter. It's been years since I bit into a Mars Bar. I've been good. I mean, it is bad to eat chocolate, isn't it?

'Good,' says the old man.

'Yeah, it's not bad,' I reply, feeling virtuous that I'm at least talking to a smelly old vagrant. 'Is your head okay?'

He nods slowly, in time to his munching.

'How did it happen?'

'Fell down. Drink too much.'

I can't help smiling. His matter-of-fact tone is comical, like someone might talk of buying shampoo or working late at the office.

'Why do you drink?' I hear myself asking, which must be at the bottom of the list of questions you're supposed to ask visiting homeless alcoholics.

'Mag . . .'

I lean closer. His clothes still stink of booze, but from his skin and hair comes the unmistakable fragrance of my Lemon Zest Body Gel.

'Maggie . . .' he says again, his bottom lip starting to tremble, and I wonder if he's about to cry.

'Maggie?' I ask, like a teacher trying to prompt the right answer from a backward child.

'Maggie.' He nods. I wonder who Maggie is. A lost love, wife or daughter? Or perhaps a favourite wolfhound. Maggie. An old name, of his vintage, buried under decades of Waynes and Portias and Courtneys.

'Who's Maggie?'

'Maggie,' he replies, which might be a deeply philosophical answer, pertaining to ideas of identity and self, Maggie indeed being Maggie. But given the way the old man is starting to rock back and forth like a fundamentalist cleric it's more likely to be due to a mental blockage, his brain having put on a record that has become stuck.

'Maggie,' he concludes.

I think for a moment about letting him stay the night.

I feel my stomach clenching around my devoured Mars Bar, that anxiousness I recall from childhood when there's something I should do but don't want to. If he stays he might steal things, or soil things, or attack me. Then I imagine telephoning Jes, and his surprise and admiration when I tell him that I've taken in a homeless man and given him a bed for the night. As I think this, I hear myself saying to the old man, 'Look, you could stay here tonight, if you've got nowhere else to go.'

I almost laugh. Of course he's got nowhere to go, Scott, he's homeless. The old man stares at me blankly again. I go to the sofa and start taking off the cushions. I can be a good person, can't I?

'You can stay here. There's a sofa-bed.'

'No!' he says, somewhat ferociously.

'It's no problem,' I lie.

'No. Sleep there!' He jerks his thumb towards the street.

'Isn't it cold?'

'Sleep there.'

I argue with him for a short time, then give him an old blanket that's lain unused under my bed for several years, which he tries to refuse but I insist, pushing it into him.

On the doorstep he stops and reaches into his pocket. He holds out his hand. In his palm is a small smooth round stone.

'Take.'

'No, really, it's all right . . .'

'Take.'

I take the stone. It's cold.

'Frank,' he says.

'Scott,' I say. We shake hands solemnly, and he walks off into the night, the bottom of the blanket dragging on the wet, muddy street.

Some time later, I take out my notepad and start writing.

NEPHEW OR NIECE

Phew!
I'm going to have a Nephew.
Or Niece,
Either would be nice,
Any size.
Will it be blue, or pink?
I think
I'll buy green, to indicate
I'm delighted either way.
I'm going to be an Uncle.
I better start buying uncool gifts,
To send the child for Christmas.

9

The following Monday, I get a letter from Dr Simon. I open it and inside is a card with a red rose on the front. For a stark moment I wonder whether Dr Simon is gay and about to confess fifteen years of love for me (I guess I shouldn't be too upset – I could use all the love I can get right now). I look at the embossed rose, which rises expensively from the high-quality card, and consider not opening it.

I open it.

Inside is a printed message with embossed gold lettering:

Dr Simon Popplewell and Dr Jane Harvey
wish to announce their engagement.
You are cordially invited to a party to celebrate this happy event
at the house of Dr Michael and Dr Sheila Popplewell,
5 Trafalgar Close, Chiswick.
Saturday 23 November 7.30 p.m.
Dress: Casual.

The invite looks expensive. Simon must really love this woman.

At the bottom he's scribbled in his indecipherable doctor's scrawl:

Who would have guessed it? Mr Single is getting hitched. Tell you
all about it soon. Cheers, Simon.
PS No puking at the wedding!

I let the phone ring as I look at the card. The answering-machine clicks on. It's my mother.

'Hello, love . . .'

She pauses for a moment, which is uncharacteristic. Normally she's so forthright, like a policewoman. I think about picking up, but I haven't the energy right now.

'I'm just calling to . . . to say . . .'

She sounds tired. Her voice is small and wavering. Perhaps she's hung-over after a retirement party. Perhaps she's got flu. If she's unwell, I know she'll never confess it: any admission of illness is seen as weakness. She often says that's why she became a pathologist – the moaning of live sick people would have driven her spare. The dead are so much more stoic.

'Oh . . . I can't remember. Old age. Call me soon. Love you. 'Bye.'

The message clicks off. I sit there.

'Love you. 'Bye.'

My mother doesn't leave messages like this. I feel a surge of love for her. I can't remember the last time she said she loved me, raw and simple like that. She's trying to make me feel better, saying it's all right about the television vomit.

I pick up the receiver. I should find out if she's feeling unwell. I should slowly, jokingly wheedle it out of her, as only I can, and see if there's anything I can do. But something stops me. I feel lethargic, apathetic. The fact is, I don't want to talk about Jes and Sam's baby.

I'll call her soon, suggest a day in London together. It's been ages. And I need to make it up to her, after putting her through the embarrassment of *Word Up!* We'll go to the Ritz for lunch and then to Harvey Nichols. Maybe I'll buy her a present.

Feeling better about my imaginary future plan, I put down the receiver.

It's a bright autumnal Thursday when I venture back to the old red-brick Victorian office block in Kensington. Lindsey Stevens reclines in her leather armchair, crosses her legs and smiles, gently.

'So tell me the news. It's been a while since your last visit.'

There seems to be a hint of reproach in her voice. She sits there in her jeans and blue sweatshirt, her breasts still ample, but I'm proud to think we've moved beyond the stage where I imagine having sex with her.

I recount my four weeks of trials and tribulations, including my puke-tastic television appearance. I talk for almost fifteen minutes, non-stop. When I stop I feel better, lighter, almost.

'Which of these events would you say has affected you most?' Lindsey asks, employing another of her manipulative smiles.

I consider this, replaying the recent mishaps, mayhem and misery in my head. Would it be the *Word Up!* fiasco? My brother and his lovely wife having a baby? Frank's strange visit? Dr Simon getting engaged without telling me?

I know which one, but I don't think I'm going to tell Lindsey.

'I don't know,' I lie. 'I think they've all affected me in different ways.'

'What about your brother's baby news?'

Shit. That's not fair. This woman is a professional.

'Yeah, that was weird. I mean, I was happy and all, but I felt kind of . . . I don't know . . .'

'Jealous?'

'I guess so.'

She's got me. I was jealous. Okay, I've always been somewhat jealous of my younger brother – he's had it so easy, so smooth, so hand-fed. But there's something about him having the baby that breaks across a boundary. It was one thing getting married to the woman he loved, but marriages can end. He could always have found his way back to single sadness. A baby changes everything. He is now definitively overtaking me, like he's had a lucky throw at Monopoly (Jes always had lucky throws at Monopoly).

As I think this, I sense another nagging feeling that there's something I need to remember, something I could and should tell Lindsey. This thing lies on the fringes of my memory, on the guest-list for my memory, but it hasn't shown up to the party yet. I search through the files in my head to no avail.

Lindsey looks at me, takes another sip of tea, then says, 'I'm going to digress here just for a second, if that's all right?'

I nod, slowly.

'I don't usually like to use my own experiences in my work, but this seems like a good occasion to break some rules. So here goes ... I have a younger sister, Sharon, whom I love very much indeed. For some reason, IQ, ambition, I don't know, I was always more successful than her, school, university, all those sort of things. But when my husband and I wanted to have a baby, we discovered I couldn't have children.'

I don't know what to say. I feel terrible for talking about Sam's pregnancy. So I just sit there and listen.

'Two months after we found out, Sharon got pregnant. And I hated her for it. Somehow I felt like it was her fault that I couldn't have kids. I blamed her for my own infertility. It was completely crazy.'

'What happened?'

'She had the baby, and I couldn't even go to see it. It took me a year or so to get beyond what was a totally irrational resentment. It's not something I'm proud of.'

'So you think I blame Jes for my own situation?'

'Some people claim that sibling relationships are more important in forming adult life than parents.'

I think about this. I suppose I blame Jes for some things. If it hadn't been for his helplessness as a child, maybe I could have been more independent, more self-assured, not always looking over my shoulder to check that he was all right.

'Let's look at it this way. Why do you think you don't have the things your brother has right now?' Lindsey asks.

'Like I said before, I've made my choices. Jes has made his. That's why we're in different places.'

'Did you choose to be unhappy?'

'Unhappy? I'm not unhappy. I've got friends, I've got my third book out. I can run a mile in six minutes. I'm not unhappy!' I bark, realizing too late that I'm raising my voice.

Lindsey nods once more. I sit there, hearing the noisy echo of my words. There's a silence during which thirty seconds tick by like a pulse. Of course she knows I'm unhappy. It doesn't take a rocket scientist or a fully trained psychoanalyst to realize this. Happy people don't go for psychiatric counselling.

'Do you remember on your last visit you said that you sometimes felt hurt because people walked out on you?'

Did I? Jesus. This is like seeing a home-video of a drunken evening and finding out what a prat you made of yourself.

'And you said you didn't need anyone?'

I nod. I vaguely recall something along those lines.

'Do you think you might have got into the habit of pushing people away to protect yourself?'

Hmmm. Protect myself. Of course I protect myself, it's the number-one thing we're taught as kids. Watch out! Be careful! Don't slip! Take that breadknife out of your mouth! We have to protect ourselves. Because people are careless, they're selfish, they lie to you, they don't come to your book launch. They walk out on you.

'Yeah. Maybe I do that,' I reply succinctly.

'So you want people to be loyal to you, not to walk away

from you, and yet part of you wants to push them away to protect yourself?'

'That's a bit of a Catch-22, isn't it?' I admit.

'It could be a problem.' Lindsey smiles.

I wonder, then and there, if Mum is right about shrinks. They put ideas into people's heads that were never there in the first place. I wonder whether I could tell her that I'm seeing a therapist.

Perhaps not.

'So, what's the answer?' I ask, sounding like a child in a classroom.

'I don't know. But I think we're getting somewhere. I want you to think about all this, and we'll talk more next week,' says Lindsey, glancing at her watch.

'Think? Of course I'll bloody think! I can't stop thinking, you stupid bloody cow!' Actually, I don't say this. Instead I thank her, pay her, and make a dash for the exit.

At the nearby Tesco, I buy a multipack of Penguin biscuits, some low-fat crisps and a Cornish pasty, something I've not eaten since childhood. I sit on a crumbly wall outside the supermarket watching cars fume and splutter in one of London's more spectacular traffic jams. I devour the pasty, then the crisps (three packets), and then a Penguin. I start to feel a little better.

As I sit there, watching the cars on the A4, I think about Frank. I feel good about myself for having looked after him. I feel like calling Jes and Sam and somehow letting it slip that I've taken a homeless man into my house, if only for half an hour. I know this is wrong, but I need some sort of validation for my benevolence.

The thing is, while Frank makes me feel better about myself, he's also a little unnerving, like a character in a Dickens novel. The Ghost of Christmas Future. Is he a warning? Or a reminder of how lucky I am? Where did he come from? How did he end up drunk and alone on a street in one of the less affluent neighbourhoods of North London? And who's Maggie?

I munch another Penguin biscuit and wonder how you get to be a homeless drunk. You'd think it was difficult, requiring some spectacular misfortune, some over-whelming tragedy involving blood and lawyers. But sitting on the old damp wall, eating my supermarket purchases, I realize that a fall does not have to be rapid. Over months and years you might not even notice the descent. You move away from your family, you lose touch with your friends. Then you lose your job, fail to meet the rent or mortgage, one drink becomes four, then a bottle and bingo!

We get used to anything, even misery.

Maybe, once upon a time, Frank was successful. Per-haps Maggie was his beautiful sophisticated English wife. Perhaps he owned an olive-oil company that went bust, or pursued an illustrious military career in the Spanish army before losing the plot when civilian life failed to compete with the thrills of warfare. Or perhaps he's just mentally ill and has been drinking since child-hood.

On my way to the tube I stop by a homeless man who looks about my age and give him a handful of pound coins and a couple of Penguin biscuits. I smile at him.

'Ta, mate,' he says blankly, and goes back to staring at everyone's feet.

Brian finally emails me – talking to me would have been too traumatic for both of us. He suggests we meet for lunch near his office in the City. At the end of the email he adds, 'PS WHO HASN'T PUKED ON TELEVISION?' Which makes me feel a little better.

The sushi bar is full of men and women in suits, booming opinions on the German economy, the terrible state of the rail network and England's latest woeful performance at some sport or other.

'You look tired,' remarks Brian, by way of greeting.

'Thanks.'

We chat for a while about Brian's work, then about Dr Simon's engagement – to my annoyance Brian has met the elusive Dr Jane, if only for a minute outside Moorgate tube station. 'She's very, er . . . direct. Probably what Simon needs. Not bad-looking, though. Nice baps.'

I smile – English colloquialisms always sound funny in Brian's resolutely American accent, even though he uses them all the time, perhaps still feeling anxious about fitting in in his adopted country. He chews a shrimp, then asks me how I'm finding counselling with Lindsey Stevens. This surprises me, because it's an unwritten rule between us that we don't talk about anything emotionally difficult. So I tell him, not too untruthfully, that it's early days.

'Lindsey's great, you know,' he says, now chewing on a spring roll before adding, without looking at me, 'She helped me a lot.'

'You went to see her too?' I ask, surprised once again. I mean, Brian gave me Lindsey's number but it never occurred to me that organised, forthright Brian would ever go to see a shrink.

'I'm from LA,' he says, with a small, weak, Brian smile. 'I had counselling in kindergarten.'

Then, after a short silence in which the American lawyer carefully considers his next words, he tells me that he went to see Lindsey Stevens for two whole years after a particularly stressful family Christmas back in California. He seems relieved to be telling me, as if I am now part of a privileged club of psychiatric patients. 'I actually punched my older brother.'

'No!'

'Yeah. Not something I'm proud of. I mean, it wasn't even a very good punch, but he still threatened to sue me.'

'Your own brother threatened to sue you?'

'He's a partner in LA's biggest law firm.'

'Why did you punch him?'

'I don't know. We never got on. He was always on my case. I guess it just built up, all those years of animosity.'

I nod slowly. I wonder if Jes would ever hit me. I don't think so. He knows how much I hate scrapping. I mean, we have our moments, but we're close enough. And we're English. We don't lash out.

'Anyway, to cut a long story short, my mum took sides, with Nathan, which meant my stepdad went the same way, and before I knew it I was spending Christmas Day alone in a motel in Hermosa Beach.'

'God. That's awful. I always thought you got on okay with Nathan and your mum.'

'Mum and I speak, but I haven't talked to my brother since the Millennium. I sent him an email last Thanksgiving, but I never got anything back.'

'I didn't know.'

'I guess it's easier cutting yourself off when you're five thousand miles apart.'

Brian stabs another spring roll with his chopstick. I think about him and his brother, the tall ex-track star Nathan with his perfect Californian jaw, trophy wife and two nauseatingly fresh-faced children. I can't imagine not talking to Jes for three years. I guess they do things differently in America.

'So, how's the love-life?' I ask brightly, having decided that the best way to stop someone dwelling on past pain is to make them dwell on present pain. Brian hasn't had a girlfriend in two years.

He laughs, fully aware of my tactic to take his mind off family woes. 'Still stagnant. But I've got big expectations for next Wednesday.'

'You've finally got a date with Winona Ryder?'

'No. I'm blowing off Ms Ryder for an evening of sixty-second dating. Have you heard of it? Barry got me a ticket. It's the best concept, man, let me tell you . . .'

Brian goes on to describe how sixty-second dating works, while I smile and nod and never get close to admitting that I, too, spent an evening with Maxine and her score cards. When he's finished we pay the bill and as we part I say, 'Good luck for Wednesday. It sounds like it could be fun.'

The following Thursday, the phone rings at three a.m. In the blurriness of sleep I wonder if it's Brian, flushed with success and happiness after his evening of one-minute dates. Then I dream for an instant that it's Ellie, wanting me, needing me, craving me, standing on my doorstep ready to forgive and give all. Or, at least, some random Swedish nymphomaniac, trying to find a single man on our family-infested street who's up for hot sex on a cold November night.

But, of course, the only news you get at three in the morning is bad.

Jes proceeds to tell me, fighting back tears, that our mother is dead. She died at one forty-five a.m. at the Chelsea and Westminster Hospital in Fulham, West London. She had pancreatic cancer. It was diagnosed six weeks ago and spread quickly. Jes had just got a call from Dickie Bennett, her work colleague. She hadn't wanted us to know.

'What do you mean she's dead?'

'She's dead, Scott. Cancer.'

For a moment, I think he's winding me up. 'She's dead?' I repeat, helplessly.

'She died from cancer two hours ago. Pancreatic cancer. Dickie said it spread more quickly than they'd anticipated. She had a gastro-intestinal haemorrhage.'

'A what?'

'Some sort of stomach haemorrhage.'

I move the words around. Our mother has died. My mum is dead. Cancer killed my mother. Mum died of cancer. She is no longer here. She is gone.

I'll never see her again.

'Mum's dead, Scott.'

I burst into tears. 'Oh, God . . .' I say helplessly, choking through my sobs. My head fills with questions, stupid questions. Why did they call Jes first? I'm the oldest. They should have called me. Why did she choose Dickie Bennett to be with her at the end? Why didn't she tell us?

Then I realize. She knew she was going to die when she came to see me on television. She didn't seem herself. Then she called me to say goodbye and I didn't pick up the phone.

'Love you. 'Bye.'

Her last words. I didn't call her. I should have called her. Oh, God.

Now Jes is crying down the phone, too, and I can hear rustling in the background, which is probably Sam.

'Sorry, Scott,' Jes croaks, as if somehow I might think it's his fault. Then he asks in a small and helpless voice, like a child, 'What are we going to do?'

'I don't know, Jes,' I manage. 'Does she know what she wants? I mean what she wanted?'

This simple shift from present to past tense starts me crying once more. When I hold the phone to my ear, the tears drip into the mouthpiece, tasting salty.

'Are you okay?' asks Jes, rhetorically.

'No. You?'

'No.'

We sit, two brothers united by grief and guilt and anger and British Telecom. After another while Jes says, 'Apparently she wants . . . wanted the funeral to be held in Edinburgh.'

'What? Why?'

'I don't know. She was born there, I guess.'

'That's ridiculous. She should be buried in Grantchester. That's her home. Edinburgh's five hundred miles away. How are we going to organize a funeral up there?'

'Look, I don't know, Scott. It's what she wanted.'

'But what about us? What about what we want?'

But we both know that what we want is impossible. She's dead. Nothing can bring her back. I have a sudden memory of Grantchester, of the sun-drenched afternoon by the river. Is this the reason it was allowed to be so perfect? Because it would never be as perfect again?

Jes speaks once more. 'We've got to call Dad.'

'Why?'

'He's our father.'

'He doesn't give a shit.'

'She's the mother of his children. He needs to know.'

'Why? Why the fuck does he need to know?' I say, my voice rising. 'He doesn't give a flying shit about her!'

'We should tell him.'

'He won't come anyway. He can never get any time off work.'

'He's retired now.'

'He is? Since when?' I hadn't known. Or, rather, I had chosen not to know.

'It's okay, I'll call him if you want.'

'Of course you will. You always do the right thing. Christ!'

'Look, there's no need for that . . .'

We tumble once more into silence. I'm angry now, angry with everyone, with the hospital for not calling me, with my brother for wanting to call my father, with my father for being an absent, uncaring, useless shit. I'm even angry with my mother for leaving me. I want to get into a car and drive away. Or crawl under my duvet and never come out.

I can't accept it!

I'll never touch Mum's wrist again. I'll never buy her flowers. I'll never taste her full-butter Highland shortbread. How can this be? Why didn't she tell us?

'Love you. 'Bye.'

We need to organize. Take control somehow. 'I guess we'll have to have the funeral next week sometime,' I say, trying to use a different voice, more sombre and professional, the vocal equivalent of putting on the black funereal suit.

'I'm meant to be going to Bremen on Wednesday,' Jes says.

'What?'

'The press trip goes to Bremen on Wednesday.'

'Why the fuck are you talking about Bremen, Jes? Mum's fucking dead. SHE'S DEAD!'

'I don't know, I just –'

'It's only a stupid fucking travel article!' I regret saying this immediately, but in my defence I'm a little rattled by the suddenness of my mother being no longer with us.

'I know it's only a travel article . . . It's just . . .'

'I know, Jes. I'm sorry . . .'

'Of course I'll cancel it . . . It's just all such a shock.'

I can hear him breathing in, trying not to cry. 'Look, Jes, let's talk in the morning. We're both too tired right now,' I say, trying to be the big brother once more.

Jes starts to cry, gasps of tears down the phone. 'I want her back,' he says, which makes me start to cry.

'Me, too.'

Lost in our tears, we hang up.

I go downstairs and press 'play' on my answering-machine. The only message is from a BT saleswoman wondering if I use the Internet. I rewind and play, rewind and play, until I've listened to the whole tape, but there is no other voice. My mother's message has been erased.

'Love you. 'Bye.'

Perhaps I imagined it.

The Third Bad Thing?

3. I feel like an orphan.

10

MUMS

Mums are like the Internet:
You'd bet on them to know the answer
To anything except
What you should wear out with Claudia Schiffer.
Everyone loves their mum,
Even terrorists and priests
And serial killers who claim
They never got sufficient maternal affection.
It's tender and tough
Being a mum.
It's sweet and rough,
Being a son.

Just outside Durham I have another Stella Artois. It's Thursday afternoon, a week after my mother died. The train up to Edinburgh is full, a mixture of business commuters and an excitable tourist crowd overdosing on Coca-Cola.

In my carriage there's a smattering of besuited men and women with mobile phones and laptops, two old ladies who evidently stopped buying clothes in 1956, and a stag party wearing matching white T-shirts that read, 'CHRIS'S SHAGFEST'.

The Shagfesters consist of fifteen thirty-year-old men acting like thirty fifteen-year-old boys. They leer and cheer at any woman who passes. They're led in boisterous fashion by Chris himself, who's wearing full makeup, a pink miniskirt and a red padded bra over his prodigiously hairy chest.

These are probably professional men, holding jobs of some responsibility, yet they're behaving like pubescent cavemen. I glare at them: these are the sort of men I write about, outlining their sensitivities, their insecurities and hidden qualities. These are the men who read my poems, my target audience. I think of my editor Eric and his insistence that my poems capture the 'inherent insecurities of modern masculinity', and I think that, actually, I don't like men very much.

I watch as a teenage girl tries to make her way to the toilet, tragically situated next to the Shagfesters' end of our carriage, and Chris hollers, 'Show us yer tits!' at the top of his drunken voice.

I recall something my mum once said: 'The problem with men is they seem to think women want what they want.'

Maybe she was right. Like children, men are often unable to understand that the rest of the world doesn't think exactly like them. In contrast, women seem to have a far too highly honed sense of what the rest of the world is thinking.

Mum never had much time for male arrogance. Perhaps

it was being one of the few female consultants in a male-dominated world. Or perhaps it was because her husband left her to raise two small boys on her own without so much as a 'see you some time'. For as long as I can remember, Mum denounced everything masculine.

'Don't be such a little man!' she would say, if I sulked, or made a mess, or cut my knee falling out of a tree. She was so adamant, so full of vitriol, that for a while I thought I didn't want to be a boy. I'd look at my little penis in the bathtub, and imagine what it would be like to be without one.

PENIS

Despite what some men think
It doesn't take a genius
To own a penis.
What I mean is,
If you're called Liz,
You're unlikely to have one.
Some men give them names,
Geronimo, Paul, or Scud,
Some women too.
But I call mine Willy
Which seems to do.

When I first began to write, I found that my clumsy short stories were almost entirely inhabited by men. Partly it was because of my inability to understand women and, by extension, any female character. But mainly it was a bid to reinstate men in my life. The problem is that, when faced with large groups of men acting like baboons, I usually find I hate them.

Then again, I hate everyone in this carriage right now, even the two little old ladies with egg-and-cress sandwiches wrapped in tinfoil and a Thermos flask covered in Skegness Holiday Park stickers. Because for them it's just a normal day, whereas for me it's a week after my mother died.

I want everyone to be as sad, hurt, angry and miserable as I am. But, of course, they're not. And I resent them all for it.

The weather is also conspiring against me. It's the middle of November, so the sky should be just like my mood – dark, stormy, prone to downpours. Instead it's blue and filled with cruel bright sunshine. We pass back gardens where children in Puffa coats play on plastic swings and mothers sit nursing cups of tea or cigarettes. The sun pours down, lighting the happy faces of the drunken Shagfesters and the two grannies as they unwrap a slice of what looks like home-made shortbread.

It's the shortbread that does me in. It's been like this, these last few days – I think I'm fine, paddling along, then it crashes into me like a seventh wave. Since three a.m. last Thursday, there has been an empty space shaped like my mum. It's filled at times by words, sounds, smells, a thousand memories, but they are empty, vacuous, unreal, just slide projections. There is nothing real there any more. Her body, which is real, but of no use to anyone now, is in a wooden coffin on a plane up to Edinburgh. I didn't know they put coffins on planes. It makes you think twice about flying, knowing some random corpse is knocking about under your Bloody Mary.

The physical lack of her is what hurts most. It's as if a cherished antique or widescreen television has been stolen from my living room. I look up every so often and I know something's missing, but it takes me an instant to remember because everything else seems normal. Then I remember what is no longer there, and the whole room changes. It's suddenly alien and hostile, no longer my own.

On the first day I didn't leave my bed, crying my eyes out – a mixture of extreme sadness and extreme guilt that I hadn't known about her illness, that I hadn't talked to her, that I'd done nothing. On the second day, I went to the Chelsea and Westminster Hospital where she'd died and wandered around the modern white building in a daze, drinking weak tea and hoping to understand. On the third day, I got drunk.

I've spoken to Jes briefly. We organized the funeral together, but only talked about timings and how many sausage rolls to order for the gathering afterwards. He said he was doing all right, I said I was doing all right, and we left it at that.

It's okay for him. He's got Sam to support him, to cry to. Who is my support? I thought about calling Ellie, but something stopped me. Even though my mother is dead, I still want to prove to her that I can be strong. Like she was.

Shagfester Chris returns from the toilet holding a can of Carlsberg and, as the train curves around a bend, he manages to spill some on our table. The two grannies look alarmed, mopping at the uriny liquid with small lace handkerchiefs.

To my surprise, I grab Chris's hairy arm and growl, 'Fuck off!'

I'm quite proud of the depth and strength of tone of my voice. I grip his arm as tightly as I can, and I don't care if he hits me, or his friends throw me out of the moving train. For the first time in my life, I feel violently powerful, because I don't care what happens to me. I clench my other fist and wait for the fight to ensue.

Thankfully, some caveman instinct in Chris enables him to grasp this. He can see that I have nothing to lose except my sense of self-preservation, which has deserted me, a fact that renders me highly dangerous. He pulls away quickly, muttering, 'Fuck you', and retreats to his friends, all of whom glare at me. My heart pounds, but I glare back, chugging my Stella as I do so.

Opposite, the two grannies don't know whether to feel more scared of Chris or me. I see them staring at me, white-faced, and at once my bristling violence vanishes, and I feel a little ashamed. So I smile as sweetly as I can, and say cheerily, 'Only another hour to Edinburgh, then.'

When the man comes round with his wobbly cart, I buy them each a chocolate biscuit.

The Belle Vue bed-and-breakfast only partly lives up to its name. There are beds and a breakfast of sorts, but the beautiful view is less apparent, unless you're the sort of traveller who longs for a vista of a Sainsbury's car park.

I wake early, head pounding, and consume the several pints of cholesterol that constitute Mrs Ferguson's Scottish Fry. The funeral isn't until three thirty. It's an awkward time: noon, I'd say, is the best funeral scheduling, giving enough time for you to wake, shower, shave, dress and feel sad, but not so long as to make you dwell too deeply on the loss and your own mortality. But three thirty was the only slot the vicar of St Dunstan's, Fairmilehead, could manage on a Friday between a coffee morning for Bosnian refugees and a concert in aid of Somalian donkeys or some such worthy charity.

So I have five and a half hours to kill in Edinburgh. Normally this wouldn't be too difficult – this is, after all, Scotland's capital with several fine museums, a castle, all the brand-name shopping you could wish for, and several hundred pubs offering a wide range of alcoholic beverages. If I was going to a wedding, it would be easy. I could meet some fellow guests for a drink, or maybe do some frivolous and expensive shopping, buy things that would enhance the mood of impending jollity and hopes of a shag with one of the bride's looser friends. But there's not much chance of getting laid at a funeral. Especially if it's your mother's.

Mrs Ferguson asks me if I'm all right, can she perhaps get me another cup of tea or would I like an extra sausage or two – the ones with Government health warnings stamped on them? I decline four times before she eventually believes me.

But I have to do something. I'm going crazy in the snug, lardy lull of the florid living room, waiting for the clock to tick round so that my mother can be buried. Perhaps this is what hell is like – eternally waiting for a horrible event that never arrives.

In the mothball-scented hall there is a wooden stand with a display of brochures. One has a penguin on the front. I put on my coat and head for the door.

As I climb the wide steps of Edinburgh Zoo, it begins to rain. At least the weather now suits my mood. Wind thrashes through the trees, which dance like demented ravers. I pay the entrance fee to a round-faced bespectacled teenager, who looks like he'd rather be splitting atoms or manipulating DNA, and enter the zoo.

By a statue of an elephant, I question my decision to leave the Belle Vue bed-and-breakfast. I'd forgotten how much I hated this zoo, trudging the concrete paths up and down the steep hills, pressing my nose against cold, dirty glass to scour the empty cages. And I'd forgotten how guilty I felt for hating it, so insistent was my mother that we should have a good time there.

It's been maybe twenty years, yet I recognize the general layout, the paths, the location of the toilets (children always remember the location of toilets). I start up the steep hill, recalling Jes and me moaning to Mum about being dragged ever upwards, and her reply: 'The best animals are at the top. You want to see the lions, don't you?'

I moaned and complained some more, and eventually, at an enclosure containing some nondescript antelope, I stopped and refused to go any further. I knew as I was wimping out that Scott of the Antarctic would have kept going past the gibbons and on to see the majestic lions, but I wanted to make a point. I think I even held on to some railings and refused to let go until we descended the hill to less lofty beasts.

Now, on the day of my mother's funeral, I set out to mend the past. I march upwards, striding past the railings, which now frame some pygmy hippos shining brown and steaming in the cold like walking turds. I find myself a little out of breath, which annoys me but, then, I haven't been for a run in a while.

Eventually I reach the top, after a couple of pauses. The lion enclosure is empty. It seems a small area, rising steeply into the volcanic Edinburgh rock, hardly a substitute for an extensive African plain or Asian desert, or wherever lions usually reside. I stand for a moment, breathing the damp air, disappointed that I don't feel more of a sense of achievement. I want to feel like some wrong has been righted, that in some way my guilt has been laid to rest, but I just feel knackered.

I peek through the grubby glass of the lions' home, hoping for a glimpse of at least a paw. A father and his son are standing there too. The father, a stocky man with a crew-cut and a shamrock tattoo on his neck, hammers intermittently on the glass in a bid to raise the lions from wherever they're lounging. His son stands by his knees, looking miserable. I feel sorry for the boy, not just because he's got an ugly crew-cut like his dad (fortunately he has no tattoo as yet, but I get the feeling this might be planned for his next birthday) and is wearing a shell-suit several sizes too big for him, but because he's had to walk all the way up the hill to stare through grubby glass into an empty cage.

I wonder where his mother is, and whether this is a divorced father spending his one day a fortnight with his estranged son. This makes me think of my own divorced father and whether he will be coming to the funeral. I don't think he would dare, the man who deserted us, who almost destroyed my mother's life, but with Edward Barron you never know. After all, there's free drink on offer. The fact of the matter is, I haven't seen him in ten years, and in my present state of mind I might punch him in the face.

The shell-suit father turns to me, nods at the empty lion cage, and says, in a thick Edinburgh accent, 'Has awah fackin sam batch!'

I have no idea what this means, so I employ a tactic learned in French lessons – I smile and nod. The father grins back, revealing an impressive gold tooth, and takes out a disposable camera, which he waves at me. The boy turns away, embarrassed, and now I know for certain that this is a divorced father clumsily trying to appear at ease, to act normally with the son he sees only once every two weeks. I know because he looks just like my father did, awkward and desperate. He's counting the time until he can return to his adult world of newspapers and pint glasses. Yet when he gets home he will wonder why, once again, he didn't fully appreciate this one precious day with his son. He'll look at the pictures he's taken and attempt to figure out why these are somehow more important to him than the actual experience.

I could tell him. It's because these pictures, placed in

carefully selected frames in his kitchen above the unused stove, help him feel like he's still a father. He's just like Edward Barron.

I take the picture for him, the father clasping the boy tightly to his thigh, the boy trying to look nonchalant. The father growls a thank-you, takes his son's hand and pulls him away, further up the hill towards a sign that reads: 'AFRICAN SAFARI ADVENTURE'.

I want to go after them and persuade the father not to drag his son to see the sad zebra and windswept wildebeest on the rainy summit. But all families are different: perhaps the boy likes hiking up cold hills in the rain to see desultory animals.

As soon as they've departed, the lion appears. He's been hiding behind a log, as if he'd sneaked there for a quiet cigarette. He paces across his enclosure, reaches the side, then paces back again. I'm sad. He's the scrawniest, most depressed-looking lion I've ever seen. His ribs show through a patchy pelt. He sits down and I can almost hear the deep sigh of melancholy. This is not the King of the Jungle, more the Junkie of the Yard.

I look around for a lioness, or at least a liony best mate, but he's there all alone. Perhaps lions are meant to be solitary animals, but this one looks forlorn. As I stare at him, he glances up, fixing me with two dark eyes. I know his look. It says, 'Why me?'

I hurry away from the melancholic lion, through the empty zoo. The rain comes down and across in spattering bursts. I shelter in a wooden café, with a cup of lukewarm tea.

It's two hours until the funeral. I have plenty of time to head back to the Belle Vue, change into the black suit, the red tie (one of Mum's favourites), and go over Psalm 23 one more time – my reading for the service. I order another toasted sandwich, then eat a Mars Bar. I begin to feel a little better.

'Goin' ta see tha penguin par-rade?' asks the spotty twelve-year-old behind the counter. He has my mother's accent, the rolling Rs.

'What's the penguin parade?'

'It's . . . y' knaw, tha par-rade of penguins. Thay git oot and walk aboot a bit.'

The penguin enclosures have changed dramatically since Jes first fell in love with the fluffy fish-guzzlers. The birds now live in a sort of penguin theme park, with sculpted pools and jaunty rocky outcrops. The only thing that's missing is a penguin rollercoaster, the Pilchard Express, but judging from the construction work at the far end of the pool, perhaps this is under development. The penguins are even sponsored now, little silver plaques adorning the wire mesh, inscribed with the names of deluded philan-thropists. It appears that, in this world of famine, war, AIDS and homeless children, there are plenty of people who want to pay to feed a penguin.

The rocks are green-white with penguin excrement, and the damp air is rent by loud penguin screeches. Apparently in Antarctica penguins live in vast colonies, up to a million birds, all shitting and squawking as one, destroying the empty, icy tranquillity of the planet's last wilderness. Perhaps I was wrong. Hell isn't waiting for a horrible event that never arrives. It's waiting for a horrible event that never arrives surrounded by a million penguins.

While the enclosure is bigger and more modern than I remember it, the smell is just the same. 'Fishy poo': that's what Jes called it, dancing up and down, shouting, 'Fishy poo!' at the top of his voice, my mother trying to calm him down, embarrassed by the people staring and laughing.

The wind hurls up in gusts from the enclosure, ripe with penguin stench. Next to me a young couple break off from kissing.

'Can you smell it?' asks the woman, holding her scarf to her big nose.

'The dead could smell it,' grins her boyfriend.

I want to tell him, 'No, you're wrong, my mother can't smell it.'

Despite the rain and the gusty wind, a sizeable crowd has gathered in front of the enclosure to witness whatever the penguin parade has to offer. The majority, of course, are families. There are middle-class dads wearing glasses and clutching guidebooks from which they lecture their offspring on the feeding habits of Emperor penguins. There are pot-bellied dads with video cameras, whose wives light cigarettes, one after the other.

The surprising thing is that the parents seem more excited than their offspring about the prospect of promenading penguins. In contrast, the children stand shuffling nervously. Perhaps this is understandable – the penguins are the same height as the kids, and evidently rivals for their parents' affections. Perhaps the kids are afraid Mum and Dad might decide they like one of the fishy birds better, and leave little Wayne at the zoo in its place.

I walk away from the gathering crowd, seeking refuge in the printed word, reading the signs on the wire mesh. There are pictures of the different species on display – the small Rockhoppers and Macaronis with their slicked-back spiky hair-dos, the tubby classical Gentoos, and the tall, arrogant, long-beaked Kings. I bet Jes would still be able to tell me all about them, all these years on. I think about calling to ask him, to rebuild some affection between us. But it seems a little strange to do this on the day of our mother's funeral. I make a note to ask him at a later date.

Displayed prominently on the wire cage are the rules of the penguin parade:

> The penguin walk has and always will be purely voluntary on behalf of the birds. They will not be coaxed or cajoled out of the enclosure, and if they choose not to come out, there will be no walk. In addition to this, we must have a reasonable number of birds to do the walk. Penguins are gregarious birds, and can become stressed if they feel separated from the group.

As the rain comes down, a group of six or seven King penguins gathers by the barrier, like Saturday-night clubbers trying to get into an exclusive venue. They rock back and forth, as if contemplating an attack on the gate.

A ripple of excitement spreads through the crowd. I look at my watch: 2.05. They're late.

As I'm wondering if I should depart and get ready for my mother's funeral rather than wait for a bunch of penguins to walk around a patch of scrubby grass, seven keepers appear, dressed in matching blue sweatshirts, blue trousers and blue baseball caps. Their leader is a big red-headed man, holding a microphone.

'Good afternoon, welcome to Edinburgh Zoo. The penguins will be coming out of the gate towards the penguin shop. Please keep behind the yellow line as penguins are quite inquisitive and they may go for your fingers. Keep all fingers out of the way, and please keep small children under control.'

Ignoring these instructions all the parents push their children on to the path. Among them I see the crew-cut man with the tattooed neck, and his unhappy son. The father has picked up his small clone, and lifted him over two other children to be planted on the Tarmac, right in front. The boy tugs at the legs of his over-long shell-suit trousers, so as not to trip into the path of any oncoming birds. Snot runs down his chin. He cowers back, but his father has pushed past the other children to block his son's exit, a hand squeezing ominously on his shoulder.

On the other side of the gate, the penguins shuffle back and forth, eager to be free.

'Now, it's a voluntary parade,' barks the big keeper. 'We can't force them out, but I think we'll have a few.'

The crowd can hardly contain its excitement. The biggest penguin, a large King with a chubby neck, stands at the front, and throws his head back like an avian Henry V about to charge the French front line. The bolt is drawn back, the adults cheer loudly, and the gate swings open. In an instant, the penguins hurtle out of the enclosure at high speed, like inmates released after ten years in a maximum-security prison. They charge on to the Tarmac path. The keepers hurry to surround them, shepherding the group, three behind, three in front. One rogue penguin darts towards the spectators, but he's quickly blocked by a fast-moving warder, and marched back to the pound in disgrace.

'Remember, keep children back!'

As far as I can make out, with my new-found penguin knowledge, the majority of the group are Kings, almost three feet high, with glistening silver backs and yellowing stomachs the colour of smokers' fingers. But there are three smaller ones with orange beaks and pink feet – Gentoos, Macaronis, Rockhoppers? I can't remember. This gang of three can't walk as fast, and have to scurry to keep up with the bigger Kings. They seem more nervous, less assured. I think I would be too, if I spent my entire life at boot level.

The concept of the parade is simple. The penguins exit their cage, walk round the three-hundred-yard path that encircles the grassy green following a single yellow line painted on the Tarmac, and return to their cage. As parades go, it's hardly Trooping the Colour or St Patrick's Day in New York, but the cameras still flash wildly as if this is the most exciting thing these people have seen all year.

It's at this moment that I remember why I hate penguins. It's not so much that they're tubby, smelly, pointless creatures who seem poorly suited to life anywhere other than the frozen wastes of Antarctica, but more that, like *Star Wars*, Britney Spears and sun-dried tomatoes, they receive general adulation far in excess of their merits.

The simple fact is, people love penguins. They go potty for them. And the penguins know it. Here they are, shuffling along, lolling left and right like the result of some strange Cold War Soviet experiment to make old men pregnant – I'm sure they could walk in a less precocious way if they wanted to.

Between the shouts, 'C'mon, pal, ovar harrr!', I can hear the slow tap of toenails as they patter along the Tarmac. At times they seem almost human, like stiff old Italian men with thick arms and long Roman noses. Then, when they stop and flap their useless wings, they are the stupidest birds on earth.

As the penguins near the first bend, the crowd of adoring humans shuffles round with them. A dozen video-cameras swing left, and women cluck and coo as if watching a parade of royal babies.

Compared to this penguin love-fest, my mother's funeral seems almost appealing. I start walking up the grassy slope towards the exit, only to be engulfed in the crowd as the penguins potter round the corner towards the small ice-cream hut, which is proudly and most Scottishly open on this freezing Friday afternoon in November.

The penguins slow, starting up the small slope. Their portly bodies lean forward as they strain uphill – I see now why no penguin has managed to climb Everest. One stops, evidently exhausted by his efforts. He is as tall as the smaller children, who form a human wall in front of him. A child screams, another starts crying. I feel for them – I mean, how would you like to stand eye-to-eye with a penguin as big as you are?

I want to cross the penguin picket line, to dash through and away, back to a penguin-free world beyond the zoo, but the stalled King penguin has created a bottleneck of onlookers and zoo-keepers. Just in front of me is the little crew-cut boy, his father pushing him forward: 'G'wan, sun, gavam ah teckle!'

'Nooo, Dad!'

The boy turns his face away, but his father grasps his head in one large, meaty hand and turns it back to face the penguin. In his other hand he holds out his disposable Fuji camera. 'Gavam ah teckle!'

The penguin is not fazed. It is used to adulation. It steps up on its podgy, webbed prehistoric toes and flaps its plastic-looking wings. The small boy screams.

'Dunnee be 'fraid, ya stupad bairn!' barks the father, pushing his son further towards the penguin. As he does so, the child stumbles, trips over his shell-suit trousers, and falls forward. He tries to stop himself, hands flailing, but the penguin lunges forward and jabs its long sharp beak at his hands. The small boy shrieks in pain and surprise, jumping back as if electrocuted. The penguin pecks again and the father snaps a picture – *flash!* – and starts to wind on the film to take another.

Something in me cracks. I can almost hear it in my head, the same sense of powerful anger that boiled up within me on the train. I step up, draw back my foot, and with a neat sidefoot that David Beckham would be proud of, I kick the penguin as it lunges a third time at the small boy. My foot connects with its pudgy stomach. The penguin totters backwards, squawking wildly. There's a gasp from the crowd, the keepers turn to stare, and the burly crew-cut father chucks down his disposable camera, takes me by the shoulders and throws me to the ground. The grass is wet and muddy. I hear my coat rip as he leaps on top of me and starts punching me in the face. 'Yer feckin' tossarr, dunnee kack thet parr barrd!'

I don't feel powerful any more. I feel physically sick. I want to run away, like I did as a child, but he is too heavy on top of me. I hold up my arms to protect my nose, turning into a foetal position so that his blows will connect with my back and neck. I hear screaming and bellowing, a whistle, running feet, and behind it all, the slow patter of penguin claws as they carry on inexorably around the path.

In the police car on the way to St Leonard's Street police station I start to cry. I blurt out, 'It's my mum's funeral. I've got to be there in twenty minutes.'

One of the officers turns to me, looks at my ripped, mud-soaked, blood-splattered coat and says, 'Assault on a penguin. Never had one of them before.'

At the police station they question me about my assault on a protected animal. I tell them more than once that I was trying to protect a four-year-old child from getting his eyes pecked out by an aggressive flightless bird, but they seem uninterested. I also inform them that my mother is being buried in half an hour at St Dunstan's Church, Fairmilehead, but they laugh and say, 'Yeah, right, of course she is.'

They put me in a cell that smells faintly of cigarettes. I am shaking, the aftershock of the fight trembling through my body. I am no brawler. What was I thinking?

As I sit there, I hear my mother's voice, clear and shrill. It makes the hairs on my neck jump and my heart thump. 'Don't sit there moping!' she says, a line uttered shortly after my father left.

The sergeant at the desk has taken my watch, so I've only a rough idea what the time is, but I know it's rapidly approaching three thirty. I shout, 'Excuse me!'

After I've counted too many minutes, a young policeman with a long nose appears and agrees that I have the right to make a phone call.

Of course, Jes and Sam's mobiles are both off. I don't know the number for anyone else at my mother's funeral. Not Uncle Jack, who has flown over from Belfast, not

Great Aunt Bessie from Fort William, who last went south of the border in 1974. Nor any of Mum's work colleagues from the hospital in Cambridge, where her death was greeted, so Dickie Bennett informed Jes, with a minute's silence.

I try Jes again.

'You're through to Jes Barron, leave a number and I'll give you a shout back.'

'Jes, please, I hope you get this somehow. Something awful's happened, I'm in a police station in Edinburgh – could you call them, tell them about the funeral, Jesus, they don't believe me . . .'

I leave the police-station number, put down the phone and place my head in my hands. The darkness is strangely comforting.

'What's up, mate?' asks the long-nosed policeman.

I look up at him, trying not to cry again. 'My mum's dead. It's her funeral today.'

He considers my words. 'Where's it at?'

'St Dunstan's. In Fairmilehead.'

'Och, that's a coincidence. My granny was buried up there last month. Lovely service they do up at St Dunstan's. What's the name of the minister again?'

I look at him, and I realize this is a clever test, and I try with all my power to recall this tiny piece of information, which has just assumed the title of *most important piece of information in the world*.

Right now, if someone offered me the choice between being told the secret of life, Liv Tyler's phone number or the name of the vicar of St Dunstan's, I would choose the

Church of Scotland minister. As I think this, it comes to me . . .

Bill Lovelace. The Reverend Bill Lovelace. A poncy but surprisingly ecclesiastical name. Thank you, God. Sorry, Liv.

'Bill Lovelace. He's quite elderly.'

The long-nosed PC looks at me. He seems a little less like a policeman. 'Is she really getting buried today?'

'Yes. Three thirty.'

'It's ten to four. I'll see what I can do.'

The Reverend Bill Lovelace shows a fair degree of surprise when a police car with flashing blue lights screeches to a halt outside his churchyard and a dishevelled bloody-nosed man in a muddy jacket and torn trousers falls out of the left-hand passenger door. He stares in mild confusion as a policeman shouts, 'Good luck, pal!' and the bloody, dishevelled man picks himself up and sprints past the crumbling graves to his side.

'Sorry I'm late. Sorry.'

I barely see the other mourners, who stare at me wide-eyed. Jes takes a step forward, then realizes he's right at the edge of the sharp deep hole where my mother's coffin is hidden by late-afternoon shade, so he totters back, holding his stomach as an anchor. 'Where the hell have you been?' he hisses, like a drag queen. Sam glares at his side.

'I'm sorry. I can explain.'

The Reverend Bill Lovelace coughs. We fall silent. 'We commend into thy hands, most merciful Father, the soul of this our sister departed, and we commit her body to the ground . . .'

I'm breathing heavily, but everything has slowed, seconds decelerating.

The vicar stoops, puts a gnarled but experienced hand into the small bucket by the graveside, and with the smooth right arm action of a champion ten-pin bowler, swings the dark brown earth from his palm into the air above the hole. The grains seem to rest in the air, just a second, before tumbling on to the dark brown lid of the coffin six feet below, scattering.

The skittering earth snatches my gaze to the hole and its silent contents. The glistening coffin lid, the length of a body. Mum's body.

'. . . earth to earth, ashes to ashes, dust to dust; in sure and certain hope of the general resurrection in the last day and the life of the world to come . . .'

Jes stoops, takes a handful of earth and chucks it in. It lands, ker-chunk!, on the coffin. I glare at him – it should have been me first, the eldest. But I suppose I've forfeited that privilege today. After all, I did just miss our mother's funeral. I wonder who did my reading.

'. . . through our Lord Jesus Christ, who shall fashion anew the body of our low estate that it may be like unto his glorious body, according to the mighty working whereby he is able to subdue all things unto himself . . .'

Sam is about to lean down, then realizes I haven't been yet so she rights herself, flushing a little. As she stands, I bend down, feeling like I'm in a strange and ancient dance that I'm only just remembering. I take the earth, which feels warm, damp and gritty. I hold it over the coffin. I grasp the soil in my hand, squeezing it tighter, wanting to obliterate it, destroy it, make it disappear. I remember, in an instant, my mother's hand on mine at the BBC studios before my television appearance. Her smooth skin. The squeeze of her fingers.

I open my palm and drop the small round ball of earth on to the coffin lid, *plunk!*

It bounces once and falls down the dark edge of the grave, the last time I will ever touch my mum.

In the car from the church I try to explain what happened, as best I can. Jes and Sam listen, and to be fair Jes only says, 'Jesus Christ,' once.

The Hunter's Inn is busy – it's a late Friday afternoon – and the back room is smoky blue-grey. It's an old pub, with a nicotine-stained ceiling, framed prints of Edinburgh in the late nineteenth century on the walls and elderly men, who seem to have stepped from a similar era, drinking half pints of pale ale. In the background a jukebox plays, Rod Stewart, or maybe U2. Mum hated rock music.

I sit on my own at a table in the corner, relieved that no one comes to speak to me. I glance, between sips of beer, at the other mourners. Some seem afraid – I think I would be, of a mad bloody-faced man who leaped from a police car to the graveside of his mother – while others, like Uncle Jack, are simply appalled by my behaviour. He hasn't said a word to me, he just glares at me occasionally over his glass, as if I'm Gerry Adams's younger brother.

Uncle Jack comes from a staunchly Protestant village in Country Antrim and his two basset hounds are named Paisley and King Billy. He's drinking Guinness, and with each sip his huge square face turns progressively more red. I'm glad he's not talking to me – he always smells of pipesmoke and stale milk, and we used to plead with Mum not to sit us beside him at Christmas dinner.

Next to him is Great Aunt Bessie, who isn't a real great aunt but the cousin of Mum's mother, a tottering eighty-seven-year-old who says little but still walks three miles a day across the Cairngorms to buy her copy of the *Scotsman*. She was my mother's favourite relative, and their relationship grew stronger after my father left us – Bessie's husband was killed during the war, and they shared the solidarity of abandoned women.

Mum always said she wanted to end up like Bessie – short on words, big on love, hard as iron.

As I look at the other mourners, I realize I know little about my mother's life beyond me, my brother and a distant past with my father. I don't recognize many of them. There are two couples of her age, well dressed, well coiffured, but mostly there are men, in sombre suits, looking grave. I assume they are mourners but, this being Scotland, it's always possible that they're just Friday-evening boozers. One man is familiar: Dickie Bennett, my mum's colleague, a tall, thin, elegant man in a dark pinstrip suit, looking a little like a secret agent *circa* 1942. He holds an umbrella and a pint, which he hardly touches. I wonder about going to talk to him, but I've always been a bit intimidated by him. He has a posh accent and steel-grey eyes, and when I was little he used to pat me on the head as if I were a dog.

I glance at the bar where Jes and Sam are chatting with Sam's brother Steven, a software engineer from Newcastle. I met him once, at their wedding. He seemed like a nice guy, the sort of man who would be Sam's brother. It was Steven who procured Jes and Sam a top-of-the-range Mercedes for their wedding car. He accepted the praise and admiration for this generosity with suitable modesty, then disappeared during the post-wedding speeches. When we came out of dinner the car was gone, and Steven was forced to admit that he'd taken it out on a test drive from a local dealership – he'd had to return it by six o'clock.

I sit at my table in the corner of the pub, hoping no one will come and talk to me. In the past I used to love occasions like this – Mum's rare dinner parties where everyone was older than me and didn't stop talking, people I could simply listen to, following on the fringes, not required to initiate anything.

Jes, of course, used to regale the chuckling doctors with tales of mishaps with his friends at school, or his prowess at inventing new flavours for the Sodastream, or the time he'd found Jeffrey Archer's dog in the river and got ten pounds for taking it to the Old Vicarage. He's doing it now, at the bar, moving from stranger to stranger, shaking hands, even kissing cheeks, thanking everyone for coming. Every so often he glances at me – it's a look that is both a reproach and a plea for assistance.

But I'm not moving. Everyone here hates me so I'm not going to disappoint them.

A few minutes later one of the old men sits down at my table without a word. He carries a pint of bitter in his shaky grasp. He ignores me and sips his pint. I gaze at his black funeral suit, his freshly shaved face, grit my teeth and decide to engage. 'Thanks for coming,' I say quickly. He looks at me, his baggy eyes damp, perhaps with sorrow. He doesn't speak. 'Funerals, hey . . .' I continue, more slowly. I feel better: at least Jes can't condemn me for ignoring everyone. I decide to open up a bit more to this stranger who knew my mother, giving so as to receive: 'She was a great mother, it's hard to imagine life without her. I'm really going to miss her, you know, the little things, like the way she used to roll her Rs, and her shortbread biscuits. Did you ever try them?'

The old man grunts a negative and takes another gulp of beer. I realize I'm going to have to try a direct question to get anything out of him. 'How did you know my mother?' I ask.

'I didnee knor harr,' he says gruffly. 'Thas as ma local. Boot A'm sorry far yar tr-r-ouble son.'

Sam rescues me. She hands me a fresh pint of lager, sits down between me and the old man and says, 'You daft bugger,' which, under the circumstances, is probably the most appropriate thing anyone could say. I accept her gentle admonishment. We sit in silence for a moment, as I try to think of an apology for everything. Then I realize I haven't even congratulated her on the pregnancy. I'd forgotten all about it, what with Mum's death, the penguin-kicking and my imprisonment. She smiles, just, and says, 'Thanks. It's a bit weird right now.'

I hadn't thought about this – that in the midst of death Sam is carrying life. I feel ashamed of my selfishness. Jes and Sam are having a baby that they will never be able to show Mum.

We sip our drinks in silence. Sam doesn't know what to say to make me feel better, and I don't know what to say to make *her* feel better, so we say nothing. Jes is still chatting away to all and sundry at the bar. He even makes Great Aunt Bessie laugh. Sometimes it's difficult to see that we're brothers. We deal with situations in such contrasting ways – I hide while Jes goes up to people, hugs them, and invites them round for tea.

As early-evening punters arrive to dissipate the heavy sadness that hangs over the room with the cigarette smoke, Jes finally sits down opposite me. Sam excuses herself – 'Pregnancy and toilets go together like rock stars and cocaine.' I know Jes has something to say, because he won't look at me directly. 'Stanley Furrows was just explaining the will.'

I look at him. He doesn't look at me. For a terrifying moment I think he's about to inform me that my mother has left me nothing. I'm terrified – not, I must point out, because I'll miss out on a large sum of money but because if I'm not in her will it'll mean she didn't love me, despite her telephone message.

'What . . . what does it say?'

'Sarah had a bit in the bank, about fifty grand, but Stanley reckons the house could be worth a million.'

'What?'

'At least eight hundred grand, but probably more.'

I don't want to think about it. My mother is dead.

Then Jes says, 'We each get a third.'

'A third of what?'

'The money.'

I'm confused. 'A third? Why a third?'

Jes sips his beer, for courage. 'Dad.'

'No? You're not serious?'

'He's the father of her children. He's our dad,' says Jes.

'But he walked out on her!'

'Yes, but –'

'He walked out on us!'

'It's in the will, Scott,' says Jes, quietly, trying to avoid a scene.

'He doesn't deserve anything!' I'm raising my voice, and people are looking at me, but I don't care. This is outrageous. 'I'm not going to stand for it!' I slam down my fist, theatrically. The pint glass shakes, but doesn't topple. I look up at Jes and he seems worried. He glances to the right, then looks back at me, as if trying to pretend his eyes haven't moved.

I look in the same direction and there, sitting at a small table in the corner, is my father, Edward Barron.

'*What?*'

'Don't be angry, Scott –'

Of course I'm angry. My father has been forgotten,

over and done with, buried in a sarcophagus that no archaeologist was ever meant to uncover. Now, on this funeral day, it's as if he's risen from the dead.

I haven't seen him in ten years. He looks shabbier, older than sixty-five. His face is saggy with deep puffy eyelids and his thinning hair is combed back. He nurses a glass of red wine in one large fleshy hand, and a cigarette in the other. He reminds me of my editor Eric, the same pose, the same pretence at being in control.

I hate him. Do I hate him?

'You should be grateful. He did your reading at the church,' says Jes, reproachfully.

'What?'

'Well, you weren't there. Come on, now . . .'

Jes moves towards him. I stand, and snatch up my pint glass as if it's a weapon. Jes says nothing, but lets me pass. In two steps I am standing in front of my father. I try not to look at him but, like a traffic accident, or a naked person, it's impossible not to.

He tries to smile. 'Hello, Scott.' His voice cracks. 'Sad day. Very sad day.'

I want to shout at him, but I'm already considered a hooligan by my fellow mourners. So I try to keep calm. And as I pause, containing fury, I look at him slyly and he seems less like the man I remember from ten years ago, the cocky, ebullient, desperate-for-the-world-to-love-him idiot. He seems on the verge of tears.

'There are no words, are there? Even for a poet.'

I've noticed his choice of wording, as elegantly and subtly slipped in as an ambassador negotiating a dodgy arms deal, but I don't want to give him the satisfaction of a reaction.

He called me a poet.

'How long are you over for?' I inquire, in a tone I usually reserve for visiting plumbers and pizza-delivery men.

'It might be a little while. You know I'm retired now?'

I nod grudgingly.

'I was wondering . . .' he sucks desperately on the end of his cigarette, careful to blow the smoke away from me '. . . could I stay with you for a few days? Down in London?'

I look at him. His hand is trembling. The cigarette is almost burned down to his fingers.

'Watch out. Your cigarette.'

He looks down. 'Shit!' He flicks the butt into the ashtray, where it lies, smouldering angrily. My heart thumps so loudly I wonder if the pub can hear it. By the bar Dickie Bennett glances over at us, a look of surprised recognition on his face. I feel like passing out.

'Why don't you want to stay with Jes?' I ask, my inflection suggesting what I believe: that Jes is his favourite and he'd much rather give me a wide berth.

He glances at Jes and Sam. 'I think they need a bit of personal space at the moment, what with the pregnancy and all. But if it's any bother, I can always find a hotel.'

I hate him. The moral blackmail. What can I say? 'Give me a call when you get down to London.'

Shortly afterwards the mourners start to leave. Jes moves to the door of the pub, shaking hands here, hugging there, kissing Great Aunt Bessie three times and making her blush. I watch him being warm, tender, interacting. I down the last of my pint, take a deep breath and walk over towards him. But I can't go all the way, I haven't got the bottle, so I hover a little way behind him. He glances round, beckons me to step forward. I step forward.

'Thanks for coming,' I say to Uncle Jack, as brightly as I can. He looks me in the eye – he has a bloodshot, drunken stare – snorts, turns and walks out of the pub. Another couple hurry past, nodding at me. They pause to shake Jes's hand. I step backwards, towards the shadows.

'A terrible loss . . .' says a voice behind me. I turn. It's Dickie Bennett, stooping as if the ceiling is too low. He holds out a long white hand. I shake it – it's surprisingly cold, considering the warmth of the pub – and he stands back. 'She was quite a woman,' he says quietly.

'Yes. She was,' I say, equally quietly, as if we're sharing a secret. He nods, turns and heads for the door. By the bar, I notice my father watching him leave, his eyes narrowed. I try to remember if they ever got on, or whether my father disliked him, as he did most of my mother's colleagues. But the past is hidden today, a protection against overwhelming sorrow.

As Jes says goodbye to the last of the mourners, Sam comes up to me. 'Need to go back to the police station?'

'No. They gave me a warning. I'm not to kick penguins again.'

'So you got off Scott-free?'

'Ha, ha.'

Sam smiles forgiveness. 'Look, we're leaving soon. Why don't you come in the car?'

'I've got a train ticket.'

She puts a hand on my shoulder. 'Come with us. It's been a tough day.'

'What about him?' I say, nodding towards my father, who is lighting another cigarette.

'He's staying in Edinburgh tonight. Some old friend of his and Sarah's from university. So you're safe.'

We are silent as Jes drives along the A701 through the Borders, the only illumination the low beam of headlights, a small pool of milky yellow light in the darkness. At one point a sheep scampers across the road in front of us and Jes jams on the brakes.

'Careful!' exclaims Sam, from the back seat.

'Sorry,' mumbles Jes, biting his bottom lip.

By the time we reach the motorway at Moffat, Sam is asleep. 'She gets tired. You know, with the baby . . .' whispers Jes, his eyes flicking from the road to the rear-view mirror so that he can see his wife curled up behind him. In this moment I feel envious of the love he has for her, of the support they're giving each other at this time. It makes me feel more alone.

Even though I know my brother's statement is an opening gambit, a bid to start a conversation between us, I don't respond. Jes bites his bottom lip once more, moving his hands around the steering-wheel as if caressing it. We both stare at the traffic ahead.

We stop for petrol somewhere after Penrith. Sam continues to sleep. I offer to pay to fill up the tank, but Jes refuses. 'I've got this one, mate,' he says, quickly. He returns from the shop with packets of pretzels, cans of Coke and some sandwiches. In the car we eat in silence. I'm surprised by how hungry I am. I finish the chicken and tarragon wholemeal. There's an extra sandwich sitting between us. Jes sees me glance at it. 'Go on. Have it,' he says.

'Don't you want it?'

'No. I'm fine.'

'Are you sure?'

'Yeah. I'm not that hungry.'

'That's not like you,' I say, then regret it – it wasn't meant to sound like an insult, but I know Jes has taken it as one.

To my relief, he doesn't strike back. 'I've not been so hungry recently. Bereavement's good for the figure, apparently.'

I polish off the second sandwich – a soggy BLT – swig the last of my Coke and burp loudly. 'Sorry,' I say.

Jes smiles for the first time since we got into the car. I glance in the back, but Sam is still sleeping.

'Mum would have killed you,' he says, more brightly.

'Yeah . . .' I almost laugh from the tiredness, tension and Tennent's lager I consumed at the pub. In this moment memories rush in like water, a fast-forward of Mum since I was little, her shouting at me for breaking her favourite lamp, her laughing when I rode my bicycle, with unhelpful stabilizing wheels, into the small ditch behind our house. I could keep these recollections to myself, but somehow it feels right to share them with my younger brother, to try to build a bridge between us. Glancing at him, I can tell that he's been flooded by the same sort of memories.

He looks pale in the fluorescent light from the dashboard, less sturdy. I need to cheer him up, make him feel a little better.

'Hey, remember when I let out that fart at the harvest festival?'

Jes nods. 'You always were a windy bastard.'

'The vicar broke off from his sermon, and made that joke about the Holy Spirit coming upon me . . .'

'Mum took us both straight home. We hadn't even had any cake.'

'She stopped my sweet money for a month.'

And we're both smiling now, cheered by the memory of my childhood farting prowess.

'Mum was like that,' I say warmly. 'Strict but fair.'

'You think?' says Jes.

'Yeah. Of course.' Although I have always felt that Jes got off more lightly, the spoiled second child.

'I don't know. I reckon she was always a bit harder on you than me,' he says matter-of-factly. This is news to me, that Jes thinks our mother treated him differently from me. Of course, I have consistently thought that she didn't push him as hard with his schoolwork, that she let him stay out later, with less boring people. But I have always felt guilty for thinking this: I reckoned I was being over-sensitive, or self-pitying.

I look at him, but he's pretending to concentrate on the road ahead. I'm about to say something along the lines of 'Don't be silly, she gave you a hard enough time too,' when my brother adds, 'But, then, you were always her favourite.'

I drop the Coke can. It rolls under my feet.

'What?'

'She loved you more than me,' he continues, in a quiet calm voice, as if announcing the football score.

'Bollocks, Jes.'

He doesn't reply.

'That's just bollocks. She loves . . . she loved both of us just the same,' I continue, with a little too much insistence in my voice.

'No. Yeah. You're probably right.'

Now he won't look at me, staring ahead at the road.

'You really think that?' I exclaim, with as much incredulity as I can muster. The problem is, I think he's right. Mum did love me differently. I just never thought it was obvious. She was always so careful to show her affection for Jes – bursting into tears when he announced he was marrying Sam, making him send her his first article for the *South London Gazette*, always taking his hand when walking with him.

'It doesn't matter,' says Jes, dismissively.

'Yes, it matters. It matters because you're wrong. She loved both of us. Equally. In fact, I think you're a little out of order.'

'All right. Forget about it.'

'What's wrong with you, Jes?'

'Me?'

'It's like you've got this chip on your shoulder. You blame everyone else for the fact you're not where you want to be.'

'Hang on. Is this me you're talking about, or you?'

'Don't change the subject.'

'Why not? *You*'re not exactly the world's happiest camper at the moment.'

'I'm fine.'

'Of course you are. That's why you got into a fight before your own mother's funeral, that's why you got locked up by the police, that's why you talked to no one at the pub, that's why you were so rude to Dad.'

'I'm not the one whining that my mother didn't love me enough. I'm not the one that sounds like some fucking yuppie on some fucking psychiatrist's couch!'

'Are we there yet?' Sam is sitting up, rubbing her eyes. 'I need a pee,' she says, with a flash of a smile. We fall silent, like guilty schoolboys.

For the rest of the journey Jes and I do not speak. At one thirty a.m. they drop me at my flat in Kentish Town. Sam kisses my cheek. Jes glares.

'See you soon,' I say, although I feel like the likelihood of this happening is up there with the announcement of a large cheese find on the moon.

I 2

On Wednesday morning, my agent telephones. I don't answer, because I'm screening my calls, an elaborate system that involves not answering any of them, however urgent. Barbara Smiles leaves a message saying she wants to outline the latest sales figures for *Men and Other Mammals*, which surprises me because I'd forgotten I'd even written it, what with everything that's happened. She sounds frosty. 'We need to talk! Call me back ASAP!'

I'm worried. I eat four slices of toast with butter and French Luxury Raspberry Preserve. When eventually I get the courage to call her – *Teletubbies*, four more pieces of toast and a sugary tea later – Barbara asks me sternly if I've seen the weekend's bestseller lists. I admit I haven't – I've successfully avoided all newspapers since the *Word Up!* débâcle. There's a pause. Then she says, at breakneck speed, 'You're at number two, hardback non-fiction, just behind Jamie! Since that stunt you pulled on BBC2, sales have been going through the roof. Eric is over the moon, they're talking about a whole new advertising campaign for you. Guess what they want the new slogan to be? "Poet Behaving Badly!" Bloody brilliant, isn't it?'

Apparently I've sold eight thousand copies in a week. The publishers are already planning a second print-run, in hardback. I'm trying to digest all this unexpected news when Barbara adds, as excited as a newscaster announcing a forthcoming celebrity wedding, 'And you've got the Northern Line! I have the letter here. The committee wants you! You've made it, Scott-lad!'

'Which poem?'

'Little Boys', of course! You should puke more often!'

'Wow. That's great, Barbara.'

I'm going to be on an underground train. I'm going to be a tube poet.

Barbara finishes the conversation by informing me that unfortunately Good Life Muesli have withdrawn their offer to print my poems on the back of cereal packets – apparently there's a clause in the contract that allows them to do so in the event of 'the artist acting in a way that might tarnish the image of the Good Life Company' – and that she doesn't give a shit. 'Cereal? For the birds! You're on the bloody Northern Line!'

As I put down the phone, I feel a bubbling excitement. This is immediately followed by a hush of sadness. I can't call my mother and tell her. Mum was always interested in my poems. 'How do you find the right words?' she would ask.

If I was feeling chipper I would smile and say, 'Genius, Mum.' And if I wasn't, I'd say, 'Luck, Mum.'

She would stare at the page of my book, then look up and ask why I'd chosen one word over another. I'd tell her, and she'd laugh and say, 'Remarkable.'

I loved her interest in my writing – she knew how much work I put into my poems. She realized that, like her with her scalpel and microscopes, I sliced, scrutinized and analysed, trying to find just the right phrase, just the right weight.

Despite what you might think, I work at my poems. Don't I, Mum?

That afternoon my father comes to stay. He tells me it's good to be back in Blighty and hands me a bottle of whisky (Bell's, not too expensive). I show him the flat, all four rooms, and he compliments me too many times on what a stylish existence I seem to be leading. Then he puts a hand on the radiator in the hallway and says, 'It's a bit parky in here. Is the heating working properly?' and I ask him when he's leaving.

Of course this hurts him, as I intended. I need to punish him. Bitterness forged in childhood is like underground lava, unseen but always there, bubbling up at intervals along its path. He sits down, in the bay window. 'I don't know when I'm leaving, Scott.'

'Well, you can't stay indefinitely, you know. I've got a life here.'

'Of course, of course . . .'

It strikes me then that while I was happy to invite a stinking, alcoholic stranger to stay with me, I can't stand my own father being in my flat longer than ten minutes. This does, even I admit, seem a little dysfunctional. 'Anyway, won't your French tart be missing you?' I say cheerily.

He looks up at me with his limp eyes. 'I don't think so.'

'Why not? She kick you out? Or have you grown tired of her, like you got tired of Mum?'

'I just . . . I just need some time away from there.'

'Why? I thought you loved France? I thought France was the bloody height of bloody sophistication and you wouldn't live anywhere else. I thought croissants and those stupid little cups of coffee were the very essence of modern fucking life! Wasn't that what you told me?'

'Mireille is having an affair,' he says, almost under his breath.

I look at him. I can see the defeat in his eyes. He didn't want to tell me this. And now I hate myself. Because I feel a tinge of happiness. 'Well, that's very Gallic, I suppose,' I say, not bothering to hide my amusement.

'It's my fault.'

I want to point out that, in my experience, most things were usually Edward Barron's fault, but even I am not that cruel. He is trying to be strong in front of me. Somewhere deep in my heart, I feel a flicker of compassion, but I try to suppress it. As a compromise I say, 'I'm sure it's not your fault.'

'It is. I'm too old.'

I almost laugh again, but manage not to. I want to say, 'Yes, Edward, that's the problem with having a girl-friend eighteen years younger than you!' Instead, I look at my watch and see that I'm late, I have to get going, which is unfortunate as I'm quite enjoying my father's discomfort. I inform him I'm off to the library to do some research and will be back to cook him supper at five.

In reality I have an appointment at the Archway sexual-health clinic, which I'm almost looking forward to since it means being away from my father for the rest of the afternoon.

At the clinic, Charles smiles beatifically as he tells me it's good news, and I wonder what's going on, all this good news in one day. Bad news must be imminent. 'The results are negative. You're free.'

It would appear that poor Cindy has caught chlamydia from someone else. I feel bad for her, but also a little elated.

I'm free.

As I walk down Junction Road the November sun shines brightly, as if just back from an exotic holiday. I'm about to start whistling to myself when I remember that my mother is dead, and that I will never see her again. I start to ache somewhere in my belly.

Is this what it's like to suffer the death of someone close? You feel guilty about feeling happy, and angry that no one else feels sad. I know Mum wouldn't want me to feel guilty and angry, but I have a long history of doing things she didn't want me to do.

I feel sick. I put my left hand on my stomach, rubbing gently, but the ache remains.

She's gone. There's nothing I can do. She will never come back.

I try to think of things to say, words that might make me feel better. But I am a bag of clichés, the phrases in my head have been said and read a billion times, everything I'm thinking seems to come from somewhere else, someone else. I don't feel like I'm in control. It doesn't feel like me.

Maybe in situations like this there are no words. Every combination of word and phrase sounds worthless and empty.

Here's one of my clichés: 'There's so much I want to say to her. But it's too late.'

What would I say to her?

'I love you, Mum.'

Why couldn't I have called her back? Why didn't she tell me about her illness? I know she was protecting us as she always did but, like numerous times in the past, I wish she hadn't been so strong. I wish she'd told me so I could have helped her in some way, however small. I wish I could have showed her that I loved her.

'Be strong,' I hear her saying.

'I don't want to be strong!' I shout in the middle of Junction Road, to the alarm of a young mother pushing her pram, who crosses the street to avoid me.

I wipe my tears, take a deep breath and set off down the street, hoping that walking will ease the pain.

By the time I reach Tufnell Park tube station, I feel a little better. I stop at the Indian shop to buy some food for supper. As I fill my basket with burgers and oven fries, I remember that I'm buying food for my father. And even though I resent him and wish he was staying somewhere else (like Beirut or Phnom Penh), I have to admit that it's satisfying having him depend on me. I toy with the idea of buying beetroot, which he hates, but I'm thirty-one years old, and bigger than that.

Back in my flat, my father is sitting in the window with three tabloid newspapers in front of him. They cover the

table, each open at a picture of me being sick on *Word Up!*
He seems cheery. 'Thought I'd, you know, catch up a bit,'
he says brightly. 'Onwards and upwards . . .'

This phrase, with which he used to wake me each
morning for piano practice, makes me wince. He holds up
one of the papers: 'Jes told me about your little . . . mishap.
Shame it had to happen on such a prestigious show. We
sometimes watch it on BBC Choice, you know, on satellite.'

I busy myself unpacking the bags. There's a moment of
silence, as loud as any shout. Then he asks, 'So, are you
going for a jog before dinner?'

'No.'

'Jes says you're always going running. A bit of a fitness
freak, he says.'

'Well, it might surprise you to hear that my little brother
doesn't know everything.'

In the kitchen I make my father dinner for the first time
in my life. As I think about opening the jar of beetroot I
slipped past my conscience at the Indian shop, the phone
rings. I ignore it, as usual, placing the chips and a burger
carefully on my father's plate. Then, to my horror, the
phone stops ringing and I hear my father's voice. He's
answered it. I could kill him. I open the jar, slap some
beetroot on to the chips and burger, and carry the plate
through to the living room.

'It's Jes,' says my father. 'Your brother.'

My heart races. I wonder if Jes is calling to make up, or
to berate me some more. As I put the receiver to my ear,
my brother sounds like he hasn't breathed for a long time.
He gasps out, 'Sam's – been – taken – to – hospital.'

'Jesus, what happened?'

'She's had a miscarriage. She's lost the baby.'

The bad news has arrived.

Morden Hospital is remarkably warm. The waiting room is painted grey, under bright white strip-lights. There are two rows of plastic chairs in front of some double doors, as if a political rally or Cub Scout slide show has just finished. There is no one else in the waiting room, except a mother and her small son.

I sit in the stuffy heat, starting to perspire, and wonder how Jes and I got to this point. How we ended up in a sweltering hospital on a Wednesday afternoon in November. It's as if something has been building, pressure within a closed space, increasing, expanding, until finally, after all these years, it has exploded.

A mother dead, a sister-in-law miscarried.

Has something caused these things to occur? Is there a path that has been followed? Or is it just the random nature of life?

Did we deserve this? Did we bring it on ourselves?

I mean, we're not evil people, really. In fact, Jes would probably be considered in the top ten per cent of do-gooders, as compiled by the Pearly Gates Statistical Company. Even I would make the top half, surely.

A nurse appears through the double doors. She tells me Mrs Barron is ready to see me. For an instant I think she's talking about my mother. Then I realize Mrs Barron is Sam, and follow her up some stairs, past a ward of motionless patients, where tinny laughter cackles from a large television, to a small private room with one window offering a truly fantastic view of a red-brick wall.

I'm nervous as hell. I don't know what I'm going to say to Jes. To my huge relief, he's not in the room. Sam lies in a narrow bed. She looks dreadful. Her face is white, she has a drip in one arm, and her hair is thick and matted across her forehead as if she's been sleeping on it. She's wearing a white nightie that makes her look like a refugee from a Dickens novel. I half expect a maid to come in with a candle.

I try to smile. 'All right, Sam?'

'Jes. Where's Jes?'

'I don't know. He's probably gone to the loo. Or to get you something from the shops.'

'He's gone for a cigarette.'

'He's smoking again?'

'The stress. Hah.' Sam sounds mightily pissed off. 'He thinks *he's* stressed . . .'

'It must be so hard. For both of you . . .'

'Why's it so hard for him? He didn't go through it.' Suddenly, she starts to cry. 'None of you understand . . .'

I don't know what to do. I step closer to the bed. 'It'll take time, Sam.'

'No, it won't,' she sobs. 'It won't take time. It's horrible, horrible.'

'You've still got each other. You can try for another baby –'

'*Fuck the baby!*'

I glance behind me, terrified someone might have heard her.

'*Fuck Jes!*'

Her hands are clenched.

'It must be so hard . . .' I say, then remember I've said this already. I need to come up with something more practical, something that will help her move on.

'Perhaps, I don't know, you just need a bit of space from each other . . .'

Unfortunately this seems to have the opposite effect to the one I was seeking. Sam starts sobbing more violently, her shoulders rising and falling, the wire from the drip jiggling up and down as if it's bopping to a rhythmic dance track. I'm afraid it might rip out of her wrist.

'It's okay, I'm sorry.' I bend down to comfort her.

'What's happened? Sam? What's the matter?' says Jes, appearing right behind me.

I turn, quickly, and almost fall on to the bed. 'She isn't feeling great.'

Jes brushes past me, and I step back. My brother takes his wife into his arms. She buries her head in his shoulder as he strokes her hair. Her sobbing subsides. Jes kisses her cheek, kisses her eyes, kissing away her tears.

'I'm so tired,' she says eventually.

'You should sleep. The medication's probably kicking in.'

He kisses Sam one more time, softly, almost religiously, on her lips. Then he gestures at me to leave. He follows me out of the room and closes the door.

We stand there, in the bright, hot corridor. I hear a clock ticking. I think he's going to shout at me, or maybe even punch me, punishing me for making his wife cry. Instead he sighs deeply, rubs his forehead with his right hand and says, 'I'm sorry, Scott. It's been awful. Just awful.'

I try to think of words, of spells that might magic away his grief and hurt, which I know are overwhelming – a poisonous blend of pain and guilt from the death of our mother and the loss of his longed-for child – but I can't think of anything other than 'Tough luck, mate,' which is completely unusable.

'Tough luck, mate,' I hear myself saying.

'Thanks for coming. I didn't know who to call.'

'I'm glad you called me.'

Tears are running down his plump cheeks. I reach out, unsure of what I'm doing, and put a hand on his shoulder, the sort of thing that a brother should do to a brother in a situation like this. It's a plump shoulder, warm and a little damp under his ragged sweater. My hand feels strange, as though it doesn't belong to me. I squeeze my brother's shoulder and he stops crying. I withdraw my hand swiftly.

'She blames me,' he says quietly. 'She says she never wanted to have a kid. She says it was all my idea, and now look at her. She says she knew she wasn't ready. There was so much she wanted to do before she became a mother. She says she feels like she killed our baby.'

I try to speak in my calmest, most big-brotherly voice. 'It's going to be okay, Jes. The important thing is, Sam's all right –'

'How did I fuck it all up, Scott?'

'You didn't.'

But he's off. He's evidently been thinking about this,

constructing a killer argument to make himself feel even worse. 'I just wasn't concentrating. I was caught up in work, in myself, wanting to go on that stupid bloody press trip to Bremen. You know, we live each day like it's not connected to the end. But it is connected to the end, Mum's death showed us that. We just let time slip by . . . and then it's slipped by . . .'

'It's going to be all right, Jes. Sam will get better, you can try for another kid –'

'Why can't you ever just listen to me?' Jes shouts.

At this moment a woman wearing a dark blue parka walks up to us holding a small bunch of yellow flowers. She's pretty, her hair cut boyishly short. Her cheeks are flushed a little from the cold. She seems younger than me, but maybe she's just ageing well. She nods in my direction, then kisses Jes on both cheeks and says gently, 'How's she doing, Jeremy?'

My mouth opens, instinctively. Jes hates anyone calling him Jeremy.

'She's pretty drowsy,' he replies, seemingly unaffected by it, 'but she'll want to see you.'

Jes opens the door to the room, then remembers me and says quickly, 'Sam said she wanted to see Rachel. I'll call you.'

Rachel glances at me again, and smiles briefly, a soft smile that seems like an apology. Then she is gone, following my brother into the private room, closing the door behind her.

I stand there, warm and exhilarated by the rush of attraction I've just felt. Then, almost immediately, my euphoria is drowned in guilt and shame. How could I be so superficial? They've lost the baby, and I'm thinking about whether this stranger is single and what it would be like to kiss her.

I hurry back to the waiting room, where my father is now sitting, with a plastic bag of Sainsbury's food between his legs. I'd told him to come to the hospital an hour after me, as I thought we shouldn't crowd Jes and Sam, and anyway I'm closer to my younger brother than he is, aren't I? He informs me he's going to cook for Jes while Sam is in hospital. I question his ability to do this, recalling the burnt fish-fingers and lukewarm baked beans of our youth. 'That was a long time ago, Scott. I've been in France, remember. Everyone can cook there.'

'Funny you didn't feel like mentioning that earlier this evening before I started making you dinner.'

'Please, Scott, not now. We need to pull together.'

He looks at me and, in a shiver of a moment, I know that expression from twenty-five years ago, a mixture of anger and pity. It makes me mad. Then he really blows it. 'At a time like this we need to be a family.'

I push past him and march out of the hospital.

I call Big Barry. He answers with what sounds like the battle of El Alamein going on in the background. 'You did know it was England–Scotland tonight, didn't you, Brains?'

The pub down the side of Charing Cross station is packed with young men, some in England shirts, screaming their heads off and spilling beer. I look to see if there are any women in the sweaty crowd so I can plan a safe route among them, between the snarling men, but of course there aren't. I try to squeeze through, getting a few shoves and fuck-off grunts even though I say, 'Sorry, excuse me, sorry . . .'

Then Barry spots me, grabs my arm and yanks me through a group of five men who growl, turn, then decide better of it when they see how big Barry is.

'IT'S THE PUKING POET!'

'Thanks, Barry.'

We haven't spoken since *Word Up!* I'm pretty sure Barry doesn't know my mother is dead – who would have told him? He downs his beer, slaps my back, shouts, 'INGER-LAND!' and orders more beer. Of course, he's got the best spot in the pub, right at the bar, with a full view of three television screens.

'DON'T TELL THEM YOU'RE A JOCK!' he whispers loudly, so everyone can hear. A couple of men turn, but Barry laughs and they turn back. England, as far as I can tell, are all over Scotland and the pub is alive with drunken anticipation. We clink glasses, Barry berates one of the England defenders, England score, the pub jumps. As he leaps up, Barry spills a little beer over a small man, who pushes him. Barry says he's sorry, and the smaller man seems to accept this as a fair response. He knows better than to mess with Big Barry, because Big Barry is the human equivalent of one of those old-fashioned cast-iron steam-rollers you sometimes see on English back roads. You know that if it ever gets into an accident everyone else is going to come off worse.

At this time I think two thoughts. First, England supporters are not into camaraderie. And second, I would like to be Big Barry – he's rich, easily pleased and too big to pick a fight with.

In the midst of all this nationalism I feel out of place. It's not simply because my mum was Scottish and I have an English father who lives in France. If anyone asks me, I always tell them I'm English. No. I think the problem is that calling myself English makes me feel out of place. No one knows what it means to be English, these days.

I try for a moment to get into the contest, but I can't help stepping outside the emotions of the game and wondering why I should care about men thumping a leather ball about with their feet. I feel like I should support one of the teams – perhaps Scotland, on Mum's behalf, but she hated football too. 'Mindless violence, and that's just the players,' she used to say.

It's funny how clear her voice sounds in my head among fifty male yells. It's funny how I feel alone in the midst of all these people, including my best friend.

I down my beer, buy us another two pints and soon it's half-time. The yelling stops and the pub is surprisingly quiet now no one's got anything to shout at.

Barry is wide-eyed. 'Magic, Brains. We're stuffing the jocks. I've got a hundred quid on three–nil. COME ON, INGER-LAND!'

Usually I would find Barry's manic intensity exhausting and even a little annoying, but tonight I need it. He takes me away from myself. I try to engage. 'How's the love-life, Barry?'

'Oh, man! Didn't I tell you? I'm banging Nancy. You know, the advertising bird from that dating thing we went to. It's been a month now. She moans like a fucking banshee . . . ooooohyaaaaaah!'

'That's great, Barry.'

'How about you? Still shagging that skinny chick?'

I think he means Cindy. I shake my head. In this moment I feel irredeemably alone. I sense tears welling up, but how can I cry among all these men, especially when England are winning?

'Whassup, Brains?'

To give him credit, Barry appears genuinely concerned. Whether it's for my well-being, or his own desire to avoid anything that might be embarrassing, is unclear. But he looks at me with what passes for compassion.

'My mum died. Two weeks ago.'

'What? No way.'

'Yeah. It's been' . . . I can't find the words.

'Oh, God, Brains. I'm sorry.'

Big Barry then does something he's never done before. He punches me gently on the shoulder. It's not hard, not even a punch, really, more of a pat with his fist. From him, I know it's a gesture of affection. Then he pulls back, tells me I need a whisky and orders the most expensive single malt in the pub. The men behind watch us.

'To yowa mam,' he says, in his best Galway accent. We clink glasses, and in that moment I feel sad but somehow happy in my sadness. For the first time since my mother's death, this seems like the right thing to do. Drinking a toast

223

with an old friend. It seems both a mark of appreciation and respect, and a celebration of life.

As we drink, the second half begins. All around us, men cheer and shout abuse at the screen. To my great surprise, Barry doesn't jump up with the throng but remains sitting, his view of the televisions blocked by gesticulating men.

'So, you know, Scott, how are you feeling?'

In the list of top-five questions Big Barry is least likely to ask me, this has to be number one – just before 'Which charity do you think I should donate to?' and 'Do you think I'm crazy going for a floral design in my bedroom?'

He's obviously a little embarrassed by his question, and seeks out a television on which to fix his attention and hide his discomfort. But he would have to stand up to get a clear view of a screen, thereby appearing highly insensitive to my feelings. So he stays on his stool, not looking at me, and sips his whisky.

To my surprise I start to tell him how I'm feeling. I explain how it's like a rug has been pulled from under me, how I'm not sure what I see when I look at myself in the mirror, these days.

'Sure . . . Yeah . . . Right . . .' says Barry, at appropriate moments, and I can tell he's making a huge effort to digest these confused, amorphous statements, seeking out something to say that might make things better for me. For the first time in ages, I find myself liking him.

'It's just so hard, Barry . . .'

'It must be, Brains. I can't imagine . . .'

He raises his glass again, to toast me and my travails – a good-luck wish. As I raise my glass one of the five men behind us lurches forward and nudges into me. I slip on my stool and knock my whisky, which spills on to my lap. Behind us, the men start to laugh, as if this has been a conspiracy. Perhaps our show of less-than-manly emotion has upset them.

'Watch out, mate!' says Barry, without the usual venom in his voice.

'Why's that?'

The man is skinny, wiry, with an eagle tattoo on one forearm.

'Look, pal, at least say sorry.'

'It was an accident.'

Behind him, the four other men chuckle. I know they're trying to wind us up. Barry knows it too.

'Look, at least buy him another whisky.'

'Why don't you? He's your boyfriend.'

'What's that?'

'You heard.'

'It's okay, Barry,' I say, and for a moment Barry doesn't react: he's trying to control himself, he knows it will be better to let it go, for us to leave and talk elsewhere. But he's not Big Barry for nothing.

'Fuck you,' he says, slowly, with menace. My heart leaps into my mouth. The man looks at him, then pushes him. His mates cheer. Barry's arm moves so quickly that none of us sees it. He punches the man in the stomach, short and sharp. The man groans, doubles over, and the other four men jump on Barry. One punches me off my stool. I try to remain upright, but I slip and fall to the floor.

It's covered in beer and cigarettes. I'm terrified, my

childhood horror of fighting returning, but I know I must try to help Barry. I try to get up, but bodies are slamming back and forth above me, men shouting, 'Fuck,' at each other. Someone shoves me down again.

In less than a minute it's over. Someone pulls me up. I hope it's Big Barry. Instead it's a big bouncer.

'You can fuck off an' all.'

I nod, shaking with fear and adrenaline. As the bouncer escorts me through the crowd, England score again. The cheers are more muted. Out in the street, my best friend is nowhere to be seen. I call his mobile three times, but he doesn't answer.

FOOTBALL

> *Boys love balls*
> *because they can be kicked*
> *without retribution,*
> *football is a solution*
> *to male frustration.*
> *Am I less of a bloke*
> *Because I like to stroke*
> *breasts not balls?*
> *Tell me, darling,*
> *If it came to a penalty shoot-out*
> *Would you let me score?*

*

Back in Kentish Town, Frank is sitting on my doorstep. The cut on his head has healed, and he seems to have made at least a half-hearted effort to comb his hair using something that might be Brylcreem, or lard. He's still wearing his black wellingtons. He even smiles at me as I walk up the five steps, sullen with fatigue.

'Hungry,' he says.

Shit. Have I become the patron saint of useless old men? First my homeless waster of a father, now the homeless old drunkard who lives in a box at the end of my street. Obviously they are attracted to me, sensing perhaps that I am like them, or have the potential to be, twenty years before my time.

I feel exhausted. There has been too much fighting for one day. 'Sorry, Frank. I'm tired. A lot's happened.' I go to the door and put my key in the lock.

'Hungry,' he repeats. 'Need food.'

The Bosphorus Café-Diner is open until two a.m., even on weeknights. It has a ragged newspaper clipping in the window indicating that it was voted Second Best Late-night Greasy Spoon by the readers of the *Camden Chronicle* in 1996. The Turkish men who run it are no strangers to late-night abuse and cholesterol, and the air is thick with steam and frying fat.

I ask Frank what he feels like eating.

'Hungry,' he says.

I order him a Gut-buster, a mountain of semi-charred eggs, bacon, chips and beans, then give in and order one for myself as well. I expect Frank to shovel in the food, but he's surprisingly dexterous with his knife and fork, holding the cutlery lightly at a jaunty angle, slicing everything into pieces before putting morsels into his mouth and chewing slowly.

I finish before him, feeling heavily, sleepily full. I sip my tea and wonder what I'm doing here, feeding a homeless incoherent drunk in North London's second best late-night greasy spoon. For some reason I think about my father, now ensconced at Jes and Sam's house in Morden, cooking *coq au vin*. And I wonder if perhaps I'm using Frank as a father substitute, my ideal of how I'd like my father to be – dishevelled and useless, someone I can control and take care of. Someone I can feel superior to.

Then I think, Maybe Frank's using me. Maybe he's smarter than he seems. What if this is the cunning plan of a lifelong alcoholic to target a weak, gullible member of society? Maybe he'll just keep coming to my house, eventually move in and take over my life?

It's all Jes's fault. If only I hadn't thought about what he would have done.

I watch Frank, his slow, measured movements, the way he sips his tea, the way he uses the paper napkins in front of him, one at a time, and he doesn't seem like a drunken vagrant. I wonder once more how he got to where he is. Whether there was a time in the past when he was like me, vaguely successful, sitting in a late-night café buying fried food for someone he thought he would never become.

'What did you do, Frank? How did you get here?'

He ignores me, slicing a piece of bacon into three.

'Were you a Czech fighter pilot in the war? The chairman of a small pencil-manufacturing company? A professional footballer? A lion-tamer? A gigolo in Amsterdam? A Vegas circus clown? A minor member of the Slovenian royal family?'

'Chocolate.'

'An enforcer for the East End mob?'

'Chocolate.'

I buy two Mars Bars and we eat in silence. From the counter, the Turkish cooks watch us with the bored eyes of late-night soothsayers who have seen it all, and then some.

When he's finished the Mars Bar, Frank stands, burps loudly, says, 'Cheers,' and walks from the café, disappearing into the night.

13

Sam is being discharged from hospital today. I thought about bringing her flowers, but somehow they seemed too funereal. So I bought a big box of chocolates and a ten-pound bottle of red wine. I want to cheer them up. Normally, perhaps, I would not be first choice to bring jollity into a traumatized household, but in the past twenty-four hours I've begun to feel if not happier then less downbeat. I'm going to make a big effort to be jaunty, light and fun. Because I want my brother to like me again.

As the train hurtles past Tooting Bec I wonder if the sadness of the last couple of weeks might bring us together. I wonder if, through the stark, tragic events of our mother's death and Sam's miscarriage, Jes and I might start to creep closer, like tectonic plates or a couple on a first date.

I know we've been crap. We've been distant, uncommunicative and fractious. But we all get stuck in our ways, don't we? It's just that some people get stuck there a little earlier than others. For Jes and me it was almost a quarter of a century ago, when he was two and I was seven. We have the thick mud of nearly twenty-five years of resentment to wade through before we can reach each other.

Jes seems flustered when he answers the door. This might have something to do with the fact that he's wearing just a pair of shorts and a grubby vest and is covered in floury dough. I glance down and his hairy hobbity feet are bare. Because of the dough, he looks a little like a corpulent ghost, the spectre of Winston Churchill, or Orson Welles. From the house I can feel hot air rushing out into the cold street.

'What's going on, mate?' I ask, but he doesn't answer. He turns and walks back down the hall. I follow him.

In the kitchen it looks like someone has let off a particularly large bomb containing many pounds of dough. There is dough on the counter, on the cupboards, on the tiled wall, on the fridge, on the table and chairs, and on the cat. Actually they don't have a cat but, if they did, it would be covered in dough.

On the counter there are several bowls overflowing with dough, and a couple of baking sheets, covered in dough. The oven hums happily to itself and there is the strong odour of what might be dough baking.

'What are you doing, Jes?'

'Making bread.'

He takes a lump of the mixture and attacks it, kneading, punching the pliant mass as if it's alive, his big forearms bulging in a way my thin ones never will. Knead, punch, knead, punch.

'Where's Sam?' I ask tentatively, placing the bottle of wine among the doughy globules.

'Gone.' Knead. Punch.

'What? Where's she gone?'

'Dunno.' Knead. Punch.

I think about sitting down, but the chairs are covered in bits of dough.

'Jes, what's going on?'

In answer, the oven timer pings. Jes opens the door, the air shimmers with heat, he takes out two loaves of bread and places them on cooling trays on the doughy table. It looks surprisingly good, Jes's bread, all moist and succulent. I feel like cutting myself a slice and smothering it in butter. As if reading my mind, Jes takes the breadknife and saws three slices, his belly jiggling as his arm swings. He takes out some butter, throws three knobs on to the bread and walks past me into the small living room.

We eat without talking. The bread is excellent. When it becomes clear Jes is not going to break the doughy silence, I ask him again what's happened and where Sam is. Without looking up, he says they had a big argument when she got home from hospital. She said she needed space from him. She's gone to stay with a friend.

'Oh, Jes. I'm sorry.'

And I am. I understand the seriousness of this situation, a wife telling her husband she needs space. In my limited experience, when a woman tells you she wants space, the sort of space she wants is one shaped like you, on a permanent basis. The only problem is, I was the one who suggested this course of action to her.

'And the *Gazette* say they're going to fire me.'

'They can't do that. Can they?'

'I've not been to the office in a week.'

Jes takes another bite of bread. I'm trying to think of something to say, to find a magic sentence that might somehow conjure a solution, but while I'm good at little poems, I'm hopeless at big advice. 'Can't you just go in and explain things? I'm sure they'd understand. I could go with you, if you want.'

He looks at me. I've given him advice, yet again. Without speaking, he stands and heads back towards the kitchen.

I sit there. This is so typical. He dismisses me. He thinks I'm selfish and didactic, whereas he's so giving and broad-minded. It's been like this ever since he was five and I refused to join in with his sponsored *Blue Peter* car-wash for the Cornish pit ponies. I follow him to the kitchen. 'I feel terrible for you, Jes. I just want to help.'

'Do you? Or do you just want to make yourself feel better? That's why you're here, isn't it?'

I know he's bruising for a fight, he needs to lash out – he's brimming with anger and dough. I also know he's partly right, that I do want to make myself feel better, but we do everything for mixed reasons. 'I came here to be with you guys. I brought you some wine, some chocolates for Sammy.'

He doesn't reply. The oven hums. I'm trying to work out a way to change the mood, to turn us down a different, sunnier, more amicable path. But it's Jes who speaks first. His voice is softer. 'I was thinking a lot last night, about Sam, about Mum, about everything, and I remembered something funny. My first bike. Do you remember my first bike?'

I don't remember Jes's first bike, but I nod slowly.

'It was my sixth birthday, my first year at school. I was so proud. It was bright red and had racing handlebars. It was the most grown-up thing I'd ever seen. When I rode it to school I felt so happy, like I was cycling on air. I couldn't wait to show my friends. I showed them, I said, "Look, this is my new bike," and Zeb laughed and said, "No, it's not, that's your brother's bike!" and all my friends laughed at me. Because it *was* your bike. Mum had just put on new handlebars and painted it red.' He sighs theatrically.

If this is an attempt to make me feel guilty, it's not going to work. 'Well, it's hardly my fault that I'm five years older than you.'

'No,' he says quietly. 'But it is your fault you still think that makes you superior.'

I try to stay calm, my heart thumping, as Jes stands there, covered in dough, like a pastry chef after a gas explosion.

'You're not the oldest any more, Scott.'

In his usual fashion, Jes has summed up the situation in a pithy one-liner.

'Is that meant to be an insult?' I ask, attempting to muster sarcasm.

'Who's insulting? I'm just telling the truth. I don't need a big brother any more. I know as much as you do, I'm just as capable as you. So why the fuck don't you stop giving me advice?'

'Oh, come on, mate, be fair.'

He snorts, loudly, in a way designed to taunt and enrage me.

'I'm just trying to help,' I continue, less calmly. 'I've spent my life trying to help you.'

'How the fuck have you helped me?'

'Don't start. What about all those nights when Mum

was gone, when I stayed with you reading you stories because you were scared? What about all the lifts I gave you when I got my car? That money I lent you for the wedding? There's so much –'

'I PAID YOU BACK!'

I know I'm being unfair. But we've embarked on hand-to-hand combat, where anything goes. 'I'm just saying –'

'God, it's always the fucking same. You just get so superior, like you know everything better than anyone. It's crazy, I mean, it's not like you're in such a great position to be giving advice in the first place –'

'Come on, Jes, let's stop this –'

'You're a fucking mess. Look at yourself. You've got no girlfriend. You've not even got any real friends. You're supposed to be this amazing poet, this great sage, but what do you know? You haven't a fucking clue. You're so locked up in yourself, you can't see anyone else!'

'I can't see anyone else? What about you? What about you and Sam? Did you see what you were doing to her? Did you see how you were pushing her away?'

The mention of his wife's name stabs him hard. Hurt and anger shudder through his big fat body. I know this is the moment where I could stop, where we could maybe pull back from the brink, but I'm on a roll so I keep going, heading towards the precipice, because I no longer care where we end up.

'You know why she didn't want to have kids with you? I'll tell you. Because you wanted them for the wrong reason. It's like everything you do. You think you can fix everything. You wanted to be the father our father never was, but you didn't think about what she wanted. And now you've blown it. Now she's walked out on you, just like he did twenty-four years ago!'

Jes stands there, face red, breathing heavily. A small dollop of dough slides from his cheek and drops, cheekily, to the floor. I stare at him, blood pumping. He wipes his face with the back of his big hand and looks at me, fire in his eyes. 'At least I've got something to lose. At least I'm not a lonely old cunt.'

I stare back at my brother, and in this moment I hate him. 'You fat fuck!'

He hits me.

I sit in my small but tastefully appointed flat in Kentish Town and pour myself another whisky. It's twelve-year-old Glenlivet, a birthday present last year from my mother. I wonder what she would make of all this – her elder son nursing a puffy crimson eye courtesy of a right upper-cut from her younger son. She'd box our ears, knock our heads together, and bark, 'You stupid little boys!'

But she's not here, and I'm afraid I'll never talk to my brother again.

I've called Jes six times, but he's not picking up the phone. All those years of rivalry, hate and unspoken love, culminating in our first ever fist-fight. Why weren't we able to see it coming? Why didn't we realize that love, fraternal or not, is something that has to be believed to be seen, not the other way round? That you have to work at it, you can't just sit back and wait for it to appear like some God-sent comet?

Without our mother to act as a negotiator in a United Nations blue beret, I'm afraid we might not see each other again for a long time. For some reason I think of Frank. Perhaps this is the beginning of my fall.

My father returns from wherever he's been – somewhere that sells newspapers, judging from the thick pile of tabloids he's carrying – and whistles on seeing my bruised, bloody face, like some Cockney chappy in a pre-war Ealing comedy. I half-expect him to chirp, 'Cor, blimey, strike a light,' but instead he sits down, places the papers on the floor and says, 'Fall down some stairs?'

I nod, finish my whisky and pour some more. I don't want to tell him what has happened. I want him to wonder, to understand that this is just the start of what he doesn't know about me. I want him to ask me questions that I will refuse to answer. But instead he remains silent. He just sits there flicking slowly through the red-tops. In the end I get so frustrated with his reasonable, detached reaction to my pulsating black eye that I tell him everything.

I'm honest, I don't paint Jes as the sole criminal. I admit my own degree of culpability, up to the point at which Jes escalated the conflict by decking me.

Edward Barron shakes his head slowly. Now I'm waiting for it, the fatherly admonitions, the talk of family and blood being thicker than water, which would be so ill-placed and ill-judged, given that he's been away for all these years, but instead he just sighs and turns another page of the *Sun*.

'That's it?' I ask, trying to feel outraged. 'No comment?

No pearl of paternal wisdom? No pronouncement from the mountain top on who's right, who's wrong?'

My father looks up at me with his baggy bloodhound eyes. 'What can I say, Scott? I've been away so long. You don't want to hear anything from me.'

He's wrong. I do want to hear something, so that I can strike him down. 'Fine,' I say, childishly. 'Enjoy the tits and football.'

'Scott . . .' he says, a little helplessly, putting down the *Sun*. I grab my coat and head for the front door. 'Please, Scott . . .' I hear him say, as I walk out of the flat and down the steps into Lady Somerset Road.

I sit back in Lindsey Stevens's leather sofa. She sits opposite, crosses her legs, and waits. And waits. I listen to the clock ticking, my heart tapping.

'It's been a while, Scott. Anyone would think you were trying to avoid me.'

'I've been busy. Work stuff.'

'So why come today?'

'I felt it was time, that's all.'

She looks at me, and I get the feeling she's trying not to smile. Inadvertently I touch my puffy eye.

'Do you want to talk about it?'

I remain silent.

'"Sunday shiners", we used to call them down Romford way. You know, after a Saturday night at the boozer.'

I nod unenthusiastically.

'So how did you get it?'

'A fight.'

'Who with?'

'My brother.'

'Why?'

'A silly little argument.'

'What about?'

'Nothing.'

Lindsey thinks for a moment, weighing her next approach. 'Did you feel better after fighting with him?'

'That's a stupid question. No, I didn't. I feel terrible.'

'How do you feel terrible?'

'I don't know. Just terrible. Jesus –'

'Ashamed? Wronged? Guilty? Come on, you're a writer. Give it a word.'

'Why don't you give it a fucking word? I'm paying you!'

'All right, Scott, let's keep it civil here.'

'Sorry.'

Lindsey takes a sip of tea, allowing the moment to defuse. After a full minute she begins again: 'Were you angry with your brother about something?'

'No, I told you . . .' My head pounds, a whisky hangover knocking at my skull. 'Yes . . . all right, I was angry with him. I'm still angry with him. Because he's had it easier than me. Because I've always had to lead. Because I couldn't be myself when I was a child, because I always had to look after him. Because he ended up with everything I want! Because he and I . . .' And as I say this, my voice rising and cracking, I see an image in my head, an image that horrifies me. It's an image I know I've seen already, like the moment on late-night television when you realize you've watched the film before.

I stop.

This is the important thing that I knew I had to tell Lindsey Stevens. The memory that just wouldn't emerge from the darkness, that wouldn't clarify and take solid, tangible form. Until now.

I am seven years old. I'm wearing striped pyjamas. It's late, and the house is still except for the grandfather clock in the hallway that 'dick-docks' as if it has a cold. I know my mum is sleeping, because she snores, ever so gently. I go into the room at the end of the upstairs hall. I stand by the small oak bed that was once mine. Jes is asleep, his two-year-old features so still and smooth and soft that he looks as if he might not be of this world, but of somewhere better, sweeter and more beautiful.

I am holding a pillow. I place it over Jes's face, just lightly. He doesn't stir, he's a deep sleeper, probably dreaming of his favourite Jammie Dodger biscuits. My heart thumps, I want to stop, but I press down on the pillow until I feel the contours of his little head.

To begin with he doesn't react, his body motionless, legs inert beneath the thin duvet. Then his head moves, his arm flings out, and I pull up the pillow and run from the room before he can see me.

I hurry out of the house and rip the pillow to shreds at the bottom of the garden, burying the pieces with a trowel. The next morning I hug Jes, over and over again, until my mother tells me to stop being so possessive.

Lindsey looks at the tears running down my face, collecting in damp spots at the neck of my T-shirt. 'What is it, Scott?'

I don't reply. I reach in my pocket, hand her a fifty-pound note and hurry from the room.

My father exits my flat to find me sitting in a blue Fiat Punto hire car. 'All right?' he says, cheerily. 'Just off to the shops to buy some aubergines for dinner. I thought we'd maybe have a little home-made ratatouille.'

'Get in the car,' I say, curtly.

'What's going on?'

'Just get in the bloody car!'

'Where are we going?' he asks, buckling up his seat-belt with boyish excitement.

I don't answer, but shove the gear-stick violently into first and screech away down Lady Somerset Road.

14

'I'm not doing this,' says my father.

I can't really blame him. I'm not sure I'm doing this, and it's my plan.

It's turned blisteringly cold, wind snapping at noses and thumbs. The children all around us are bundled up like spacemen, except for a small group of hardened boys under the age of twelve in short-sleeved football shirts – blue and white, I've no idea which team – their coats tied defiantly around their waists. Two are sucking on cigarettes behind the chimpanzee cages. I'm glad they're here. Suddenly my plan seems possible. Maybe.

I approach the diminutive smokers with an offer of cash. I have my parka hood tied tightly so the furry fringes almost conceal my face, and I'm wearing sunglasses, even though the sky is November grey.

'Twenty each and a tenner for your friends.'

They look at each other. One has big ears that are turning blue gradually in the cold. He sucks on his Silk Cut as if it might be the last breath he'll ever take. Neither of them seems surprised or threatened. They nod. I hand them the cash. It's three twenty-five p.m.

The London Zoo penguin pool is much smaller and more stylish than the one in Edinburgh. It's a modernist oval of white concrete surrounding an aquamarine sunken pool complete with two white spiral ramps sweeping around each other into the water. It looks like a Hollywood swimming-pool, except that instead of scantily clad starlets sunning themselves, there are small black penguins preening their backsides.

I look round for CCTV cameras, but there don't seem to be any.

There's a fairly decent crowd at the pool, which is surprising, considering it's a freezing Tuesday five weeks before Christmas. There are the shaven-headed kids and their burly teachers (he dressed in tracksuit, she in combat trousers and black coat like a terrorist commander, which, given the somewhat revolutionary behaviour of some of her pupils, I suppose she is). And there's a well-groomed group of private-school boys with bright, red-faced complexions, standing around in their red and grey uniforms.

The two groups exchange wary glances, each intimidated by the other. Between them stands a cluster of old people, huddled together under a tree for warmth. They're dressed as old people always seem to be when it's very cold – in flimsy winter coats designed for an era when hardship was considered a good thing. They wear ill-shaped bobble hats and badly knitted gloves. I can feel their chill.

I look around for my father, and spot him lighting a cigarette by the rhino enclosure. In some ways he looks like the under age smokers – the same shiftiness, the same bent back as he tries to light up. I wonder if he'll try to stop me. I wonder if he knows he won't be able to.

I stand at the thin low white wall of the penguin pool.

There's a four-foot drop to the terracotta-painted poolside. It's not going to be easy, but heroic deeds never are.

There must be about twenty penguins in the pool. The sign says they are Jackass penguins from South Africa. I never even knew they had penguins in Cape Town. The Jackasses (the perfect name for a penguin, in my opinion) are small, about eighteen inches high, with black feet and stubby black bills, white tummies and a white curve around their heads like a hood. They seem quite content, hanging out on their curved ramps, being admired by the gesticulating private-school boys and glared at by the inner-city kids.

As I survey the penguins, I notice one bird on its own towards the back of the pool, nearest the zoo exit. He seems different from the other penguins, isolated, his back turned away from the water, facing the wall. It's almost as if he's been excluded, like a naughty schoolboy sent to the corner. He's about two feet tall, with pink feet, an orange bill and a splash of white across the top of his head, from eye to eye. He stares at the wall as if depressed. I watch him for a moment, and something about his wings dangling sadly by his sides and the way the other penguins are ignoring him makes me feel sorry for him.

But there's no time for sentimentality. It's starting to get dark. I have to hurry.

I move round the back of the crowd, adrenaline racing. I get to the far end of the pool by the solitary penguin, where there are fewer people. Beyond, my father tries to appear invisible. But he needn't worry. No one's noticed him, or me.

I stand there, heart thumping. This is how a bank robber, a kidnapper, an assassin must feel, moments before the deed. The sense of power is immense. No one else knows what's about to happen. Not even my paid employees.

As I raise my left hand, our agreed signal, the small boy with the big blue ears vaults over the low wall at the opposite end of the penguin pool. He lands on the terracotta poolside in a crouch. The onlookers gasp. 'OI! STOP THAT!' someone shouts.

The boy stops in front of a small penguin and screams theatrically. 'YOOWAAAH!'

The penguin stares at him, as if wondering why he is being abused in such an ugly fashion, then jumps into the pool.

The burly teacher in the tracksuit shouts at the top of his voice, 'RYAN!'

The female terrorist leader shrieks, 'RYAN! GET OUT OF THERE RIGHT NOW!'

At once, another shaven-headed boy leaps over the wall, skidding on the wet poolside, almost tumbling into the water. He bends down and taps a Jackass penguin on the head. The penguin squawks and dives into the pool. Other penguins follow, like lemmings off a cliff. From the other side of the enclosure, another boy leaps down on to the poolside, hollering. A man shouts. Someone blows a whistle. The penguins flap their stubby wings.

The three boys run back and forth around the pool, screeching, 'WAAAHAAAYAAAAH!' while the other shaven-headed children lean over the wall, chanting like

Romans at a gladiatorial combat, 'YEAAAAAHAAAAH!'

The private-school boys look on, their red faces redder with shock. A keeper tries frantically to unlock the gate. As he does so, one of the boys slips and falls head first into the pool. The burly tracksuited teacher clambers over the wall, skids on the poolside and jumps into the pool to save him, discovering as he does so that the water is only three feet deep.

I can't believe my luck. I open my parka, lean as far as I can over the wall, grasp the solitary penguin, close my coat and walk away quickly, leaving the sound of shouting, water splashing and whistles blowing behind me.

The penguin struggles in my hands, but I grasp him tight. He wriggles, wings straining to push free. I grip him firmly through the pockets of my parka. I can feel the bird tremble. I feel sorry for him, but there's nothing I can do. He is my only hope.

I keep walking.

'To the car! Now!' I hiss at my father, who stands there wide-eyed and open-mouthed. He follows dutifully, like a son, and for a brief moment I feel all-powerful.

At the zoo exit the news of the penguin carnage has spread and staff are running past me towards the enclosure.

The hire car is parked opposite the zoo. For a horrible moment I wonder if I put enough money in the meter, and if the blue Fiat will be clamped. It's not. We're almost free.

'Open the door!' I bark at my father. He hesitates. 'Open it!'

He opens the door. On the back seat is a square box of

the toughest cardboard I could find – an old computer-monitor box discovered lurking at the back of a cupboard. I lean over, undo my coat and push in the penguin. I close the lid and the penguin pokes his head up through the hole I've cut to allow his head to be free so that he can breathe easily.

'Hand me the tape!' I shout at my father. I take the masking tape and stick down the lid. The penguin tries to peck at me, but he's held firm by the cardboard. I feel like cheering. So far my plan is working perfectly. The penguin rocks back and forth in the box, like a high-security prisoner on a psychiatric ward. I throw a small sheet over his exposed head.

My father waits by the passenger door, his white face stricken.

'Get in!'

He pauses. 'Why are you doing this, Scott?'

I look at him, my heart pumping. 'It's for Jes. It's going to make everything all right!'

'How?'

'Just get in the bloody car!'

He gets in, I take a deep breath and pull away slowly and calmly as a police car screeches to a halt outside the zoo and two large policemen dash through the gates, truncheons at the ready.

15

Strictly speaking, I don't know how stealing a penguin is going to make everything all right. I don't know anything right now. It just seems, after everything that's happened – Ellie's departure, Mum dying, Sam's miscarriage, Jes punching me in the face – that kidnapping a flightless bird is the right step. It could be my last chance.

I hope the penguin understands.

My father hasn't said a word since we left the zoo, fifteen minutes ago, which is fine by me. The penguin's been pretty quiet too under his sheet. He's behaving like an experienced kidnap victim, the chairman of a major company with dealings in Colombia, deliberately not inter-acting with his captors, remaining silent and still. He may, of course, be dead.

Like many kidnappers, I can't help feeling a little sorry for my hostage. I mean, I don't know anything about him. The strange thing is, he doesn't look like the other penguins, with his orange bill and pink scaly feet. I don't even know if he really is a 'he'. But I've given him a name. He's Norman II.

I try to keep to the quieter roads, the back-streets, away from the bustle of London's West End. We head past King's Cross, up Pentonville Road, then along Old Street to Whitechapel. I want to keep east, close to the carpet warehouses and clothing emporiums where large card-board boxes on back seats are not uncommon. Thankfully nobody glances into the car. This is London, after all, the capital of anonymity.

I keep looking in the driver's mirror. As we head past Liverpool Street station, the cardboard box rocks once more and there's a sound of squirting penguin excrement. I breathe out with relief. At least he's still alive. My father groans theatrically.

You get used to the smell. Sort of.

We sit in a traffic jam at Monument, still not talking to each other. I look at my watch. Four thirty. I've timed this terribly. It's rush-hour. I want to get there quickly, to get Norman II comfortable – I'm thinking salt water and a tin of pilchards. I also want to get as far away from the scene of the crime as I can. It will take them a while to notice he's gone, but when they do all hell will break loose. A child going missing is one thing, but a missing penguin is the definition of tragedy. The British love their animals.

I pull out to overtake a slow-moving Vauxhall estate. My father awakes from his sulking silence. 'Why didn't you signal?'

'Look, it was safe, I was just –'

'You didn't signal. How could he have known you were going to overtake?'

'Look, I do know how to drive!'

'He might not have seen you!'

'IT WAS PERFECTLY SAFE!'

'Just like your mother.'

He stops. He knows he's overstepped a mark, mentioning Mum. I feel the anger boiling inside me, not just because he insulted me but because I remember how he used to criticize Mum's driving (she was a nervy and over-cautious driver, especially at traffic lights), making her cry on more than one occasion. I think about shouting at him some more, but I manage to hold myself back. I need all the allies I can get right now. Eventually he speaks again: 'I'm sorry. I shouldn't have said that.'

I let him stew as we edge across London Bridge. It's dark now, the misty cold damp night descending on London like a dark fog. People are shivering at bus-stops.

Suddenly, ahead of us, blue lights are flashing.

'Shit!'

I brake once more. Beyond is a police car, two policemen in fluorescent coats standing beside it. My heart races. Are they stopping cars? Is it a roadblock? Maybe they've heard about the penguin kidnap and are searching all cars heading south of the river. I try to calm myself. Maybe it's just a random breathalyser test. Or vehicle licensing.

My father says nothing, staring ahead. I breathe out – it's just a minor accident, the policemen are waving cars on. I drive by them, eyes ahead, hands gripping the steering-wheel. They don't give the blue Fiat a glance.

I glance into the rear-view mirror, and I can sense the penguin watching me through the sheet, head still, eyes focused. I get the feeling he wants me dead.

'I can't believe Sarah's gone.'

'What's that?' I ask, turning to look at my father, unsure if I've heard him correctly.

'It was all so sudden, such a terrible shock.'

I feel angry once more. Where is this coming from? Why the hell is he talking about Mum as we drive into South London with a stolen penguin on the back seat? This isn't about Mum. It's about Jes.

I try to contain my anger, hoping the moment has passed, but he continues talking, almost to himself: 'I guess Sarah knew best, not telling anyone about the illness. It was a brave thing in a way, it prevented us suffering all that pain with her. She was a strong woman. Too strong, maybe . . .'

I'm about to tell him to shut up when I notice his eyes are watery. I'm surprised, shocked almost. Is he crying? What the hell does he have to cry about? It should be me who's crying.

Doesn't he realize what a shock it was for me, for her, when he walked out on us? Doesn't he know that he screwed up our lives, pushing us from each other? Doesn't he know that when I was a child I considered killing my younger brother?

My father takes out a handkerchief. Old men with handkerchiefs always make me feel sad, they reveal such tender vulnerability. My anger dissipates slightly. He looks out at the line of red brake-lights along the road and says, 'God, I miss her, Scott.'

You could have knocked me over with a sardine. Even Norman II seems surprised: he shuffles in the box on the back seat, and shits again. The smell is terrible, but my father seems not to notice. 'I thought she was invincible. It was me . . . I . . . I was always meant to go first . . .'

He's crying bigger tears now. There were many times, in the past, when I dreamed of my father crying like this.

I wished for it like some children wish for ponies or violent video-games, so that I could laugh in his blubbering face. But now I can't laugh. I hate to admit it, but I feel a tiny bit sorry for him.

'It's funny. When you were born, Scott, our lives changed so dramatically.'

Now it's my turn to feel tears welling, as we edge towards the Elephant and Castle. My mother never talked about my birth. I try to be strong. I don't want to show him any emotion. But he's not looking at me. Instead he stares out at the giant red dancing elephants on the side of the desolate shopping centre.

'I remember the first time she spoke to you, just after the birth. She took you in her arms and said, "I'm here." She had a new voice, a voice I'd never heard before, as if a hormone or something had suddenly made her a mother.'

I know that voice too. It's the one I hear still.

My father continues, as if something in him has broken, releasing a stream of memories: 'She kept calling you "my son, my son". I wanted her to say "our son". But she never did.'

I am her son, I feel like saying. Not yours.

He's smiling now, but it's not a smile of joy, more the sort of smile that tries to conceal anguish. 'She was so protective. I'd let you crawl across the floor, and she'd scream at me for putting you in danger. I'd pick you up and she'd take you from me because I wasn't holding you properly. She used to drive me mad sometimes.'

'Is that why you walked out on her?' I'm sorry. I couldn't help it. It's a little flare of fury, lighting up inside.

'No. Not exactly.'

Now I feel it's my turn to remember. Yet my memories are angrier. I feel them burning up inside me, like a hot curry after six pints of strong lager. 'She went through hell after you pissed off to France!'

'Yes. I know. It can't have been easy.'

'It was fucking awful. For all of us!'

He's silent again. His jowly jaw is taut as if expecting pain. I don't want to disappoint so I proceed to tell him my version of the past. My bitter memories. On the back seat Norman II sits and listens. He has another shit and starts to gasp, small penguin pants.

I tell my father of the pain I felt. Of how I thought it was my fault, that I'd done something wrong. How I went over and over in my seven-year-old head the things I'd done in the days and weeks leading up to his departure – my sloppy maths homework, spilling a plate of baked beans, kicking a football into the vegetable patch, saying, 'Bloody hell,' when I slipped and tapped my head on the banisters.

I vomit it all out as we crawl along Kennington Park Road towards the Oval. To my surprise it feels good. I'm less combative than I'd imagined. My outpouring is slow, choked, like the grumbling stop-start London traffic.

I tell my father how our world tipped upside-down the day he left. How it hurt so much – the kids teasing at school, the cars passing our house with two parents smiling in the front seats, the fatherly shadow that turned out to be Mum's coat hanging in the hall. And I tell him about the smaller sufferings, the everyday misery.

'I got fat after you left. I couldn't stop eating, especially chocolate. Mars Bars mainly.'

'I like them too,' says my father, a little too amicably.

'I wasn't very happy,' I continue, but he isn't listening.

'You know, I was chunky as a boy,' he says, lost in thought. 'I could show you pictures . . .'

I stare ahead, jaw clenched, despairing that he can't even listen to me just once. Suddenly I wonder if this is what Jes feels like with me.

My father glances over, noticing my clenched jaw. 'Sorry. Sorry. Go on,' he says hurriedly, trying to hand the power back to me.

I think about remaining silent, to punish him. But I need to talk, I need to let him know about the past and how much he hurt us all. So I continue, more angrily now, 'Our world turned upside-down.'

I tell him how, after he left, Mum stopped letting us do things that he had been happy for us to do. In the twenty-four hours following his departure, football by the french windows was banned, as was running naked in the house. Spoons were only for desserts, we had to use a knife and fork for the mashed potato. And we had to be tidy. After he left, Mum became a tidiness freak. And because I wanted to make her feel better, I took to the new clean regime with vigorous dedication.

I'd berate Jes each day for leaving toys on the floor of his room. I told him one time that if he didn't clear up his Lego Mum would take him to the orphanage and leave him there. It's no wonder he threw a fit and told her he wanted to go and live at Zeb's house.

'I used to get mad at her because I didn't have a dad like my mates. I acted like it was all her fault.'

'Maybe it was.'

He says this so quietly that for a moment I'm unsure if I've heard him correctly. 'What did you say?'

He remains silent. He shakes his head, quickly, as if he's made a mistake. In that instant, my recent more tender feelings towards him explode in a *Lethal Weapon* fireball. 'For God's sake! You walked out on her! In case you don't remember!'

He looks at me. His face has hardened, the soft, flabby, ageing flesh tautening with more youthful anger. 'I've had enough of this, Scott! Yes, I walked out on her, as you put it, but it wasn't all my fault. It takes two to screw up a marriage.'

'Bollocks! You couldn't hack it, so you pissed off!'

'I couldn't hack it for a reason.'

'What? What fucking reason?' He is silent. I want to punch him, stab him, crush him. 'God, you make me sick!'

He looks at me, a short sharp glare. 'Your mother was having an affair.'

I almost crash into the back of a bus. I brake heavily, the penguin box slams into the back of my father's seat, my father shouts, 'KEEP YOUR EYES ON THE ROAD!' I pull out and swiftly overtake the bus, Tom Clancy's face glaring down at me from the side.

'Is the penguin all right?' I ask.

My father looks back. Norman II is panting again, like an unfit long-distance runner.

'His sheet's come off.'

'Put it back on.'

My father reaches behind and the penguin pecks him. He curses, and throws the sheet over its head.

'I don't believe you,' I say, quietly and menacingly.

'I promised myself I wasn't going to tell you. I'm sorry, but I've had enough of you hating me.'

'You're so full of shit!'

'It's true!'

'I don't believe you! Mum didn't have an affair!'

I didn't think it was possible to hate him any more than I have up to now, but it is. It must be a rare and wonderful talent, the ability to make people loathe you, shared only by a privileged few, like Judas Iscariot or Margaret Thatcher.

He remains silent. I start to feel a little better. He's just making it up. Maybe it's his idea of a joke.

'You're not very funny, for your information.'

'I'm not joking. Sarah was sleeping with someone else.'

'Is this the best you can do? Some soap-opera story about adultery? Jesus, you're worse than I thought, and I thought you were pretty bad.'

'You need to know the truth, Scott.'

'What truth? That you're a delusional old bastard who's spent nearly twenty-five years trying to think of an excuse for walking out on your wife and two small sons, and all you can come up with is some ridiculous hackneyed bollocks about her having an affair, when we all know she didn't have time to go shopping for shoes for herself, let alone screw some bloke on the side!'

'Not some bloke. Dickie bloody Bennett!'

I burst out laughing. This is the funniest thing I've heard

in years. Stooping, big-nosed Dickie? The secret agent? The man who dresses as if he's stepped out of an Edwardian dining room? 'Oh, please . . . Dickie Bennett?'

'Call him. Ask him. The bastard won't hide it. He'll admit to it, with his bloody English upper-class sense of fair bloody play. Except it wasn't fair play, was it? He stole my wife.'

Perhaps my father is a better actor than I've ever given him credit for. He's got all the emotions down pat. But, I remind myself, he's had almost twenty-five years to come up with this story. He's just gambling – one of his favourite pastimes – on me being too nervous or too protective of my own integrity to call my mother's ex-colleague and ask him if he was screwing her when we were kids. I decide the best method of defence is attack.

'I'd rather ask Mum. But, oh, what a shame, the one person who could easily verify your sordid little fantasy is now six feet under in an Edinburgh cemetery. That's convenient, isn't it?'

'Look, I'm sorry I told you, but it wasn't all my fault. Let's just leave it at that.'

'No, let's not just leave it at that. Let's just tell you to fuck off and leave us alone, once and for all! ALL RIGHT?'

On the back seat Norman II has shaken the sheet from his head. He is staring at me, a little shocked by my harsh tone. My father gazes out of his window.

We drive on in silence down the Clapham High Street to Clapham Common where there's another traffic jam. Images race through my head – my mother and father dancing, Dickie Bennett at our house in Grantchester, my mother's tears at the dinner-table as Jes and I stared down at our fish-fingers. Suddenly I remember her words after Edward Barron left us: 'It's not you, Scott, my love. It's me.' I remember her eyes, wide, crazed almost. Now, for the first time, I recognize that look. It was guilt.

As we head along the side of the common my father mutters something, then falls back into his hard-faced stare at the line of blinking red tail-lights, like so many angry eyes. 'I guess I just didn't make her happy.'

In this moment, somewhere past Balham, South London, my heart sinks, and I start to wonder if it's true. And the more I wonder, the more I get the feeling it *is* true. Something in my father's voice, the gravel, the emotion. Maybe people have a different voice when they're telling the truth, even good liars.

I remember Dickie Bennett at the wake. There was something in his look, the way he shook my hand, that exuded nervousness and culpability. He was like a child trying to cover up something he shouldn't have done.

I feel sick, as if I'm going to vomit up the three coronation-chicken sandwiches I consumed at the car-hire office. Not because my mother had an affair – the physical act seems so distant and unconnected from us now – but because the past I have considered so sacred, so solid and immutable, the past that in some ways I have founded my present and future upon, is crumbling. It's almost gone, a ship on the verge of sinking beneath the waves. Just as death robs us of a future, so my father's revelation has stolen my past. I feel like I'm falling, tumbling through empty space.

On the back seat the penguin pants, a deep rasping sound. He doesn't seem well.

'Why's he doing that?' asks my father, worriedly.

'He's stressed. They get like that when they're away from their colony.'

'I know how he feels,' says my father, trying to be funny.

The traffic is flowing more easily now. We're almost there. I turn past South Wimbledon station, down London Road, and finally left on to Hazelwood Road. As I park I look in the driving mirror. Norman II is staring at me, accusingly. My father looks across, as if wanting me to say something. But I'm not ready to admit that I believe him. Perhaps I never will be.

He takes his cigarette packet and opens the door. 'Well, you'd better get on with it, then.'

16

I stand outside the blue front door. There is no sign of
life from the house. I glance back at the car. On the back
seat, Norman II seems a little traumatized by his cross-
London journey. He rocks back and forth in the box like
an old Hasidic man. The box is sodden. Fishy poo has
seeped out on to the dazzling upholstery, complementing
the spearmint colour scheme. The Fiat smells of rotting
sardines. I am beginning to worry about my five-hundred-
pound vehicle damage excess.

It's six thirty p.m. People are returning home, bundled
against the cold, struggling with too many shopping bags.
Still I stand there, unable to ring the doorbell. My father
watches me: he's standing by the Fiat's passenger door
dragging on a cigarette. 'Come on,' he says grumpily. 'Get
a move on.'

I stretch out my arm, a finger crooked to push the bell.
I could turn and leave, but I need to see him. I want to
atone. I need forgiveness. Now more than ever. All I have
to do is ring, and everything could change.

I press the doorbell. The bell tinkles shrilly, a somewhat
effeminate ring. Nothing. I press it again. There is no
sound from inside the house. I push once more, long and
hard and a little bit angry. Next door a lace curtain twitches.
A car passes, drum and bass music pumping.

I ring one last time, for ten seconds.

This time the door opens. Jes stands there in black tracksuit trousers and a large white T-shirt that hangs over his belly like a veil. He seems surprised and more than a little annoyed to see me. He's wearing purple slippers, like a grandfather. 'Piss off!' he says, and begins to close the door.

I grab hold of the door frame. A splinter cuts into the palm of my hand. 'Ow!' I pull back my hand, and Jes slams the door. There is a spot of blood in the middle of my palm. I try to pull out the splinter with my teeth, to no avail. I hammer my other fist on the door in desperation. 'COME ON, JES! OPEN UP!'

Unsurprisingly, the door remains closed. The lace curtain trembles. A woman glances out of an upstairs window across the street.

'That's enough, Scott. I think we should be going,' says my father, more anxiously.

I pound Jes's front door with my fist. 'COME ON, JES! PLEEAASSE! JUST LISTEN TO ME!'

The door opens once more. Jes glares at me. I wonder if he's going to hit me again. 'Piss off! Both of you!'

'Listen to me!'

'What?'

'I've got something to show you.'

I take a step back to the car. He looks at me, mistrustfully, as if I'm ten years old again and about to lure him into doing something he doesn't want to do, like being tied to a tree so the Lone Ranger (me) can rescue him from Mexican *banditos* (also me).

'Come on. Just look. Please?'

He steps forward, glances to where I'm indicating, and stops. He leans in as if inspecting a painting. The penguin looks up from the back seat. It sees Jes and starts to rock and pant again.

'God!'

Jes peers through the car window, shading his eyes from the street-light reflection. The penguin stops rocking. It fixes Jes with a disgruntled stare. Jes stares back. For a moment I imagine my fat brother as a penguin, six foot tall and sixteen stone. It's a comforting image.

'Where did you get it?'

'London Zoo.'

'Jesus Christ!'

'This afternoon.'

'Why the fuck did you take it?'

I am silent. I had reasons. One big reason. But now, here, that reason seems small and petty and childish. 'I've given him a name. He's called Norman II.'

Jes looks at me. Then he looks at Norman II. 'You have lost your mind.' He turns and strides into his house. He slams the front door shut. The penguin squawks.

'You've got to do something with that bird,' says my father.

The drive back across London is tense. I now have the air-conditioning on and the windows open in an attempt to cool down Norman II, who has been panting more heavily with the sheet finally returned to his head. The cold air seems to be working, although my father is shivering. He tells me to wind up the windows, but going against his advice is still proving enjoyable.

Norman II rocks back and forth in his box, once more trying to shake loose the sheet that's supposed to be covering him. I try to convince my father to sit with him and hold the sheet firm over his head, but he declines. I can't blame him: the back seat is encrusted with penguin excrement.

Norman II gets more excited the further north we travel. Crossing Blackfriars Bridge, he swivels his head to look at the spotlit landmarks of London – Tate Modern, St Paul's Cathedral, and beyond to Tower Bridge. There is something childishly innocent about the way he bobs his head back and forth, viewing the city beyond his penguin pool for the first time.

'Come on! Cover him up!'

'It's dark, no one can see him!'

'Cover him up!'

Reluctantly, my father reaches behind and tries to place the sheet over Norman II's head. The penguin pecks him once more. My father curses. The air-conditioning hums. I speed up like a criminal in a getaway car, which I suppose I am.

My father tries one last time to conceal Norman II, thrusting the sheet at him like a matador. Norman II dodges his advance and pecks back. For a few seconds they continue this dance, back and forth, the penguin hampered somewhat by being constrained in a cardboard computer box, until at Smithfield Market my father is victorious, casting the sheet over the penguin's head. 'You have to sort this out!' he barks, bristling with anger as he nurses his bruised right hand. I ignore him and continue up Farringdon Road. As we pass the *Guardian* newspaper office, I consider stopping and leaving Norman II at Reception, imagining the headlines.

'PENGUIN KIDNAP THWARTED!'

'ILLEGAL ANIMAL TRADE EXPOSED!'

'POET IN PENGUIN LOVE TRIANGLE!'

But I can't let him go. He hasn't served his purpose yet.

I park outside my flat in Kentish Town. It's eight o'clock. I look up and down the road, but there doesn't seem to be anyone around. I open the door just as the hippie couple from next door come round the corner pushing their old-fashioned Oxfam pram. I freeze as if this is some childish game of musical statues. They stop at the steps down to their basement flat. I nod at them, which is about as friendly as you're supposed to be with your neighbours in London. They nod back. I wait as they unpack hippie-baby, which is dressed in a mini black kaftan, like a tiny Ayatollah, and disappear into the bowels of their vegetarian cellar.

The coast is clear.

I open the back passenger door, reach in and take hold of the penguin box. It's sodden with watery excrement. As I take it, Norman II angrily shakes off his sheet and grabs my forearm with his orange beak. His grip is surprisingly firm.

My father watches from the street, inhaling a cigarette. 'I don't think he likes you.'

Unable to come up with a witty retort, I ignore him, concentrating more on the penguin gripping my arm. I wriggle a little, trying to shake him loose. I take his head with my other hand, around the back of the neck, and try to prise him off my arm. But he's fixed there, refusing to budge. So I lift the box and the penguin from the car, the bird's beak still clamped to my forearm.

'Shit!'

I'm standing with a boxed penguin attached to my arm in the middle of Lady Somerset Road, NW5, a street not renowned for its Antarctic wildlife. At least it's dark, but somehow Norman II's eyes seem to gleam in the orange light of the street-lamp, like some Satanic child. I clasp the poo-soaked box in the crook of my right arm with the penguin still attached to the left, and hurry up the steps to my front door. As I get to the top, I realize that my keys are deep in my pocket and I'm going to have to put Norman II down to get them out.

'Where you went?'

I almost drop Norman II. Sitting at my front door is Frank. He's wearing a different suit, a shabby tweed number, with his black wellies, and his hair is even more debonairly slicked back than normal. He staggers to his feet. The penguin wants to look at this new threat, but he's still gripping my left forearm, which is now unhealthily numb. 'Er . . .' I say, helplessly.

Frank stares at Norman II. Until now I've considered Frank unshockable, even a little lobotomized, but he seems perturbed to see a real-life penguin on his street in North London. He starts to stammer, 'Pen . . . pen . . . pen . . .', spit flicking from the corner of his mouth. I'm afraid he's going to have a seizure.

'The thing is . . .' I mumble.

Then, just as suddenly, Frank stops stammering and reaches out a gnarled blue-veined hand, pausing just in front of the penguin's head. His hand is dead still, not even a tremble, and his eyes are now focused sternly on the bird. A strange cooing sound emanates from his scraggly throat.

Norman II releases my arm, and swivels his head to encounter this new enemy. But instead of pecking Frank's eyes out, or snapping at him, he shakes his head from side to side, then fixes the old man with a defiant stare. Frank, in turn, stretches out his hand further and scratches Norman II under his bill. The penguin lifts it and Frank continues to tickle its neck. Through the box I can feel Norman II vibrate like a cat or a mobile phone. He may even be purring.

'Gen-too . . .' stammers Frank, still tickling. I stare at him, amazed at the old man's way with flightless birds.

'Gen-too . . . peng-guin. Penguin!' he shouts happily.

'Not so loud, Frank.'

'GENTOO PENGUIN!' yells Frank.

'Be quiet!' I hiss furiously, like a pantomime villain.

Frank stops tickling Norman II, turns, pushes past me and hurries down the steps. He looks back once then walks away as fast as his ancient spindly legs will carry him.

The soggy box breaks as soon as I step into my hallway. Norman II falls through the bottom, hits the floor with moderate force, and topples over. He seems surprised and a little dazed. He struggles to right himself as I discard the shitty cardboard, then scrabbles upright and starts waddling down the hall, towards my bedroom. I dash after him, just managing to close my bedroom door. Now the only place for him to go is the bathroom, which is where I usually house penguins when they come to visit. He skitters into the small room, I follow him in and close the door quickly.

He's cornered. He backs away to try to hide under the wash-basin, panting. I run the bath with cold water, sprinkle in some salt, and open the window to give him cool air. I just pray he'll calm down. At least, with the window open, November in North London feels a little like the Antarctic.

I manage, somehow, to herd him up and into the bathtub, where he stands shaking his stubby wings, flinging water everywhere. I take a pilchard from the tin I've opened, wash off the tomato sauce and drop it into the water. Norman II looks at the sinking fish with disdain, then proceeds to kick and thrash at it, churning up the bath-water into a brown fishy stew.

'What's going on in there?' My father opens the bath-room door. 'Oh, God!'

'It's fine.'

My father stares at Norman II, mouth open. Then he says, 'Really, Scott, you have to take it back.'

'I can't,' I reply, sounding unintentionally childish. 'He's a present for Jes.'

'You haven't thought this through, have you?'

As my father says this, Norman II leans forward and

squirts out a stream of green liquid from his rear end. It splatters against the side of the bath and up on to my father's shirt. He exits the bathroom at full speed. It smells foul, like month-old fish stew.

I feel like laughing hysterically. I want to shake Norman II by the wing. He's dispatched my father, just as I wanted to, only with more style than I could ever have mustered. Even in my wildest fantasies, I never dreamed of crapping on him.

I take another pilchard and hold it as a trophy in front of the penguin's bill, but he doesn't make a move to snap at the fish, which dangles between his eyes. It's as if he's wilfully choosing not to eat. Perhaps he's on hunger-strike.

I drop the pilchard into the water and exit the bathroom. Through the crack in the door I spy on my new house guest. He remains there, upright in the tub, rocking back and forth.

I spend most of the night on the Internet. I can't sleep, turning over in my mind the two secrets I have recently uncovered.

I attempted fratricide (half-heartedly) at the age of seven.

My mother had an affair.

The first I can deal with. It's not unnatural to want to kill your siblings, is it? I mean, I was only seven. It was just a reaction to the hurt and abandonment I was feeling at the time. Honest.

But my mother's infidelity is harder to dismiss. I still want to believe that my father is lying, that he's the delusional old bastard I've always thought him to be. But somehow I know he's telling the truth. It's not just the evidence – my mother's words, her look of stricken guilt after Edward Barron left, Dickie Bennett's appearances at the house, his contrite handshake at the wake. It's more the feeling I have now. As if something that was previously a little off-centre has slotted into place.

I feel dizzy. I'm not disgusted that my mother had an affair – in fact, I'm a little relieved she had a bit of romance to compensate for all her hard work, bringing up two young boys on her own. But I am upset. There's so much I don't understand. Why did she keep this huge secret from me? Could she not have told me when I reached my eighteenth birthday or on some other auspicious occasion? Did she not trust me?

Did she not love me?

I think about our relationship. I've always thought we were close. Closer than some mothers and their sons, at least – Brian hasn't talked to his mum in months and Barry has never, to my knowledge, even admitted the existence of someone who gave birth to him.

I try to picture those times when we exhibited closeness. I want to catalogue the soft-focus moments when we shared secrets, feelings, when we were undeniably open with each other. The problem is, I can't think of any.

We'd have lunch together, dinner reasonably often, we'd celebrate birthdays, Christmas. She came to my book launch, and to *Word Up!* But there was always a distance between us. She would always gently, but insistently, push me away.

In reality, it was rare that we talked about emotional stuff, of hopes, needs and fears. Thinking about it now, I wonder if maybe we were scared of being too open with each other, lest the chink in the protecting barrier became a crack, then a hole, and the whole horrible painful mess of the past came rushing in, like a flood through a dam in a 70s disaster movie.

I wonder now. Did I simply invent this picture of my caring, open-hearted mother? Did I create a false image of our tightly knit little family unit, strong against the world?

Questions race through my head. Did she love Dickie Bennett? What attracted her to that tall, thin, awkward man with the big nose? Did the affair continue after my father left? Did she love us any less because we were a constant reminder of the man she no longer wanted?

I wish I could speak to her, delve into her emotions. I wish I could do an autopsy on her, the pathologist, and discover the reasons why she did what she did. I wish I could slice into something, put it under a microscope and say, 'That's it!'

But the histopathologist kept her secrets well hidden.

I want to call her. I pick up the phone, and her number is still programmed under MUM. I push the button. The number dials. My heart pounds for a moment, deluded into thinking she might answer, that this has all been a dream, like in a Shakespeare play, or a ratings-topping episode of *Dallas*.

'This number is no longer available,' says a curt recorded female voice.

This mother is no longer available.

270

I surf the web for penguin information as my mum walks in and out of my mind, both real memories and imagined settings, conversations I've had and others I invent as the night deepens. I stare at dozens of web pages, the screen glowing brightly in the darkness.

There are too many websites about penguins. There are children's school projects – crayon drawings lovingly scanned on to pages by admiring parents, showing blobby shapes that look more like Teletubbies than birds – penguin gift clubs (no, you can't give a penguin to someone – although imagine what a lucrative business that would be), and live web-cams from penguin pools around the world. Even the scientific papers, concerning latitudinal variations in wing size, still seem to worship the stubby birds, showing countless snapshots of the darling avians.

As I click through penguin cyberspace, I come across one site dedicated to Scott of the Antarctic. I dwell there for a few moments, seeking reassurance, clicking through the black and white photographs familiar to me from childhood. Scott stands in each frame looking so resolute, so tough, so clad in ragged fur, with various dumb-looking penguins in the background.

It was easier back then. In his day you didn't have to deal with emotions, needs and desires, with partnership issues and personal space. You just had to cross a thousand miles of frozen wilderness wearing shabby animal skins, and die heroically for your country. Compared to making a modern-day relationship work, marching for a hundred days across Antarctica, then freezing to death in a tent was a breeze.

I click off Scott and find a more friendly page. www.penguinfacts.com.

Here I discover that there are seventeen known species of penguins, ranging in size from the one-metre-high Emperor penguin to the Little Blue penguin of Southern Australia, which is the size of a coffee mug. All of them live in the southern hemisphere (no wonder Norman II is disorientated), apart from the Galapagos version, which resides on the equator in ninety-degree heat.

To my surprise, Frank seems to have been right about Norman II. He is a Gentoo. Gentoos come from the sub-Antarctic islands where they live in colonies of up to a thousand pairs, which might explain why Norman II is feeling a little lonely. Gentoos are two feet tall and weigh twelve to fifteen pounds – five to seven kilos. Apparently, the penguin on Penguin books is a Gentoo. What was Gentoo Norman doing in a pool of Jackass penguins?

I read the bit about Gentoo diets carefully. 'All penguins eat fish such as sardines, anchovies and pilchards, as well as squid. For Gentoos, the staple diet is krill.'

Damn. We don't have a krill shop in Kentish Town. You'd probably have to go to Kensington for that.

The final section of the site concerns penguin mating habits.

'Penguins usually mate for life, which is between ten and fifteen years. In some species the male will bring the female a stone, placing it at her feet as a gift to strengthen the bond between them. The female will then use these stone gifts to build her nest.'

I glance over at my CD shelf. There, next to the half-empty bottle of Glenlivet, is the stone Frank gave me, smooth-polished grey.

At three a.m. I creep into the bathroom with a fresh tin of pilchards. Norman II is not asleep, but at least he seems calmer. He stands at the far end of the tub staring at me. His eyes glint in the moonlight. I sit down on the toilet and wash a pilchard under the tap, carefully cleaning off the tomato sauce like a priest performing a religious ritual.

I hold out the fish. The penguin inspects me as if we're on a first date and I've just invited him back for coffee. He makes no move to grab the pilchard. A wave of despair washes through me.

Normal, sane people, when they need to apologize to someone or encourage someone to forgive them, send flowers or buy the person in question an alcoholic beverage, maybe even a slap-up dinner. I stole a penguin.

'What the hell was I thinking?'

Jes liked penguins when he was four years old. He's now twenty-six.

'Fuck, fuck, fuck!' I shout to myself, as Norman II watches me, pitifully. Then, swiftly, he grabs the pilchard, nipping my fingers.

'Ouch!'

I pull away my hand, my fingers throbbing. The penguin holds the fish in his bill, for a moment, still watching me, then tips back his head and gulps it down.

I look at him. He stares back at me.

'Thank you,' I say, quietly.

Some time later, I go into my bedroom and wake up my father. He groans and looks around him, trying to figure out where he is. 'What time is it?' he asks grumpily.

'Why did you just run away?' I ask.

'What?'

'Why didn't you stay around, at least for me and Jes?'

'It's four in the morning.'

'You should have stayed. You should have talked to us, helped us through it. You were just a bloody coward! Why couldn't you have been a man about it?'

He looks at me in the half-light, his eyes sleepy and confused. 'Be a man about it? What does that mean?'

For a moment he has me. I haven't a clue. It's just an expression. But I don't let this hold me up. I gather my forces once more, and ride back into battle. 'Why the fuck didn't you tell me about Mum before?'

'What? You believe me now?'

'You should have told me!'

'I was scared.'

'You are so bloody selfish. You should have told me. You should have told Jes. Maybe it would have changed things. Maybe it would have made a difference!'

'I'm sorry, Scott.'

'You've already taken my father away from me. Now you're trying to take my mother too!'

With this, I slam the door and go back into the living room where I angrily pull out the sofa-bed, making as much noise as I can. Something in me is hoping that he will follow me here and sit down to talk, like he did when I was scared of the dark as a child. But there is no sound, no footsteps. He remains in the other room, as separate from me as he has always been.

17

I wake from a terrifying dream in which I am stampeded to death by six-foot-high penguins who then use my head as a football while my mother laughs hysterically. The doorbell is ringing. I make the tough but necessary decision not to answer it. It rings again. I glance at the clock. Eleven thirty a.m. My father shouts something at me from the hallway. I put my pillow over my head and close my eyes. I hear him go to the door, some muffled voices, then nothing, until a voice grumbles, 'Get up, Scott.'

When I look up from my sofa-bed refuge, Jes is standing in the doorway. He's wearing jeans and a cardigan Sam gave him last Christmas. 'Where's the penguin?'

My heart leaps. Perhaps he has forgiven me. Perhaps it's all going to be all right after all. 'In the bathroom. Why?'

'Have you seen the news?'

'No. You woke me up,' I counter grumpily.

'It's on every channel,' says my brother, a little smugly.

'What happened?'

Jes doesn't answer but picks up the remote control and flicks on the television. On BBC News 24 the last headline, read by a stern-faced Moira Stewart, concerns the kidnap of an Argentine penguin from the world-famous penguin pool at London Zoo. My father starts laughing. My heart thumps.

The report features an eager young reporter 'live' at the London Zoo penguin pool. He stands in front of a group of solemn Jackass penguins, who resemble politicians after an election defeat.

'Yesterday at London Zoo the unthinkable happened. A young penguin was snatched by an unknown assailant . . .'

The reporter explains that the penguin wasn't just any old flightless bird. He was a recent gift of the Argentinian government – a peace-offering on the twentieth anniversary of the Falklands War.

'Shit,' I say, a little panicked. My father chuckles. Jes stares blankly at the television screen.

The picture cuts to fuzzy CCTV footage. My panic doubles. Where were the cameras? I didn't see any cameras. The penguin pool is shown, the crowds around the wall. Luckily the camera doesn't seem to have covered the area at the far end of the pool where Norman II was standing, and where I lurked before carrying out the heinous crime. As we watch, the first shaven-headed boy leaps over the wall into the enclosure.

'It seems that the boys acted as some sort of decoy . . .'

My father and Jes lean forward to see better. The three boys run round the poolside, then one slips, I think it's the blue-eared boy. He falls into the pool. The penguins dart away, the burly schoolteacher leaps into the water. It's actually quite exciting, like a North London episode of *Baywatch*.

'The boy, Ryan Masters, fell into the pool but was saved by

276

his teacher, David Stone, who heroically dived in after him.'

The footage shows Ryan Masters and his teacher now standing up in the pool, somewhat embarrassed to discover that it's only three feet deep.

'Both pupil and teacher were taken to the Royal Free Hospital for check-ups but were discharged soon afterwards. While police are keeping an open mind concerning the theft, they don't believe there is any connection to the Falklands conflict. One source I spoke to earlier said it was possible that Pedro was stolen to order, perhaps by a European rare-animal collector. Police are appealing to anyone who was at the zoo yesterday to come forward.'

The picture cuts to a square-faced, earnest young woman with straight dark hair wearing a green London Zoo sweatshirt.

'Zoo vets say they are very concerned for Pedro's health. Late last night head keeper Betty McCallister made an impassioned plea for the penguin's safe return.'

Betty McCallister speaks into a wad of microphones and tape-recorders held in front of her face: 'I want to ask whoever has taken Pedro to return him as soon as possible. Penguins are very sensitive. They are sociable birds and can be easily stressed on their own. Pedro might die if he is not returned to his colony.' At this point, Betty McCallister starts to cry. It's subtle, not a full-blown sob, but her eyes become shiny, and she wipes them with her hand. When she speaks again, her voice cracks: 'I ask you, whoever you are, please give our penguin back.' With that, she bursts into tears. The microphones and tape-recorders pull back a little, and an arm appears on her shoulder.

The picture cuts back to the grave-faced reporter: 'The Argentinian embassy has just issued a statement expressing hope for the speedy return of the bird known as the Peace Penguin. Police are today carrying out a forensic examination of the area here at the zoo in a bid to find any clues. They have to work fast, as time is running out. Back to you in the studio, Moira . . .'

'All that carry-on for a bloody bird!' snorts my father.

'How could anyone steal the Peace Penguin?' says Jes, cheerfully. 'It's awful.'

'What are you doing here, Jes?' I ask, glaring at him. 'Why didn't you just call to say we were on telly?'

'I wasn't on telly. I had nothing to do with this!' my father interjects angrily.

'I thought you should know. That's all.'

As the BBC news cuts to an item about sausage-making in Shropshire, I realize I'm starving.

'Hadn't you better check on the penguin?' Jes asks.

'I will. I just need some food first.'

I make myself some porridge. I offer Jes a bowl – he loves porridge, with lots of butter and brown sugar.

'I'm not hungry.'

'Come on, just a small bowl.'

'I'm not hungry. All right?'

My father also declines, preferring instead to smoke a cigarette on the steps outside. I eat my porridge in under a minute, then make myself another bowl. Jes watches as I eat. 'Tapeworm?' he asks, without humour.

'Must be.' I finish the bowl and chug down a glass of

orange juice. I wonder about telling Jes of our mother's affair, socking it to him right here and now. That would wipe the grin off his face. But just as I'm about to he says, 'I'm going to check on the penguin,' and heads off to the bathroom.

The sight that greets us upon opening the door is fairly spectacular. My bathroom now resembles a Jackson Pollock painting. The room is completely sprayed with green shit. There are lines of fishy poo across the tiles. There are little pools of poo on the floor. The room smells foul. Both Jes and I gag.

'What have you done to him?' asks Jes, appalled.

'I fed him. He seemed happy enough.'

'Yeah. Shit happy!'

To be honest, I'm simply glad the penguin is still alive. I was expecting him to be lying in the tub, scaly feet in the air, having breathed his last in the night.

'"The Peace Penguin".' I snort, derisively. 'That's the stupidest thing I've ever heard!'

'You have to take him back.'

'They'll arrest me.'

'I wonder what you'd get for stealing a penguin.'

'Thanks for your support.'

I get out a pilchard and wash it, then hold it out to Norman II, who eyes me, then Jes. He steps forward gingerly, takes the fish from my fingers, and gulps it down. 'You see?' I say triumphantly. 'He likes me.' I watch the bird swallow the fish and wonder if the Peace Penguin can possibly bring peace to me and my brother, after all these years.

As if answering my thoughts, Jes shakes his head and says, 'Why the hell did you steal it?'

'I don't know.'

'Was it for me?'

'I don't know.'

'To say sorry or something?'

'I don't know.'

'You're so strange.'

'I know.'

My father enters the bathroom and almost chokes on the smell. 'Jesus wept!' The penguin backs away in the tub.

It's quite crowded now. My father remains by the toilet. Jes chooses the open doorway. I stand by the wash-basin. Norman II rocks back and forth at the end of the tub.

We watch him. He watches us.

'*Three Men and a Penguin*,' says my father, in a tone that suggests he thinks he's being funny.

'*And a Baby*, Dad,' says Jes.

This annoys me immediately, the way he calls our father 'dad', so easily, so blamelessly.

'What baby?'

'It was *Three Men and a Baby*. With Tom Selleck.'

'Yes, I know. I was making a joke. You know, to try to lighten the mood.'

We fall into silence. Four hearts beating, one of them avian. We all feel uncomfortable, but no one makes a move to depart. It's as if we've sought refuge in this small, stinking bathroom. It's as if this is our shelter from the outside world, the world where women abandon us, or die.

I've not been so physically close to my brother and father since I was seven.

'This is strange,' says Jes. My father and I nod, for want of anything better to say.

After a minute or so, my father coughs and declares, 'Last time I was with you two in a bathroom you were tiny.'

'That was a while ago,' says Jes, attempting a smile.

'Yes. A long time,' says my father. 'A very long time.'

Jes looks at me, a quick raise of the eyebrows as if to say, 'Great, the old man's cracked.' In that shared glance I feel closer to my brother than I have in ages. It's as if we're tapping into a secret language, a code learned as children that has been forgotten and now remembered. It feels . . . warm. We both look away, a little embarrassed.

'Oh, well,' says my father, by way of conclusion. He falls silent, perhaps lost in memories of us as children when we were as short as penguins and he could carry us in his arms.

Norman II looks at us. If he could speak, I know what he would say: 'What a bunch of losers!'

Instead, the Peace Penguin opens his bill and coughs out a long stream of green slime, which drips into the bathtub. We watch in growing horror as the slime continues to stream from his mouth, like he's an extra in some low-budget horror movie.

'What the hell is that?' exclaims my father.

'Half-digested fish,' says Jes, as if this is so obvious it hardly bears mentioning.

'That's the most disgusting thing I've ever seen,' continues my father. Norman II finishes spewing up pilchard and squawks proudly.

'Maybe it's a gift,' I say, brightly. 'To thank us for looking after him.'

'I'm not cleaning that!' says my father, shaking his head. 'You have to take him back!'

'That's what I said,' adds Jes, smugly.

'HE'S MY FUCKING PENGUIN! I'M NOT TAKING HIM BACK!' I shout, manically.

Before either of them can react to my outburst, the doorbell rings. We all jump, hearts racing, terrified that it might be the police, or the Argentinian government, or an irate bunch of London Zoo keepers ready to beat the shit out of the cruel, evil man who stole their penguin.

'Don't answer it!' I whisper.

The bell rings again, loud, long and ferocious.

'You'd better see who it is,' says my father.

'Why?'

'It might be important.'

'I'll go,' says Jes. 'I'm not implicated.'

'No,' I say vehemently. 'I'll just check who it is. Keep quiet. If necessary, we can pretend no one's home.'

At the living-room door I crouch down, then slide along the floor on my belly – I never used to have a belly – like a soldier behind enemy lines. I'm more scared now. What is the penalty for stealing a penguin? A fine? A year's community service? A five-year stretch in Wormwood Scrubs?

I pull myself up at the window, just enough to be able to see who's standing at the front door.

It's Big Barry. He's never been to my flat before. I didn't even know he knew where I lived. I open the door. 'All right, Brains. It took me bloody ages to find this place. You really do live in the suburbs, don't you?'

He looks awful, like someone who hasn't slept for forty-eight hours, and there's a not-too-faint scent of alcohol and cigarettes clinging to his wool coat. His eyes are puffy, the bags under the big lids like yellowing bruises, and his hair is ungroomed – which is a little like the Pope deciding not to wear a crucifix.

Suddenly I'm afraid he's seen the penguin theft on television and somehow worked out it was me. Now he's here to blackmail me – although why someone who earns ten times what I do would want to blackmail me isn't yet clear.

'What's up, Barry?'

Barry looks down at his feet, then runs a large hand through his greasy hair. 'I dunno. I just . . .' He looks away down the street, unable to meet my gaze. Then he turns back, his big nose sniffing like a bloodhound's. 'What the fuck is that smell?'

The Bosphorus Café-Diner is a scary place in daylight. The walls reveal grease-stains that would be of great value to nutritional archaeologists seeking to determine the diets of Kentish Town citizens over the last sixty years. Between the oily splats are curling posters of various esoteric Turkish landmarks, such as a motorway bridge in Ankara and a waterfall outside Erzurum that looks like it might be the result of a burst drain.

As for the staff, they seem even less friendly in the

283

daytime, if this were possible. On the morning shift, the short, muscled Turkish men – four moustaches and a toupee – stand behind the counter and glare at the customers as if daring them to take a swing.

Barry nurses his tea and three sugars while I tuck into a large Breakfast Special. In the confines of the café, surrounded by builders and traffic-wardens on their extended lunch breaks, and little old men reading the *Sun* from back to front, Barry seems smaller. He hunches over the table as if he's cold. His hand trembles as he raises the tea to his lips. Then he runs his hand through his unkempt hair again. 'I'm sorry, Brains. I don't know.'

'What don't you know, Barry?'

Barry stirs his tea again, even though the sugar has long since dissolved. 'They fired me.'

I munch my forkful of sausage. I bite through the crisp, almost plastic exterior, then chew into the fat-juice interior that's it's best not to think about in case you start imagining what it might contain. I'm buying myself time to think.

There are two unique things to consider here. First, Big Barry has lost the job he seems born to do. Second, he's telling me about it.

I put down my fork and look at him. 'But you're their best broker.'

'They fired our whole department. New York's cutting back. It's been on the cards for months.'

He looks at me, eyes wilder now. I realize that, for the first time in the thirteen years since I've known Big Barry, he's scared.

'What am I going to do?'

'You'll find another job.'

'No one's hiring.'

'They'll hire you. You're the best.'

'Not any more.' He stirs his tea one more time, then looks up. 'What will Nancy say?' His voice is surprisingly small.

'You haven't told her?'

'I can't, Brains.'

I think about this. Until a minute ago, I'd have thought Barry would be more worried about losing his income, his status and his company Porsche than the opinion of a big-breasted brunette he's only been screwing for a couple of months – after all, he has never had a shortage of big-breasted brunettes, not to mention most other hair colours. There is only one conclusion to be drawn: he must be serious about her.

Now, I don't know Nancy at all, but from the brief time we spent together at sixty-second dating she seemed like a woman partial to rich men in gainful employment. 'You guys have been getting on pretty well, haven't you?'

He nods sadly.

'Well, then, she'll be fine about it. She isn't going out with you for your cash.'

'No?' he mumbles, as if trying to convince himself.

'Tell her about it, Barry. Don't hide it. I mean, it could bring you both closer together.'

'You think?'

I've no idea. What do I know about women?

'Definitely. You can't pretend everything's okay when it's not. You have to be honest.'

Listen to me. The king of pretending everything's okay when it's not. But I'm changing. Aren't I?

'I can't tell her.'

It's suddenly clear to me that, for Barry, explaining his situation to Nancy will be the same as explaining his situation to himself, so he's decided on secrecy.

'You have to. Put yourself at her mercy.'

'What do you mean?'

'Tell her everything. Then see what she decides to do. Maybe she'll surprise you.'

'You think?'

'Definitely.'

At Kentish Town underground station, Barry hugs me. I can't remember him ever having hugged me before. Come to think of it, I can't remember him ever having travelled by public transport before. He informs me that he's now saving money, but doesn't explain the hug.

It's dark as I make my way back to the flat. I sit on the low wall at the top of Lady Somerset Road. I need a breather.

Like Norman II, I feel like I'm in the wrong hemisphere. Everything's upside-down. Jes is looking thinner, I'm looking fatter. My mother had an affair with a man who looks like Sherlock Holmes, and I'm taking care of my long-forgotten father. And, by all accounts, I'm happier than Big Barry for the first time ever. What's going on?

The past that was so set, that seemed as if it would dictate the present for ever more, has gone. It's like one of those newspaper stories you believe, only to find a few weeks later that the whole thing was an invention or a

286

mistake. There should be a retraction: 'We wish to apologize for the error in printing this version of the past. It was in no way correct. We are sorry for any inconvenience.'

Maybe I was wrong. You don't have a thousand futures, but only one past. You have a thousand pasts, but only one future.

As I sit under the streetlight, watching a leaf on a green-barked tree shiver in the wind, Frank appears from his alleyway. He shows no surprise to find me sitting on the wall. He's holding something to his chest like a shield. He shuffles up and hands me a large hardback book. I look at the cover: *A Children's Illustrated Book of the Animal Kingdom*.

'Look!' he says, emphatically. He sits down alongside me and starts to turn the pages, carefully, almost reverentially, like an old monk with an ancient illuminated manuscript seeking to show a novice the secrets of his order. The paper is faded, tattered at the corners. Some of the pages are ripped or stained with a brown substance. He stops at a page marked with a thin black plastic comb. He takes the comb, places it in his pocket, and points at the book. 'Gentoo penguin!' he says proudly.

He's right. The double-page spread depicts a happy Antarctic scene, populated by cheerful penguins of various species. And there, on the right-hand page, standing proudly on an icy outcrop is a Gentoo penguin – the spitting image of Norman II, with the white splodge over his eyes and his small pink feet.

'Read,' he says, emphatically.

'I've got to go, Frank.'

'Scott, read!'

'Frank . . .'

'Scott, read, please!'

His voice is insistent, desperate almost. I feel responsible. I take the book from him. He sits back, expectantly. I clear my throat: '"Penguins live in Antarctica, the coldest place on earth. They have two layers of feathers and a layer of fat to keep them warm. They spend much of their life in the water, and their bodies are perfectly shaped for swimming. Look at the Gentoo penguin here . . ."'

Frank glances at the page.

'"Can you see how he is different from other birds?"'

'Little wings!' states Frank, categorically.

'"He has little wings,"' I read. '"They are stiff and act like paddles when he's swimming."'

Frank nods gently. 'Stubby tail!' he barks.

'"He also has a stubby tail, which he uses as a rudder. He can move very fast through the water . . ."'

As I read, I hear my mother's intonation, her measured expression, as she sat by my bed reading *Highland Stories for Boys*. I finish the penguin page and stop, shutting the book slowly. 'Well, Frank, I'd better be off now.'

'More.'

'I really have to be –'

'More!' He grabs the book, opens it to a double-page spread on the African savannah, populated by wildebeest, lions and giraffes. '*More!*' he shouts.

I'm tired. I want to go home. I've done my bit, I've been patient, I've done more than most. 'Look, I'm sorry but it's late, I've got to go . . .'

I stand. He stares at the African savannah, engrossed

in the lurid portrayal of a lion tearing a hyena to pieces.

'Well, I'll see you around . . .'

Frank looks up again. *'Scott, read!'* he shouts with surprising violence.

'No. I'm going.'

'Read!'

I suddenly feel angry. I've been kind to him, patient and giving. Why can't he just leave me alone?

I decide to turn the tables on him. 'Where did you get this book?'

'Read!'

'Was it a present? Did you steal it? Did you find it in a tip?' In this moment I am possessed by the desire to know more, fed by anger and irritation and my continuing curiosity. I want to know his secrets, his story, the reason he's alone and slow and uncared-for, with only a tattered children's book to keep him company. 'Where do you come from, Frank? What's your story? What's your past?'

He looks down at the book once more, avoiding my questioning.

'Who's Maggie?'

'Shut up,' says Frank, a sudden two-syllable growl.

'What did you say?'

'Shut up!'

'There's no need to be rude –'

He snatches up the book and, with surprising agility, leaps to his feet. 'Shut up!' He pushes past me and walks away down the street, murmuring curses to himself. To my shame, I'm relieved.

*

Back at the flat Jes sits at the table in the window, staring out into the dark street. His face is white, his shoulders hunched. He seems more fragile than ever, his normal cheerful mass shrunken. I pray it's not more bad news. My father follows me in. 'Sam left a message on his mobile,' he whispers, conspiratorially.

'What did she say, Jes?' I ask quietly.

My brother doesn't look up. 'She's staying with her friend Rachel. In Camden.'

'Rachel?'

'You met her at the hospital after . . . you know . . .'

I do know. I feel a flash of excitement in my belly. 'Camden's just down the road,' I say, a little too enthusiastically.

'She doesn't want to see me. That's what she said in the message.'

He sounds so sad, without hope. I feel an immediate compulsion to cheer him up.

'Women always say that,' I declare, with absolute conviction, 'but they don't always mean it.' I glance at my father for affirmation.

'Sometimes they mean it,' he says helpfully.

'How do you know if they mean it?' asks Jes, his eyes flicking back and forth between us, like a child seeking wisdom. My father and I stand there, silent – as if we're a stepfather and natural dad, competing over the boy we both call 'son'.

My father is about to speak when I interrupt, fearing his next enlightenment: 'Look, I could come with you to Camden. You could talk her into coming back.'

Jes fixes me with a disdainful stare. 'What would I say? She didn't want this baby, but she definitely didn't want to lose it. I can't just call her up and tell her everything's going to be okay, not to worry, let's just get back to normal.'

I try to think of a response, something, anything to make him feel better. Nothing comes.

I retreat to the bathroom with a tin of mackerel. Norman II looks up as I enter. He seems almost pleased to see me. I sit on the toilet seat once more. After a short while he waddles up the bathtub towards me, then stops, two feet away. He looks at me, tenderly, I think. I take out a piece of mackerel, wash off the oil and hold it out for him. He takes it and swallows. I pick out another chunk. 'I'm sorry about all this,' I say gently.

Norman II looks at me.

'I hope you understand. It wasn't personal.'

The penguin cocks his head to one side, as if listening. To my surprise, tears are welling in my eyes. I want to hug him. But I manage to restrain myself. I've put him through enough already.

He takes the fish.

'You do understand, don't you?'

Norman II squawks once, and I feed him the rest of the can of mackerel.

At ten p.m. I make myself some pasta – no one else seems hungry. I ask Jes if he wants to stay the night. He agrees, reluctantly. And so it is that I share a bed with my brother for the first time since holidays when we were eight and three respectively, while our father sleeps in the living room. We are a family reunited. Sort of.

I lie there, trying not to think. It feels good to be horizontal. I don't feel so dizzy. So much has happened. So much has been uncovered. My past has been sliced open.

I want to tell my brother about our mother, her infidelity and the real reason our father left us. I want to confess how I placed a pillow over his innocent, childish face, but I don't want to freak him out any more than he is already. There will be a time for the past to be reworked when the present is more stable. If the present ever becomes more stable.

I lie next to my fat brother, aware of his bulk, turned away from me. We are so close, barely a foot apart, yet it's like there's a steel partition between us.

As the night minutes tick by, we each listen to the slow tapping of Norman II pacing back and forth across the bathroom floor.

None of us sleeps well.

18

Dawn is softening the orange glow of the London night. Low mist whispers between skeletal winter trees. A dog barks. On the back seat of the Fiat Punto, the penguin sits quietly in a fresh cardboard box (Waitrose Andalusian Clementines, sturdy but compact).

I'm sitting with my brother in a car park on the north side of the Outer Circle of Regent's Park. It's freezing outside, but we have the windows open to prevent Norman II overheating. Our breath billows in the cold air. We hug ourselves, trying to keep warm.

As light yawns into the sky, we can see frost glisten among the grass. There's ice on the puddles. A milk float groans past, shuddering in the cold.

Jes looks exhausted. He cradles a cup of coffee made while it was still night in my tiny kitchen. I'm munching a Mars Bar. I've offered Jes some three times, but he's refused. In the twenty-four hours since he turned up at my flat he hasn't eaten anything, despite my urging.

He woke me at five, insisting we take the penguin back to London Zoo. 'It's not fair!' he whispered ferociously. 'He needs to go home!'

'He's fine. He likes it here.'

'We have to take him back!'

And so we are sitting here in silence at six fifteen on a

293

November morning. I wonder if I should start up a conversation, but I'm too tired. I don't want to take Norman II back, I feel sort of attached to him, but I know Jes is right. I guess I was always intending to return him. It's just . . .

I can't believe it. I used to hate penguins.

We sit in awkward silence. Jes opens the passenger door and pours the dregs of his coffee on to the frozen Tarmac, which steams like a mini primeval swamp.

'When do you think someone's going to arrive?'

'I don't know. I reckon we should wait till six thirty. Then we take him over there.'

On the back seat Norman II starts to pant a little. 'Maybe he's excited to be going home?' I say lightly.

'He's fucked,' Jes says, more brutally. 'Poor bird.'

I think about arguing with him, pointing out that the penguin has had a fine old time on his short luxury break in Kentish Town, but I know Jes's moods. He's tired, depressed about Sam, and spoiling for a fight. Instead I look out, towards the entrance to London Zoo. An early-morning jogger is approaching, head down, pounding the streets. I feel a sudden twinge of guilt. I haven't run in two months. I haven't had the energy.

'I still don't know why you took him,' mutters Jes.

This annoys me, despite my attempts at positive feelings. I thought we'd established why I took the penguin. It was supposed to be a symbol, a gift of apology and love. I thought Jes knew this. I thought it was understood between us. But now he wants to push me away again, here in our blue Fiat Punto at six twenty-two in the morning. I think about spelling it out for him, about digging up the subtext: 'Okay, Jes, I wanted to give you the penguin to say sorry for all those times in the past when I hurt you, physically and emotionally, and in particular that time when I tried to kill you by putting a pillow over your head.'

But I say nothing. As usual.

Jes stares sullenly at the jogger running past. Once again I recognize we are at a moment where things could go either way. I could start to dig my trench, set up the artillery and embark on the conflict as I have done many times in the past. Or I could wave a white flag, hold out the olive branch and release the white doves.

There's only one way to go. Negotiate.

'All right. I admit it wasn't the best idea I've ever had.'

As if in confirmation, the penguin starts panting again, more deeply this time. Jes turns to look at him. 'He's fucked. I'm getting him some help.'

With that my brother gets out of the Fiat, opens the back door and reaches in to pick up the Waitrose box.

'Wait.'

He pulls the box out of the car, steps back, the bottom falls out and the penguin tumbles to the grass.

'Shit!'

By some miracle of physics, Norman II lands on his tiny pink scaly feet. He seems surprised. Jes grabs for him, but the penguin has realized he's free and is not about to pass up such an opportunity. Like an Energizer Bunny he sets off across the grassy verge in the direction of Camden Town. He moves quickly, waddling from side to side as he runs, small pink clawy feet scampering.

'Great, Jes . . .' I say, getting out of the car. I start to run after our errant captive. Jes just stands there, open-mouthed, still holding the box, watching the sprinting penguin.

Norman II is nearing the second car park. I'm gaining on him, but I'm puffing already, cursing my recent inactivity. Beyond are some railings and a main road where, even at this hour, cars are lined up, forming a nascent rush-hour traffic queue.

I catch up with Norman II as he reaches the second car park. I holler at him, 'Here, boy! Here, boy!' like some demented shepherd. He turns abruptly. A man glances over from his car, eyes wide at the sight of a small penguin sprinting across an empty car park chased by a six-foot man in a parka.

To my relief, Norman II starts heading back across the car park towards the Punto. Jes drops the box and heads to cut off the penguin from the road, waving his arms like a football referee denying a penalty.

'Hey-ho!' he shouts.

I close on Norman II. Jes moves quickly, blocking his path. We've almost got him. Norman II makes a dash for the gap between the Fiat and Jes's left leg. I throw myself at him in a clumsy rugby tackle and fall to the ground with my hands around his fat little stomach. Norman II wriggles, but I just manage to hold firm.

'Sorry, mate,' I murmur apologetically. In reply Norman II lifts his backside and a warm spurt of penguin poo hits me between the eyes.

Jes runs up with the box and places it over the penguin's

head. 'Ay-carumba!' exclaims Jes, staring at my poo-stained forehead. 'That was a great shot.'

We drive to the zoo entrance and I carry the box from the car. I am about to place Norman II on the ground outside the locked gates when the jogger rounds the corner. My heart hammers in my chest. The jogger slows, then stops, remaining a few feet away, as if he might catch something. He's in his late thirties, with thinning hair and expensive running shoes. I hold the cardboard box. The penguin's head swivels round to look at the sweating man.

'What are you doing with that penguin?' asks the man, accusingly.

I try to think of an answer, but I can't. He's got me. He's seen the television reports, read the newspapers. He knows this is the Peace Penguin. I feel sick to my stomach, not because I've been caught (it's a relief, almost), but because it's my fault that my brother's also been caught. I'm supposed to be the eldest, the responsible one, and I've just dragged him down with me.

'It's worming season,' says Jes, gruffly.

I turn quickly, not a little alarmed. My brother is eye-balling the purple-suited jogger as if he might be the most annoying man he's ever met.

'We have to worm them,' he continues drily. 'It's not pleasant.'

'Oh,' says the jogger. 'Really?'

'Yes. It's their summer, you see, in Antarctica, and that's when they get worms. In their anus.'

'Oh.'

'You have to clean them out. It's not a pretty job.'

'Oh, yes. Our dog got worms last year.'

'So you know what I'm talking about.'

'Yes.'

'Well, if you'll excuse us . . .'

Jes steps towards the locked side-gate into the zoo, takes out a bunch of keys.

'Sorry,' says the jogger. 'I just thought . . .'

'We really must get to work,' says Jes, pretending to fumble through his keys. 'There's another forty to do before tonight. It's going to be hell.'

'Right. Of course,' says the jogger, resorting to the English default of mumbling deference.

'I think I picked up the wrong keys,' says Jes, turning to me. 'Do you have yours?'

'Shit. I think I left them at the surgery,' I say, warming to the pretence. 'I can go back and look.'

'Good luck with the worms,' says the purple jogger, hurriedly, and runs off, faster than ever. Slowly I place the box on the ground.

'Wow,' I say.

'Let's get out of here,' says Jes.

At 6.47 a.m., at the side gate to London Zoo, a large woman in a cleaner's uniform approaches the cardboard box. In the hire car parked further down the road, Jes and I watch in silence. She stops, mistrustful. She's probably afraid it's a terrorist bomb. Then Norman II sticks his head out of the hole. The woman jumps, as if in a cartoon, her feet seeming to leave the ground for a second. She bends down for another look. Norman II nods to her, almost regally, and she dashes past him into the zoo.

After a minute or so, the woman returns with two men in keeper's uniforms who walk slowly, oozing scepticism. Then Norman II pokes his head out of the box once more, the two keepers take a step back, have a quick discussion and carry the boxed penguin into the zoo.

We remain for a while, listening to the whir of the Punto's heating system. The road is busier now, more cars zipping by, thinking they've found a cunning short-cut until they reach the jam leading from the traffic-lights at the Marylebone Road. It's daylight, a thin, milky sky. I miss our penguin already.

'I should be going,' says Jes, eventually.

'You're more than welcome to stay at mine.'

He says nothing.

'Look, I know it isn't my business, but maybe you should call Sam. You know, try talking to her.'

'I did.'

'When?'

'Last night. One in the morning.'

'What did she say?'

'Nothing.'

'She said nothing?'

'To begin with. Then she cried a bit.'

'That's good, isn't it? Crying's good. She misses you.'

'She said it's over. She doesn't want us to be together any more.'

I feel a thud in my stomach. I was wrong. I don't want

Jes to be single like me. Sam cannot leave him. I can't imagine my brother without her. They love each other. They are my shining light, my golden couple, my example of what could be. If they split up, what hope is there for anyone?

'She said she definitely wants to break up?' I ask, my voice trembling a little.

He looks out at the traffic, the puffing line of cars. 'Sort of.'

'What does that mean?' I say hopefully.

'She doesn't want to see me. She's not sure what to do. She thinks maybe we shouldn't talk for a while.' He's trying to hold back tears.

For the second time in my life, I put my hand on his shoulder. 'It's going to be okay, Jes. Really it is . . .'

He pulls away, almost violently. 'No. It's not going to be okay.'

I take a deep breath, trying to stay calm, to be strong for him. 'Look, why don't I talk to her? We get on well, maybe she'll listen . . .'

'What? Like she listened to you at the hospital? When you told her to get some space from me? No fucking thank you!'

Oh dear. Here's another fine mess I've got myself into. I hurry to attempt an explanation: 'I was just trying to make her feel better. I'm sorry, I didn't think she was even listening to me . . .'

'Why do you have to get involved, Scott? Is it because you're jealous? You want to fuck it up for me?'

'I just wanted to help.'

'Don't talk to her!' He's turned to me, eyes narrowed. 'Don't make it any worse than it already is! I don't need your help! I'm sick of you trying to help me!'

'Come on, Jes . . .'

'You're just like Mum. Always trying to control me. Jesus, it's like you think I'm still five years old!'

'There's no need to bring Mum into it.'

'You never listen to me, do you? God, it's so pathetic! It's like I don't even exist!'

'I listen. Of course I listen.'

Jes breathes out, an exaggerated sigh, like a church-hall actor. I get the feeling he's playing out a role he's already rehearsed, words he's already written. 'I'm going to tell you something that I don't want to tell you, but maybe it'll help you understand a little bit. Maybe it'll finally get through that thick, selfish skull of yours.'

'I'm listening.'

'You, Scott Barron, my big brother, have been my hero ever since I can remember. My biggest hero. Yeah, funny, isn't it? Have you any idea what it's like to have your hero think you're an idiot?'

I'm his hero? You could have fooled me. Maybe this is just a tactic to set me on the defensive, to make me feel guilty. I wonder if he's inherited this approach from our father, Edward Barron, the king of making you feel guilty.

'Come on, Jes. I'm not your hero. You think I'm a selfish git. You think I'm a narrow-minded, conservative arsehole. Most of the time you can't even stand me.'

He looks at me with what he wants to portray as pity in his eyes. 'No, Scott. That's how you feel about yourself.'

'Ouch,' I say, with exaggerated sarcasm, trying to pretend that he hasn't hurt me.

'Mum always said it,' Jes continues, sounding almost smug. '"Scott doesn't even realize you worship him,"' she said to me once. Imagine how that made me feel? That my own mother saw how dependent I was on you, and how you didn't give a shit about me!'

'Well, Mum was full of surprises, wasn't she?' I can't quite believe I'm doing this. Before I can stop myself I say, 'Did you know she was sleeping with Dickie Bennett?'

As soon as it's said, I wish with every nerve ending that I'd kept my mouth shut. Jes's face turns white, but I can't turn back. It's like I'm watching myself sitting there, changing our lives for ever. 'Yeah. Dad told me. Spilled the beans, as it were. Mum was having an affair. That's why Dad left us.'

Jes looks at me, aghast. He's breathing heavily, like a stressed penguin. His hands are trembling. 'Dad told you? Shit . . .'

'Two days ago. I'm really sorry . . .'

'I can't believe he told you.'

'What?' Now it's my turn for the blood to drain, my heart to spin. Jes glances out of the window at the gathering traffic. 'You knew?'

Jes shakes his head, but I know it's not denial, more disbelief at the suddenness of a situation he hadn't envisaged ever having to deal with. I can't breathe.

'Yeah.'

'How long?'

'Dad told me about six, seven years ago, in France.' He

looks at me, now trying to show compassion in his eyes. 'I'm sorry. He said he wasn't going to tell you.'

'What? Why?' My voice is small and lost.

'He thought it was best.'

'I can understand him not telling me . . . But you?'

'I was going to. But somehow I couldn't. You loved Mum so much.'

I am stunned. My little brother has been holding this huge secret from me. He's been trying to protect me by keeping me in the dark. What right has he to control me like that? What right has he to patronize me? With every breath my anger doubles. Jes is stammering now, flailing like someone who can't swim: 'Yeah, look, I should have told you. I'm really sorry. But at least now you know.'

'Get out!'

'I'm sorry, Scott –'

'Just get out!'

I reach over. He jerks back, an impulse I recall from childhood when occasionally I would lash out at him or try to snatch one of his penguins or his blanket. I tug at the passenger-door handle, my elbow nudging into his big fat stomach. 'Get out,' I implore, sounding less enraged.

Jes just sits there, looking at me with his big brown eyes. 'You see now why I'm so shit scared about Sam leaving? Maybe she'll find someone else – like Mum did.'

I let go of the door handle and fall back into my seat. Suddenly I don't feel for myself but for him. He needs Sam. He's feeling so frightened. At this moment I am frightened too. Maybe nothing will be the same again. Maybe we have ruined everything.

'I'm sorry,' I say. I can't think of any more words. I sit there, alongside my brother, hoping that he will say something, take the initiative like he usually does and lead us back to the Promised Land.

Instead he opens the passenger door. Swiftly he squeezes his bulk from the seat and steps out. 'Where are you going?' I ask, timidly.

He puts his big meaty hands on the roof, leans in and says, 'You're right. The penguin was a fucking stupid idea.' Then he walks away.

I try not to watch him go. Then I look up and see him moving steadily towards the line of stationary traffic. He crosses the road and marches into Regent's Park. As he disappears from view, I start to cry.

I return to the flat at ten thirty a.m. after driving around North London looking in vain for my fat brother. I know he's gone south, back home, but I don't have the courage to follow him across the river.

As soon as I enter the hallway of my flat, things seem different. Out of habit I go to touch the cold radiator and snatch back my hand. It's hot. The heating is on. The boiler is humming smugly. Then I sniff the air. It smells fresh and piny, like a hotel. I look in the bathroom, expecting to see the aftermath of the Third World War and the walls, floor and bath are spotless, shining like some 'after' shot from a bathroom-cleaner commercial.

In the living room my father is sitting by the window holding a book. He looks up as I enter. He blushes a little, as if caught doing something he shouldn't. He turns the book down, so I can't see what it is.

'The heating's working,' I say, with a raise of my eyebrows.

'I forgot to tell you, I called a plumber,' says my father, a little guiltily. 'He came at eight thirty. It was pretty straightforward. Too much limescale in the pipes. It took him twenty minutes.'

'I see,' I say, confused.

I try to see what book he's reading, but he's still hiding it. He coughs and asks quickly, 'The penguin get off okay?'

'Yeah. The zoo took him back. Thanks for cleaning the bathroom.'

'Oh. No problem. It came off more easily than I thought. Did Jes go home?'

I nod. I wonder about letting things go, about leaving the past behind. But fixing my boiler and cleaning a shitty bathroom do not excuse my father from his prior sins. 'We had another fight.'

'Oh. Sorry to hear that.'

'Why didn't you tell me he knew about Mum?'

My father looks out of the window, then at his shoes. 'I'm a bit of a coward, aren't I?'

'Yes. You are.'

Suddenly I feel immensely tired and in need of a lie-down, alone, on my bed with the door locked and the lights out. I turn to leave. As I get to the living-room doorway my father speaks hurriedly: 'You know something, Scott?'

'What?'

'Your poems . . . they're very funny.'

I look at him. He's holding up the book he's been reading. It's *Men Matter*. 'Thanks,' I say swiftly, then turn and quickly walk from the room. In my bedroom, I lie down and feel warm in my flat for the first time in months.

I stare at the ceiling, admiring a single thread of spider's web that dangles like a mini Miró mobile, jiggling back and forth in the hot-air currents. I watch the tiny spider dash up and down, and envy his dedication and certainty.

I can't sleep. I feel ashamed that I tried to hurt Jes by telling him about Mum's affair, and ashamed that I thought I knew everything, when in fact I knew nothing.

I think about Mum, about her secret. I want to cry again – she feels so far away. I sense myself slipping into despair once more, the aching sadness rising through me.

I remember the touch of her hand at the BBC studios. I remember the bottle of '71 Château Pétrus we drank on her sixtieth birthday. I remember her voice: 'Love you. 'Bye.'

I lie on the bed, staring at the ceiling like a madman in an asylum. I picture us having lunch at Claridges before Christmas carols at the Albert Hall, walking by the spring sea in Devon, her laughter when I read her *Uptown Guys* from cover to cover, one summer Sunday of rain. I see us sitting on the bed in my Laura Ashley Spanish-bordello bedroom after her sixtieth birthday lunch. I felt close to her. She kissed my cheek.

Words fill my head, like the chants of spells, her words, Jes's words, my words. I hear Sam, standing in the sun by the river in Grantchester: 'It's a choice you make once, to love that person, to be with them whatever they do, however they behave.'

Can I choose to love my mum, despite the past?

I close my eyes, hugging myself gently in the warmth of my freshly heated bedroom. I did love her, I say to myself. I still love her. And she loved me too, in her own way. 'At a time like this we need to be a family,' says another voice in my head.

I jump out of bed and rush into the living room. My father looks up, alarmed. 'Where's the phone?' I yell.

'By the stereo.'

I pick it up and punch in J-E-S. It rings. Jes answers. 'It's Scott. I'm really sorry –'

He puts down the phone. The angry buzzing of the dial tone. I dial again. It's engaged. I ring ten more times. Each time I get the short shrill stabs of the busy signal.

'He must have taken it off the hook,' says my father. 'We could go and see him in Morden?'

I shake my head. I feel so tired. I'm not courageous enough to go and see Jes. Maybe at the end of the day I am a coward like my father.

19

I am a coward like my father.

In the middle of the night, I drove the Fiat Punto to the Edgware Road and left it in the hire office car park: I couldn't face the wrath of the spotty man behind his plastic desk. The back seat is badly stained and there's a discernible smell of regurgitated fish clinging to the upholstery. My vehicle damage deposit is definitely at risk. I put the keys through the letter-box with a note attached, saying, 'Why aren't you open twenty-four hours?'

In the taxi back to Kentish Town, I stare out at the orange night of London, wondering whether Jes's fears that he and Sam will break apart like my parents did are justified. I wonder whether history does indeed repeat itself, or whether we can break free of the past. And I wonder why I am feeling so hungry. I get the cabbie to drop me off at the Bosphorus Café-Diner. I order the chicken kebab special and double chips. By the time I've scraped the plate clean, I feel a little better.

I wake late on my sofa-bed, a refugee in my own flat. It's almost three weeks since Mum died. Jes still hasn't called back.

I stare at the phone. After a while I pick it up and punch in the three letters M-U-M. Her number appears. With a faltering hand I select the erase option. My finger remains over the OK button. I imagine pushing it, clearing the number.

I can't do it. Not yet. I press cancel.

I call Jes again. This time I get the answering-machine. I leave a stilted message saying I'm sorry once more, and suggest that we meet up to talk soon.

Among my postal delivery of bills and glossy envelopes containing offers of immense loans with no apparent need for repayment, there are two handwritten letters. When I was a child I used to complain to Mum every time I got handwritten mail. I longed for official-looking letters in my name, typed and franked, not stamped. Such letters would define me as a grown-up, with their connection to large financial corporations.

Now, of course, I dread machine-processed post. I long for envelopes with someone's real-life scrawl on them, denoting personal contact rather than corporate ano-nymity. I open the two handwritten letters with childish excitement. One contains a wedding invitation from Dr Simon. It is written to 'Scott Barron and One' in a jaunty slanting script that seems designed to taunt me. The wedding is in three weeks, just before Christmas. The chances of me finding an 'and One' by then are as slim as a supermodel's finger.

The second letter is from Eric Maloney, my editor at Oak Tree Press. He has written to me in his own small insectoid calligraphy (rather than a typed letter) to show me how important I am to him. In his letter, he praises my talent as a modern-day poet before outlining the 'magnificent sales figures' (first print-run sold-out, nine thousand copies of the second print-run already shipped). He wants me to do more TV interviews (a possibility of *Richard and Judy*). And he wants to sign me up for my next book 'with an increased fee that would reflect your best-selling status'.

At the end of the letter he adds a PS: 'Scott – think women! Huge potential market for you!'

I turn on the television and watch the lunchtime news. The last report is from outside London Zoo. There are pictures of Norman II at the zoo's hospital, being fed with a syringe. There is an interview with Betty McCallister during which she bursts into tears once more. And finally, the Argentinian deputy ambassador appears outside a plush house in West London to express the relief of the Argentinian people that the Peace Penguin is safe and well. 'It is good we have a happy ending. *Muchas gracias.*'

My father enters. He's freshly shaved, wearing a jacket and tie. I ask him where he's going. 'The bank. I need to sort out my finances.'

'Do you need money?' I ask, before I can stop myself.

'I'm fine, Scott, but thanks.' He turns to go, then stops. I pretend to be fascinated by Michael Fish and his sweeping arm movements predicting a bold frontal system storming in from Ireland. It's as if my father is trying to find the courage to say something, and I'm afraid of what it might be. I don't want to feel any more emotions for a while.

'Look, Scott,' he begins, and my heart sinks. It's going to be one of those conversations. 'I've been thinking . . .'

'God help us.'

'I wonder if you should give Samantha a quick call.'

'Why don't you?'

'You get on well with her.'

'Jes doesn't want me to. He was quite categorical about it,' I say, proud of my talent for understatement.

'Yes, yes, I know, but maybe we should take our own initiative on this. I'm afraid if they don't start talking to each other again soon, it might just end up being too late.'

I look at him, and feel a pang of love for the old bastard. He's so worried that Jes and Sam will repeat the mistakes he made with Mum, that his younger son will be left alone like him with regrets at the age of sixty-five. I can see the fear in his eyes. In this moment, my father is no longer the arch-villain who has dwelt in my head for two and half decades, but merely a tearful old man. For the first time we are less like enemies forced to share the same prison cell, and more like intimate strangers – brothers reunited after a world war, for example.

'I don't know if it'll do any good,' I say.

'We have to do something.'

'Jes will kill me. That would be it, game over. He already thinks I try to control him all the time.'

'When to act, and when to lie low? I've never figured that out myself. But, for what it's worth, I think we have to try.'

'We? It's me who'll get in the shit.'

He breathes in, seeking strength. He looks at me, his grey-blue eyes narrow. They look much like my eyes. 'When I left, you lost a father, Scott, but I lost my two sons.'

I meet his gaze. We remain there, in silence, staring at each other like two gun-slingers squaring off.

'I'll be back this evening,' he says, and leaves.

Well, at least I won that showdown.

I stare at the phone. It stares back, the receiver like some small dark grey alien head, mocking me. I think I can hear it laugh, a stringy cackle. I pick up the receiver and press the redial register. Three numbers come up. I press the information button. One has the time of the call listed as 0100. One in the morning. The time Jes called Sam. It must be Rachel's number in Camden.

Before I can get too scared, I dial. The phone rings. I have no idea what I'm going to say. To my horror, an unfamiliar female voice answers. 'Hello?'

'Er . . . this is . . . er . . . Jes Barron's brother.' I sound like a stammering psychiatric patient, unsure even of my own identity.

'Oh. Yes. Hi. How's it going?' Rachel's voice is friendly, gentle, sexy.

'Yeah, fine, thanks. I was just . . .' Wanting to ask you out for a drink? '. . . wondering if Sam's around?'

'Oh, sorry. She's out. I think she went swimming. I can take a message, though.'

'Good. Right. Well. Maybe you could . . . er . . . ask her to call me?'

'No problem. Does she have your number?'

'Yes. Actually, maybe not. Can I give it to you?'

'Hang on. I'll just get a pen.' She's going to write down my number. 'Shit, I can't find one . . . Oh, here's one. Sorry.'

She laughs, briefly, at herself. I want to climb down the phone-line and kiss her, but I've put on a bit of weight recently so instead I give her my mobile number.

'Got it. I'll pass it on to Sam.'

'Thanks.'

'Any time.'

'So . . . I'll wait for Sam to call.' Good, Scott, that's very debonair, very sophisticated, trying to prolong the conversation.

''Bye, then,' she says.

'Oh. Yeah. 'Bye.'

She puts down the phone. I listen to the dial tone. It purrs sweetly. I look around me. The room seems larger and brighter. I forgot to tell her my name. The room shrinks once more.

That afternoon, I try to find Frank. I want to know that he's okay after his little tantrum. But I'm apprehensive about finding him, because I'm feeling increasingly responsible. And responsibility, along with diarrhoea and athlete's foot, has never been one of my favourite sensations.

As I tramp the damp streets looking for my tramp, I find myself getting tired – how much weight have I put on? A bus pulls up at the stop in front of me and I hurry to catch it, thinking that I can hunt for Frank from the top deck like a safari tourist.

As I reach it I am met by Stephen King, who glares down at me with his dark, menacing eyebrows. His long face is splayed across the bus, advertising his latest block-buster. I pause, the driver nods at me to inquire whether I want to avail myself of his vehicular services, and I get on, despite not having enjoyed one of Stephen King's books since puberty.

The bus heads down towards Camden and I scour Kentish Town Road for signs of Frank. I think that, unlike my editor Eric, I wouldn't like to have my face on a double-decker bus. It seems so . . . prosaic. Victor Hugo had a boulevard named after him while he was still alive, and a million Parisians attended his funeral under the Arc de Triomphe, but today the height of literary achievement is a plug on public transport – a poem on the Underground, or your mug on a big red bus.

I take another bus back up to Kentish Town, but there's still no sign of Frank. I walk up and down Kentish Town Road, looking in doorways, cafés, pubs and McDonald's. Then I start to worry. What if my questioning panicked him? What if I have forced him to confront terrible memories that might have been suppressed by drink and mild dementia? What if I have undone years of psychiatric treatment?

Frank must be in his late sixties. He might even be in his early seventies. Why does he like penguins so much? Did he ever visit the South Pole? Was he a brilliant Romanian Antarctic scientist studying the embryos of Emperor penguins, who fell in love with a beautiful assistant called Maggie, who then tragically fell through the ice to her death? This seems unlikely, given that his penguin knowledge is derived from *A Children's Illustrated Book of the Animal Kingdom* and he appears to travel no further than Café du Nord on the Kentish Town Road. Perhaps he had a pet penguin once (the rules on domestic animals were much more lax in the olden days, when you could keep tortoises or alligators in your bathtub without anyone batting an eyelid.)

Or perhaps he's just one leg short of some trousers.

At the top of Lady Somerset Road, my mobile beeps twice. It's a text message from Sam, asking me to meet her the next morning at Café Juju in Camden.

20

It's a blustery early winter day, sun and showers, the sort of day when the last leaves are tugged from the trees. I decide to make the most of the sunshine and walk to Camden. I know I'm going to be early, whatever I do.

As I near Sainsbury's, my mobile rings. I answer it hurriedly, worried it might be Sam calling to cancel, or Jes acting on some sixth sense that I am meeting his wife behind his back.

It's my agent. Barbara Smiles cackles as she informs me that newspapers and magazines are queuing up to interview me. 'The *Sunday Times* wants a profile, but I've also had a call from the *Telegraph*. We may be able to start a bidding war. And *Elle* wants a photo shoot. I've a call in to *Hello!* magazine, I think they should send you somewhere exotic.'

'Great. Thanks, Barbara,' I say, looking at my watch.

'What's wrong, Scott-lad? Don't you want to be bloody famous?'

'No, it's just I'm about to go into a meeting.'

'Really? Anything I should know about?' asks Barbara, suspiciously.

'No, nothing like that. I'm just meeting a friend for brunch. When's the first interview?' I ask, wanting to calm her inquisitive mind.

'I've got one lined up for next week. One of the slag-mags, but it does have a circulation of two hundred thousand.'

'Great. Which one?'

'*Zap!* They're sending one of their fashion people to talk to you, so you'd better find some decent clothes to wear. I can recommend a stylist, if you want.'

Before I can protest, or even ask for clarification on whether this means Ellie is coming to interview me, I hear another phone ring in the background. Barbara shouts, 'Sorry, Scott. Got to go!' and disappears.

The brown and cream exterior of Café Juju seems resolutely contemporary, but once inside the feel is more Cotswolds tea room, apart from the loud rap music and the punkette with red Mohican behind the counter. I sit in the back room pretending to read the *Guardian*, trying to think of things to say to Sam.

I am extremely nervous: my hands shake a little as I hold the newspaper. I feel pressure weighing on me like chain-mail. It's like I'm about to go into an exam, and I know I haven't done anywhere near enough revision. I know I'm probably going to fail, but if I get a couple of lucky breaks I might just be able to scrape a pass. I'm nervous because I want to say the right words to Sam. I want to persuade her to return to my brother.

To calm myself, I order four pieces of toast with jam. When I've guzzled these, I order four more. I'm just finishing them when Sam arrives. She smiles, almost. 'Hey, Scott.'

'Hey, Sam. You're looking good.'

'Thanks.'

I'm not entirely truthful about this. She seems thinner, tired, her face drawn. She has no makeup on, and her hair is bound in an orange headscarf. She wears a light brown suede coat with furry edges, faded jeans and Puma trainers – a little more 'street' than I've seen her in Morden. She orders an Earl Grey tea. 'I didn't know where to meet,' she says, a little nervously.

'This is great.'

We sit for a moment, listening to some tripping garage music. I wipe toast crumbs off my sweater.

'So . . .' she murmurs, glancing from her teacup to the stained glass of the window, without making eye-contact.

'I didn't know whether to call you. Jes didn't want me to,' I stammer clumsily.

'I know. It's okay.'

I should have a great opening line to knock her sideways, to kick her passion into life and rekindle the love in her heart. But I don't.

I launch in anyway. 'I don't have any answers, Sam. I just want to tell you what you already know. He loves you. More than anything.'

She remains silent. I really wish I'd planned this better. I wish I had a list of cogent arguments, killer points to persuade her to return to Jes. Instead, I've got a bagful of clichés.

'That's not enough,' she says eventually. This seems like a line she's been repeating to herself, a mantra to make her feel stronger.

I wade back in with another from my collection of bland and meaningless statements for use in complex emotional situations. 'He needs you.'

'This isn't just about Jes.' I nod, I hope sympathetically. She seems to soften slightly. 'I know you think Jes and I are so great together, but maybe we're not. Maybe you just like to think we are, because you –' She stops.

'Because I what?'

'Because you need us to be together. You need us to work, after everything that's happened with Ellie, with your mum dying . . .'

She's right. I do need them to be together. I need them to prove that relationships can work and that real love exists outside Mills and Boon books. Is this clouding my judgement? How do you know when two people are right for each other? It's not like there's a chemical reaction and they both turn the same colour – although that would be a profitable invention.

Sam looks away again, staring at the stained-glass window. I know I need something, I need some words to stir the tenderness in her heart. Then it comes to me. 'Do you remember what you told me on Mum's birthday in Grantchester, that loving someone is all about choice? That's what you said. A choice you make every day for the rest of your life.'

She sits there, fixated on the stained-glass window and the blurred shapes walking to and fro like coloured ghosts.

'You were right,' I continue. 'You have to make that choice, to take someone as they are, warts and all, whatever their problems, their imperfections, their hang-ups. Because everyone has them, don't they?'

Sam looks at me, a little puzzled, perhaps wondering why I suddenly sound like I'm on a mid-morning television talk-show. I bluster on: 'Okay. I don't know if you're perfect for each other. But I know Jes has chosen you, and he'll choose you every day for the rest of his life, whatever, however you are. The question is, can you decide to choose him again?'

To my surprise and relief, this seems to work. She bites her bottom lip, gently, just like Jes does. I think she's fighting the desire to cry. She's trying to be strong. I want to put my arms round her and tell her she doesn't have to be strong, that we spend too many hours and too many days trying to be strong.

The music changes, a haunting, depressingly classical piece. Sam still stares at the window. Then I remember another line from Grantchester and I go for gold: 'Look, you said yourself that loving someone is harder than not having someone to love . . .' This time it works: she bursts into tears.

Outside the café my sister-in-law breathes in deeply – the fumes from the constant Camden traffic jam can't be good for her – and stops crying. 'Sorry, Scott. I just . . .'

I put my arm round her and she leans into me. People pass by and I'm sure we look like a couple, fresh from an argument, about to make up. But the strange thing is that, even though she's a very attractive woman and I'm holding her tight and I can feel her skinny body and small breasts against me, I feel no sexual attraction. I just feel compassion, the desire to protect her, to make her feel better. I feel like . . . I don't know. I feel like her brother.

'Want to go for a walk?' I suggest brightly. She nods, smoothing her fingers across her eyes. I hand her a Café Juju napkin. She blows her nose.

'Could we go to the zoo?' she asks, like a small girl. 'Rachel and I were meaning to go, but we just haven't got round to it.'

My heart pounds. I look at her red eyes and wan face. 'Why not?' I say, taking her hand. 'I haven't been there in ages.'

As I buy two tickets at the zoo gates, I try not to panic. What was I thinking, agreeing to bring her to the scene of my crime? What if someone recognizes me? What if Sam senses my nervousness and realizes I'm the one, the Evil Penguin Nabber – Sam has "Female Intuition Plus", the new improved Female Intuition with added Perception.

Fortunately, my nervousness is countered by my desire to make her feel better, to take care of her. This makes me stronger. And, curiously enough, I really want to see Norman II again. I want to check he's all right.

The woman at the ticket office doesn't even look up.

The zoo is fairly busy. There are several tourist groups, some families and one nursery-school outing of tiny children who hold each other's hands as they straggle from cage to cage. Sam gazes after them as they disappear into the Reptile House. I steer her gently the other way.

We pass the ape cages, the gorillas glaring and the

chimpanzees screeching. I talk a lot, so Sam doesn't have to. I talk about my father coming to stay. I talk about how perhaps, somehow, we are edging slowly towards a small reconciliation – trying not to hint too obviously that she and Jes could do the same.

'So how's it been, staying with Rachel?' I inquire nonchalantly.

'All right. She's a sound girl,' says Sam, happy to be talking about something other than her problems and my family. 'She's been very supportive.'

'She seemed nice, when I met her at the hospital . . .' I mumble clumsily.

Sam stops. She looks at me and says, somewhat reproachfully, 'Scott . . .'

'What?'

'You fancy Rachel, don't you?'

'No, of course not.'

Sam starts to laugh.

'What's so funny?'

'You.'

'Why?'

'Sometimes you're so bloody obvious.'

'About what?'

'Rachel.'

'What about her?'

'You fancy her. You great lummox!'

'No, I don't.' I can't help blushing. 'I just thought she looked nice.'

Sam looks at me intently, a mischievous smile on her pale face.

'So, would you . . . you know, put in a good word for me?' I say, like a lovelorn teenager.

Sam snorts, theatrically. 'And subject her to another of the Fabulous Barron Brothers? Not bloody likely!'

It takes me just a second to grasp that she's joking. She laughs again and walks on, striding forth with more Sam-like vigour.

We wander past some cages containing small furry animals of unclear origins. Sam asks how my book is doing. I tell her about the prospective interview with Ellie's magazine.

'It's perfect!' she declares resolutely. 'She's coming grovelling to you. You're the big success.'

'It's just so weird.'

Sam stops. 'No, no, no!'

'No what?'

'You're not getting back together with her! She's not worth it!'

I look at the strange furry animals, which seem to be a kind of miniature hirsute pig. Sam looks at me. 'You don't still want her back, do you?'

I think about this. My automatic reaction is to say yes. But since seeing Rachel at the hospital, I don't know. Maybe Ellie no longer has the power to wring my heart like a sponge. Maybe I'm free of her.

'Do you?'

'No,' I say, without huge conviction.

'Good. Don't show any interest in her. Tell her how well you're doing, and then boot her out of the door!'

As we pass some shivering flamingos in a murky pool,

I attempt to turn the conversation back to her and Jes. Subtly (I think) I ask her if the *Telegraph* wants her back at work soon. She sighs and says her sick leave runs out the following week, and that she's not looking forward to it. 'I hate the bloody office. All those writers travelling all over the world, and I'm stuck there in that stupid bloody tower in Canary bloody Wharf!'

Ahead are the lion enclosures, crowded with onlookers. We decide to avoid the congestion, and stop at a less popular window featuring a fat, bored leopard sprawled across a branch, its huge paws dangling apathetically.

'It's like he's the one watching us in our cage,' remarks Sam, with a smile. We look at the leopard, who stares back at us with big black vacant eyes. He yawns, as if he's watching a television programme that has failed to live up to its billing.

'Did you ever see my graduation project?' asks Sam, out of nowhere.

'Maybe. Actually, I don't think so.'

'"Incarceration". That was the theme. I spent a week at Marwell Zoo. I did all these pictures of keepers and vets in the cages, like they were on display.'

'Sounds interesting.'

'A few of them worked out okay.'

The crowd has thinned slightly, so we move on to the lion enclosures, an expansive area befitting the lions' billing as the stars of the zoo. A number of mothers stand alongside toddlers in brightly coloured push-chairs. I notice Sam glance at them, breathe in quickly, then turn her gaze to the two young lions playing by the small lake that prevents them jumping into the crowd and biting our heads off.

One lion roars, the other jumps forward and slaps his face.

'They must be brothers,' I say quietly. Sam smiles, looking intently at the lions, and I wonder if she's mentally framing them, choosing shutter speeds.

'Do you miss taking pictures?'

'Yeah.'

She smiles, to herself, the sort of smile that is self-reproach rather than satisfaction. But when she speaks, there is energy in her voice. 'I'd love to take more pictures. Actually, I'd love to try to make a living from it, one day. You know, go freelance. Just to see . . .'

'Why don't you?'

She laughs mockingly. 'We couldn't afford it.' She looks at the lions, who are still slapping each other playfully with their huge soft paws. 'Oh, well.'

I think about this for a moment. 'Would three hundred thousand pounds help?'

'What?'

'That's what you and Jes would get if we sold Mum's house.'

'You can't sell the house.'

'Why not?'

'It's . . . I don't know, it's the past. It's your family history.'

'The past is less important than the future,' I say.

Sam bursts out laughing.

'What's so funny?'

'Oh, Scott,' she pats my arm, 'you're all right, aren't you, pet?'

'Not too introspective?'

Immediately I wish I hadn't said this, but Sam just smiles. 'You're all right.'

She heads down the steps to the penguin enclosure. My heart starts thumping. She's going to see Norman II. I think about calling out to stop her. I could tell her I was thirsty, or hungry, or simply feign a mild heart-attack. As I'm debating this, she reaches the pool and I hurry down the steps to join her.

I wish I'd worn a hat. I know it's unlikely anyone will think I'm the perpetrator of the penguin crime of the decade, but I still feel guilty. What if Norman II recognizes me and goes berserk? He has every right to, after all I put him through.

A large crowd of onlookers surrounds the pool, huddled together at the far end. Children point, their parents take pictures. There, in his accustomed territory by the back wall, is Norman II, standing proud, munching a piece of mackerel.

'Pedro!' shouts one man, his camera raised. 'Come on, Pedro!'

'It's him!' says a young pigtailed girl, in a stage-whisper.

'I want to see! I want to see!' shouts her small brother, struggling to pull himself on to the ledge. I glance over at a hastily erected sign on the wall: PEDRO THE PEACE PENGUIN RETURNS TO LONDON ZOO!

'Wow,' says Sam at my side. 'I didn't know they'd found him.'

'Who?' I ask, feigning ignorance.

'Pedro the Peace Penguin. I'm glad he's safe.'

For a moment, I think about confessing to Sam my role in Pedro's abduction, but something holds me back. It feels like an unfinished story.

'Penguins are Jes's favourite,' murmurs Sam, watching Norman II as he swallows the fish and flaps his stubby wings, to the delight of the enraptured audience.

'Yeah. I never quite understood that.'

'I think it's because he's a bit like them.'

'How's that?'

'I don't know. Soft and cuddly. And he likes a crowd . . .' Sam tails off. She seems embarrassed to have been so tender about her husband. I hope this means there's hope. But I don't want to push it. 'The bastard's been sending me letters,' she says, quietly, almost to herself. I wait for her to elaborate but she doesn't. Instead she pretends to start reading the penguin information on the ledge in front of us. I keep watching Norman II, like an anxious parent at the playground gates. But I needn't worry. He seems to be doing a little jig, shamelessly milking the crowd. There's even applause from some of the onlookers. He seems much happier than the last time I saw him here. Perhaps his trip to my Kentish Town bathroom was just what he needed.

As I watch, Norman II dives into the pool, everyone cheers, and I'm amazed at how graceful he is, a small, stout, black and white missile, shooting through the water.

I feel proud.

'It says here that penguins can't be on their own,' declares Sam quietly, breaking our awkward silence.

'What's that?'

'Penguins. It says they're the most sociable of all birds. They have to have other penguins around.'

'That makes sense.'

'"Penguins have very strong pair bonds",' she continues reading. '"They recognize each other as individuals and have ways of greeting each other after a period of separation . . ."' She stops suddenly. We both know why. We're both thinking about Jes and Sam's separation. Will they have a chance to show their way of greeting?

We gaze into the enclosure, silent again. As I watch the waddling birds in their Hollywood pool, I realize for the first time why people like penguins. It's because we are like them. We shouldn't be on our own. It's too stressful. We need each other.

'I should get going,' says Sam, looking at her watch. 'I'm meeting Rachel for lunch at one.'

I nod.

'Maybe I'll put in a word for you,' she adds, with a quick smile.

'Thanks, sis.'

'It was good seeing you.' She kisses my cheek. Her lips are cold. She steps back, waiting for me say goodbye.

'Will you call him?' I ask quickly.

She looks at me, her face white, with small dark hollows beneath her pretty eyes. 'I don't know. It's his birthday next week. Maybe I'll speak to him then.' I'd forgotten this. Of course it's Jes's birthday. He'll be twenty-seven years old. 'Perhaps you shouldn't tell him we met up. You know?'

'Sure, Scott. Whatever.'

With this, Sam walks quickly away. I stay for a few minutes watching Norman II with his friends. He stops pecking for fish and seems to look up at me, just for a second. I raise my hand until I realize I'm waving at a penguin.

21

I think about calling *Zap!* and talking to Ellie about the interview and her motives for doing a story on me. I dial the number once, but hang up. Then I call Brian.

He seems surprised to hear from me. 'Where have you been?'

'Nowhere.'

'It's been a while.'

I suggest lunch. He seems pleased. As I put down the phone, I wonder why I don't call him more often. It seems to make both of us feel good.

We meet up at Lucy Sushi in the City. Brian's even earlier than I am for events, which is one of the reasons I like him. He stands up as I enter and gives me a hug. This happens more commonly with him than it does with Big Barry, but not since my thirtieth birthday. 'Sorry about your mum,' he says solemnly.

'Thanks,' I reply gravely.

We both sit down, a little relieved we've got that out of the way. Brian talks quickly, saying he's just completed a big pharmaceutical deal and he'll pay for lunch. Since I'm not Stephen King, I agree graciously and order the second most expensive sashimi on the menu.

As soon as our beers arrive, I find myself outlining my

role in the kidnap of Pedro the Peace Penguin. I don't know why. Perhaps, having kept silent with Sam, I need to confess.

I talk non-stop. To his credit Brian listens to my tale of penguin abduction with the utmost patience, stabbing slices of raw fish and popping them whole into his mouth as if mimicking the penguin protagonist of my story. When my confession is over, he asks me why I did it. He is a lawyer, after all.

'I don't know.'

'Come on, Scott. You have to admit it's pretty weird, stealing a penguin.'

'Yeah. I suppose so.'

I try to pick up some rice with the chopsticks, but the grains fall to the plate. 'I stole the penguin to give to my brother so he'd like me.'

'Come again?'

'Okay. I lost the plot a little. But Jes always liked penguins. Somehow it seemed logical.'

'Did it work?'

'How do you mean?'

'*Does* Jes like you?'

'I don't know. We had a fight. He hit me.'

'No shit.'

'Yeah. He's having some problems with Sam. It's hard for him right now.'

'You want my advice? Let him be. You've made your gesture. It's his turn now.'

'What? Like you waiting for Nathan to get back in touch?'

Brian sees that this is not a very good comparison. 'I guess so,' he says, quietly.

We fall into silence, each thinking of our respective brothers. Brian stabs another piece of sashimi and drinks the last of his beer.

'So what's your news?' I ask eventually.

'Well . . . I'm dating someone.'

'Wow. That's great!' And it is. I feel genuinely happy for him. Brian needs a girlfriend. Every time he saw Ellie he'd ask her if she had any single friends. She always complained about this when we got home, outraged that he would think any of her friends would go out with someone as nerdy as him.

'Yeah. You'll never guess where I met her.'

'A billion-dollar business deal? The gym? No, wait. I've got it. Starbucks! You always said that was the best place to pick up women.'

'Sixty-second dating.'

I laugh.

Brian blushes, a little. 'It's true. We just hit it off. In fact, it didn't even take us the whole minute. It was more like twenty-second dating. We've been going out for four weeks now, and it's so good, Scott, I can't tell you. We just click.'

I can't believe it. One of my friends finding a girlfriend at a stupid dating evening is strange enough. But two of them? I laugh some more.

'What's so funny?' Brian asks, a little taken aback.

'Nothing. It's just Barry met someone there too.'

'I know. That's why he told me to go. He said it was really great.'

I stop laughing and think about this. I'd assumed Barry had encouraged Brian to go to sixty-second dating as a joke. But maybe he was serious. Maybe he believed it would help. Whatever the motivation, it's obviously made Brian's year.

'So what's her name?' I ask, intrigued.

'Cindy. Cindy Shavers.'

I almost choke on my tuna roll. I start to cough violently. 'Are you okay?'

I splutter, heaving in air. I feel like choking to death might not be a bad thing right now. Can I tell my friend that I have slept with his new girlfriend before being sick in her room-mate's wicker wastepaper basket? I should, shouldn't I? Because I should tell him about her case of chlamydia. You can lie to your best friends, but you can't mess with matters of sexual health.

'She said you'd be surprised,' continues Brian, lightly.

'What?'

'I didn't want to tell you about her, but Cindy's great. She said we should just be open and honest.'

'Why didn't you want to tell me?' I ask, feigning innocence.

'Because you two . . . you know? Shagged.'

I blush bright red. I feel doubly guilty – once because I had sex with his new girlfriend, and twice because I mocked him for going to sixty-second dating, in the full knowledge that I, too, had hoped to find true love there. 'Look, Brian, it was a drunken night . . .'

'Don't worry. It's okay. Cindy told me all about it. She's so honest.'

How honest? I wonder. Should I raise the small matter of her STD? I decide discretion is the better part of valour. 'She told you everything?'

'Yeah. Of course . . .' He looks at me with growing suspicion, his eyes narrowing as they must do over mahogany negotiating tables. 'At least, I think so.'

'That's great.'

'What are you getting at, Scott?'

'Er . . .' Can I tell him? Can I break a habit of our thirteen years together and actually confront something difficult? 'I mean . . .'

'What is it?'

'Have you, you know, slept with her yet?'

'No, but I will. She drives me crazy. Maybe tonight . . . I'm feeling lucky.'

'Oh.'

'Jesus, Scott, what is it?'

'Nothing.'

Maybe it's better to let sleeping STDs lie.

'You're not jealous, are you? I mean, that wouldn't be fair. After all, you walked out on her.'

I blush pinker than the sashimi. 'No, no, it's not that. I'm really happy for you. For both of you. It's nothing, really.'

'I know, I know!' Brian sounds childishly pleased with himself.

'It's nothing.' Now I fervently wish I'd never started this whole honesty kick. It's unhealthy.

'It's that thing about the . . . you know . . .'

'No, it isn't.'

'Yes, it is.'

'No, it isn't.'

'You don't even know what thing I'm referring to.' Brian grins, and I get a glimpse of what he must be like in his legal world, playing cunning games of contractual cat and mouse. I decide to plead the Fifth Amendment and remain silent in the hope he will let it go. Of course he doesn't let it go.

'I don't blame you,' he continues, now positively smirking. 'I wouldn't want to talk about a dose of chlamydia either!'

Then something strange happens. Maybe it's a natural lull in everyone's conversation, or maybe an angel is simply passing by, as my mother used to say, but, whatever the reason, just as I bristle with indignation and embarrassment, almost rising from my chair and knocking over our bottle of Tingzu mineral water, the whole restaurant falls silent.

'I DIDN'T GIVE HER CHLAMYDIA!' I shout as loudly as I can.

Silence. The world stops turning. Faces stare at me, some with open mouths. A waiter pauses: the plate he's carrying is suspended in mid-air. Even the coat-check lady is leaning out of her booth. It's like one of those Victorian cartoons in which everyone is looking aghast at the hapless wrong-doer, under the title, 'MR JENNINGS SAYS HE PREFERS THE FRENCH MUSTARD!'

I laugh, nervously, blushing bright purple. Brian smiles broadly, admiring the faces looking at me.

'I know, Scott. I was just winding you up.'

Thankfully, everyone starts talking once more. The waiter moves on, and the world turns. My blush has spread to my chest and hands. Brian looks at me. I look at him. Then we both burst out laughing.

I return to Kentish Town feeling happy for my American friend, a soft happiness that's not simply due to lunchtime drinking. He deserves it, after his long periods of loneliness and self-doubt. Maybe there is a law of karma after all. At least, for some people.

As I think about him and Cindy together – actually, they're a well-matched couple, not too trendy, but both independent of spirit – it dawns on me that, for the first time in fifteen years, my three closest friends are in love. It's amazing. Just think of the money I could have made putting a bet on that.

As I near my flat I slow. I'm wondering why I still feel happy. In the not-too-distant past, this situation, whereby my friends have found romance while I'm about as far from coupledom as a newborn baby, would have left me resentful and self-pitying. Something has changed.

Before I get anywhere near deciphering what it is, I almost fall over Frank. He's curled in my doorway, arms crossed, leaning against the wall. He seems to be asleep. I bend down, inhale a rasp of cheap whisky. He's been bleeding again, from a cut on his chin. I place my hand on his shoulder. He doesn't move. I shake his shoulder gently. He snores loudly. I think about touching his face, but it's snotty and bloody and specked with white beard stubble.

As I turn my key in the front door, he wakes. He looks up at me, trying to focus. 'Come on, Frank. I'll clean you up,' I say encouragingly.

'No clean.'

'Don't you want a nice shower?'

He shakes his head, obstinately.

'But you're hurt.'

'No hurt.'

'Are you sure?'

'Food.'

Oh, no.

'Chips.'

'Look, I'll take you to the hospital.'

'Need chips.'

'You need to see a doctor.'

'Chips!'

As I help him up, I notice he has a new pair of wellington boots, coloured a sprightly electric blue. They glint for a jewelled instant in the wintry late-afternoon sun.

The stocky Turkish men nod to me as if I am a regular. They smile almost benignly as Frank returns from the toilet with his face washed and his hair slicked back. He eats the vast amount of fried food without a word, chasing chips and mushrooms around the plate with the fork as if playing some strange intricate game of his own making.

Two more cups of tea and a Mars Bar later I decide to try and make conversation. 'You remember my penguin, Frank? I took it to the zoo.'

He doesn't look at me, instead choosing to analyse the checked pattern on his mug.

'Have you ever been to the zoo?'

He sips his tea, making an exaggerated slurping noise that may or may not be genuine. Then, almost slyly, he reaches into his large pockets and takes out his animal book. He opens it carefully in front of me. He points to the page with the penguins. 'Penguin,' he says, helpfully.

I wonder, just for a moment, if he's playing me. Maybe he's not a homeless, drunken, retarded man, after all. Maybe he's just pretending, maybe he's an actor sent to wind me up.

Or is Frank simply a crotchety old foreign geezer with mental-health problems? I need to know. I need to know his past. I need to find out.

'Who's Maggie, Frank?' I ask loudly.

'Penguin.' He points at the picture with his gnarled finger, a little more insistent this time.

'Who's Maggie?'

Frank jabs his finger at the penguin picture again. 'Gen-too penguin!' he barks, angrier now.

'I want to know, Frank. Who is Maggie?'

He looks at me and scowls, his forehead furrowed. Maybe this is cruel. Maybe it's even a little risky. Maybe he'll tell me to shut up once more and boot me in the shins. But I don't care. I'm in a mean mood. I want to push him. 'Who is Maggie?'

He thinks for a moment, or perhaps his brain has simply shut down, taking a breather after an information and memory overload. I wait for the boot in the shins, a curse or two. He looks up at me as if he's made a difficult decision. 'Maggie gone.'

My frustration vanishes. I feel instant compassion for him because I know how he feels. His wavery old man's voice, low and grumbling, seems to sum up the pain of separation. I see in his face the flicker of anguish that is attached to the memory of a loved one like a nerve. 'Maggie gone,' he repeats.

Maggie gone. Mum gone. Jes maybe gone.

'What happened? Did she die? Did she leave? What happened, Frank?'

I want to know the details, I want to unlock his past and make a diagnosis of the present.

'Maggie gone.'

We walk in silence up Lady Somerset Road, Frank lagging a couple of steps behind me in his bright blue wellies. I'm nervous. I should invite him in, clean him up a bit, but after that I don't know. I can't look after him on a longer-term basis. I'm sorry, but I just can't.

Then it hits me. Maybe I can help Frank find somewhere to stay, if he wants it. A hostel or something. There must be charities. I'll even pay for it. It'll be my New Year resolution.

We get to the steps of my flat. There are no lights on inside. My father must have gone out. I take out my keys.

'You can stay here tonight, Frank. What do you say?'

He looks at me with that stark stare of his. For the first time, I see that his eyes are green.

'You can take a shower. You can sleep on the sofa-bed. It's pretty comfortable.'

In a mischievous way, I'm quite looking forward to Frank meeting Edward Barron. Maybe he can borrow my father's Brylcreem.

Frank continues to look at me.

'You stay here now,' I say, trying out the monosyllables of Frank-speak.

He shakes his head. 'Go,' he says.

'What? Go where?'

'Go home.'

'Home? What home?'

'Need money. Go home.'

'What money? What home?'

'Home. Need money.'

What home could he possibly have? Is he delusional? Are we both delusional? He's speaking faster now, more agitatedly, spit flicking from his lips. 'Need money. Go train. Train good. Train home . . .'

'Where? Where is your home?'

'Train. Now! Train good!'

He's babbling, I want to slow him down, or shut him up. Unable to curb my frustration, I say sharply, 'What are you talking about, Frank?'

He doesn't reply. He looks down at his blue wellingtons. Then he reaches into his pocket and takes out a scrap of paper. It's yellowed and crumpled, like an ancient relic. He holds out his palm and smiles at me as if giving me a gift. I take the crumpled scrap of paper.

Written on it is what seems to be a telephone number.

The city code is 01792. I have no idea where that is. 'Come on,' I say purposefully. 'We are going to sort this out.'

Frank sits on my sofa, with his knees together. He reaches into his overly large coat pocket and takes out *A Children's Illustrated Book of the Animal Kingdom* and turns to the penguin page, which he stares at stubbornly, expressionless, unmoving. I take out the phone directory and check the city code: 01792 is Swansea, Wales.

I've never been to Swansea. I've never even been to Wales. It's always seemed so . . . Welsh. I dial the number. It rings and a woman's voice answers in a singing Swansea accent: 'Hello, Silvia Evans.'

To my surprise my heart is racing. 'Hello, my name's Scott Barron, I'm calling about a man called Frank in London, I don't know his surname, but he must be in his sixties. I was wondering if you know him.'

There's a silence at the other end of the phone. Then she speaks again: 'Please. Is he dead?'

'No, no, nothing like that.' I hear an exhalation of relief. I continue quickly, wanting the story out. 'It's just, well, he's been living rough near my flat and we've sort of got to know each other, and he gave me a piece of paper with your number on it.'

'Is he all right? Please tell me he's all right,' says Silvia Evans, her voice rising and falling, excitement and fear zipping down the line.

'He's fine. I think he just wants to come and see you. He keeps talking about "home".'

'Oh, my. Oh, my. I can't believe it. Franco. My brother's alive.'

'Your brother?'

Silvia Evans proceeds to tell me the story, breathlessly, as if she wants to get it out of the way in order to ask more questions about her errant sibling. The story is not quite as exotic as the ones I'd invented. She tells me that Franco was born in Malta before his father packed the family on to a boat to Swansea, where she herself was born. Her brother was always a little backward. He never really had a proper job, he was always a bit of a drinker. He ended up in London living in a bedsit in Camden. After a bad fall, he was taken in by social services and eventually ended up in a psychiatric hospital in Enfield. She says she hasn't seen him in ten years, ever since he had to leave the hospital because of a bed shortage. She and her husband Terry tried to find him after he disappeared – they came to London five or six times to search the streets, before Terry convinced her that it was a hopeless quest. Half-way through her account, Silvia starts to cry. 'Please forgive me. It's just I've been waiting every day for someone to ring and tell me that Franco is dead. I just can't believe he's still alive.'

I look over at Frank. He's still staring at the penguins, as impassive as a shabby statue. 'He's fine,' I say reassuringly. 'He's got this children's book of animals that he likes. It seems to calm him.'

Silvia laughs, despite herself. 'He loves his animals. Ever since he was a lad. We used to go up to Bristol Zoo all the time. Our mother used to take us.'

I smile at the thought of Franco and Silvia as children, staring at an empty lion cage in the hope of a glimpse of the King of the Jungle, just as Jes and I did, and our children, if we ever have any, will do. Then I think of the one thing I have to ask Silvia, the burning question, the controversy of the year.

'Sorry, Silvia, but he keeps mentioning someone called Maggie. Have you any idea who Maggie might be?'

Silvia thinks for a moment. 'No. Sorry, love. Not a clue. Maybe it was someone at the hospital.'

She asks if I can look after Frank until she comes down in the morning to pick him up.

'Of course. He can stay here tonight.'

'No! Train now!' barks Frank, looking up from his animal book.

'Come on, Frank.'

'TRAIN NOW!'

It's six forty-five and I am standing on platform eight of London's Paddington station, handing a homeless man a bag containing two sandwiches, a couple of Mars Bars and a large bottle of 7-Up, his beverage of choice. I have bought him an open ticket so he can return to the capital any time he chooses. I hand him a hundred pounds in cash. He says nothing as he puts the envelope quickly into his threadbare pocket.

I show him to his seat on the train. The other passengers eye him nervously but he sits down quietly, and begins to lay out his sandwiches, chocolate, 7-Up and a plastic cup neatly on the table. I hand him his ticket. 'Show this to the guard, okay?'

He nods.

''Bye, then, Frank. See you soon.'

Frank nods once more. He reaches inside his coat and takes out his book. He opens it carefully, and turns to a page showing an Amazonian rainforest.

A guard comes through the carriage and I ask him to look after my grandfather on the journey west to Wales. He looks at Frank, then at me, smiles and says he'll pop by every so often to check he's all right.

Frank doesn't say another word. He nods one last time, then starts rearranging his sandwiches and plastic cup. I pause for a moment. 'Come on, Frank. Let's play this one last time. Who's Maggie?'

Frank turns the page of his book. The picture now shows the Australian bush, complete with kangaroos and koalas. He doesn't look up.

'Oh, well,' I say, and turn to go, realizing as I say it that these are the exact words, said in the exact tone, that my father always uses on occasions of gentle disappointment.

'Maggie Thatcher,' says Frank gruffly. I spin round. He's still looking at his book.

'What did you say?'

'Maggie Thatcher,' he repeats, without looking up. 'Stupid bitch.'

I'm still laughing as I stand on the platform and the train eases forward, taking an old man back to Swansea to see his sister for Christmas. I wave, but Frank doesn't look up from his book.

*

When I get back to my flat, my father is cooking spaghetti sauce. It smells surprisingly good. He tells me he's been trying to get hold of Jes. He even went down to Morden and knocked on the door, but no one answered. He says he's worried. I say nothing. What is there to say?

'Do you think Sam will go back to him?' he asks, quietly.

'I don't know.'

'Oh.' He looks down, deflated. I think about going up to him and putting my arms around him, but I'm not ready for such proximity. Not yet.

'I think maybe we should sell the house in Grantchester,' I say quickly. He looks up. 'Sam wants to chuck in her job, try freelance photography. But she can't because they have no money. This way they get the money, she gets to take pictures, she's happier, Jes is happier. It could work. What do you say?'

My father doesn't answer. He looks out of the kitchen window down the row of gardens lit by other kitchen windows where families are sitting down to dinner. His face suggests he's thinking, all wrinkled brow and pursed lips. I'm suddenly worried. He's going to object, he's got his own plans for the house, and he's going to use it as a way to re-establish his position as head of the family. After an uncomfortable silence, he looks back at me. 'I think it's a bloody marvellous idea.'

'Really?'

'Why not? Liquidate our assets.'

'We can send the money to Nice.'

'I'm not going back to Nice.'

'What?'

'I'm not going back. I decided last night. I want to go travelling.'

'Travelling?'

'Why not? I got this brochure.'

My father reaches down to a bag by the bin and snatches out a glossy brochure, as if by magic: *Overland Expeditions*. 'There's this amazing trip across East Africa.'

'What?'

'They start in Mombasa, then head down into Tanzania, you travel all together in a converted Mercedes truck.'

'East Africa?'

'I've always wanted to see Africa,' he says, a little defensively. 'Ever since I was a boy.'

'What about Mireille?'

He thinks, just for a moment. 'She can go fuck herself.'

I burst out laughing. My father looks at me as if he's going to admonish me as he did when I was a child, then he starts laughing too.

Later that evening, my father helps me clean the flat. We talk a little, about Jes, about Sam, about the past, about the penguin, and about what vaccinations he'll need for Africa. We are careful to avoid any unpleasant memories, any contentious subjects. For long periods we clean and scrub without talking. At one stage he stops dusting, picks up a book from the living-room shelf, and starts flicking through it. I ask him what he's doing.

'I used to love Steinbeck,' he says, by way of explanation. '*Tortilla Flat* was my favourite. It's been years since I read it. Do you think I could borrow it?'

I nod, struck by the weirdness of the situation. Just

three months ago could I have imagined lending my father a paperback? Then, something else strikes me, a bolt from the past. 'Did you read a lot, in Grantchester, when we were little?' I ask, trying not to sound too inquisitive.

'Now and again. I had a whole shelf of books downstairs. I guess your mum chucked them out after, you know . . .'

I laugh, an exhalation of memory.

'What is it?' he asks, a little concerned.

'Nothing,' I lie. I laugh again. The books that nourished me through my childhood, that I'd revered and cared for thinking they were my mother's, were his. His legacy to me. I wonder if I should tell him the truth. There seems no reason not to. 'She didn't chuck them out. I had them in my bedroom.'

It's my father's turn to laugh. 'She kept them?'

'Yeah. I read them all. Steinbeck was one of my favourites too.'

'Well, I never. That's funny, isn't it?' he says.

'Yeah. It is . . .' I say, with a smile.

When the cleaning is finished, my father says he's tired – he is sixty-five, after all – and feels like going to bed. We have a little argument about where he should sleep, which I win. I let him have my bed. He thanks me, and takes *Tortilla Flat* into the bedroom.

I sit in the living room eating some of his tastily spicy spaghetti accompanied by a half-decent bottle of wine. Soon I hear him snore. I sit there, cradling my wine glass, listening to his breathing, as he must once have sat and listened to my childhood slumber. After a while I get up and go to the bedroom door, which I push open gently.

347

He is lying there, on his side, one hand still clutching the copy of *Tortilla Flat*. I reach down, prise the book gently from his fingers and place it carefully on the bedside table. He stirs briefly, then rolls over and starts snoring once more.

Back in the living room, I pour myself a third glass of wine and take out my notepad.

MY OLD MAN

My old man's getting older.
Like a clock ticking,
He still winds me up.
My old man's getting shorter, five millimetres a year,
It's a fear,
Third Age Shrinkage.
But I'll still love him, however little, brittle
And bitter he becomes,
Because he's my father.
I bet if I sold him at Sotheby's he would fetch a record price.

22

It's Jes's birthday, 6 December. He's a Sagittarius. Apparently that means he quests after knowledge, loves to travel, and can be standoffish when dealing with strangers. He would, so the books say, make a good salesman.

If he's having a party, I haven't been invited.

The day starts strangely. There are days like this in life, I have found, when I lack control, even more so than normal. However much I concentrate and try to avoid mishap and mayhem, things go bizarrely astray.

It is days like these that make me believe that God might exist, because on such days I feel like forces beyond my control are speeding me along, even though I try to forge my own path. On days like this, I am a cork on a wave.

I log on to my laptop and there's an email from Brian saying he has called his brother Nathan in Los Angeles.

It wasn't so bad. He said he'd been meaning to call me too (maybe he was lying but I chose not to think so). We're going to talk next weekend. It feels good.

In the morning post, I get a letter from Big Barry. I have never received a letter from Big Barry in all the years I've known him. Let's just say that he's more of a verbal communicator.

Barry's letter covers two pages with neat but expansive

handwriting, in which he thanks me for being his friend, for listening to him in his time of need, and for my advice. I try to remember what my advice was. It was evidently something to do with Nancy, because he goes on to say that Nancy has said she loves him despite his unemployed status. In fact, she's giving up her marketing job and the two of them are going off round the world for six months. They hope to end up in Australia, where they will look for work together.

I have to read the letter twice. Big Barry has never travelled anywhere, other than to five-star resorts in which his interaction with the surroundings is limited to ordering the local dish of the day. The image of him with a backpack is as alien to me as the Queen with a plastic bag. He concludes by inviting me to dinner at his flat the following week. He claims he's going to cook. He signs the letter, 'With thanks to my best friend, Barry.'

In the bathroom I step on the scales. The gauge reads thirteen stone four pounds. I have put on a little under two stone in three months. Twenty-six pounds to be precise – or twelve kilos. I'm now the heaviest and fattest I've ever been.

The funny thing is, I don't mind.

I go for a haircut in Kentish Town, before my *Zap!* interview. I want to look my best, to combat Ellie. At the desk I can't remember who cut my hair the last time – they're all from Sweden or Italy or both, and they all have piercings and clothes that seem to have been ripped on purpose. The manager gets exasperated when I can't come up with a name, so I end up with a woman called Loti, who has bright pink hair and a bright green shirt slashed down one side to reveal a red bra. As the haircut proceeds in stark silence – Loti is quite defensive about her English, or lack of it – I begin to wonder if I might be her first ever customer. My request for a 'choppy style' in the Ethan Hawke mould has been reinterpreted in an admittedly original way: there seem to be bald patches among tufty bits, and the fringe is as jagged as a lightning bolt. I ask her to even it up a bit, but she just throws her hands in the air and barks, 'You want choppy! Choppy I give!'

With a slop of gel delicately mashed into my hair by Loti's firm fingers, I look just about passable, and in my haste to leave I tip her an extra three pounds. An hour later, in the Somerfield supermarket on Kentish Town Road, two small children point at me and laugh. Shortly afterwards it begins to snow.

As I arrive back at my flat the snow is starting to settle. I find my father sitting in the window watching the flakes dance and pirouette, the snow putting on quite a show at a venue in which it hasn't performed for several years. He doesn't seem to notice my haircut.

'Up to anything today?' he asks.

'I'm doing an interview this afternoon.'

'Fantastic. Who for?'

'*Zap!* magazine. It's a women's mag.'

'Really? Never heard of it but, then, I am an old-age pensioner.'

'It's not exactly a household name.'

'Well, I'm sure you'll be brilliant. You'll have all those women swooning over you . . .'

'Dad . . .' I say, reproachfully. He looks at me. I look at him. This is the first time I've called him 'Dad' in years.

'You do know it's your brother's birthday today?' he asks.

'I sent him a card and a case of wine,' I say hastily.

'Good idea. Sustenance.'

I start looking for a hat to cover Loti's cut-and-blow-dry disaster. I am trying not to worry about the impending interview and seeing Ellie again. As I'm rummaging in my cupboard, my father appears behind me, coughs and says, with feigned disregard, 'He's having a party, you know.'

I see now where Jes gets his acting talent from. 'Really?'

'Somewhere called the Place in Soho. Seven thirty, I believe.'

'How do you know?'

'His friend Zeb told me.'

'Oh. Right.'

'Just so you know.'

At two o'clock, I take the Underground into central London for my interview with Ellie and *Zap!* Despite my good intentions, I'm wearing one of the cashmere sweaters she gave me, and my favourite Levi's. I also sport a black running hat to cover my hair, in the hope I might be able to pass it off as a fashion statement. I think Ellie might laugh. But for some reason I'm not nervous. I think about Mum and Sam, and then about Rachel, and I feel strong. Just.

In the carriage the heat is turned up high and there's the solid smell of sweat clinging to the ragged seats. It is almost empty, just a couple of schoolkids playing truant and the ubiquitous drunk at one end singing 'Danny Boy' quietly to himself. I remove my hat for a moment, look at my hair and wonder whether I should find some barber's shop in town and ask them to shave my head.

At Warren Street station, a pretty girl gets on and sits down opposite me. I glance at her, then away, then to one side of her, then to the other side of her. Sometimes it's so hard being British. I'm sure if I was Italian, I would fix her with a lascivious stare until she could bear it no longer and either snog the gob off me, or slap me in the face and get her brothers to knife me in a darkened alley.

Instead I glance six inches above her pretty blonde head, and almost fall off my seat. By the coloured spaghetti of the London Underground map, is a poem.

LITTLE BOYS

I was a little boy, once,
About a week ago but
I grew up yesterday
when my father left us
and someone told me love is not eternal
before she put her tongue in my mouth
for free.

Underneath are two words: 'Scott Barron' and a date: '(1971 –)'. I want to scream out loud, 'THAT'S MINE!' but

I'm too self-conscious, so I just sit there, waiting for someone to glance up and read it. Two stops later, when I get out at Tottenham Court Road, no one has.

The fake leather sofa in Barbara Smiles's waiting room is uncomfortable, a cheap piece of furniture that sags alarmingly as you sit so that you end up hunched like a rabbit. I sit there, trying to remain upright but constantly sliding down, and I glimpse the flabbiness in my stomach, the small bulging line. I sneak a quick pinch of my waist, and there's more than an inch.

I've not been running in nearly three months, and I have no desire or motivation to get out my Nikes. I'll have to make several stringent New Year resolutions.

But that's for January. Today, on 6 December, I'm happy to accept two chocolate biscuits and a sugary tea from Barbara's assistant, the long-suffering Julie. I take off the black hat and run my fingers through my chewed-up hair.

I haven't seen my agent since my book launch. She is wearing her trademark black suit, which seems sharper than ever. Her hair is cut shorter, with blonde streaks, looking even more fashionable than normal. She kisses me on both cheeks, like a bird pecking worms. Thankfully she doesn't mention my haircut. I tell her about seeing my poem on the train.

'Bloody marvellous. It's what you always wanted, isn't it? You lucky little bugger!'

Is it what I always wanted? I guess so.

Barbara looks at me. 'What's up, Scott-lad?'

'Nothing, Barbara. I'm happy.'

'So you bloody should be! Now, the slag-mag hack is here. It might be an idea to flirt with her, they usually write about it. You have your reputation to think of, Mr Poet Behaving Badly!'

'Barbara . . .'

The door to the office opens and a woman walks in. It's not Ellie. 'Hi, I'm Susy.' She's short, despite her high-heeled boots, wearing a roll-neck sweater with a cardigan and woollen skirt.

'Wh-where's Ellie?' I stammer.

Susy looks at me blankly, as if I might be a little bit backward. Then something clicks. 'You mean Ellie Masters? She's on her honeymoon, the cow. Seychelles or somewhere.'

I blink, six times.

'Do you know her?' Susy asks, intrigued at my reaction.

'No . . . no. Not really.'

'She's away for a whole month. Her husband's loaded.'

Ellie's married. I feel for a moment as if I'm out of my body, watching the scene of Susy, Barbara and myself standing there in awkward silence. My heart beats fast, but I don't feel sick. I just feel, I don't know . . . light.

'Well, I'll leave you to get on with it,' says Barbara cheerily. 'We agreed one hour, Miss Bartlett. Mr Barron is a very busy man.'

Barbara departs, Susy sits down, takes out a tape-recorder and a notepad, looks up at me and says, 'Cool hair. Didn't Leonardo get that cut last month?'

The interview goes well, by which I mean swiftly – in

under thirty minutes. Susy is clearly bored by talking about anything but fashion, and does little to hide her amusement at my lack of clothing knowledge. She asks me the usual questions about my writing and my poems, then kindly helps me fake a few answers about my wardrobe and lets slip in passing that she doesn't really like Ellie and that her husband isn't that good-looking. 'He's no George Clooney,' she says, cheerfully.

Despite my new-found maturity, I'm relieved. I'm no George Clooney either, but it suits me to think that I might be a little more handsome than Ellie's new hubby. I thank Susy as she leaves. 'I really enjoyed the interview,' I declare, without a hint of fabrication.

Barbara congratulates me on making the slag-mag woman fall in love with me. I say I liked her. 'Should I get her phone number, Scott-lad? I can do that, you know, for you.'

'No, thanks, it's fine. It just feels good to be talking about my work again.'

Barbara's eyes brighten and she asks me if I've thought more about my next book. I tell her I'm considering writing some poems about women, as Eric suggested.

'Bloody marvellous!' declares my esteemed agent. 'Women buy shit-loads of books!'

Outside it's dark and the snow is still falling in big fat flakes. The streets are turning white, sound and light softened by this rare London snow. People laugh and holler, looking up at the sky as if angels might appear. A businessman in a suit tries to catch a snowflake on his tongue.

I stand in the cold and think about Ellie. She's on her honeymoon in the Seychelles or somewhere, with a wealthy man who is no George Clooney. Three months after we broke up, she is married.

We probably weren't right for each other, were we?

At six thirty I find myself walking down Poland Street into Soho. I know where I'm heading, but I can't admit it to myself yet, so I wander the streets and everyone seems intoxicated, which is normal for Soho, but tonight it's a more childish exhilaration that Londoners only get when they are drunk in the snow.

Several office Christmas lunches have evidently just finished, and men in suits and women in black dresses are lurching along the pavements wearing flashing red reindeer antlers and tinsel. The men try to make snowballs to throw at the women, others scoop snow off cars to put down their colleagues' backs. There are shrieks and howling laughter. Christmas lights shine in the whiteness, decorations glimmer in shop windows. My shoes crunch as I walk.

I pass a pub where a crowd of men in England shirts watch football. I didn't even know England were playing, but there's no mistaking the look of rabid camaraderie that Englishmen get when supporting the national team. I look up at the TV screens and England score. The pub goes wild. Down the road I hear similar shouts, guttural and raucous. Then some of the men in the pub start singing the theme from *The Great Escape*, chanting, 'Inger-land!' at the end of each verse. Their raucous voices boom out into the snowy streets. I want to go in and shout at them to stop. I hate the way football does this – drags men back into an idealized past (a false past, a past that exists only in their heads) where England still rules the world, and our Tommies kick Jerry and Froggie and Eyetie and Nip to kingdom come in the name of Blessed Majesty and Dame Vera Lynn. 'Get over it!' I want to shout. 'We have to move on!'

But there are at least a hundred of them, and they're bigger than me.

I've calmed down by the time I reach Old Compton Street: the headquarters of Gay London, it is immune to such football-induced passions – other than for Michael Owen's thighs. Here, even the sex shops are festive, decorated with cheap coloured lights. In one glitzy window a male mannequin sports a rubber Rudolph reindeer head on his penis. Rudolph's red nose pulsates intermittently. I can't help laughing.

I look around, worried that someone might have seen me staring at the mannequin's groin, and spot a couple walking along hand in hand. They seem happy. It's Brian with Cindy Shavers.

I think about shouting hello, to give them my symbolic blessing. But just as I think this, they stop opposite me and kiss, long and hard. I duck back into the shop doorway.

I stand there, watching them. Brian's face is a little flushed, and his perfect teeth gleam as he pulls away. Cindy laughs. She takes his hand, and swings it like a child. I keep silent in my doorway refuge. I don't feel embarrassed. I just don't want to interrupt their evening. They look happy.

As they pass a parked car, Brian scoops some snow off the roof on to Cindy's head. She squeals, he laughs, and runs off down the street. She laughs too and takes off after him.

At seven thirty-one, I am standing outside The Place. The windows are misted with the hot, happy breath of drunken drinkers. I try to peer inside, but I can't make out many faces. I can't move. I don't know if I want to go in, or turn and run all the way home. What would Scott of the Antarctic do? Or Rupert Brooke? Would they be man enough?

I am still outside the bar at seven forty-seven when Zeb arrives carrying a square box wrapped in gold paper. He's six foot three and wearing a long khaki Mod parka jacket *circa* 1972 that's just a little too short for him. I like Zeb. Even when he was three foot six and wearing furry orange pants, he seemed cool, at ease with everyone and the world around him. I shuffle to one side, hoping he won't recognize me, but he grins a wide crooked-tooth grin and holds out a hand, cradling the box in his other arm. 'Poet-man! Great to see you. Jes didn't say you were coming.'

'I'm not, really. I've got something else on. I just thought . . .'

'Come on, Wordsworth, let's get the bevs in. It's the big man's birthday.'

With that Zeb pushes me forward and, before I know it, I'm through the heavy doors and into the thick damp heat of the pulsating Soho bar.

Jes doesn't see me at first. He's at the bar with Dan the

Man and Mad Michael, with what look suspiciously like tequila shots lined up in front of them. He's wearing a faded denim shirt and well-cut baggy trousers. He looks pretty good. Dan the Man is sporting a Sainsbury's supermarket T-shirt and ripped jeans, his shaven head glistening in the bar heat. Mad Michael, all five foot two of him, sits on a stool to look taller, the beginnings of a goatee sketched on his chin. Music is pounding, and I automatically try to decipher the song. Jes and his friends always know every track. I never do.

Zeb pushes through a small crowd of dancing women towards the bar, as if drawn by the magnetic lure of his friends, oblivious to anyone else around him. The women glance up at him, his mop of unruly black hair, his chiselled jaw, his fine, almost aquiline nose, and giggle among themselves, but he seems not to notice. Luckily he's so intent on reaching the bar and the round of tequila that he forgets about me for a moment. This gives me the chance I've been looking for. I stop and hide behind the group of dancing women.

Zeb gets to the bar, drops his birthday box in front of Jes and hugs him. Then he turns and looks for me. I duck down, but he spots me and points. Jes looks over. I wonder if I should crouch, or even throw myself to the beer-sticky, cigarette-crusty floor, but before I can my brother sees me.

I hold up my hand limply, as if admitting to a minor schoolroom crime. He stares at me for a second. Then he nods, once. Not with welcome, but not with malice either. Just a simple nod, matter-of-fact, an acknowledgement of my presence. Zeb beckons me with his long hands, like an airport worker guiding in a 747.

I get to the bar and find myself blushing, but as it's so hot no one notices. 'Happy birthday, Jes,' I say quickly.

'Thanks.'

'I know you didn't . . .' I'm stammering. 'It's just Dad told me about the party.'

Luckily, Zeb interrupts me, his desire for drunkenness all-consuming: 'DRINK!' he shouts, handing me a tequila and raising his own glass. 'TO JESSICA!'

Despite myself, I smile. I'd forgotten their pet name for my brother.

'TO JESSICA!' they all shout, my brother joining in – I remain silent, not wanting to offend Jes, I'm not one of his childhood friends – and we all down our tequilas. I feel my stomach do a tiny flip. Sweat trickles down my forehead and neck, but I can't take off my hat to reveal Loti's choppy disaster, even if Leonardo di Caprio did get a similar cut last month.

'What's with the hat?' Jes asks, suddenly. His friends turn to look, as if viewing me for the first time.

'Oh, nothing, I was just cold in the snow,' I stammer. What's the point? I might as well get it over with. 'Okay. I had a really bad haircut.'

'Go on, let's see.'

Jes is looking at me, eyebrows raised, a challenge. I could refuse, I'm five years older than these four boys, I'm the grown-up, I don't have to be part of the gang.

'Only because it's your birthday.'

I take off the hat. They try not to laugh.

'What happened?' says Jes. 'Did they use a cheese-grater?'

With this he smiles a big Jes smile, which makes me want to smile too. I catch a glimpse of myself in one of the numerous mirrors behind the bar. My hair is smoothed down with sweat, which only serves to accentuate the scrappiness of the cut. It looks like some rodent has chewed small chunks out of my head.

'Loti didn't speak English very well,' I say, meekly.

The four men start to laugh, and within the four different laughs I hear my brother's laugh largest and deepest of all. But instead of feeling hurt that they're laughing at me, I feel a small warmth. It must be the tequila.

Zeb embarks on a complicated but funny story about his car radio and the Kylie-loving mechanic down the road in Balham who only has four fingers on his left hand, and I thank him silently. I get the feeling he's sensed the tension between me and my brother, and he's seeking to quell it with his silky conversational skills.

Beers have miraculously appeared and we drink and listen to Zeb, and then to Dan the Man as he recounts how he inadvertently fell into a sculpture exhibit of shining metallic balls at the Hayward Gallery. Everyone is laughing, and I find it easier to laugh along with them. On the sound system I think I recognize the song – it's by some Scottish band who had a big hit that I don't know the name of.

'What's this?' says Zeb, when Dan has finished his story. 'Brothers' night?'

'How do you mean?' asks Jes, a hint of worry in his voice. I try not to look completely baffled.

Zeb gestures to the speakers above the bar. 'First the Jackson Five, all brothers. Now the Proclaimers, Craig and Charlie Reid from Leith, brothers. All we need now is a bit of Liam and Noel and we have a theme night.'

'Brotherly hits!' says Dan the Man, warming to the idea.

'Yeah. You guys should dance,' says Mad Michael, nudging Jes and grinning at me.

'Boogie Brothers!' cackles Dan the Man.

'Fraternal Funkmeisters!' howls Zeb.

Jes looks at me, and for a moment I think he wants a lead, for me to tell him what to do. But I know I can't: not only is this his night, and I've promised myself to stop offering advice, but I'm petrified of dancing. I can't do it. I can't expose myself to ridicule.

To my relief, the music changes, something more funky.

'Any brothers involved?' asks Dan the Man. I glance at Zeb.

'No. It's Prince, "Alphabet Street". We've moved on to midgets,' laughs Zeb, who has always been the leader of the pack.

'Mikey, on the dance floor now!' shouts Jes, and they all start to howl with laughter once more. Mad Michael growls at them and orders more beers. Zeb places more tequilas in front of us, salt, drink, lemon. We shake our heads like dogs as the evil oil goes down. We sip more beer to take away the toxic taste, then Zeb and Dan head off to the toilets. Mad Michael leans over the bar to harangue the insolent Spanish barman for more drinks.

Suddenly it's just me and my brother, a foot apart. We both stare out at the dance-floor, the women jiggling and giggling to Prince.

I take a long sip of warm beer, swill it round my mouth and swallow. I ease my weight on to my right foot, which propels me inwards towards Jes. 'So . . . how's the birthday going?' I ask, brightly.

'Not so bad. Thanks for the wine.'

'Any time.'

Jes keeps watching the dance-floor, his left fingers tapping out the beat on his large thigh. I want to ask him about Sam. As if reading my mind, he glances at me and says, 'Sam sent me a present.' He turns to show off his denim shirt and well-cut trousers.

'Looks good.'

'That's Sammy.' He leans back against the bar. There's a moment of silence. Then he says, 'She said you'd been to talk to her.'

Oh, no. This is where it all goes horribly wrong. 'I just . . . Look, I'm sorry, I know you didn't want me to.'

'It's okay. She said it was good to see you.'

He turns back to watch the dancing women, one of whom is now on a chair, gyrating her ample hips. We stand there without speaking. The barman turns up the music volume and the women cheer as one.

'I went to see the penguin today,' says Jes, over the din.

'Really?' I say, surprised. 'How is he?'

'He seemed pretty happy, you know, with the other penguins.'

'That's good.'

Jes looks at me. I look at him. 'No more stealing penguins. Okay?'

'Okay.' We both smile.

Zeb returns and orders another round of tequilas to go with the beers. The music thumps. My head is dancing. The four friends are joking, shouting, Zeb has his arm round Jes and I feel a tinge of jealousy, but it passes almost immediately. Zeb's his oldest friend. I'm his older brother.

I notice women eyeing up the gang, the prettiest concentrating their furtive flirtatious glances on Zeb, who, despite his current single status, seems unaware of them. I admire their solidarity, these four musketeers. Thank God Jes has this, I think. It's not like he gets it from his family.

I finish my beer (my fifth? sixth?) and realize I haven't been to the toilet since I arrived an hour and a half ago. As I head off from the bar, I find that somehow my legs have had the bones removed. I can't walk straight. I'm more drunk than I'd anticipated. I'm more drunk than I've been since throwing up live on national television.

I'm having a piss in the shining metal toilets, happy that no one else is there and I can take my time, when I hear heavy footsteps. Jes appears by my left shoulder. 'Hey,' he says, noncommittally.

'The Barron bladder,' I say lightly.

He mumbles something, shuffles along the urinal and starts to pee. We are six feet apart, and I have a sudden flashback to when we were children and we'd piss into the toilet at the same time, trying to splash each other.

We both stare into the urinals. Jes starts to hum the

Proclaimers song. I finish, zip up my trousers and step away. Jes does the same. Then he says, 'What I said about you not being the oldest any more. It's not true. You're still my older brother. You always will be.'

'Thanks,' I say softly. I look at him, my brother. 'You know what's funny?' I ask.

'What?' There is suspicion in his eyes.

'I might be the oldest, but I'm the one who's spent twenty-odd years wishing I was you.'

'What?'

'It's true. You've lived your life so much better than me. You're happier than me. And for fuck's sake, you're a much better writer than me!'

'Bullshit.'

We both step to the wash-basins. I turn on the tap and continue, 'I just got lucky. I don't know what I write about. It's just little ditties. You care about what you write.'

'Bollocks. You're brilliant. At least, that's what I tell everyone.'

I look at him. He bites his bottom lip quickly. I see him as a child with the same nervous reaction. In this moment, I love him. I want to say so many things, I want to pour out twenty-seven years of love. We wash our hands in adjacent basins. We step to the twin hand-towel dispensers, and each pull down a towel. Ceremoniously we rub our hands in unison – the British Synchronized Bathroom Display team.

'Listen, Jes. I'm sorry I called you fat.' I'm suddenly terrified. Why did I have to say that? Why did I have to remind him? The last time I called him fat, he decked me. Jes throws his paper-towel ball into the bin. In the row of mirrors I see four of him. In the neighbouring mirror I see myself. We look more alike than we've ever been – he slimmer, me heavier.

I know that this is the moment when, if he is still angry with me and has no desire for reconciliation, he will put me down. It is the moment when he has the power to push me away, to reject me for ever. I have reached out to him and I need him to accept my apology. A rebuttal now would strike straight to my heart. For an instant he runs his hand over his bulging belly. Then he says, 'You're looking a bit porky yourself, these days.'

I look at him. He grins. 'Come on. Let's get another drink.'

Back in the bar, Zeb and Dan the Man are dancing. Mad Michael is nowhere to be seen. I buy two more beers and hand one to Jes. 'What's the toast?' I ask.

'To the fat brothers,' says Jes, raising his beer bottle.

'To us.' I smile, and we drink, together.

The room is shrinking now, until my entire universe is the bar counter and my fat brother sitting on the tiny bar stool. I look at him, his belly hanging over his birthday trousers like a happy fleshy waterfall, and I want to grab it and hug him to me and envelop his large flabby mass in my arms.

The music changes. A more upbeat track comes on.

'Oh, yes!' shouts Jes. 'Come on, brother!'

'What is it?'

But Jes is up and slipping past drinkers to the tiny space

of the dance-floor, barging past Zeb and Dan the Man to assume his rightful place at the epicentre of his birthday celebrations. It's remarkable how easily he moves for a man of his bulk. He throws one arm in the air, finger pointing, and strikes a disco pose. Around him people laugh, but he doesn't care. I finally recognize the track – 'Staying Alive' by the Bee Gees. Jes is pretending to be John Travolta.

At the bar I feel the forces of the past clinging to me, holding me back here, out of the way, where I always remain, watching, never entering in. 'COME ON, SCOTT!' shouts Jes, over the music. 'IT'S MY BIRTHDAY!'

I smile and wave at him. I don't want to go. I'm going to stay put.

Jes waves again. I don't want to make a fool of myself in this cool bar in cool London, to have people laugh at me. 'COME ON, MATE! COME AND DANCE!'

It's his birthday. But I don't dance. I never have. I can't, can I?

'Come on, Scott!' he shouts.

I stand. My heart races. I find myself walking from the bar. I pass several drinkers, who don't even look up. This isn't so bad. As I get to the dance-floor I see people look at me. I hesitate, standing there. I could go back to the bar, to the past, but then Jes waves once more and his gravitational pull hauls me through the dancing couples. Zeb and Dan the Man part to let me reach the centre as one of the Gibb brothers squeals something about mothers and brothers.

Jes steps back, smiling at me, to allow me space. He

strikes the Travolta pose once more. I stand there, arms limp at my side, moving my feet slowly, woodenly. I see faces watching us, laughing at us, Zeb and Dan now standing and pointing and laughing, but Jes doesn't care. He's really going now, spinning round, pointing his finger up and down, legs apart, head snapping this way and that, and his belly seems to rotate in time to the music. I am standing there, in the centre, the whole room watching and laughing. I glance over at the bar, and the empty stool where I would normally sit, and suddenly I don't care what anybody thinks.

I launch into a strutting move, passing Jes, then spinning on one foot (quite dexterously, I think) and prancing back towards him. I throw my head back, stand with my legs apart, point my right index finger to the heavens and in a deep raucous voice that seems new and hopeful I exclaim, as loudly as I can, 'Yeah, Brother!'

It's late. Somehow I'm on the handlebars of Jes's red Marin mountain bike, wobbling at high speed up the snowy pavement on Hampstead Road towards Camden Town. Jes is pedalling furiously. I'm a little hazy on how we got here. We come down off the kerb, kerchunk!, then up another kerb, kerdunk! We skid and wobble violently.

'YOU'RE TOO HEAVY!' shouts Jes. 'LARDASS!'

'WATCH OUT FOR THE BIN!' I scream, laughing my head off. A police car slows, then speeds off lights flashing.

'WAAAOOOOOOH!' we shout, hurtling through the snow-laden night.

'E.T., PHONE HOME!' shouts Jes.

'HERE IT IS! HERE IT IS!' I scream, then remember I'm meant to be quiet: we are on a mission. 'It's Arlington Street,' I whisper, then hiccup loudly.

Jes stops suddenly. I slide off the handlebars, stumble and fall into a small hedge in someone's front garden. A pile of snow lands on my head.

'SSSSSSSH! BE QUIET!' barks Jes, before he, too, recalls that we are supposed to be undercover. He places the bike carefully against some railings, takes out his keys, then drops them in the street. 'SHIT!'

He kneels down, scrabbling in the snow. A light goes on in a window down the street. I pull myself out of the bush, reach down and pick up the keys triumphantly. 'YOU'RE DRUNK!' I exclaim, happily. He grabs the keys.

'IT'S MY BIKE! MY BIKE!' he growls. He starts locking it, then drops the keys again.

I look around me, trying to get my bearings. Ahead is a row of terraced houses, opposite some old industrial units. As I look, my vision predictably hazy, I see a huge penguin looking down at me. I look more closely. There's no doubt about it. It's a ten-foot-high penguin – not something you can easily mistake.

I wonder for a moment whether this is God, floating in the air like an Antarctic Virgin Mary. I wonder whether, three weeks before Christmas, He has chosen to reappear on earth in the form of a large flightless bird. I step into the street for a better look. I slip in the snow, almost fall, but just manage to right myself. As I get closer the penguin becomes a picture on a billboard. It's an Emperor penguin standing next to a flaming gas heater. The slogan reads: 'Keep warm this winter.'

I stand there staring at the penguin, which looks out at me with a small but saucy grin. Jes appears at my side. His breath is silver in the street-light. 'Norman lives,' he says happily. 'Come on.'

He turns and heads across the street to the line of houses. I want to stay here, protected by the watchful gaze of the giant penguin, but I know I must be at my brother's side. I must be his friend and ally in this most challenging and dangerous of deeds. I must be Scott of Kentish Town.

Jes rings loud and long on the buzzer. I manage to decipher the figures on my watch: 23.44.

I hope this is an auspicious time. I hope that the planets are aligned and the entrails of some chicken in Mongolia are suggesting positive things.

Jes rings again. There's a sound from inside the house. Footsteps walking slowly down some stairs. Are they angry? Surprised? Delighted? We can hear out hearts beat.

The door opens. Standing there is Rachel. She's wearing jeans and a green T-shirt. She looks even prettier than I remember.

Before she or we can say anything, Sam appears behind her, in a dressing-gown and pyjama bottoms.

'What are you doing here?' she says, her tone not revealing whether she's overjoyed or mad as hell.

My brother opens his arms wide as if wanting to hug the world, and shouts, 'I LOVE YOU, SAMMY! I LOVE YOU MORE THAN ANYTHING!'

Across the street a group of people heading home from the pub have stopped on the corner and are watching, captivated by the unfolding drama. Sam glances at them, then at me – I nod and smile in what I hope is an encouraging way – then at her errant husband. 'Why are you here?' she says, in a tone that suggests she knows.

'Because I need you,' says Jes, firmly. From his pocket he takes a red carnation stolen from the bar. It's almost dead. He hands it to her.

Sam looks at him. As if by some predestined plan, they both exhale at the same time, their breath mixing in the silver light. I pray to a God I've not spoken to in a long time that everything is going to be all right.

'You're pissed.'

'It's my birthday.'

She clasps her arms around herself, for warmth and protection, weighing the incontrovertible truth of what he's just said. It is his birthday. The day it all began. 'You look like shit.'

'Please, Sammy. It's fucking freezing.'

Sam looks at him for a moment. Something shifts. The planet turns. 'Come on. I'll make you a cup of tea.'

She starts to go upstairs. Jes watches her, then steps

forward, past Rachel, and disappears into the house. I'm about to speak when I hear him trip and fall *thud* on the staircase. Sam laughs quietly from the darkness. 'Come on, you daft bugger. Get your arse up those stairs.'

The people across the street move on, giggling as they

amble around the corner. I am still standing on the door-step. Rachel is still holding the door open. She smiles at me. 'We were never properly introduced,' she says softly. 'I'm Rachel.' Her voice is gentle. I could wake up to that voice.

I smile back at her. 'Hi. I'm Scott. His fat brother.'

She laughs quickly, a beautiful laugh, and I follow her into the house, closing the door behind me.

It starts to snow again. By morning the city will be covered. As the flakes swirl and waltz, fat and content, across the road the giant penguin looks down, continuing his watch over the sleeping men and women of North London.

MY FAT BROTHER

My brother's fat, like a chunky KitKat,
an obese rat
or Salman Rushdie's hat.
For many years I forced tears
From him, in creative ways,
Shame you might say
But that's brothers for you.
We hide love (and concern)
Under iron gloves, cuffing.
Yet over time, I've learned, slowly,
To speak to him with words, not bashing.
I'd not choose another.
He's my fat brother.